Maureen

eternity base

Bob Mayer

Other books by Bob Mayer

Eyes of the Hammer
Dragon SIM-13
SYNBAT
Cut-Out

BOB MAYER

eternity base

LYFORD
Books

Copyright © 1996 by Bob Mayer

LYFORD Books
Published by Presidio Press
505 B San Marin Dr., Suite 300
Novato, CA 94945-1340

Library of Congress Cataloging-in-Publication Data

Mayer, Bob, 1959–
    Eternity base / Bob Mayer.
       p.   cm.
    ISBN 0-89141-509-2 (hardcover)
    1. Riley, Dave (Fictitous character)—Fiction. 2. Antarctic regions—Fiction. I. Title.
PS3563.A95227E86   1996
813'.54—dc20   95-53729
                                            CIP

Printed in the United States of America

eternity base

— prologue —

ANTARCTICA, APPROXIMATELY 575 MILES EAST OF MCMURDO STATION, 21 DECEMBER 1971. "The last load," the army major in the gray parka remarked.

"Amen to that," Captain Reinhart muttered. Through the scratched Plexiglas windshield, he glanced at the frozen runway splayed out in front of his plane. To his left rear, a staircase descended into the cargo bay of the C-130 transport where his loadmaster was securing the few pallets of luggage the passengers had carried on board. Along the walls, the major's soldiers, bundled up in cold-weather gear, were seated on red web seats, ready to get started on the long journey out of here.

Reinhart couldn't blame them. He'd brought them here four months ago from Vietnam via McMurdo Station and then spent the intervening time flying back from the Station every opportunity the weather gave, bringing the men equipment and supplies for whatever they were building here in the frozen wasteland of the Antarctic. A week ago that process had reversed and he'd started bringing out equipment and people. The outflow in equipment and supplies had been considerably less than the inflow. Reinhart was anxious to go.

The sky was clear and the wind had died down. The weather report from McMurdo looked good, but Reinhart had long ago learned that the Antarctic was one place where weather reports could be counted on about as far as the report itself could be folded into a paper airplane and thrown. The only constant in the weather here was change—and the change was usually for the worse.

Reinhart wasn't sure who the major worked for. The name tag on the major's parka read Glaston. All Reinhart knew was that four months ago he had been ordered to do whatever the man said. Glaston had been there waiting to receive their cargo every time they'd landed at Eternity Base—the code name of this unmarked location. Today even Glaston was going out with them. If anyone was remaining behind, Reinhart did not know and cared even less. It was their last flight from Eternity Base, and successfully completing it was his only concern.

On what served as an "airstrip," the plane sat in a large bowl of ice surrounded on three sides by ice ridges and intermittent towering mountains punching through the thick polar cap; the strip pointed toward the one open side. The hulking C-130, with four powerful tur-boprop engines mounted on its broad wings, was the most reliable cargo airplane ever to fly, and Reinhart felt confident in its abilities. Bracketed over the plane's wheels were sets of skis that allowed them to negotiate the 2,000 meters of relatively level ice and snow that these people called a runway.

"Closing the ramp," the loadmaster announced in Reinhart's head-set. In the rear of the plane, the back ramp lifted from the thin, pow-dery snow as hydraulic arms pulled it up. Descending from the high dark hole that led to the uplifted tail came the top section of the ramp. Like jaws closing, the two shut against the swirling frozen air outside. The heaters fought a losing battle against the cold as they pumped hot air out of pipes in the ceiling of the cargo bay, ten feet overhead.

Reinhart turned to Glaston. "We're all set, sir."

The major simply nodded and clambered down the steps to take his seat in the rear.

"Let's do it," Reinhart told the copilot. Carefully, they turned the nose straight on line, due south. As Reinhart increased throttle, the plane slowly gathered momentum. The propellers and skis threw up a plume of snow behind.

Reinhart waited until he was satisfied they had enough speed and then pulled in the yoke. The 130's nose lifted and the plane crawled into the air. Once he reached sufficient altitude to clear the mountains, Reinhart banked hard right and headed west. In the distance, out the right window, the ice pack that hugged the shore of Antarctica could be seen as a tumbled broken mass extending to the horizon. Reinhart turned over the controls to his copilot. Two hours and they'd be at McMurdo; the passengers would be off-loaded for transfer to another aircraft, and he and his crew could begin the long, stop-filled flight back to their home base in Hawaii. After four months down here, they were more than ready to see loved ones and celebrate a sunny Christmas.

This whole mission had been strange from the initial tasking back in early September. Reinhart and the four members of his crew had flown the Hawaii–Pago, Pago–Christchurch, New Zealand–McMurdo Base, Antarctica, run several times in the past. Almost every cargo crew in their squadron stationed at Hickam Air Force Base received the honors every so often. But four months ago they'd been tasked "for the duration of the mission" to support Glaston. They'd met him at a dirt airstrip outside a classified Special Forces camp in Vietnam, only to be told to fly to the U.S. Antarctic research station at McMurdo and take on transloaded cargo from other C-130 cargo planes coming in from New Zealand, then fly the cargo out to this site. What had been especially interesting about the mission was the fact that as far as their parent unit knew, they were still in Vietnam. All their mail had come through that theater before being forwarded down here.

"I've got the beacon clear," the copilot informed Reinhart.

As long as they kept the needle on the direction finder centered, they'd come in right on top of McMurdo. That was another odd thing. They'd flown every mission on instruments in both directions, never once using a map—not that maps were very useful over the frozen wasteland of Antarctica. As any worthwhile pilot would, Reinhart had a reasonably good idea of where Eternity Base was, based on both flight time and azimuth. Satisfied that all was going well, he settled back in his seat for a nap. He'd need the rest if he was going to take the eight-hour leg from McMurdo to New Zealand.

Two hours later a nudge on Reinhart's shoulder awakened him. "McMurdo," the copilot announced.

Out of the left window Reinhart saw the sprawl of buildings that made up the largest human habitation in the continent. With the onslaught of winter just a few months away, the population would drop from its summer high of six hundred to less than a hundred care-takers. Out the right window the massive form of Mount Erebus, an active volcano, filled the horizon twenty-four miles away. Directly below lay the edge of the massive Ross Ice Shelf, more than five hundred miles from its southern origin at the foot of the Queen Maud Mountains.

The copilot swung them around for a final approach to McMurdo's ice strip. As soon as the skis touched, he reduced throttle and upped flaps for maximum stop. They slid down the runway, using the tail to keep them on line. Slowly the aircraft's speed dropped.

Reinhart could see two other C-130s sitting near the field's operation tower. One of those would take their cargo and passengers for the trip back to Vietnam, and then they would be free to go. After radioing the tower for instructions, they taxied over to the designated plane and idled the engines. A forklift was waiting to take off the pallets. As soon as the ramp was open, the soldiers stomped across the snow and onto another plane while Reinhart's two enlisted crewmen rolled out the pallets.

Glaston was the last to leave, waiting in the cockpit until all had been crossloaded. "Anxious to get home, I suppose?"

Reinhart grinned, the adrenaline of pleasant anticipation flowing. "Damn right. We're talking white beach and tanned women back in Hawaii."

Glaston nodded. "Have a good flight. We've appreciated your help. My superiors will be forwarding letters of commendation for you and your crew to your headquarters."

That was the least they could do, Reinhart thought, to pay them back for spending four months living in a damn Quonset hut buried under the snow at McMurdo and flying a load every time the weather cleared. Of course things could have been worse: they actually could have been flying missions in Vietnam. "I appreciate that, sir."

The major disappeared down the stairwell, and the loadmaster slammed shut the personnel door behind him.

Reinhart turned to his copilot and navigator. "Do we have clearance to go?"

The navigator's face split in a wide grin. "We have clearance, and the weather looks good all the way to New Zealand, sir."

"All right. Let's head for home."

They turned their nose into the wind and powered up. Soon the plane was in the air and over the ice-covered Ross Sea. New Zealand was eight hours away, due north.

Reinhart piloted the first three hours, as they slowly left the white ice behind and finally made it over clear ocean, speckled with small white dots far below, indicating icebergs. At that point, Reinhart turned over the controls to his copilot and got out of his seat. "I'm going to take a walk in back and get stretched out."

He climbed down the stairs. The loadmaster and his assistant were sleeping on the web seats strung along the side of the plane. The only cargo remaining was the pallet that held the crew's personal baggage, strapped down in the center of the large bay.

Reinhart walked all the way to the rear, where the ramp doors met, rolling his head on his shoulders and shaking off the strain of three straight hours in the pilot's seat.

His mind was on his wife and young daughter waiting for him in Honolulu when the number two engine exploded with enough force to shear the right wing at the engine juncture. The C-130 immediately adopted the aerodynamics of a rock and rolled over onto its right side. Reinhart was thrown up in the farthest reaches of the tail as the plane plummeted toward the ocean 25,000 feet below. He blinked blood out of his eyes from a cut in his forehead and tried to orient himself.

His primary thought was to try to crawl back up to the cockpit, but his legs wouldn't obey his mind. There was a dull ache in his lower back and no feeling below his waist. He grabbed at the cross beams along the roof of the aircraft, trying to pull himself forward with his hands.

Reinhart was twenty feet from the front of the plane when the surface of the water met the aircraft with the effect of a sledgehammer slamming into a tin can. There was no need for Reinhart to worry about immersion; he was crushed into the floor of the aircraft. He was dead well before his remains began sinking under the dark waves.

COLORADO SPRINGS, COLORADO, 20 DECEMBER 1971. The man in the black suit picked up the phone on the first ring. "Peter here."

The voice on the other end was distorted by both distance and scrambler. "This is Glaston. The final link has been severed. Eternity Base is secure."

"Did you receive the last package?"

"Yes, sir. The courier brought them in on the final flight, but I don't understand why—"

The man cut him off. "It's not your place to understand. Did you secure them?"

"Yes, sir. They're in the base."

"The courier?"

"Taken care of."

"Excellent."

— One —

CHICAGO, ILLINOIS, FRIDAY, 18 OCTOBER 1996. The volley of shots was ragged, five going off at the same time, the other two rifles sounding like a car backfiring shortly thereafter. Riley had expected the sharp crack of the blanks so he wasn't startled, as were some of the other people surrounding the grave.

His black army raincoat was unbuttoned and the stiff wind was blowing it about, but he didn't notice. The battered green beret scrunched down on his head was soaked from the freezing drizzle that had been falling for the past half hour, but Riley seemed unaware of it.

The second volley was slightly better—only one shot a split second behind.

To Riley's left, Col. Mike Pike, U.S. Army Retired, was very aware of both the weather and Riley's condition, and he didn't like either. In thirty years in the military, Pike had attended more than his share of funerals, but this one was different. He'd never been to the funeral of a woman killed in the line of duty, and he'd never had to comfort the man she'd left behind. It had always been the other way around.

Not that Pike thought any words could comfort Dave Riley at the moment. Riley's slight frame was ramrod straight, and his dark eyes were focused on the plain wood coffin suspended over the yawning hole in the ground. The short black hair under his beret was matted and poked out at strange angles around the dark skin of his face, the complexion an inheritance from his Puerto Rican mother, as his name was his inheritance from a father he never knew.

7

The salute was done, and a police bugler began playing taps. Pike had spent so many years isolated in the military that he had never really considered the fact that the police community was very similar to that of the army—close knit and banding together when one of their own went down. The last notes of the bugle were ripped away by the wind, and then it was over. The coffin was slowly lowered. Riley stepped forward, grabbed a handful of mud, and opened his fingers to let it fall on the coffin, not even noticing that most of the mud stuck to his skin.

The commissioner was the first to walk by, shaking Riley's hand and saying something that was swirled away by the wind. The line of mourners continued, and Riley greeted each mechanically until there was no one left.

Pike waited. He didn't mind the freezing rain splashing against his leathery face and rolling down inside his collar. There'd be plenty of time to get warm later. As he'd been told thirty-three years ago as a young buck going through Ranger school, "The human body is water-proof." He knew that Riley was just as hard, so it wasn't physical stress that Pike worried about now. It was emotional stress: that was a minefield few warriors felt comfortable traversing.

"Do you want to be alone?" Pike asked.

At first he thought Riley hadn't heard, but then the other man turned his head slightly, as if considering the question, before speaking. "No. She's dead. Standing here isn't going to change that. It's just making her death seem real—standing here, seeing this. I didn't believe it when they called me. I didn't begin to believe it until I saw her body in the funeral home."

Pike remembered the phone call from Riley three days ago. It had been succinct and to the point: "Donna's dead, sir. They just called me from Chicago. She walked into the middle of some punks ripping off a deli and got shot."

That had been it. Pike had driven the five hundred miles from Atlanta to Fort Bragg that evening, making it in time to fly up to Chicago with Riley. They'd learned more about the incident, as the police referred to it, from the detective handling the case. Donna Giannini had been going to lunch at her old neighborhood deli as she had done almost every day at work. There were two teenagers in the store holding a pistol and a shotgun on the owner in the back room, trying to get him to open a small safe. When she called out from the counter to her old friend the owner, her answer was a blast of buckshot to the chest.

It hadn't killed her outright. She drew her gun, stood back up, and shot the kid with the shotgun three times, killing him. Then she collapsed and died. The second kid ran out the back of the store.

"We'll get the other one," the detective had told Riley and Pike. He looked at them and glanced around; then, in the manner of one professional to another, he continued in a lower voice: "He won't be brought in alive. Everyone on the street knows it, he knows it, we know it, and I just want you to know it. Donna was good people and a damn good cop. We don't let cop killers walk here or go cry in the courtroom."

Donna Giannini *had* been good people, Pike reflected. The best. He had gotten to know her well when she and Riley had come to him for help the previous year after running into trouble with rogue elements of the Witness Protection Program. He had known Dave Riley from his time in the Special Forces; years earlier, under Pike's command, Riley had run direct action missions into Colombia to destroy cocaine factories. The two had kept in touch over the years.

Pike had been happy about the two of them being together. He knew they'd had plans: Riley was going to finish out his twenty years next spring, then retire, move up to Chicago, and go back to school. That was something Pike had heartily approved of. It was as if Riley had come out of his shell and become alive, ready to start a new life after the trials and darkness of his life in the Special Forces. But now—now, Pike didn't know what was going to happen to his friend.

Pike had been relieved when the detective assured them that the second man wouldn't be brought in alive. He'd feared that Riley would stay in Chicago and exact his own vengeance. At least now he could get Riley out of town without tripping over bodies.

Riley turned from the grave and looked out over the cemetery. He seemed reluctant to leave, but the inevitable was sinking in. "All right," he finally said. "Let's go."

They walked slowly over to the rental car, each lost in his own thoughts. As Pike got behind the wheel, Riley slumped down in the passenger seat and looked out the window, keeping the fresh mound of dirt in sight until they turned a corner. Then he faced front. "I put in my papers," he said, as flatly as if he were announcing the sun coming up.

"You what?" Pike said, surprised.

"I'm on terminal leave. I've got enough days of leave saved up to run me through my retirement day next year. I was going to stay on active duty and cash in my leave when I retired—to pay for my first year of school—but that no longer is neces . . ." Riley paused, and Pike kept his eyes straight ahead on the rain-soaked road, not wanting to see the tears.

"What are you going to do?" Pike finally asked. "Take some time to—"

"I don't want time and I don't want to think," Riley snapped. He turned to his old friend. "Sorry, sir. I know it might be too much to ask, but do you have any jobs I might be able to do?"

Pike ran a security consulting firm, with clients all over the United States and overseas. He was glad that Dave was turning to him for help. "Hell, yeah. I'd love to have you come work for me."

"Just keep me busy," Riley said. He looked over his shoulder one last time. "Just keep me busy."

— TWO —

NATIONAL PERSONNEL RECORDS CENTER, ST. LOUIS, MISSOURI, 22 NOVEMBER 1996. The National Personnel Records Center in St. Louis consists of seventeen acres of paper hidden underground with an eight-story office building housing other federal agencies above it. Papers tucked away in the building range from old social security records to the original plans for Fat Man, the first nuclear bomb. The U.S. government runs on paper, and the National Personnel Records Center is the temporary storage place and clearinghouse for every imaginable type of government record.

Unclassified records are in folders placed inside cardboard boxes, which are stacked on rows and rows of shelves. The secure "vault" contains all the classified records. Every scrap of paper produced by the numerous organizations, and every piece of paper relating to any person who ever worked for the government, are kept in the Records Center. Personnel records are normally kept for fifty-six years, organizational records for twenty-five unless marked for longer keeping. Once that time limit is up, files marked as permanent records are moved to final storage in the National Archives in Washington, D.C. Nonpermanent records are held until the time limit stamped on them, at which time they are reviewed for either destruction or movement to the Archives.

At the moment, it was organizational records that held the attention of Sammy Pintella. Actually, it would be fairer to say they occupied

11

the time but not the interest of Sammy. Her tall, slender form was perched on the edge of a metal folding chair next to a line of rollers. She sported short red hair, cut almost punk style, and a freckled complexion. Her expression betrayed supreme boredom with her job.

A cardboard box of army unit histories would come rolling down to her every thirty seconds. She would look in and quickly scan the contents under the bright glare of the fluorescent lights overhead, making sure the material matched the computer printout she had taped to the edge of the platform. She had a good memory and referred to the printout only every dozen or so cartons. Satisfied that the box held what the printout said, she'd send the box on its way to the other end of the conveyer, where a pimply faced college freshman would remove the box and place it on a pallet. Once the pallet was full, it would be taken by forklift to the loading dock. When enough pallets accumulated, a tractor trailer would be filled and sent to the National Archives.

Sammy had been at it for almost two hours now and had finished six cart loads. She enjoyed working alone and she didn't talk to the men who brought the carts or took away the pallets. The Records Center was a giant library of tempting unknowns to her. She could get lost in the stacks for hours on end, looking through various files, reading the stories of people and organizations that the tides of time had swept away or carried on to different places. The assembly line work bored her but had to be gotten out of the way so she could disappear back into the stacks tomorrow.

Two divorces, no children, and thirty-six years on the planet gave Sammy a different attitude from the college students who worked part-time in the unclassified stacks. This job was her sole means of support, and she was glad to do it in a place where she could be alone most of the time. Getting paid to deal with the records of people she'd never meet and places she'd never go suited her just fine.

She flipped open the lid on the next box and was so benumbed by the endless, bland file folders that she almost pushed it on to oblivion. But in the back she spotted the edges of some black and white photos stuffed into one of the folders. That was unusual: typically the histories were dry recitations of the barest facts—just enough to satisfy the army regulation requirements. Curious, Sammy reached in to pull the file. That brief halt caused the first disruption of the afternoon as the next box crashed into the one in front of her.

"Hold it!" Sammy yelled down to the front end worker. "Take a break."

The slider shrugged, sat down on the edge of his cart, and pulled out a dog-eared paperback to read. The man on the other end took the time to restack his boxes, preparing the pallet for the forklift.

Sammy opened the folder and laid out the photos on the conveyer belt. The twelve photos showed a desolate winter landscape and bundled-up men working on some sort of structure dug into the snow. Several photos obviously had been posed seriously; in others the men were goofing off for the camera.

Sammy picked up one photo. About forty men were gathered around a crude sign drawn on cardboard: B COMPANY ETERNITY BASE. Behind the men, all that could be seen rising above the snow was a metal shaft with a door in the center. Farther in the background, three massive mountains rose from the ice-covered landscape, blotting out most of the horizon.

Sammy flipped the picture over. The date was printed on the bottom edge: 17 NOVEMBER 1971. She retrieved the folder and looked at the faded label: 67TH ENGINEERS. UNIT HISTORY 1971. LT. FREELY, HISTORIAN.

She turned it back to the front. Eternity Base. Sammy frowned. She'd never heard of such a place. After working here for eighteen years, ever since graduating high school, she thought she'd seen just about every type of army record that existed and was more familiar with army terms, units, and bases than most generals. She checked the rest of the folders in the box, but they were just the normal histories of other army units in 1971, none of them appearing particularly interesting or containing pictures. Sammy put the folder to the side.

"All right. Let's finish this off." She slid the box down the line.

As the second hand hit twelve, aligning with the minute hand, the workers at the Records Center broke from the chains of the job. They moved for the stairs, to spread out into the city of St. Louis until eight the next morning when they'd be drawn back by the siren call of the time clock. Sammy stayed behind. She had nowhere in particular to go other than her apartment to stare into the aquarium sitting on a stand beside her bed. She figured the fish would be all right for a while without her. She often stayed late, thumbing through interesting files and finishing the tasks that never seemed to get done in the required eight-hour workday.

Her supervisor, Brad Tollander, a history Ph.D. who ran this section of the Records Center, stopped by her desk as he headed out. "What are you working on, Sam?"

Sammy and Brad were the two old-timers of the Center. They'd come in together just after the famous fire that had badly damaged the top floor of the building. They'd been here when many of the eighteen wheelers filled with records had driven up to the loading dock. They'd helped unload carton after carton, year after year. Between the two of them they knew where almost every record was.

Despite the recent valiant attempt to list everything on a computer database, there was no substitute for the years of knowledge in their two heads. Sammy often wondered what would happen when they both retired. There would be records sitting in boxes that no one knew were in the stacks. Computers were fine, but some things just couldn't be quantified into the little sections on the database.

Sammy shrugged. "Just going through some of the unit histories we cleared today. A few looked kind of interesting."

Brad nodded. Reading files was one of the perks of the job. "All right. I'll see you in the morning." He trudged up the stairs.

Sammy turned back to the computer screen. As soon as the door swished shut behind her supervisor, she punched into the unclassified database, accessing armed forces installations. She started with the army. It took her ten minutes to determine that there was no listing for Eternity Base. She moved on to the air force and then the navy, with similar results. On the off chance the marines might not have told its mother branch, she checked the corps records too. Nothing. That meant that this one file folder of photos was the only mention in the entire Records Center of such an installation. Or at least in the unclassified records, she reminded herself.

Sammy had put the photos in time sequence earlier, and she noticed that the dates on the back had spanned four months—from late August through December 1971. Judging from the pictures, Eternity Base was some sort of structure constructed under the snow cover in a cold-weather area. That led Sammy to her second avenue of investigation. She accessed the database on Alaska and tried cross-referencing. Again she drew a blank.

She wondered if Eternity Base might be part of the Defense Early Warning (DEW) line constructed across northern Canada—maybe even in Greenland. Her fingers flitted over the keys of the computer as she checked that, but no cross-reference showed up there either.

Sammy then took a different route. She turned off the computer and moved into the stacks. She went directly to the section that held army organizational records—every army unit's record, from battalion level on up. Finding the section that held the engineer units, Sammy followed the number of the battalions as they went up. She pulled the cardboard box labeled 67TH ENGINEERS, 1970–1974.

Kneeling on the floor, she tugged out the thick folder for 1971. It was bulging with copies of orders, promotions, citations, operations plans, and the various other forms of paperwork that army units churned out in the course of business. Sammy slowly peeled through the pages and stopped at a stamped set of orders. The orders deployed the 67th Engineer Battalion (Heavy Construction) from Fort Leonard Wood, Missouri, to Vietnam on 20 June 1971.

It didn't take a Ph.D. to know that Eternity Base wasn't in Vietnam. She continued through the rest of the folder, looking for a set of orders detaching B Company from the battalion for the Eternity Base operation. Such orders would list the destination, but there were none to be found. As far as she could tell, the 67th Engineers had been attached to the III Corps Tactical Zone, doing various construction jobs throughout the area until redeployment to the United States on 18 May 1972. The unit had been disbanded in early 1974 during the big drawdown in forces after the war.

Sammy ran a hand through her short hair as she considered the puzzle. She knew the army paperwork system very well, and it was unheard of for an entire company to disappear for four months and not leave a paper trail. Why was Eternity Base so important that it could pull an engineer company out of a war zone for four months?

After another thirty minutes of going over the 67th's records for 1971 in more detail, Sammy still could find no hint of where B Company had gone. All references to that unit simply ended in August and reappeared at the end of December. Another person might have been frustrated, but Sammy was intrigued. This was a challenge. She slid the folder back into the box and replaced it on the shelf. Then she wandered out among the twelve-foot stacks, slowly making her way to her next destination, on the far side: the TDY records.

TDY is military jargon for Temporary Duty, and every time any army element—from the individual on up—was assigned away from the parent unit, a set of TDY orders had to be cut authorizing it. Since B Company had obviously been separated from the 67th Engineer Battalion, Sammy felt reasonably confident that a set of orders would be there, listing where the unit had gone.

She narrowed her search to the folder containing all TDY orders for III Corps, Vietnam, July–August 1971. Finally she found a mention of the phantom company. A single sheet of wrinkled paper—Department of Defense Form 1610—detached B Company, 67th Engineer Battalion, from III Corps, effective 18 August 1971, to the operational control (OPCON) of MACV-SOG.

Sammy's eyebrows raised at the last term, and her pulse rate quickened. She knew very well that MACV-SOG stood for Military Assistance Command Vietnam—Studies and Observation Group. What had MACV-SOG wanted with an engineer battalion? Despite the innocuous name, Sammy knew that SOG had run Special Forces cross-border missions throughout the war, along with many other classified operations. Some of the records for that unit were in the vault, requiring a top secret Q clearance to even take a look.

Checking SOG records was out of the question. Sammy looked at the rest of the orders. There was no termination date in the appropriate block. It just read: UNTIL MISSION COMPLETION. Destination was listed as CHI LANG, VIETNAM.

Sammy shook her head. She didn't care what the orders said; those pictures had not been taken in Vietnam. So where had B Company really gone? She replaced the orders, put the box back on the shelf, and headed for her desk. Her mind was clicking along, sorting all the data she had sifted through today, as she pulled on her leather jacket and headed up the stairs. She used her access card to open the door and stepped out into the lobby.

The guard casually looked her up and down as she left. His interest was not sexual. Not only were there numerous classified documents in the vault, but the personnel records were not for public dissemination. Nothing came in or out that wasn't authorized. The previous year, one of the part-timers had been fired for trying to take Elvis's army medical chest X-rays. Sammy wondered how American taxpayers would feel if they knew that Elvis's X-rays were now locked in a classified vault along with the original plans for the first atomic bomb.

She swung open the glass door and walked across the parking lot. Straddling a Yamaha motorcycle, Sammy put on her helmet. The engine roared to life and she cruised out of the lot, the cool fall air knifing into her despite the leather jacket. She cut through the back streets of St. Louis, eventually arriving home. She rented an apartment on the top floor of a garage behind a family house; it was small and cheap and, most importantly for her, it was quiet. She'd lived there for four years now. Sammy parked the bike and bounced up the stairs.

The first sight to greet her eyes as she locked the door behind her was the flashing red light on the answering machine. Sammy turned on the small electric heater and stood next to it for a few seconds, trying to get the chill out of her bones. She reached over and tapped the message button on the machine.

"Hey, big sister, it's me. I've got the late shift tonight—midnight to four A.M. Turn me on if you're still up. Gotta go. Bye."

The double beep sounded, indicating no more messages. Sammy put a pot of water on the stove and turned the heat on high. While waiting for it to boil, she stepped over to one of the many bookcases that lined the walls of her one-room apartment. This particular bookcase held row upon row of nonfiction—everything Sammy could find or order about the war in Vietnam. The book she wanted sat in the center at eye level: *Green Berets at War* by Shelby Stanton.

She checked the index. There were five references to Chi Lang. The last one was what she was looking for. Chi Lang had been a post on the Vietnamese-Cambodian border where Special Forces troops had launched classified reconnaissance missions. According to Stanton's research, the post had been shut down on 23 September 1971 due to extreme Vietcong pressure.

Had B Company been used to close out Chi Lang? Sammy immediately dismissed that thought. There was no snow at Chi Lang, and it certainly wasn't Eternity Base. So why then the orders? For the first time that day, Sammy felt a tremor of unease. More than twenty-five years ago, someone had gone through quite a bit of trouble to hide the whereabouts of B Company, 67th Engineers, for four months. If it hadn't been for some lieutenant with a camera and one roll of film, there would have been no anomalies in the unit history and the whole thing would have disappeared into the Archives in Washington, most likely never to surface again.

Before returning the book to the shelf, Sammy turned to a well-marked place in the back. Appendix A was titled SPECIAL FORCES PERSONNEL MISSING IN ACTION. Eighty-one names were listed in alphabetical order along with a one-paragraph description of the circumstances surrounding each incident. The entries weren't numbered; Sammy knew there were eighty-one because she had counted them one day and the number had stayed in her mind. Thirteen pages in from the first name she stopped. She knew the words by heart, but still she read:

Samuel Robert Pintella, Staff Sergeant, reconnaissance patrol member, Command & Control, MACV-SOG. Born 6 April 1941 in St. Louis, Missouri. Entered service on 23 July 1961 at St. Louis, Missouri.

Missing in action since 6 January 1972, when patrol inserted 4 miles inside Laos west of the DMZ; past initial radio contact, no further contact was ever made.

Sammy slowly put down the book and blinked the sudden tears out of her eyes. She looked up to the next higher shelf. A photo of a grinning young man astride an old Harley-Davidson motorcycle sat next to a photo of the same man wearing tiger-striped fatigues and sporting a green beret.

Sammy shifted her gaze to the clock. It was almost seven. Five hours until her sister, Conner, came on the TV as anchorperson for the Satellite News Network (SSN). Sammy decided to set her alarm so she could wake up and catch the first hour of Conner's broadcast. Her sister had moved up to the front desk only last week, and Sammy had watched her twice so far. It was strange for Sammy to see Conner on national satellite TV, even if it was the graveyard shift. Conner certainly was on a different life track, but Sammy felt no jealousy for her sister. Sammy believed that experiences shaped your life, and her experiences had been much different from Conner's.

She thought of a line she had once read: "It's not the sins of the father but rather the grief of the mother that is so damaging." Sammy disliked the word *damaging* because of its implications, but she did agree that their mother had been greatly affected by their father's actions and even more by his disappearance.

Their dad had wanted sons and had accepted the births of his daughters with a certain resignation. Their mother had initially acquiesced to his attempts to defeminize Samantha and Constance, the most immediate result being the adoption of the nicknames Sammy and Conner.

As the elder, Sammy had spent more time with their father, and her idolization had found an outlet in dungarees and tree climbing. She'd shied away from their mother's desire to slow her down and clean her up; as a consequence, their mother's hopes for a ladylike daughter had fallen on Conner.

Sammy had spent time with their dad whenever he was home. She remembered living in the trailer court outside of Fort Bragg among the other enlisted families in the 1960s. He'd taken her out to the woods camping. He'd also taught her martial arts—a practice their mother had rolled her eyes at and curtailed every time dad went overseas.

While Conner was spending her afternoon at ballet class, Sammy was catching tadpoles and playing war. She'd learned the pleasures of solitude, and her present position could be seen as a direct result of that. Conner, on the other hand, had taken a different path; her position as newswoman had had early seeds.

The age difference between them had loomed large when their dad was reported as missing in action. Sammy was devastated. She had been close to him; to Conner he was a distant symbol.

The four years between them had become an unbridgeable gap when Sammy got her driver's license. That was the year Sammy discovered that living and moving fast were inexplicably entwined. She had climbed into the '64 Mustang and never really looked back at the twelve-year-old girl dressed in taffeta and lace, tapdancing to a tune

Sammy would never understand. That summer Sammy, always a bright student, rejected the idea of college in favor of the Records Center. She'd had her own demons to exorcise, and the Records Center had beckoned with a possible solution.

Sammy had avoided her mother; she filled her days with work and her nights with men who would never be her father. When she finally realized that no man was better than the wrong man, she attained an uneasy peace with herself. She knew she could take care of herself—her dad had taught her that early on. Once she understood what was causing the many bad relationships, she stopped them like snapping her fingers.

Conner was tough too, but in a different way. She was driven to succeed, but Sammy wasn't sure her sister knew where that drive was taking her or if it would make her happy. Sammy was sure Conner would figure herself out eventually; it would just take time. She also knew she shouldn't judge her sister, since she herself was still struggling with an old ghost—one that the mention of the acronyms MACV-SOG and MIA had sparked in her today.

Sammy turned away from the memory-laden bookshelf, grabbed a package of instant noodles from the cabinet above the stove, and poured the contents into the boiling water.

— three —

NATIONAL PERSONNEL RECORDS CENTER, ST. LOUIS, MISSOURI, 23 NOVEMBER 1996. It had come to Sammy in the midst of watching Conner's first hour stint on the news, early in the morning with only the reflection from the small bulb on top of the aquarium mixing with the flickering glow of the TV. The organizational records of the 67th Engineers might not have yielded the information on where B Company had truly gone, but there was another avenue to pursue, albeit a more risky one. Watching her sister's discourse on the latest pathetic world situation, Sammy had made up her mind to pursue that route.

Now, back at work, she was following through on her decision. She went to the aisle where the files for the 67th Engineers were located, pulled the 1610 TDY order, and flipped it over. More than forty names were listed on the back—the men of B Company. Sammy copied the names of the four officers onto an index card and slipped it into the pocket of her jeans.

So far she had done little more than scratch at the surface, using unclassified data that was simply lying on the shelves and stored in the computer. Now, for the first time, she was stepping over the line. She had seen other workers do it for various reasons, mostly checking out personnel records of someone they knew; although forbidden by the rules of the Center, this usually was unofficially tolerated.

After her first year here, Sammy had asked Brad to help her pull all the classified information on her father's last mission. What they'd found had agreed on the surface with Stanton's book, but the records

21

were sketchy, which had bothered her. She discovered that her dad had been on a four-man special reconnaissance team named Utah, composed of two Americans and two indigenous personnel. She found out the name of the other American on the team, only to learn that he'd been reported as missing in action more than two months prior to her own father's disappearance. There was no explanation on the records for this time difference, nor had there been any reply from the Pentagon to her many letters.

That kind of gap in the records didn't surpise Sammy anymore. She had found more than enough documents that disagreed with the commonly accepted view of many of the events of modern history. And there was the fire that had destroyed the top two floors of the Records Center in 1973. It had burned the personnel records for those men involved in the government's nuclear testing in the late '40s and '50s and also the records for those troops exposed to Agent Orange in Vietnam. The destruction of the records was convenient when the government was faced with numerous lawsuits involving ailments claimed to result from those two government actions.

Over the years, Sammy had kept quiet about several discrepancies that might have embarrassed the government. The link between Eternity Base and MACV-SOG was beginning to get under her skin, however. There were too many facts that just didn't fit, and it was too similar to her father's case.

She had finally given up trying to find the "truth" concerning her father's disappearance when she'd realized how anxious it made her mother. Whether her mother's desire to keep the past buried was an attempt to avoid personal pain or to protect the pride of her new husband, Sammy was never sure. Sammy had even managed to forgive her mother for the ultimate betrayal—having her father declared legally dead so she could marry Nelson Young, M.D. That was the same year Sammy left home, so her stepfather had never assumed much of a role in her life.

Conner, on the other hand, had been only twelve and had accepted Nelson Young with love and exuberance to fill the gap created by her father's two tours of duty in Vietnam. Nelson, in turn, gave her his name and a fine education. He'd made the same offer to Sammy, but she had turned down the latter because she thought it was a package deal. Sammy now knew that Nelson would never have insisted she take his name in exchange for his love and support, but she also realized that there was more to it: she hadn't wanted his fathering and had let him know it. It was a decision she had made out of youth and pride and loyalty, and although she now knew it had been the wrong decision, she didn't regret it.

Sammy pushed her chair away from her desk, clearing her mind of memories and focusing on the present. She left the Records Center and took the elevator. She was sure Brad wouldn't miss her. He knew she put in more than her required forty hours a week, and he didn't begrudge her the flexibility to take care of personal business once in a while.

The seventh and eighth floors of the building now housed RC-PAC; the Reserve Component–Personnel Administration Center. Entering the foyer on the seventh floor, Sammy pulled her ID card out of her wallet and showed it to the guard at the desk. She was waved through into the hallway where secure doors stretched off in either direction. Sammy's access card wouldn't work on these doors, so she picked up one of the phones hanging on the wall and dialed.

"RC-PAC. Tomkins here."

"Tom, this is Sammy."

"Hey, how you doing, wild woman?"

"I'm in the hall."

"I'll be right out."

She hung up the phone and waited. Soon a set of doors whisked open and a short, balding man stepped out. His face broke into a wide smile as he walked up to Sammy. Handing her a visitor's pass, he guided her into the room.

"What brings you to my part of town? Misplaced some social security records?"

Sammy waited until the doors shut before answering. She'd worked with Tomkins dozens of times in the past; RC-PAC transferred the records of military personnel over to the Records Center every fiscal quarter when the designated individuals were no longer to be held in the reserve files.

"I need to check on a couple of people."

Tomkins gave her a curious glance. "What for?"

Sammy sighed. "That damn computer. We've got some gaps in the database and Brad wanted me to check it out." It was weak, but she also knew Tomkins would do just about anything for her on the off chance she might finally agree to date him. She hoped it didn't come to that. He was one of those men who needed female attention like a leaky raft needed air: Sammy knew she could pump him up every day, but he would never be strong enough to float on his own. She had long ago learned the bitter lesson that people who couldn't stand on their own made miserable partners in life, dragging you down with them.

"So how're the fish?" Sammy had invited Tomkins to her apartment once for a small party for some of her coworkers, an invitation he had made much too significant.

"Still breathing."

"Uh-huh." He led her into a larger room—an above-surface, miniaturized version of the Records Center. All the records for military personnel no longer on active duty, but who were or had been part of the reserves—either in a reserve unit or the IRR (Individual Ready Reserve)—were kept at RC-PAC. "OK. What do you need?"

Sammy pulled out the index card. "I need whatever you have on these folks."

Tomkins looked over the names. "Army, eh? All right." He led her to his desk. "Take a seat." He punched into his computer for a few seconds, then the printer whirred. He grabbed the printout. "I'll be right back."

Sammy licked her lips nervously as he disappeared into the labyrinth of records. She remembered when two of her fellow workers had unearthed information on Ferdinand Marcos in the Records Center. At a party one of them casually mentioned what they'd found to a reporter for the *New York Times*. Once the media got hold of the information, the publicity train had run down the tracks. Marcos's fabricated history of being a resistance fighter in the Philippines during World War II had gone up in smoke. That had been fine for the media, but the two workers were no longer employees of the government.

"I've got 201 files for the first two." He handed them over and disappeared again.

Sammy opened up Capt. Louis Townsend's record. He had been the commander of B Company from April 1971 through January

1972. His Officer Efficiency Report (OER) for the time period of Eternity Base made no mention of the base and made it sound as if he had been in Vietnam his entire tour of duty. He even had a Bronze Star for the Vietnam tour. The citation read:

> For numerous heavy construction engineering assignments under adverse conditions in hostile territory.

She looked at the other file. It was Lieutenant Freely's—the picture taker. His record held no hint of Eternity Base either. Tomkins returned with the other two lieutenants' records and Sammy went through them. Nothing in either one referred to Eternity Base or cold weather or held even the slightest indication that the men had been deployed out of Vietnam for four months in 1971.

Tomkins was sitting on the other side of the desk, pretending to look at his computer screen. When Sammy closed the last file, he raised an eyebrow. "Find what you needed?"

Sammy shook her head. "No."

"Maybe if you tell me what you're looking for, I can help you find it."

Sammy closed her eyes and thought furiously. "How about medical records?" Medical records for military personnel were considered government property; when an individual went off active duty, the entire folder for his career time was sent to St. Louis.

Tomkins stood up. "Yeah, we got the active duty ones for those people. You want all four?"

While he was gone, Sammy wrote on her index card the last known addresses for the four officers. She had just finished when Tompkins returned. She found what she was looking for in the second folder: Lieutenant Freely's. The entry was hand written on a diagnostic form dated 19 November 1971:

> SM suffering from severe frostbite, second and third digits, left hand.

The consulting physician's name was typed at the bottom of the page: Doctor John Reynolds, Major, U.S. Air Force. She had two more pieces of the puzzle, although it wasn't clear where they fit:

Freely hadn't gotten frostbite in Vietnam. And why had he been treated by an air force doctor and not an army medic?

"Do you have any records on an air force major—name John Reynolds? He was a doctor. Social security number 185-35-9375."

Tomkins typed for a few seconds and then looked up. "Nope. You have it all. He got out of service in '75. Died in '83."

With these new items, Sammy took her leave quickly, short-circuiting Tomkins's attempts to make conversation. She already knew the next thing she had to check.

"Want to go to lunch?" Brad stopped by her desk.

"No thanks," Sammy answered.

Brad didn't leave right away. He perched on the edge. "Are you all right?"

Sammy looked up in surprise. "Of course."

Brad shook his head. "I don't know. You've been acting a little weird lately. Are you sure everything's OK?"

Sammy gave what she hoped was a reassuring smile. "Everything's fine, Brad. Just a little tired, that's all. I watched my sister on the news late last night and didn't get much sleep."

"How's she doing?"

This time the smile was true. "She looked really good."

Brad stood. "Well, when you talk to her again, give her my best wishes. She seems to really be on the way up."

That was an accurate way to describe Conner, Sammy reflected. When Brad was out of sight, she headed into the stacks. Unerringly she went to the correct shelf. Doctor Reynolds's 201 file was in a box containing those of other former air force officers who had died in 1983. Sitting down cross-legged on the concrete floor, Sammy opened the file and started reading, going from his medical school and commissioning through his various tours of duties. The man's professional life was open before her.

From late 1968 through 1970, Reynolds was stationed at Bethesda Naval Hospital in Maryland. As 1971 began the doctor was still in Maryland. Then she found what she was searching for. In May 1971, Maj. John Reynolds, M.D., USAF, was given a set of TDY orders assigning him to a place called McMurdo Station for six months.

Sammy had heard of McMurdo Station. She frowned in thought for a few seconds, then it came to her. McMurdo was the United States' primary research station on the seventh continent. Eternity Base was in Antarctica.

— four —

SNN Headquarters, Atlanta, Georgia, 24 November 1996.
"What about the hearings?"

Stu Fernandez shook his head. "We've got that covered. They're going live on most of the channels anyway."

Conner Young tapped a finger on her desktop. Stu was an assistant producer for the Satellite News Network (SNN) twenty-four-hour news, and as such he was in the same position as she—one step away from prime time. "But what about a different angle? What if we—"

Stu held up a hand. He'd been here four years now and had heard it all, or at least thought he had. "Conner, listen to me. The senate hearings are dead. People are tired of them. We need something totally different. This is an up or out business. You either make it—and keep making it—or you're out."

Conner had graduated from the local news in Chicago to SNN only three weeks ago, and already the pressure was on. This was not a place where you could take a moment to pat yourself on the back. That attitude started at the top and insinuated itself into every room of the large building in Atlanta that headquartered the network. It made for great ratings and a high burnout rate.

Conner's physical appearance belied the inner strength necessary to fight one's way into this building, much less the stamina to endure and survive. Many adversaries were still smoking in the ruins of their underestimation of Conner's tenacity. She wasn't a woman you glanced at, but rather a finely made specimen who caught your

28

attention and held it long enough to create admiration. Her facial features were elegant and classic—thin, finely sculpted nose; wide, evenly placed dark eyes; and a generous, well-defined mouth surrounded by a soft, creamy complexion that caused fingers to clench with the desire to touch.

Conner's trademark, though, was her hair—thick, black, and cut in a short geometric style. She had Sammy's height and slender body, but, as if God couldn't find enough gifts to bestow, Conner also had a full bosom that her slim hips only accentuated. She was beautiful and she knew it. Although her looks mattered little to her, she was always aware of their effect on others and used that to her advantage.

Stu was beginning to lose the glassy-eyed look he'd had the first week Conner was here, and for that she was grateful. She hated it when people spoke to her about professional matters yet stared in that way she had grown accustomed to—distracted by her appearance.

Stu turned to leave. "Listen, I've got to get to the tape room. I'll see you later."

Conner didn't have an office. She had a cubicle, just off the main studio where the news was fed out nonstop, every hour on the hour. The schedule was brutal. Not only did the anchors have to do a four-hour on-the-air shift five times a week, but they also had to research and present two five-minute special features a week. It was the ability to put together these features that separated the good reporter from the pretty face that could simply read a teleprompter. Conner knew she had to prove she was one of the former; the latter didn't last long at SNN.

Conner sighed as she continued working the computer's mouse, searching the extensive SNN database for something she could suck up, refine, and use. SNN used not only the United Press International (UPI) and Associated Press (AP) lines but almost every other source of information available, both human and machine. The chief executive officer of SNN, J. Russell Parker, liked to boast that the SNN mainframe computer contained more up-to-date world information than the National Security Agency's.

The buzz of Conner's phone saved her for the moment from the eye-numbing green tint of the screen.

"SNN. Conner Young."

"Hey, Constance."

There was only one person who called her that, and to be honest, Conner hated her given name. But she'd never tell Sammy that. "Hey, Samantha. How're you doing?"

"All right."

There was a long pause. Sammy had never called her at work before, even when she'd been up in Chicago. "Are you OK, sis?"

"I'm fine."

Conner waited, aware of an awkwardness that was always present in their conversations. Well, then, what the heck are you calling me for? she thought. "How's mom?"

"All right. She's in England with Nelson." Conner frowned. Sammy had never called Nelson dad even though her mom had married him more than nineteen years ago. It bothered Conner.

This father issue had always been a wedge between them. For Conner, middle childhood had been like growing up in a house of mourning—a strange situation, since the loss of her father meant nothing to her. It was hard for her to miss something she'd never really had. But even as a child Conner could see how devastating it was for Sammy. Whereas their mother was able to replace the husband she lost, Sammy couldn't replace her father.

Sammy had fallen victim to her mother's inability to start a new life without negating the old. It was as if the only way her mom could make room in her heart for Nelson was to destroy all the emotional evidence of the young soldier she had loved. Sammy felt betrayed. Conner had always thought this was what had driven her sister into two quick marriages and that dismal job she couldn't seem to leave.

Her own situation had been much different. With Nelson, Conner had found a man who was hungry to love and be loved. His younger step-daughter became the focus of his life, and he made sure she had few wants. Though Conner felt on the surface that Sammy had thrown away a chance for paternal affection, the selfish child in her was glad that she'd never had to share Nelson with her sister. In Conner's mind, Sammy had tied herself emotionally to a dead man, which seemed a foolish thing to do. The differences in the way they lived seemed ample evidence of Sammy's folly.

It took Conner a moment to realize that Sammy was still silent even though she was the one who had called. For the first time Conner could remember, her older sister was hesitant. Conner decided to wait it out. She returned her gaze to the computer and clicked the mouse, looking at a new screen.

Finally Sammy spoke. "Conner. Listen, I've found something strange in the Records Center."

"Yeah. What?" Jesus Christ, Conner thought as she read her screen, the UPI had actually carried a story on UFO landings in Idaho. Idaho of all places! How come the damn things never landed in Central Park?

"There's this place, it's called Eternity Base, and it was built by the military in 1971, and there's no record of it anywhere."

"If there's no record, how do you know it exists?"

"I've got photos of it. That's what started me on it. I found this file in unit histories and then . . ."

As her sister related her search, Conner forgot about the computer screen. She was surprised at Sammy's investigative skills. When her sister finally drew to a close, though, Conner was confused.

"Antarctica? Why would the army build a place in Antarctica?"

"I don't know. But they certainly went to a lot of trouble to hide it."

"Well, even if they did, what's the big deal? I mean we're talking twenty-five years ago. Who cares? Maybe it was just some temporary thing and it's gone now."

Sammy's voice was sharp when she answered, and Conner belatedly realized her mistake: everything that happened twenty-five years ago was important to Sammy. "That may be true, but the simple fact that the United States built something secret down there is pretty significant."

"Why?"

Sammy sounded surprised. "It violated the treaty."

"What treaty?"

"The 1959 Antarctica Treaty the United States signed along with seventeen other nations. It suspended all territorial claims for thirty years and also specifically prohibited any military presence in Antarctica. It's the one place on the planet where weapons are outlawed."

Conner considered that. "Did these engineers have weapons with them?"

"Well, no, not that you can see in the picture. But that's not the point."

"What is the point?" Conner didn't like asking so many questions. It seemed to give Sammy an edge.

"The *point* is that something was built down there in 1971, something that somebody took a lot of trouble covering up, to the extent of altering and hiding official records. Something that was important enough to pull an army engineer company out of a war zone to build."

"So what do you want me to do about it?" When she heard Sammy's reply, Conner realized that her tone must have been harsher than she intended.

"I don't expect you to do a damn thing about it. I just thought that maybe you could use something interesting in your new job to get a leg up, but obviously you don't need any help. I shouldn't have called you in the first place. Bye."

The phone went dead. Conner slowly put down the receiver and considered what her sister had said. Why did Sammy think she needed a leg up? For a second she felt a flash of irritation at an offer of help from a woman who lived above a garage. Maybe it was her sister's way of hanging on: by helping her, Sammy could feel some personal sense of responsibility for Conner's success. Conner had felt it before—the subtle innuendos meant to remind her that self-reliance and competence played a small part in her current position. Conner knew she had earned her way to this tiny cubicle, and she didn't want to hand anyone else—even her sister—any share of that.

But Conner couldn't completely deny her professional interest. Sammy had always seemed to possess an innate ability to sense the hidden and darker sides of the world around her. As soon as her sister had mentioned the acronym MACV-SOG, Conner had known that Sammy would hold onto this issue like a dog with a bone until she sucked it dry of every piece of available information. Her sister would continue to dig; if she unearthed more, there might very well be a story. Maybe not the one Sammy wanted, but one that could push Conner out of the cubicle and into an office with a real door. As Stu had said—it was an up or out business.

Antarctica. Maybe there were other hooks that could be tied in. The environmental group Our Earth might be interested in something involving that area of the world. Conner had done a story on an Our Earth protest about pollution in Lake Michigan, and she'd been impressed with the group's ability to generate publicity.

That thought reminded her of Devlin, the man who had run the protests. He was the only person in the four years she was in Chicago who had managed to penetrate her professional cloak, albeit only for a brief moment. She remembered that he'd talked for a while about Antarctica, even mentioning that he'd spent a winter down there.

Conner grabbed her Rolodex and flipped through to O. She dialed the number for the Our Earth headquarters in California. A cheery sounding young woman told her that Devlin was currently in Australia. With a little coaxing, the girl gave an overseas number where he might be reached.

Conner looked at the clocks posted on the wall. It was after midnight in Tokyo, which she guessed was somewhere near the same time zone as Australia. She dialed the international code and then the number. When the phone was picked up on the other end, she was surprised at the clarity of the transmission.

"Hello?" a voice with a rich Australian accent answered.

"Is Devlin there? This is Conner Young calling from the United States."

"The United States, eh? Must be early in the morning there, isn't it?"

Conner rolled her eyes. "It's a little after eleven."

"It's a little after midnight here." The voice waited for an apology, then, getting none, moved on with a sigh. "All right. I'll see if I can track him down for you, missy."

There was a thump as the phone was dropped, and Conner started tapping her fingers on the desktop. After three long minutes the phone was finally picked up.

"I didn't expect to hear from you again."

Conner was startled at the reaction the deep voice brought out. "Devlin, how are you doing?"

"Not bad. How are you, Conner?"

"All right."

"Where are you calling from? Charlie said it was the States."

"Atlanta."

"Atlanta? What happened to Chicago?" Devlin asked.

"I moved over to SNN."

There was a light whistle. "So you've made the big time. Congratulations."

"Well, actually I'm on the periphery of the big time." Conner shifted to the task at hand. "That's what I'm calling you about. I remember you talked about having been to Antarctica several times."

"Yes. Four times. I also wintered over at the Our Earth base there three years ago. Why? What's up?"

"I received information about something, and I was wondering if you could give me some help."

"What's the information?"

"I've been told that the army built a secret installation, called Eternity Base, in Antarctica in 1971."

"What kind of secret base?"

"I don't know."

"Where exactly was the place built in Antarctica?"

"I don't know. That's why they call it a secret, Devlin."

"Well, I've been down there and I've also talked to a lot of people stationed down there, especially at McMurdo, and I've never heard anything about a place called Eternity Base. It would be pretty difficult to cover up something like that, although '71 was a long time ago."

Conner was interested in impact first, details later. "What I want to know is—if this Eternity Base did exist, and no one knew about it, how big a story would that be?"

Devlin whistled. "It'd be big, Conner. First, it would have broken the '59 treaty. Any base that is built down there, even if it is temporary, has to be open for inspection by any of the other signees of the treaty. If a base is hidden, well then it certainly isn't open for inspection.

"Second, if the army built it, then it's probably some sort of military base. If it still exists, that would be a gross violation of not only the letter of the current 1991 accord governing things in Antarctica but also the spirit of the accord. Our Earth has really been upping the pressure there, and we have a few things planned in the next couple of months. Discovering something like this Eternity Base would be great publicity."

Conner backtracked a little. "Well, other than a few nebulous records, I have no real proof of anything. I just wanted to find out if this was worth pursuing."

"It's definitely worth pursuing. If you need any help, don't hesitate to call me." Devlin laughed. "Even if it is after midnight. I remember the last time we talked after midnight."

Conner didn't want to discuss that right now. "I'll do some more checking, and I'll get back to you if I come up with something."

"All right. I'll be at this number for at least another two days. After that, I'm not sure where I'll be."

"Bye." Conner slowly put down the phone. She'd never even asked Devlin what he was doing in Australia. She shrugged. There'd be time for that if she talked to him again.

Damn Sammy. Conner swung her bulky purse up on the desk and started rummaging through, looking for her personal address book. She thought she had Sammy's work number in there but she wasn't sure. There it was—under S. Conner punched in the number with her pencil.

"Records Center. Samantha Pintella."

"All right, I'm sorry. I've had a rough day."

There was no trace of anger in Sammy's voice. "It's OK. I shouldn't have called you anyway."

"No. I think it's an interesting story. Will you get in trouble if we do something on it?"

Sammy's voice was tentative. "Well . . . I was thinking that you wouldn't have to say you got it from me. You could probably talk to one of those men in the engineer unit who built the place and maybe they would tell you something about it. You wouldn't have to tell them that you first heard about Eternity Base from records in the Center."

Conner got a clear screen on the computer and hit the speaker button on her phone. "All right, give me the names and addresses. I'll see what they have to say."

After Sammy was finished relaying the information on the four officers, she added: "Let me know what you find out, all right? I'm interested in this thing. The tie-in with MACV-SOG is kind of strange."

"Sure. I'll get back in touch. Bye." Conner hung up. She was right about Sammy's special interest in this case. Sammy just couldn't give up on the possibility that her father might still be alive. She was always reading anything to do with the MIA issue or Special Forces operations in Vietnam.

Conner felt a moment's guilt for suspecting Sammy of a hidden agenda. This story could help her career—Sammy was right about that. In this business one tended to be paranoid. There was always someone right behind you on the ladder waiting for you to screw it all up so they could stomp over your shattered career to take your place.

Conner shook thoughts of Sammy's fixation out of her head. I have my own fixation, she thought, smiling. She immediately called information and started working on the first name on her list. Using his last known address, she tracked down Captain Townsend's number.

The phone was answered by a woman who told her to hold on and she'd get her husband. At last the phone was picked up. She wondered if the man was in a wheelchair, it had taken him so long.

"Hello?" said a man's voice, tremulous with old age.

"Is this Louis Townsend?"

"Yes."

"This is Conner Young. I'm with SNN News and I'm doing some research on army installations. I'm particularly interested in something your unit was involved with in 1971."

"The army? '71?" There was a pause. "I was in Vietnam in '71. What project are you talking about? We did a lot of work shutting things down there that year."

"I'm not talking about Vietnam, Mister Townsend. I have some information that your company was sent on temporary duty to Antarctica for four months near the end of the year. Could you shed any light on what you were building in Antarctica?"

There was a long pause, then Townsend's voice came back, sounding very distant. "I'm sorry, ma'am, but you've received bad information. We were in Vietnam from June of '71 through May of '72. A man doesn't forget something like that even if he's as old as I am."

"I know that's what your unit is listed officially as doing, Mister Townsend, but I do have some evidence indicating that—"

"Ma'am, I really have nothing else to tell you. I have to go now."

The phone went dead. Conner felt a lot better about this hang-up than she had about her sister's. There was a story here. She could feel it. Old soldiers loved to tell war stories, yet this guy had hung up on her.

She quickly tracked down the second name on the list, but there was no answer. She moved on to the third. Conner checked the map on the wall as she called—the area code was in New Jersey. The phone was picked up on the third ring by a woman.

"Hello?"

"May I please speak to William Freely?"

"He's at work. May I take a message?"

"Could I get his work number, please?"

"It's 654-9329."

"Thanks." Conner dialed the new number.

"Freely's Building Supply. This is Anita. How may I help you?"

"Is Mister Freely in?"

"Hold on. I think he's out back on the loading dock."

While she waited, Conner drew up a blank screen on her computer and began typing questions.

"Bill Freely here." The voice sounded slightly out of breath and very deep.

"Mister Freely, this is Conner Young from SNN news. I'm doing research on army installations and I'm particularly interested in a project your unit was involved with in 1971."

"Yeah?" The voice was not friendly. "Which project? We did a whole lot of stuff that year."

"I'm interested in what B Company, 67th Engineers, built down in Antarctica between August and December 1971."

There was a long pause. "I'm sorry, miss, but you've got your facts wrong. We were never in Antarctica. I surely would have remembered that."

"I'm sure you would have, Mister Freely, especially since you were treated for severe frostbite on two fingers on your left hand at Mc-Murdo Station, Antarctica, on 19 November 1971. Tell me, did you get frostbite while taking those photographs of Eternity Base? The photos I have copies of?" Conner waited. The fact that he didn't hang up right away was a good sign.

Freely's voice was sharp. "Listen, lady. We were told that everything about Eternity Base was classified. I mean, it was a long time ago and all that, but still a guy can get in trouble. I forgot all about taking those pictures."

Conner leaned forward in her seat. "I have them here on my desk and they have your name on the back."

Another long pause. Finally Freely came back, his voice resigned. "Yeah, I took those damn pictures. I don't see what the big deal about the whole thing was anyway. They told us not to talk about it—national security and all that—and we were just so happy to be out of Vietnam that everyone went along with it. At least in the beginning. But after a couple of weeks down there in that hellhole, Vietnam started looking like a good deal."

Conner thought quickly. She'd learned to keep people talking by shifting subjects. They were so busy thinking about the answers that they'd forget the importance of what they were saying. "What about the aircrews that flew you in there? Do you know where they were from?"

"There was only one aircrew. I think they were home-based in Hawaii."

Conner cut back to something else that might get a reaction. "How's your hand doing?"

Freely's voice rose an octave. "That was part of the bullshit about that mission. We'd just finished off-loading the plane and it had headed back when I got hurt. I'd been working on the surface shaft doors and I got careless. You'd think I'd have known better after three months, but . . . anyway I got the bite bad and needed to be medevacked.

"Well, this major who was in charge wouldn't send another plane out to get me. I had to wait until that particular plane got back to McMurdo, set down, refueled, and came back out to pick me up. Probably wasted about three hours because of that.

"Since the whole thing was classified, they wouldn't medevac me out of Antarctica after I received my initial treatment. So I had to go back to Eternity Base with my hand like that until the entire unit was pulled out. That's what really screwed up my fingers more than anything else. And that's why I only have three fingers on my left hand. I had to have the sons of bitches amputated eight years ago. The civilian doctor who did it said it was because they'd never healed right due to the prolonged exposure. So you can take the goddamn army and its station down there and shove it. I don't want to have anything more to do with it."

"I can understand that you are somewhat bitter, Mister Freely. You spent the entire four months there in Antarctica?" Conner coaxed.

"Yeah."

"When did you leave?"

"About four or five days before Christmas."

"Where were you stationed? At McMurdo?"

"No. Like I said, we only went to McMurdo for emergencies—we didn't have a doctor with us. We were stationed right there at Eternity Base."

"Where was Eternity Base?"

"I don't know."

"What do you mean you don't know? You didn't know where you were?"

Freely's voice took on that *"I'm talking to an idiot"* tone that Conner hated. "I mean, I knew we were in Antarctica, but I couldn't tell you where. We weren't allowed any maps. When we flew, they blacked out the windows in the hold of the C-130. No one in the company knew where the hell we were."

"You had to have some idea. East, west, north, or south of Mc-Murdo?"

"Lady, you ever been to Antarctica?" Freely didn't wait for an answer. "The goddamn place is one big jumbled-up mass of ice and mountains. North or south?" Freely laughed. "Compasses don't work too well down there. Do you know that the magnetic pole is farther north of the true South Pole than McMurdo? In fact, magnetic south from McMurdo is actually west if you look at a map. That was the most screwed-up place I've ever been. All I know is that the site was a little less than a two-hour flight by C-130 from McMurdo. You look at the pictures and you got as good an idea of where that place was as I do."

"What did you build there?"

"We didn't really 'build' anything. We put together a Tinkertoy set. It was all prefab," he explained. "They flew it in by sections. Someone with a lot more brains than we had in our outfit designed that thing. Each piece could fit in a 130, yet when we put it all together it was pretty big. Of course there were a shit load of 130 loads coming in. Hell, they spent almost an entire week just bringing in fuel bladders. That plane flew every moment the weather allowed."

"What was it you put together?" Conner asked quietly, hoping she could keep Freely going.

"My best guess is that it was some sort of C & C structure—Command and Control. We just put the buildings together. Before we were even done, they brought in more guys to put in other stuff. I remember a lot of commo equipment. They sealed off sections of the place as we finished, so I really couldn't tell you what it looked like on the inside when it was completed.

"We stayed in two prefab Quonset huts on the surface, and we broke those down and took them back out with us when we left. All you could see when we took that last flight out was the entry and ventilation shafts. Everything else was underground."

"What did it look like underground?"

"There were twelve of the prefab units."

"How were the units laid out?"

"We set them up in three rows of four, about eight to ten feet apart, and roofed over the space between, which just about doubled the underground area of the main base."

"That took four months?"

"What took the most time was digging out that much ice and snow even before they brought in the first unit. We also dug two really big tunnels on either side for storage and two areas for fuel. Plus the long tunnel and area for the power station."

"Do you have any idea who occupied it?"

"You know, that was the funny thing. That last day when we flew out, I really don't think there was anybody left behind. There was this major who was in charge. He was a real strange fellow. Spooky. Anyway, he was on the last flight out with us."

"Do you remember that major's name?"

"I don't know. Claxton or something like that. He made everyone nervous—always sneaking around, checking on people."

Conner was confused. "Why go through all that trouble to build something if no one was going to use it?"

"Hey, you got me, lady," Freely snorted. "I'm just a poor tax-paying schmuck like everyone else. I don't know why the government spends money like it does. I'll tell you one funny thing though: the last two weeks we were there, the project was basically done—you know, the buildings and all that. We spent the remaining time in the tunnels storing a whole bunch of supplies off-loaded from that C-130."

"What sort of supplies?"

"All I can remember is a lot of food."

"What about—"

Conner's streak had run its course. "Listen, lady. I already said too much."

"I really appreciate your help, Mister Freely. I was wondering if perhaps I could send someone to talk to you and—"

"Lady, I just told you. I want nothing more to do with this. Don't call me back. And if anyone asks, I didn't tell you squat." The phone clicked.

"Asshole," Conner muttered into the dead receiver.

"Anybody I know?"

She looked up, startled. Stu was standing there with a smile on his face. "Sounds like you were having an interesting conversation."

Conner made a snap decision. "It was. I have something kind of weird that I want to run by you. You have some time?"

Stu made a great show of looking at his watch. "Well, I suppose I could spare twenty minutes for my newest reporter. Shoot."

Conner concisely briefed him on the entire development, occasionally using the notes she'd been making on the computer while talking to Freely. When she ground to a halt she looked expectantly over at Stu, who was perched on the edge of her desk. "Well, what do you think?"

"About what?"

Conner felt a flash of irritation. "About the story."

Stu shook his head. "You don't have a story."

"What do you mean?"

"What are you going to do?" Stu sighed. "All right. Let me lay it out for you. The idea that the government built some secret place down in Antarctica is all very unique, but you have two major problems. One is that it was twenty-five years ago. People aren't going to care that much.

"Even more basic than that, though, is you have no solid source. You say you can't use your sister's stuff because she'll lose her job. And this guy Freely doesn't sound like he's willing to come forward. Maybe you could dig and come up with somebody else, but even then we need to backstop with something stronger than somebody remembering what happened that long ago."

Stu stood up. "It was a good lead, though. Your sister sounds like she might be sitting on a gold mine of information there at the

Records Center. Keep up the link. I'd be careful about the Our Earth people, though. They'll do damn near anything to get a story. They'd just get you hooked so they could talk about the whales getting killed."

As Stu disappeared, Conner swiveled her chair thoughtfully back to her computer. Stu was right about the Our Earth people. But it wasn't just them. She thought of what she had done, or would do, for the sake of a story. Conner had always known that ambition was a card with a flip side. That other side was the sheer capability to do anything, damn the consequences. Conner had the ability to play that card. And this, plus her looks, would eventually get her everything she wanted.

Stu was dismissing the story too easily, she thought, but she had to admit he was right about not having a backstop. They'd get blown out of the water if they put what they had on the air. She had a feeling about this, though. The government had tried too hard to hide this base. Even though it was twenty-five years ago, who knows what they might have done. Conner scrolled the computer screen back on her notes, looking for another door to try.

It took her less than forty-five minutes to find it.

NATIONAL PERSONNEL RECORDS CENTER, ST. LOUIS, MISSOURI.
Sammy slowly put down the phone. Her sister had acquired quite a bit of information in the last couple of hours. She considered the request Conner had made and looked at the in box perched on the corner of the desk. She was behind—a rare event. She'd spent a few hours this morning using the computer to try a few different avenues of approach on Eternity Base. The fact that she'd come up without even the slightest mention of the name made her recognize the extent to which the information had been buried.

Conner's suggestion that she try to track down the aircrew of the plane that had made the runs from Eternity Base to McMurdo made sense, but Sammy wasn't exactly sure where to find the information. She figured that Hawaii—where the plane was supposedly based— was her best bet.

Twenty minutes of work yielded two C-130 squadrons stationed at Hickam Air Force Base in Hawaii at the appropriate time: the 746th

Tactical Airlift Squadron (TAS) and the 487th TAS. Sammy stood and stretched her back, preparing for the plunge into the stacks.

She pulled the 746th's records first. An hour and forty minutes later she was familiar with the operations of that unit in 1971 but had found no record of flights to Antarctica. Her luck changed with the 487th. The records showed that C-130s from that unit had regularly made runs from Hawaii, across the Pacific, and down to McMurdo. But there was nothing to indicate that one plane had been detached for four months to the Antarctic, so Sammy went to her old standby—TDY records.

She was halfway through the folder that held the TDY records for the 487th and about to turn a page when something caught her eye. Sammy's breathing grew faster as she read the DD-1610. It detached one plane and crew on 15 August 1971 to the operational control of MACV-SOG, Vietnam, for the duration. It was too much of a coincidence. Sammy quickly copied the tail number of the plane and the name of the five crew members.

Returning to her computer, she accessed the personnel database and punched in the name of the pilot. The screen glowed with the reply. Sammy quickly checked the other four crew members of that C-130. Their entries all read the same. With a shaking hand she dialed her sister's work number.

"SNN. Conner Young."

Sammy wasted no time on preamble. "Constance, what was the last day that engineer lieutenant told you he was down there? The day they flew out?"

"Hold on." Sammy licked her lips as she waited for her sister's answer. "Well, he didn't give a date. He just said it was four or five days before Christmas."

Sammy looked at the date on the screen and felt her stomach lurch. "And Freely said that only that aircrew knew the location of Eternity Base?"

"He said that crew and some major named Claxton or something like that. Why?"

Sammy told her sister what she'd just uncovered. There was a long silence on the other end.

— five —

SNN HEADQUARTERS, ATLANTA, GEORGIA. "You have fifteen minutes, Conner," Stu Fernandez whispered in her ear as they entered the conference room. "Make it good."

J. Russell Parker presided at the end of the table. Only forty-eight years old, he had made SNN the leading news network after outlasting and outcovering all the competition during the Gulf War. With a prematurely balding forehead, set off by large bushy eyebrows, he looked more like a friendly uncle than a CEO. He disarmed his competitors by his amiable appearance, but the mind behind that face was razor sharp.

Parker was flanked on either side by his primary assistants, John Cordon and Louise Legere. The latter was generally hated by all the reporters even if she was good at her job as special features editor. Legere was as strong as Conner in the ambition department but was less graceful, stepping on toes as she pursued her goals. Cordon, the executive vice president of operations, was considered more a flunky than an executive. He seldom spoke, but for some reason, when he did speak he had the boss's ear.

Conner took her position at the other end of the table facing Parker. Stu sat in the middle of the three chairs on the flank, next to Cordon. Conner noted that careful choice of position: Stu wasn't throwing himself totally in her camp until he saw which way the wind blew.

44

Parker greeted her, starting the clock. "Ms. Young, Stu tells me you've dug up something interesting and that you think it's worthy of more investigation."

"Yes, sir, I have." Without further ado, she presented her information, laying it out concisely and in what she hoped was an intriguing manner. The three let her speak for five minutes without an interruption.

Done, she leaned back in her chair and waited. No one spoke, waiting for some indication of how Parker felt. The man in question rubbed his chin and then smiled. "Very interesting. Sounds dark and mysterious. I like that. *But.*" He pronounced the last word very clearly. "But, we really don't have anything solid to run with. You say your sister does not wish to be used either as a source or even as an anonymous conduit of hard copy information."

"They check people going in and out of the Records Center," Conner explained. "Even if she was able to sneak out the photos, if we used them in a story, it wouldn't be hard for the government to find out where they came from and backtrack that to Samantha."

"What about one of these engineer fellows?" Cordon asked.

Legere cut in, not allowing Conner to answer. "No good. We're talking about something that's twenty-five years old. People aren't interested in some old fart standing in front of a camera recounting a story about a mysterious base in Antarctica."

"However," Legere beamed a frosty smile down the table toward Conner, "if we did have something solid—a document, say, or especially these photos—I think it might make a good five-minute spot. We might be able to stir up enough reaction to justify further digging by one of my people. Antarctica is an interesting topic as far as audience reaction goes. The last frontier sort of thing."

Conner pressed her case. She wanted more than a five-minute spot, and it was *her* story. If Legere got her way it would basically mean that Conner had wasted everyone's time here, and she was sure Parker would remember that in a negative light. "I think we might be able to work the treaty violation angle."

Parker was tapping a finger against his upper lip. "My big question is: what did they build down there? We're talking 1971. Nixon is president. Vietnam is going down the tubes. The country is in bad shape and we have something secret being built in Antarctica. Maybe some sort of radar setup?" Parker roused himself from his musings. "Oh, well. It doesn't matter. We don't have enough to go with, I'm afraid. You really don't have any hard evidence, Ms. Young. Nice—"

Conner took the plunge and cut in. "The tail number of an air force plane that was reported missing in action on 21 December 1971 in Vietnam is the same tail number of a plane that filed a flight plan out of McMurdo on 21 December 1971." Conner knew she was speaking too quickly and tried to slow down. "I checked FAA records. Those men were the only people who knew where Eternity Base was, and all five are currently listed as MIA in Vietnam." Conner had the room's undivided attention. "Whatever they were doing was important enough to cover up the loss of five men. And those men did not disappear in Vietnam." Conner looked Parker in the eye. "What if I find out what was built there?"

Legere swiveled her gaze at the reporter. "How?"

Conner played her last card. "I go there."

"What!" exclaimed Legere.

"We send some people down there and find the place."

"That's if it still exists," Legere countered.

"I believe it does," Conner said.

"Huh? You *believe!*" Legere shook her head. "Young lady, do you know how much it would cost to mount a team to go to Antarctica? It's the end of the world, for God's sake."

"We could get logistical support from Our Earth." Conner had just finished talking to Devlin and he'd promised his help. But she knew that these people would be as leery as Stu about getting mixed up with Our Earth.

Parker raised his bushy eyebrows. "Our Earth? How are they involved?"

"They're not involved, sir. But they have experience in the Antarctic. They run a year-round station near McMurdo Base, and McMurdo served as the supply conduit for Eternity Base. They are the only non-government organization to have such a setup on the continent. They have both ship and plane capability. The only expenses we would incur would be transportation to New Zealand. Our Earth would take care of logistical support from there on out—with no professional compromise. We can do the story however we like.

"Additionally," Conner continued, "even if we somehow don't find Eternity Base, we still can pick up enough other stories to make the trip worthwhile. There's the French airstrip story. The Japanese and Korean whaling fleets, which those countries claim are operated only for scientific purposes. The new treaty and its effect on research down there." She'd been told it was best to have more than one plan when you briefed Parker. She could see him finally crack a slight smile.

"How will you find this place if no one knows where it is?" Cordon asked quietly .

"I'll find it," Conner answered firmly.

"But how?" Legere dug in. "We can't send you off on some wild goose chase."

Parker smiled fully then. "Who said it would be you, if we sent anyone, Ms. Young?" He didn't wait for an answer. "All right. I think the cover-up on the loss of that aircraft is significant enough to make it worth our looking into. People haven't totally forgotten the MIA issue, and that could be a good lead-in. Even if you don't find the base, the story on the plane might be worthwhile if you can find out something more."

The CEO turned to Legere. "Do it. One standard overseas team." He looked into Conner's eyes. "You can have ten days from departure to return. Get me something." With that he stood and left the room, followed by Cordon.

Legere paused in the doorway. There was no smile on her face. "I'll contact you first thing in the morning about your team." Her voice dropped the temperature in the room a few degrees.

Stu was left sitting there with his newest reporter, not having said a word the entire time. Now he looked at her and shook his head. "Jesus Christ, Conner. Do you know what you just did? I mean, even if you find the damn place, who's to say there's anything important there now? It could be a garbage dump for all we know."

Conner knew she'd put her entire career on the line. "You're the one who said this was an up or out business, Stu. You can go up only if you take chances." She gathered her files and left the conference room.

As she walked back to her cubicle she thought about what had just happened. If she didn't find Eternity Base she'd be lucky to find a job reading the local news on a small-town cable channel. Conner shook her head. Now was the time to think positively. If—no, not if—but *when*—she found Eternity Base, she was determined that she would have a story, whatever it might be.

Conner was at the end of her rope. The phone had turned into an enemy for the past hour, eliciting no useful information. She picked it up one more time and dialed.

"Records Center. Samantha Pintella," a voice drawled on the other end.

"Sammy, I need your help."

"What's up now?"

"I received permission to lead a news team to Antarctica to do a story on Eternity Base. The only problem is that I still don't have any idea where it is."

"You're going down there? That was quick work. What do you need from me?"

Conner spun her chair away from the computer screen. "I've got to find Eternity Base and I'm having no luck. I've called all four people on that list you gave me and they won't say a thing. Freely won't even come to the phone to talk to me. He threatened to contact the FBI if I called again. Is there anything, anything at all you can think of that might help?"

"To be honest, no. There's no other record of Eternity Base here that I could find. The 67th Engineer's unit history had just those photos in it, no paperwork that might have had a location listed on it. You could try the enlisted personnel in the company, but from what Freely said, nobody in the unit really knew where they were or why they were building what they were building.

"Besides, I've got to put that file back in the box first thing tomorrow morning. The load's getting picked up and taken to Washington."

Conner sighed. "Can you think of anything I can do?"

"The only thing I haven't done yet is access the restricted database and the vault. That's the classified area of the Records Center. But if I do that and you break the story, people are going to know right away that I was in on it. Plus, accessing the computer may alert someone that we're onto the base—I'm sure that d-base is monitored."

"I really need your help," Conner pleaded.

Sammy's voice was cautious. "Tell you what I'll do. I'll do some runs on the computer. See how it goes."

"All right. Thanks for the help."

"Sure."

"Right, bye." Conner hung up. She rummaged through the piles of paper on her desk until she found the stick-em note with the phone number of the Our Earth office in Australia. She dialed the international code and then the number. Devlin made it to the phone more quickly this time.

"Devlin, it's Conner."

"What's up?"

"I'm coming to Antarctica with a team."

His reaction was more positive than her sister's. "Great!"

Conner gave a quick synopsis of her meeting with Parker.

Devlin immediately got to the heart of the matter. "So you need help finding this place, right?"

"Right."

"Well, there's not much I can do for you right now. You really have nothing except that it's a little less than two hours out from McMurdo by C-130. I mean, we don't even know if it's south, east, or west. Most likely south or east, though."

Conner typed that into her computer. "Why do you say that?"

"If the U.S. Army built this thing and wanted to keep it a secret, as you've said, then they'd probably want it to be far away from any other countries' stations. The Russians had a base in 1971, Leningradskaya, about five hundred miles to the west of McMurdo, and the French had one farther along the coast in that direction.

"South from McMurdo there's nothing until you hit the South Pole itself. So that would seem like a good place to hide a base. Maybe in the Transantarctic Mountains.

"East from McMurdo is Marie Byrd Land, and there was nothing permanent out there for almost two thousand miles in '71, although in '73 the Russians put in a base, called Russkaya, right on the coast to the east. But if it was 1971 and I was going to build some sort of secret base, that might be a direction I'd go."

Conner made notes of all that. "Anything else you can think of that might help?"

"When are you arriving in New Zealand?"

"I don't know yet. I should get my itinerary tomorrow. Probably this weekend sometime."

"Give me a call and let me know when you'll be landing. I'll meet you there and have things ready to go."

Conner decided to test the waters a little. "It'll be good to see you."

Devlin laughed. "I haven't heard from you in over a year, but, yes, I'll be glad to see you, too. I enjoyed our night together. I've thought of it a lot. It's not often I meet someone I can talk to so openly. I won't ask why you never tried to get in touch with me again."

Devlin's voice shifted gears. "Anyway, that's the past. I'm interested in this story of yours. It has the potential to make people think about Antarctica, and we certainly need that. A large part of our environmental legacy as a race may depend on how we deal with the last untouched frontier on the seventh continent."

Conner wasn't sure herself why she'd never gotten back in contact with Devlin, but the reverse was also true, and he was offering no explanations. "All right, but remember I have to be objective."

"I know. Listen, I've got to get back to work. Call with your flight info. If I'm not here, leave a message and I'll be there to meet you. All right?"

"All right."

"Great. Bye."

"Bye." Conner slowly put down the phone. She realized there was one more important thing she needed.

COLORADO SPRINGS, COLORADO. The flashing light on the secure phone drew the old man's attention from the picture postcard view of the Rocky Mountains outside his window. Despite his years there was still a bounce to his step as he walked over to his desk. He was tall with a stomach flat as a board. His silver hair framed a distinguished face that attracted women a third his age and made the men around him choose their words with care. A long finger reached out and hit the speaker button. A brief whine and a green light on the phone indicated the line was secure from eavesdroppers.

"Peter here."

"This is Andrew. I am calling you as per instructions, sir."

Peter looked down at the caller ID—it was scrambled. He recognized the code name though; it belonged to one of many people in the government and other organizations whom he kept on his payroll to funnel information to him. Peter had long ago learned that information was much more valuable than money, and it was getting more valuable as the electronic net encompassing the people of the world grew. "Go ahead."

"My people have detected an inquiry into the secure database that you have coded for alert."

Peter's slate gray eyes focused on the phone as he bent forward slightly, the muscles in his forearms rippling as he leaned on his desk. "Subject?"

"Eternity Base."

The old man's eyes closed briefly and then opened. "Source?"

"National Personnel Records Center in St. Louis."

"Who is inquiring?"

"A Samantha Pintella," Andrew replied. "My records indicate she's a section chief there with a Q clearance."

"A sanctioned search?"

"No, sir. It looks more like she's just fishing on her own."

"Anything more?"

"Negative."

"Thank you."

"Do I need to be concerned?" Andrew asked.

"I will take care of it." Peter hit the off button and flicked a switch on the desktop before walking over to one of several exercise machines set up near the windows. As he sat down and began a set of arm pullovers, the door on the far side of the room opened. A stocky man with an expressionless face distinguished only by bright blue eyes walked up to Peter, halting a respectful five feet away, silently awaiting his instructions.

After the tenth repetition, Peter smoothly let the weight slide to a resting position and looked up. "My dear friend Lazarus. How are you today?"

"Fine, sir."

"Good. I need you to make a trip to clear up some old business."

— six —

Louise Legere looked up briefly from the computer printout. "You're going to rack up quite a few frequent flyer miles on this trip." The special features editor read the grueling itinerary with relish. "Depart Atlanta this evening at six, straight through to San Francisco. Depart San Francisco for Honolulu. Depart there for New Zealand. Hmm, you cross the international date line en route, so there goes one of your ten days. Arrive in Auckland, New Zealand, on Saturday evening at seven." She slid the paper across the desk. "That's the end of the commercial flights and my involvement. Your friends from Our Earth have to take care of you from there on out."

"How much time in the air is that?" Conner asked.

Legere's fingers flew over the numeric keypad on her computer. "Let's see. Rounding everything off, you have five hours from here to San Fran. Another five to Hawaii. That's ten. Ten from Hawaii to New Zealand. That's twenty."

Conner shook her head. "How about a longer layover in Hawaii? At least to let everyone get a night's sleep."

Legere didn't even consider it. "My dear girl, you can sleep on the plane. Time is money, and your little trip is already burning more than it's worth."

Conner knew she shouldn't have bothered asking. "When do I meet my crew?"

"This afternoon at one in conference room three," she said coldly.

Conner wanted to get this meeting over with as quickly as possible. "When is the return flight?"

"You head for home on the fourth from New Zealand."

"But if you add in the two days to go to Antarctica and back up to New Zealand, that only leaves me with four days to search for Eternity Base," Conner protested.

"Mister Parker gave you ten days. I've given you ten days from leaving Atlanta until returning."

Conner felt a small knot of panic form in her stomach. "I need more than four days."

Legere wouldn't negotiate. "No. Those crew members will be on special duty pay. Do you know how much that is per day? The commercial plane reservations are already made.

"Now, also, don't forget your communication requirements. Your commo man knows about it, and he'll have the frequencies and satellite information, but it's your responsibility to make contact with us here on schedule. *Everything* on this trip is your responsibility. Do you understand?"

Conner looked into the face of the older woman, noting the lines around her eyes and the sharp red gash her lips made in the pinched face. "I understand."

Legere slid a folder across the desk. "Here's your authorization and tickets. Stop by Miss Suwon's desk down in records for your background packet and personnel roster. I'll see you when you get back."

Conner picked up the folder and left the office. She took the elevator down to the basement where the large mainframe computer for SNN was housed along with its human servants. She found Miss Suwon seated in a large office that made Conner's cubicle look tiny. A massive desk with four separate computer terminals on top dominated the room. A sophisticated laser printer in the corner of the room was spewing out a piece of paper every few seconds.

Miss Suwon was a young Asian woman with the petite figure that women from that part of the world seem to have stamped in their genes. She was dwarfed by all the electronics. Her hair was straight and long; cascading to her waist in a graceful line that even Conner had to envy. Suwon was dressed very well for someone in a basement office, and Conner wondered if maybe she had chosen the wrong job in this organization.

Suwon smiled as Conner came in the door. "Miss Young. I am glad to finally meet you." She swiveled in her chair and frowned at the computer screen. "I do not yet have your roster—there have been two other crews requested this morning, and personnel is still trying to rework their schedule. I assure you that you will have a good crew and they will be at your meeting this afternoon."

Miss Suwon passed over a bulging binder. "This was the best I could do on such short notice. I hope it will be helpful."

Conner looked at the label on the cover: SNN/CONNER YOUNG/ ANTARCTICA/BACKGROUND DATA/25 NOVEMBER 1996. She flipped through, amazed at the amount of information it contained and how well organized it was. There were sections on the history of Antarctica, the weather, environment, exploration, political status— everything Conner could possibly need as background for a story.

"Thank you very much. I've heard so many good things about what you do here, but this is truly amazing."

Miss Suwon smiled demurely. "I am glad to be of help. If you need anything else, please feel free to stop by." She held out a 3.5-inch diskette. "This is all the information in the binder on disk so you can cut and paste on your laptop if you need to." She then slid across several large brown envelopes. "These are maps of various scales of Antarctica, which might prove useful."

With a final thanks, Conner made her way back to the news section.

NATIONAL PERSONNEL RECORDS CENTER, ST. LOUIS, MISSOURI. The phone was ringing as Sammy approached her desk, still shivering from the motorcycle ride to work. "Records Center. Samantha Pintella."

"It's Conner. What'd you get?"

"Well, good morning to you too. I got nothing, to put it bluntly. I did a search using all the information you'd uncovered. As far as the classified d-base is concerned, Eternity Base never existed.

"What I did find backed up the cover stories for both B Company, 67th Engineers, and the aircrew. Both are listed as being in Vietnam working for MACV-SOG."

"Shit," Conner muttered. She wasted no time getting to the next angle of attack. "Sammy, I need those photos."

"Why?" Sammy asked.

"Because if any of them have something in the background, especially a significant terrain feature, we might be able to triangulate the location from known features." Conner was obviously looking at a map—Sammy could hear paper rustling in the background. "There're a lot of mountains and glaciers down there. We might be able to recognize something in the photos."

Sammy remembered the three peaks she'd noticed in the background of the group picture. "I put the folder back in the box and it's on the loading dock. It might even be on the trailer and on the way to the Archives in Washington."

"Could you check to see if it's there at least? Sam, my job rides on this story. Please."

Sammy sighed. "All right, all right. I'll check. Hold on."

Sammy put the down phone and headed for the back of the basement. She went up a ramp to the inside loading dock. There were twelve pallets of records sitting there. Sammy immediately saw that the one holding the 67th's unit history was still in the same place. She retrieved the record and took it back to her desk.

"I've got it, but I can't take the pictures, Conner. They'd hang me. Digging around in the computer is one thing. But taking documents from the Center is a direct violation of the rules."

"I won't use them on the air, Sammy. I promise."

"No." Her sister was making good money at SNN, but Sammy needed two more years of government service to get her minimum retirement pay. "There's no way I'm removing these from the file."

"How about a photocopy then?"

Sammy frowned. "Photocopy?"

"I'll take anything I can get, Sam. Can you copy them and fax them to me right away?"

Sammy thought about it. There was a copying machine right near her desk. She could easily hide the copies under her shirt and go to a nearby store and fax them. With the originals still in the file, it wouldn't be a direct violation of the rules. "The quality will be pretty crummy, you know. You promise not to use them on the air or even refer to them in a story?"

"I promise."

"Give me your fax number."

Sammy copied the number.

"I really appreciate this, Sam. I'll talk to you when I get back, OK?"

"All right." Before Conner could hang up, though, Sammy continued. "Listen, Conner, I want you to be careful. Somebody went to a lot of trouble to hide the existence of this place. Even though it was twenty-five years ago, that doesn't necessarily mean it's a dead issue. The fact that my boss couldn't find anything in the classified files worries me more than if he had found something. Do you understand what I mean?"

"Yes."

"All right then. You take care and be safe."

Sammy hung up the phone. She took the photographs and copied them, then returned the folder to the loading dock. She went to the ladies' room, where she slid the pictures under her T-shirt and tucked it back in. At her desk she put on her leather jacket, then went over to Brad's office to tell him she'd be out for a little while.

She made it past the guard without arousing any suspicion and hopped on her motorcycle. There was an office supply store less than three blocks away. Sammy roared over there and parked her bike between two cars out front. She hurried in and gave the copies to the lady behind the counter along with Conner's fax number. It all took less than a minute. Then she tore the copies into little pieces and deposited them in a trash can on her way out.

Sammy opened the door with a feeling of relief that this whole episode was now out of her hands and into Conner's. As she grabbed her helmet off the motorcycle seat, she noted a Chevy van blocking her in. Sammy put the helmet on and cranked the engine, waiting for the driver of the van to take the hint and move. After thirty seconds she beeped her horn. She couldn't make out the truck's occupants through the tinted windshield.

"Goddamnit," Sammy muttered. She got off her bike, walked up to the passenger side, and rapped on the door. The cargo door slid open and a man leaped out. He wrapped her in a bear hug and rolled back into the rear of the van, the door sliding shut.

Sammy kicked backward, feeling her boot strike home, but the man holding her didn't make a sound. Sammy struggled desperately, but her arms were locked to her sides with a grip of steel. She felt a prick in her wrist and looked down to see a needle sliding into the flesh. As she watched, the plunger was pushed.

The last thing her conscious mind processed was the van pulling out into traffic.

— seven —

COLORADO SPRINGS, COLORADO. The phone woke the old man out of a deep sleep. The young woman who was sharing the bed rose without a word and slipped toward the door, not even taking the time to put on a robe. As the door closed on her pert rear end, the man hit the speaker button.

"Peter here."

"This is Lazarus. I've checked out the Pintella woman. She knows little other than that the base is in Antarctica. The exact location is secure. She found some old photos in a file from the engineer unit that built the place. I will secure the photos."

"Good."

"We have another problem, though." The man's voice paused and then continued. "Pintella told someone about what she found."

"Who?"

"Her sister. Conner Young. She's a reporter for SNN. Apparently SNN is planning to send a news team down to Antarctica to check out the story."

Peter sat up in the bed, flexing the muscles in his right arm as his eyes focused on the phone. "I already know about the SNN contact. Is that the only person she told?"

"Yes, sir."

"All right. I'll handle SNN. You take care of your end there in St. Louis."

"Yes, sir."

Peter terminated the conversation. He sat for a long time, thinking of options. He knew better than to react immediately—there were possibilities to be explored. And, of course, he already had a plan in place at SNN to provide damage control. After forty minutes and several phone calls, the course of action was determined. He dialed Atlanta.

SNN HEADQUARTERS, ATLANTA, GEORGIA. "I'm Conner Young. I will be the team chief for this trip." Conner looked at the three men assembled around the conference table. "I'd like each of you to introduce yourself."

An overweight man with thinning gray hair took the initiative. "I'm Les Lallo. Cameraman."

Seated next to him, a young man with a sallow face under an unruly mop of blond hair bobbed his head nervously. "Tom Kerns. Sound."

The last man's voice rumbled. "Keith Vickers. Satellite communications and computer." Vickers was a large man and looked as though he spent all his time off in the weight room. The muscles under the black skin of his arms rippled and flowed. His shaved head reflected the fluorescent lights in the ceiling.

Conner reached forward and hit a button on the remote built into the tabletop. The men studied the map that appeared on the screen. "What are we going there for?" Lallo asked as he recognized the location.

"The purpose of our trip is to find a place called Eternity Base. It was constructed somewhere in Antarctica in 1971 by a U.S. Army engineer company."

"What do you mean 'somewhere in Antarctica'?" Lallo pointed at the screen. "That's a pretty big place."

"Right now, all we know is that this place is a little less than a two hour plane ride from McMurdo Station." Conner wanted to keep the information about the faxed pictures to herself for the time being. Sammy's warning had made some impression.

"What kind of place is this Eternity Base?" Kerns asked. "And why do we want to find it?"

"It's a group of buildings constructed under the ice. We want to find it because the existence of the place has been secret."

Lallo was interested in her first sentence. "If it was built under the ice, how are you going to find it?"

Conner fixed him with a stare. It was time to establish the chain of command. She'd found that men tended to usurp control unless firmly kept in their place. "You're here to work the camera, right?"

Lallo shrugged. "Yes."

"How we find Eternity Base is my problem and I'll take care of it. The purpose of this meeting is to work out the logistics of getting from here to Antarctica."

Lallo obviously felt put in his place, and he shut up. It was Kerns who asked the next question. "How do we even know it exists?"

"Because there were photos taken of it."

The communications man, Vickers, stirred for the first time. "Do you have the photos? I'd like to take a look."

Conner shook her head. "I don't have them yet."

Lallo and Kerns exchanged a look. The older man spoke very carefully. "Ms. Young, may I say something?"

She nodded.

"We're going to be working together for ten days. Now, I know this is probably a very important story to you, since you're new here. Tom and I . . . well, we want to help you out as much as possible. For this to work, you've got to tell us everything. That goes from the day-to-day stuff to the story. The better we understand how you are approaching the story, the better we can help you with the shots and the sound. We're all a bit behind the power curve here because we got notified of this tasking less than an hour ago, so you're going to have to bear with us a little bit."

Vickers agreed, pointing at the screen. "Mister Lallo is right about the location. This is a very big area."

Conner tapped the map. "We're pretty certain that the base is to the south or east of McMurdo Station." Her long, manicured finger swept across a large white area labeled Ross Ice Shelf and came to rest on the far side. "It's probably somewhere here in the Transantarctic Mountains or in Marie Byrd Land. Maybe even in the vicinity of a base that was abandoned in 1972: Byrd Station, located right here." Her finger was resting in the middle of what appeared to be a vast expanse of nothingness. She'd studied the map; based on what Devlin had told her and her own common sense, this was the best she could come up with.

"We will be met in New Zealand by an expert on Antarctica, and with his help, and the information we do have, I feel certain we'll find the base. We have four days from arriving at McMurdo, and we will have access to a plane from Our Earth the entire time to help us in the search."

Lallo nodded slowly. "Can I add something else, Ms. Young?"

Conner considered him for a long second and then nodded.

Lallo leaned forward in his seat. "I know you're new here, but I've been on this kind of fishing expedition before. Sometimes Mr. Parker seems to get a wild hair up his ass, and he sends a news team out on some crazy story. Most of the time they come up with nothing, but every once in a while they hit pay dirt." Vickers turned to his young partner, Kerns. "Tom, remember Mexico?"

The soundman put his hands over his eyes. "Oh, God! Don't remind me. I still have nightmares about that."

"What happened in Mexico?" Conner inquired.

"We went down there because someone had some information—or so they claimed—about the lost treasure of Cortez," Lallo explained. "We spent two whole weeks crawling through jungle and climbing mountains. Tom damn near had a heatstroke hauling his gear."

"Yeah, but at least we still have a job," Kerns threw in.

Lallo agreed. "Correct. That poor reporter we went with—what was his name? Hornacek or something? Anyway, Parker fired his ass the moment we got off the plane for coming back with nothing. That man uses people like sponges."

Conner looked at the map once more and turned back to the room with a big smile. "Well, you won't have to worry about heatstroke this time." She pulled the itinerary out of a folder. Time for business—not war stories. "We depart from Atlanta at six this evening. Nonstop to San Francisco. Then from there to . . ." Conner ignored the dismayed look on all three men's faces as she ran through the brutal travel schedule. "If all goes as planned, we arrive at Auckland International on Saturday evening at seven. From there we will be met by a representative of Our Earth, who will arrange transportation down to their base in the Antarctic."

She put down that piece of paper and picked up another, a copy of which she handed to each man. "This is the list of equipment I want brought." She looked around. "Are there any questions?"

Three heads indicated negatively. Conner felt good for the first time in a while. She was in charge, and that always gave her confidence.

NEW YORK, NEW YORK. The aide to the North Korean ambassador to the United Nations looked through the printout, as he did every day, seven days a week, every week of the year, marking the lines with highlighters. Blue meant forward to higher headquarters; green meant requires more information before forwarding; and yellow, no significance and delete.

Three-quarters of the way through the printout a four-line entry caught his attention:

News team to be dispatched 1130Z, 26th, from Atlanta to Antarctica to investigate report of U.S. Army base constructed there circa 1971. Code name of base: Eternity Base.

The aide reread the lines again. He was intrigued—as much by what wasn't mentioned in those four lines as what was. If his agent at SNN, Loki, had more information on Eternity Base, it would have been included. The lack of information meant that this was the first mention of Eternity Base that Loki had come across. Most interesting. The aide used his green marker and moved on to the next item.

— eight —

ATLANTA, GEORGIA. Conner crossed and uncrossed her legs. She was already feeling cramped and they hadn't even boarded yet. She turned her attention to the portable computer on her lap. She'd spent most of the afternoon packing and checking with Stu and hadn't had a chance to run through the data Miss Suwon had given her. With twenty hours in the air, she would have plenty of time to examine it all in depth and try to condense the copious amount of information into a usable format. For now, she was fascinated with the history of Antarctica, something that hadn't been taught in school. A continent without any native population didn't lend itself to inclusion in standard courses.

The lesson was interrupted as they were called to board. As soon as she'd checked the tickets, Conner had noted that they were traveling economy class. She had a feeling that the long hand of Louise Legere would follow them throughout this journey.

Conner followed the crowd onto the plane, slipping between businessmen hanging their suit bags and grabbing pillows. She claimed the window seat, Keith Vickers the one next to her. After they took off, she reopened her laptop and went back into the history of the seventh continent. By the time they were cruising west at 35,000 feet, she was totally engrossed, and the miles passed below, unnoticed.

EAST ST. LOUIS, ILLINOIS. Sammy had been regaining consciousness for brief interludes over the past hour, but every time she approached lucidity, a large wave of blackness had again engulfed her. This time, though, as she opened her eyes, she could actually think. Vague memories flitted about her brain, trying to tell her something had happened over the past several hours that she needed to recall, but try as she might, no concrete memory would form. There were disturbing visions that seemed like very bad dreams, but as she took in her surroundings, the present nightmare banished thoughts of the immediate past.

With slow sweeps of her eyes, she checked out the situation. She was lying on the floor in a filth-strewn room. A single lightbulb burned in the ceiling, casting long shadows across the room. A wooden door was the only link to the world outside. Her wrists were handcuffed behind her, the steel cutting uncomfortably into her skin.

She was considering sliding her hands down her back and pushing her feet through to at least get her hands in front of her body when the door opened and the man from the van walked in.

Sammy was truly scared now because the man made no attempt to disguise his identity. He had hair cut tight against his skull, his bright blue eyes emanating both intelligence and malice. After staring at her for a few minutes, he finally broke the silence: "Good day, Miss Pintella. You don't have to worry. I've already gotten what I needed from you." At Sammy's confused look he smiled. "It's part of the miracle of modern medicine. The first shot I gave you caused unconsciousness. The second one made you talk." He squatted down and gazed into her eyes. "You don't remember talking, do you?"

Sammy didn't answer. She curled up in a tight ball, her knees to her chest. The man poked her in the shoulder. "There's no need for you to play dumb. I know quite a bit about you—one of the perks of the job. You told me everything I asked for. I know about your sister, but that's no longer my problem. You also told me some very interesting personal information."

Sammy closed her eyes and starting rocking back and forth. He slapped her on the face. "Don't tune me out." He smiled, but it was only a moving of muscles in his face that didn't touch the coldness of his strange eyes. "It's kind of like looking into someone's soul. Imagine being able to ask someone any question you want and get an honest answer. Psychologists ought to use my techniques. It would save a lot of time. Of course there's too high a percentage of adverse side effects to make it feasible in the real world."

His eyes were flashes of blue, catching the light from the bulb above them. He pulled a pistol with a bulky barrel out of his shoulder holster. He put the muzzle against Sammy's temple and stared at her with a crooked smile. He stayed like that, his eyes boring into hers, for a very long minute, then put the pistol away. "We need another two hours for the drug to clear your system. Wouldn't do to have that found by some enterprising coroner. Might make people ask too many questions." He stood up and looked down at her. "You understand, don't you?"

Sammy gazed back blankly.

He stood and began pacing about the room. "You didn't do very well with your life. Couldn't even keep a husband. Maybe in your next life you'll do better."

Sammy whispered to herself.

The man spun about. "What did you say?"

Sammy muttered again. The man knelt down next to her and reached for her shoulders, pulling her to her knees. "Speak up."

She pressed her chest against his.

"That's not going to work," the man said, as she leaned into him.

Sammy kept her eyes on his. She could feel him growing hard against her stomach. Despite his protestations, he was staying close.

"Not in the head," she said softly.

For the first time the man was confused. "What?"

"Please don't shoot me in the head. I'll make it worth your while. Anywhere but the head."

The man stood up and moved a few feet away. Sammy awkwardly shuffled toward him on her knees until he was against the wall. She pressed her face into his crotch. He was most definitely hard now. Sliding her tongue up the zipper, she flipped out the steel tab and gripped it with her teeth.

Sammy slowly pulled down the zipper. He wasn't wearing underwear, and she could feel flesh for the first time. She pushed in harder, moving her head until she found the tip of his cock, then she drew it into her mouth.

The man moaned. She took it in as far as she could and then let it pop out. She started licking one of his balls gently and then started sucking him again.

"All right," the man muttered as he leaned back against the wall. "I knew you liked to do this. The needle made you tell me all about what you like to do."

Sammy clamped down on the flesh in her mouth with all the power in her jaws, and the man's scream echoed off the walls as he doubled over. Sammy rolled away to the right, tucking her knees to her chest and sweeping the handcuffed wrists down her back, over her feet, and up in front. Staggering to her feet she ran for the man; he was still doubled over, blood pouring over his hands as he grasped his groin.

Sammy first struck him in the face with her manacled hands, then, looping her hands behind his head and pulling down with all her might, she slammed her left knee into his face, doubling the strength of the blow. His teeth clicked shut and his head rocked back. Blood exploded in a spray from his shattered nose.

Sammy snaked her hands inside his jacket and retrieved the pistol as he belatedly tried to stop her. She dove away as he blindly struck out with a flurry of punches. She held the gun in front of her with her manacled hands and pulled the trigger.

There was no sound of a shot—just a sickening thud as the side of the man's head exploded in a spray of brains and blood, adding its own gory mark to the wall beyond. His body crumpled to the ground; an arm briefly twitched and then he was still.

Sammy felt her stomach flip, but the nausea quickly passed and a black sense of calm swept over her. After taking a few deep breaths, she went over to the body and searched the pockets until she found the key for the handcuffs. Holding the key in her teeth, she freed herself. She grabbed a thermos the man had brought and washed out her mouth and cleaned the blood from her face. She took his wallet and key ring and strapped on his shoulder holster. Then she retrieved her crumpled leather jacket from a corner of the room and put it on. Without a backward glance, Sammy left the room and headed out of the abandoned tenement.

AIRSPACE, WESTERN UNITED STATES. Two and a half hours out of San Francisco, and Conner was still working on her laptop, summarizing and organizing the data Miss Suwon had drawn out of the SNN computer. All those pages and pages of notes would result in maybe three minutes of airtime in a fifteen-minute spot if she did find something.

"Do you know all you ever wanted to know about Antarctica now?" Vickers interrupted her thoughts.

"Not yet," Conner answered tersely.

"Want to tell me about it?" Vickers asked with a smile.

Conner looked at him. "Tell you about what?"

Vickers pointed at the computer. "Antarctica."

"Why?"

Vickers shrugged. "I've never been there or really seen or read anything about it. Besides, it will do you good to verbalize all this information. I've always found that putting thoughts and ideas into words clarifies them."

Conner realized this was a chance to show him that she wasn't just another pretty face, and he would undoubtedly relay that information to the rest of the team. Sometimes she grew very tired of having to prove herself. "What do you want to know?"

"Well, for starters, why is it named Antarctica?"

Conner started tapping keys on the computer, but Vickers interrupted. "How about from memory?"

Conner stopped and looked at him, considering the subtle challenge. "All right." She turned off the power, shut the lid on the computer, and put it under the seat in front of her. "Arctic comes from *arktos,* which is the Greek word for *bear*, referring to the northern constellation Ursa Major, the Great Bear, more commonly known as the Big Dipper. As you know, the region surrounding the North Pole is called the Arctic region. Well, the prefix *ant* means opposite or balance, so basically Antarctica means opposite Arctic or, literally, opposite bear."

Vickers didn't seem overly impressed with her mastery of language. "Tell me about the continent."

Conner mentally sorted through all the numbers and facts she'd been steeped in for the past hours and imagined herself facing the red light of a camera. "Antarctica is the fifth largest continent, encompassing more than five and a half million square miles."

"Is that land or ice?" Vickers asked.

"Almost the entire place is ice covered," Conner replied. "The extent of the land underneath is at best a guess. A lot of people don't realize it, but the North Pole is ice on top of the Arctic Ocean, not a land mass. Antarctica is a true land mass, and it holds ninety percent of the world's ice and snow. It is the only continent not to have its own native population."

"How many people are at McMurdo?"

"It's the middle of the short summer down there, so there will be about seven or eight hundred folks—mostly scientists working on a variety of projects."

"How about at this Our Earth base?"

Four people are there every winter. How many are there in the summer, I don't know."

"How well mapped is Antarctica? I mean how could this Eternity Base, if it's there, have remained hidden for twenty-five years?"

Conner didn't appreciate the "if it's there" qualifier. "If you wanted to hide something, the best place in the world would be Antarctica. Although it's the size of Europe and the United States combined, less than one percent of it has been seen by man."

Vickers was skeptical. "Even with overflights?"

"Even with overflights. From 1946 through 1947 the U.S. Navy ran a mission called Operation High Jump, using more than five thousand men, thirteen ships, and numerous helicopters. They took so many pictures that some of them were never developed. Despite all that equipment and manpower, their coverage of the interior was very limited and they managed to photograph only about sixty percent of the coastline."

"What about satellites?"

Conner nodded. She'd thought about that herself. "Satellites weren't as significant back in '71, but even then it was the same situation as now. Satellites are either in synchronous orbits, which means they move at the same speed as the rotation of the earth, thus staying relatively over the same spot, or they have their own orbits. As far as I know, there are none in a synchronous orbit above Antarctica—no reason for one to be. There are no weapons allowed down there, thus no military presence.

"Some satellites run the north-south route and cross the poles, but two factors work against their picking up much. First, quite simply, no one has been that interested in Antarctica, so the satellites don't often scan that part of their orbit. Second, the weather is terrible down there and it's rare that the sky is clear."

Vickers leaned forward. "Have you factored the weather into our search?"

"Yes."

Vickers seemed to wait for more, but Conner said nothing. Finally he spoke. "Well, what did you find in your computer about the weather?"

Conner sighed. "It's usually bad. Very bad. Antarctica is the highest, driest, coldest, windiest continent. Wind gusts of a hundred and fifty miles an hour are not unusual."

"What do you mean driest?" Vickers asked.

"It hardly ever snows or rains there. But a layer of snow covers the ice, and the snow gets blown about a lot, causing white-outs and blizzards."

Vickers pointed at her computer. "Lallo said you have all that stuff in hard copy. Would it be possible for me to look at it?"

Conner pulled out her briefcase, retrieved the binder, and handed it over. Anything to keep him quiet. She didn't want to talk about negative what-ifs. For the next two hours, she worked in silence until she couldn't stand it anymore. She closed her computer and repositioned her pillow to try and catch some sleep. The last thing she saw before weariness claimed her was Vickers leaned over the binder in the darkened aircraft, slowly turning a page.

EAST ST. LOUIS, ILLINOIS. "Damn!" Sammy slammed down the pay phone in disgust. SNN had confirmed that Conner had already departed on her trip, but the woman on the other end wouldn't divulge her sister's itinerary. Sammy also knew that telling Conner what had just happened wouldn't deter her in the least; on the contrary, it would whet her appetite for the story.

Sammy leaned against the wall of the Minute Mart as she considered her next move. She knew she was in East St. Louis because she could see the Gateway Arch in the distance against the setting sun. The van that had been used to kidnap her was parked nearby; using the keys taken from the dead man, she'd driven the van to the first phone booth she could find.

The thing that scared Sammy the most was not knowing who the man she had just killed was working for. That fact had kept her from immediately calling the police. Sammy knew she needed help, though, and that gave her the first positive thought of the evening. She pulled out her wallet and searched for a business card she'd been carrying for years. She dialed the home number that had been penciled in below the business number.

"Pike here."

"It's Sammy Pintella."

The gruff voice mellowed. "Sammy, how the hell are you?" Colonel Pike had been her father's team leader during his first tour in Vietnam. After her dad was reported MIA, Pike had helped the family in every way he could and had stayed in touch over the years.

He had taken a special liking to Sammy and had tried to help make her missing father a peaceful ghost. He was the one who had given her the names of the other Americans on her dad's team, but he had had no explanation for why the two were listed as lost on separate dates.

Hearing her friend's warm voice, tears welled up in Sammy's eyes. She steeled herself, knowing that she couldn't let her emotions take over. It was difficult enough to think clearly in the aftermath of the drugs she'd been given. "I need help."

"What's wrong?"

Sammy gave a quick synopsis of the events of the day, and Pike was quick to agree with her initial assessment. "You're in deep shit. For all you know he could have been working for the U.S. government, so you did right not calling the police. The spooks would be hooked into them for info. Don't go back to your apartment either. Is there a place you can wait until I get someone up there?"

"I've got a van I can stay in for a while."

"All right. Go to the airport. Once you get a parking space, call me back with your location. I'll have my man meet you in the parking lot. He should be there by midnight. Once you two make contact, we can try and figure out our next move."

"OK."

"I'll talk to you soon."

Sammy hung up the phone and headed for the van.

— nine —

NASHVILLE, TENNESSEE. The ribbon charge blew in the center of the door, leaving the edges still attached at the hinges and lock. Four figures, clad in black, slipped through the seam, splitting left and right into two-man teams. The men wore black balaclavas covering their faces and were armed with M16 rifles.

"Clear left!" the lead figure yelled.

"Clear right!" the second man confirmed.

The right team moved out of the foyer and headed down the hallway, rifles pointing across each other's front. Reaching the first door on the right, one man used a sledgehammer to break the lock; the other man kicked the door, and they entered. The second team moved up the hallway and did the same thing on the first door on the left. More men were coming in the front now, taking up the vacated positions.

"Clear!" the first team yelled as it came out of the room. The two moved to the next door. Again the lock was slammed out, and they sprinted through the door and froze.

"Don't shoot! Don't shoot!" A young woman dressed in jeans and a sweatshirt ran toward them. Another figure was lurking in the shadows near a door on the far side of the room.

"Down!" yelled one of the men, but the women continued to the door. He grabbed her and shoved her behind him. "Freeze!" he screamed at the other figure in the room as he and his partner leveled their M16s.

The roar of automatic fire just behind them caused both men to start and turn. The woman stood there, Uzi in hand, a smile on her face. As the brass from the blanks tinkled onto the floor, she said: "Bang. Bang. You're dead."

"Everyone down and cuffed. Everyone!" Riley came out of the shadows, shaking his head. There was a look of frustration on his face, visible even beneath a three-day growth of beard. The two policemen lowered their weapons. Their faces were red as he walked up to them.

"Bring everyone in." Riley slumped down in an armchair to await the gathering of the rest of the members of the Nashville Police Department HRT Team—or what the Nashville police were trying to make into a Hostage Rescue Team. As evidenced by the recent exercise, they had a long way to go.

Riley looked at the woman. "Good job, Luce." He wearily rubbed his eyes as the ten policemen he and his partner had been training for the past week gathered together in the abandoned building they'd been using for practice.

Riley was hungover and tired. He'd spent a late night the previous evening in the lounge of the Sheraton Hotel, his temporary home, trying to figure out consecutively better approaches to the female bartender. She'd deflected every attempt while slapping the beers on the mahogany and picking up his money. In the end she and the alcohol had won, and he'd staggered off to his room alone in the early hours of the morning. He wished he could get a drink of water now, but the building had no water.

A day that had not started well wasn't going any better. Luce had practically kicked the door down this morning to rouse him from his deadened stupor. Then they'd been at it all day long, practicing their entry procedures until they had them down pat in the daylight. Now they were getting in a little night work.

Riley swallowed, trying to draw up a little moisture. His throat hurt like hell. "All right," he rasped. "First. Luce show them where the gun was."

The compact woman lifted the back of her sweatshirt and slid the mini-Uzi into the harness strapped around her body. She smiled demurely and swiftly drew the submachine gun back out. Then she put the gun down on the ground and lifted the right leg of her jeans. A small automatic was cinched to her right calf. She lifted the front of her sweatshirt slightly. Unsnapping her belt buckle, she folded out the knife on the reverse side.

Riley bowed in her direction. "I won't even begin to tell you what she has in her bra."

The cops laughed nervously, not sure if he was joking.

He walked over and stood next to her. "Just because she's a woman doesn't mean she can't kill you." He slashed forward with his left hand in a karate strike for her throat. She easily blocked it, grabbed his hand, and then twisted underneath, locking his elbow over her shoulder, the pressure on the joint lifting him up to his toes. Riley tapped her with his free hand and she released him. "In fact, studies have shown that female terrorists are much more ruthless than men. Thanks, Luce." She turned and left the room.

Riley shook his head. "Rule number one. Everyone gets cuffed. Everyone. Hostages included. The easiest thing for a bad person to do if they want to get out alive is play the victim in this situation. It doesn't look good on the news to have cuffed hostages, but it beats being dead." He coughed and cleared his throat. After a brief glance around, he walked over to the window and spit.

"All right. The entry was good. Let's remember something though. We've got to work this up to where you can do it not only at night but wearing gas masks. Your normal crook in a hostage situation is going to be relatively unprepared, so it's to your advantage to gas your objective. That's why we've designated your blooper man and had him practice putting his tear gas rounds through windows out on the range.

"But let's also worst-case things. If your intelligence indicates you're up against professionals, then you have to expect they're wearing gas masks too." Riley's head hurt. Every time he taught this stuff he started getting into this worst-case cycle. "So then you're back to square one. But that's what—"

"What have *you* done?" A burly policeman, his bulk enhanced by the flak vest he wore, had asked the question.

"Excuse me?"

The cop's gray mustache twitched as he spat the words out. "We've been listening to you prattling on for four days now about what we should and shouldn't do. Well, I've spent eighteen years on the streets here. I've been in three shoot-outs, and I just want to know what your qualifications are."

Riley sighed. "I spent three years in the 10th Special Forces Group. Then three years in a classified counterterrorist unit overseas. I've been to—"

"Yeah. I heard all that the first day," the cop interrupted. "But what I want to know is if you've ever been shot at or if you ever shot anyone. Eh?"

Riley looked at the man for a long time as he considered his answer. Finally he lied. "No."

The cop nodded. "I thought so. Well, I have, and you can tell us all this, but it don't make a bit of difference when the shit hits the fan. You stand there and—"

"Riley." Luce was in the doorway with the portable phone in her hand. "The colonel's on the phone for you. He wants to talk to you now."

"All right. You take over. Do another run through." Riley could feel the eyes of all the occupants of the room on his back as he took the phone from his partner. He walked down the hallway and stepped out into the brisk fall weather.

"This is Riley, sir."

Colonel Pike wasted no time on pleasantries. "I want Luce to finish out the contract. I've got a friend in trouble and I need your help."

Riley didn't hesitate. "Yes, sir." He knew the colonel was worried about him and that Luce had been assigned as his partner to keep an eye on him, but Riley felt that he did his job well enough. What he did in his off-duty time was his own business. He'd been at this job for a little more than a month now, and although it had kept him busy, there were still times when there was no work and the four walls of the hotel room closed in. Those times were the worst. He wondered what the colonel had conjured up for him now.

"Your tickets will be waiting at the Delta counter at the airport. The flight takes off in forty-five minutes, so get moving. Give me a call when you get on the ground."

AIRSPACE, PACIFIC OCEAN. As the western coastline of the United States disappeared behind them, Conner allowed her mind to drift ahead to the landing in New Zealand and then back in time. She wondered if Devlin would be the same as she remembered him from Chicago more than a year ago.

She'd first seen him chained to the outlet pipe of a factory that poured thousands of gallons of polluted water into Lake Michigan every hour. Devlin and three other members of Our Earth had stayed there for four hours, letting the filth pour over them, while other members of the group held banners and protested nearby. Finally, even the security men for the plant couldn't take it anymore and they had moved in with bolt cutters to break the chains.

Conner had already gotten enough footage for a good minute-and-a-half spot, but she still followed the police wagon down to the station, where Devlin and his partners were booked for unlawful trespass. She was impressed with the efficiency of the Our Earth organization as the men were bailed out in almost record speed.

Devlin was coming out of the courtroom, still clad in his filthy overalls, when he spotted her standing by the door. He walked over to her and smiled. "The news lady. Channel 4. How much time do we get tonight? Thirty seconds?"

Conner looked up at his grime-streaked face and decided he was worth more than a perfunctory two- to three-minute chat. She already knew some background and hoped to coax more from him. Randall Simpson Devlin was almost more of a story than the group to which he gave all of his time and the majority of his money. And money was the key to Devlin—his family was loaded, thanks to a hardworking great-grandfather, good family marriages, and efficient tax attorneys.

She knew from her research that Devlin's childhood had been spent in East Coast mansions surrounded by the best primary caretakers money could buy. His first toy car was large enough for him to ride in; his first pet was a pony. His father had hoped he would enter the family business after the Choate–Ivy League route, but Devlin at eighteen had turned away from his family's money and connections to make it on his own. Conner's theory was that in Our Earth he had found a way to assuage his guilt and thereby enjoy the fruits of his ancestor's labor.

Standing there outside the police station, Conner was impressed that he both knew who she was and had spotted her at the plant. She wanted to know more. There was a great story standing in front of her and she meant to get it. "No, sixty seconds. But I can make it ninety if you let me buy you a drink and then talk to me."

She wasn't sure why she had asked him out for the drink. It just seemed like the right thing to do. It was far more than the story. The facts that Devlin was attractive, rich, and would be gone from the city in the morning and out of her life were very enticing.

Devlin smiled at her. "I'm not exactly dressed to go out. How about we go back to my hotel while I get changed. I'll take that drink and talk when I'm clean."

Conner was not surprised when the cab dropped them off at the most expensive hotel in downtown Chicago. Devlin smiled at her look, as though he expected some comment about his extravagance. "I figure four hours in that filth is worth this, wouldn't you agree? As a friend of my father's used to say—'never complain, never explain.'"

Conner smiled back. "Henry Ford."

Devlin seemed slightly surprised. His eyes lingered on her face. "You're no dumb mouthpiece, are you?"

"No, Mr. Devlin, I'm no dummy."

Devlin remained silent until they were in his suite. He showed her where to make the drinks and left to take the much needed shower. Conner was flipping through a thumbed copy of short stories when he returned to the living room wearing loose khaki pants and a tight polo shirt. He looked very good with all the gunk removed. His blond hair was just beginning to thin but was a nice contrast to his blue eyes. He had a muscular body. Conner was swift to note that it was his natural build and not one he worked on. He had the beginnings of that soft look that comes from an easy life and middling ambition.

She held up the book. "Fitzgerald. So, Mr. Devlin. Is it true? Are the rich really different from me and you? Or should I say me?"

He shot her another dazzling smile and pulled her into his arms. She felt him grow hard beneath the pants. "No, not at all. I'd say the rich aren't very different. The main luxury is more time to think about things."

Conner pulled away and sat down on one of the overstuffed damask sofas. "The rich seem to skip a lot of preliminaries."

Devlin sat across from her and picked up the drink she'd made for him. She noticed the manicured nails before she noticed how fine the hands were. "I'm sorry, Conner. May I call you Conner? I hope I didn't seem rude, but you are an incredibly beautiful woman and well read on top of that. I guess I got carried away."

Conner nodded an acceptance to his apology and pulled out a notebook. "Devlin—may I call you Devlin? Or do your friends use your first name?"

He showed a set of perfect teeth. "Devlin is fine."

"So, Devlin. Tell me about a life of environmental activism after a youth of unparalleled luxury."

Devlin leaned back, crossing his legs and putting both arms on the back of the sofa. He looked for all the world like the scion of a wealthy family. "The hounds of the press appear to skip a lot of the preliminaries also."

"I've always found a good interview to be an excellent preliminary," Conner remarked, her eyes meeting his.

Devlin talked for a long time.

Later, when they were lying in a tangle of linen on his king-size bed, he asked her about her newscast that night. She looked down at him, pushing aside the tendrils of dark hair that had fallen across her eyes, and informed him that if she didn't show up at the station on time they knew she was on a story.

Devlin wrapped his hands around her thin waist, looked up at her, and replied: "Well, I'd definitely say you're on a story now."

At the time, Conner had found the comment amusing, and she had silently agreed.

The next day a bouquet of roses was waiting on her desk at work. Conner became irritated when her coworkers looked at her curiously, and the whole incident began to seem like a mistake. She knew that the flowers put the burden on her to get in touch with him, but she didn't. She had her life planned, and a relationship with Devlin—or anyone—would just get in her way.

Conner sometimes wondered if she'd made the right decision, but then came the offer of the job in Atlanta and she'd thought about nothing but work since then—at least until the other day when she'd picked up the phone and called Devlin.

With the click of the computer screen locking upright, Conner banished that memory and went to work to ensure that her future would be as successful as her past.

St. Louis, Missouri, 26 November 1996. "Come in," Sammy called out, pressing her back against the far wall of the van and pointing the pistol at the back door. The metal door swung open and a figure was standing there, silhouetted against the parking lot lights.

"Whoa!" The man dropped a duffel bag he'd been carrying and held his hands away from his body. "Take it easy. I'm Riley. Colonel Pike sent me."

"Come in and shut the door," Sammy ordered.

Riley threw in his duffel bag and then followed it. With the door swung shut, the inside was almost pitch black. "Could you put down the gun, please?" Riley asked.

Sammy slid the pistol back in the shoulder holster. It had been an anxious four hours waiting here in the dark. She'd started doubting reality in that time, not wanting to believe she'd killed a man earlier this evening. Then she'd started getting paranoid, wondering if even Pike was to be trusted. When she'd called him with parking lot information, the colonel had relayed to her Riley's name and approximate time of arrival. She'd spent the interim trying to figure out what steps to take next. Although she might be relatively safe for the moment, she knew her sister was heading into something much more dangerous than she expected.

"The colonel told me to keep you safe and not much more," Riley remarked as he sat down on his duffel bag. "Care to fill me in on what's going on?"

For the second time that evening Sammy related the events that had occurred since leaving the office supply shop. Riley also had her backtrack a bit and give him all she knew on Eternity Base. When she was done he sat silent for a few moments, then spoke. "We need to get rid of this van and the gun. They're the two things that can link you to the body."

Sammy shook her head. "Our first priority is to warn my sister."

Riley shook his head in turn. "No. At least not through SNN— that's the most likely source of the leak reference Eternity Base. Think about how those places operate. They've got more people getting paid off than any South American government. It's the perfect conduit for intelligence organizations to sink a line to fish for information. If you try getting in touch with her through SNN, you might as well advertise your presence, and from what you told me about your sister, she would probably continue on with the story anyway."

"Then we catch up with her," Sammy declared firmly.

"What?" Riley blinked in the dark.

It was the decision she had come to more than an hour ago, and she was determined to follow it through whether Riley agreed or not. "We catch up with her and warn her. You can protect her along with me." Sammy leaned forward. "The colonel told me not to go to the cops. You're telling me not to go to SNN. I agree with both of you. Either way we could be putting our heads in the lion's mouth."

She continued. "We don't know who that man worked for, and until we do, we won't be safe. The only way we're going to find out who is behind this is by linking up with Conner and helping her find Eternity Base."

Having said what she'd needed to, Sammy watched Riley in the dim glow from the windshield, waiting to see how he'd react. Pike had only said that Riley was ex–Special Forces and did good work. He was a far cry from the Rambo type so commonly portrayed in films, but Sammy had expected that because her own father had been slight of build and a quiet, thoughtful man.

The one quality Riley had—a quality Sammy noticed in almost every ex-SF man she'd ever met—was a sense of quiet competence and confidence. He looked as though he'd had a rough couple of days, with his growth of beard and his red-rimmed eyes, but then she had no idea what he'd been doing, so that didn't bother her. Something about him told her that he'd know what to do, and that he'd do it without his ego getting in the way. Underlying that, she also sensed some other deep emotion, but right now she couldn't put her finger on it. She only hoped that he would be willing to go along with her plan.

"I need to check it with the colonel," was Riley's only reply to her words. "Let's make a call."

Sammy followed as Riley led the way over to a pay phone in the terminal. She could hear only his side of the conversation and was impressed that Riley gave his boss just the facts with no editorializing. Most men she'd met had seemed to feel that no matter what a woman said, they could think of a better idea.

"He wants to talk to you." Riley held out the receiver.

"Mike, it's Sammy."

The colonel's voice rumbled in her ear. "You heard what Riley told me?"

"Yes."

"Is that what you want to do?"

"I think it's the only thing we can do," she replied.

The colonel chuckled. "You sure have your daddy's smarts. He was always a good one for coming up with some harebrained scheme. The amazing thing was that they usually worked. I'm alive today because a few of his ideas worked when mine wouldn't have.

"I can't order Riley to go with you. I'm going to tell him I'll pay him double his usual salary, but that won't mean much to him. If he decides to go, it'll be because he wants to—not for money. That's all I can do. If he decides against it, I suggest you two come here to my safe house and I'll try using some of my contacts to sort out this shit storm. Is that all right?"

Sammy knew it was the best she was going to get. "Yes."

"All right. Put him back on."

She handed the phone to Riley; he listened for a few minutes, not saying a word. His eyes continually scanned the airport and the parking area outside.

"Talk to you later, sir." Riley hung up the phone and then looked at her. "The colonel says your dad was in Special Forces. MACV-SOG. And he's MIA."

Sammy nodded.

Riley looked over her shoulder at the deserted ticket counters. "We won't be able to get our tickets until they open up in a few hours. I say we get some sleep in the van before then. I also need to get rid of the gun. Can't take it with us."

Sammy held up her hand. "Tickets to where?"

Riley gave a hard smile. "Antarctica. Where else?"

— ten —

INTELLIGENCE SUPPORT AGENCY (ISA), HEADQUARTERS, SOUTH-
WEST OF WASHINGTON, D.C. Bob Weaver was a third of the way
through his in box when he came upon the encrypted fax from Falcon.
He quickly decoded it and then stared at the resulting message for a
few seconds before turning to his computer:

> Request ID on Antarctic base, code-named Eternity Base.
> Established 1971 by army. Investigative team dispatched P.M.
> 25th to locate Eternity Base.
> Falcon 2200Z/11/25/96

Weaver accessed military records and quickly searched the database. After twenty minutes of fruitless effort, he was convinced of one
thing: there was no record in the ISA's classified database of an Eternity Base.

The Intelligence Support Agency was the military's secret version
of the Central Intelligence Agency (CIA). Lavishly funded by the
Pentagon's multibillion dollar black budget and accountable to no one
but the National Security Council, it had tentacles in every domestic
and foreign source of information. The ISA was more than a gathering agency, though. It also acted on the information it received, implementing numerous covert actions both in the United States and
overseas in the name of national security.

The ISA had contacts throughout the business world, men and women in critical places who worked with the ISA to forward the interests of the military and, concurrently, the massive industrial complex that supported the military. The ISA was the covert arm of the military-industrial complex that President Eisenhower had so feared, and its power was far greater than even those briefed on its existence dared believe.

Weaver encoded a message and electronically dispatched it to Falcon's handler, stationed in Atlanta. He had no idea when it would be relayed to Falcon, or even who Falcon was, but that wasn't his responsibility. He picked up the next piece of paper in his in box and went to work on that.

ST. LOUIS, MISSOURI. The hand on her shoulder woke Sammy out of a deep sleep, and she was momentarily disoriented as she took in her surroundings.

"We're boarding," Riley said quietly. His eyes were red rimmed from not having slept at all, either in the van or in the terminal.

Sammy stood up and stretched. She had nothing but her wallet and the rumpled and stained clothes on her back. She'd managed to wash off most of the blood on her shirt and jeans in the airport ladies' room, and since both garments were dark, what remained wasn't noticeable.

Riley held out a newspaper and cup of coffee. "Not a thing in here about a body being found, so that's good."

Sammy accepted the paper and watched as the herd moved toward the boarding gate. "The colonel said you'd been in Special Forces."

Riley nodded as he sipped his coffee. "I had almost twenty years in."

"Officer or enlisted?"

"Enlisted, then warrant officer."

"Why'd you get out?"

Riley looked at her for a second before replying brusquely. "I retired. Is that OK?" He didn't know what Pike had told her and he didn't want to talk.

"So you think I shouldn't ask questions?"

Riley was surprised at her directness. "I'm sorry. I didn't mean anything by what I said. I mean, you asked me why I got out and I told you."

Sammy relaxed. The loudspeaker in the waiting area announced final call for boarding. Riley pulled out the tickets. "Window or aisle?"

Sammy blindly grabbed one and looked at it. "Aisle."

AUCKLAND, NEW ZEALAND, 27 NOVEMBER 1996. Conner threw bags into the back of the pickup truck while Vickers, Kerns, and Lallo carefully stowed the cases containing their electronic gear. It was hard to believe their seemingly neverending flight from Hawaii was finally over.

Conner didn't know what to make of Devlin. For some reason she'd remembered him differently. About six foot four, tanned, with blond hair cut in a carefully casual style and rugged good looks, he would have been perfect for one of those beer commercials—kayaking down whitewater rapids while several beautiful women awaited him at the other end. Perhaps that's what bothered her. He looked as though he came from central casting. She hoped there was more to him than that.

There was a curious intensity about Devlin that was offset by a congenial, perfect smile. Conner had not remembered that smile, and it made her slightly uneasy. She had to give him credit for one thing, though—he ran a very smooth operation. Within forty-five minutes of landing, they had all their gear gathered together, were through customs, and were ready to move.

Conner slid in the passenger side of the pickup while Vickers and Lallo joined Kerns for the ride in the van. They rolled around the perimeter road of the runway until they came to a small hangar.

"Here we go," Devlin announced, getting out and sliding the hangar doors open. They drove in and parked. Two planes were sheltered inside. Conner got out and joined the rest of her party.

"This is our bird," Devlin announced, standing in front of the nose of a sleek-looking twin-engine plane. Conner noted the skis bolted on over the three wheels and the extra fuel tanks hanging under the wings. "And this is our pilot, Peter Swenson."

The pilot, who was toiling over the left engine, acknowledged his introduction with a grimy wave. Swenson looked as though he'd done more than his share of hard living, his graying hair and lined face indicating a life spent in the outdoors. "Swenson was originally a bush pilot from Australia, but he's done quite a few Antarctic runs for us," Devlin added. "We'll leave the gear here. Let's move into the ready room and get coordinated."

Conner was trying to get over her jet lag while at the same time trying to sort out her feelings. Her greeting with Devlin after getting off the plane had been awkward, somewhere between a lover's hug and the polite handshake two professionals would bestow on each other. There was no doubt now, though, as the team settled into metal folding chairs in front of a tacked-up map of Antarctica, that Devlin was all business.

Conner stood in front of the group to lead things off. "Devlin and I have decided to depart tomorrow first thing in the morning."

"How long a flight is it to where we're going?" Lallo asked.

"We'll be in the air almost ten hours," Devlin answered. Ignoring the groans, he turned to the map. "By the way, the base that Our Earth runs down there is called Aurora Glacier Station. It's located here, on Ross Island, about fifteen miles from McMurdo Station, right next to—what else?—Aurora Glacier. Right now we've got eleven people down there, but seven are out on the ice shelf doing research and won't be back for a while, so we'll be able to squeeze in without much trouble."

Conner stood back up. "The plan is to fly down there and start the search immediately. I faxed Devlin some xeroxed photos of the base when it was built, and he has some ideas about where to look."

As Conner sat back down, she felt a little disoriented. The sun was setting in the west, yet her body felt it was time to be getting out of bed.

Devlin used his finger to point on the map. "Eternity Base appears to be set in a sort of basin, surrounded on three sides by mountains. Based on the flying time I was given—two hours—I've estimated it to be about five hundred to six hundred miles from McMurdo, straight line distance. That places it in one of three locations: to the south here at the edge of the Ross Ice Shelf in the Transantarctic Mountains; to the east at the edge of Marie Byrd Land where King Edward the VII Land juts out into the Ross Sea; or to the northwest here along the Adelie Coast.

"The order in which I've just shown you these possible sites is also the order in which I think we should look. Six hundred miles from

McMurdo along the Adelie Coast puts you almost right smack on top of the French Station, Dumont d'Urville. I doubt very much that Eternity Base is in this area for several reasons. First is simply that it would have been built too close to an already established base—d'Urville. And the Russians also had a base in '71 farther east along that coastline, here—Leningradskaya.

"Additionally, I and many of my colleagues from Our Earth have been in this area several times conducting protests over the airstrip the French have been trying to build there for the last four years. We have made numerous overflights of the area and spotted nothing. Also, there's no doubt the French themselves have extensively searched that area.

"It's possible the base is here along the coast to the east, but I like the location in the Transantarctic Mountains, because if the purpose was to hide this base, putting it there would locate it much farther south than any known existing bases except for Amundsen-Scott Base, which sits right on top of the geographic South Pole itself. This area is along the original route explorers used to reach the South Pole. Both Amundsen and Scott traversed the Ross Ice Shelf and traveled up glaciers into that mountain range. Nowadays, though, expeditions bypass the mountains, going around either to the east or west. The area has not been extensively explored. Therefore it is my recommendation that we look first in this region.

"What I've done is make a montage of the silhouettes of the mountains around Eternity Base along with azimuths at which the pictures were taken. Fortunately we were able to determine this from the shadows. Then, as we fly along the mountains, we'll try to match the outlines."

Devlin held up a piece of paper with an outline of three jagged peaks poking above a sea of ice. "This is the view we should see along a due north azimuth. Mountains whose peaks manage to make it above the ice are called nunataks. As you can see in this picture, we have three very distinctive nunataks—two large pointed ones on the flanks of this rounded one. This three-mountain setup is what we should be looking for."

"How common are nunataks?" Vickers asked.

"Not as common as this map would make you believe with all these mountain ranges drawn on it," Devlin replied. "The Antarctic ice sheet averages more than twenty-five hundred meters thick. That's more than eight thousand feet. So a mountain has to be very high to clear the ice sheet.

"If we can find these three—and they are rather unique—and line up exactly on azimuth, then we will be along the line that Eternity Base lies on. In fact, I think there might be someone from our organization at Aurora Glacier who might even be able to identify these mountains and save us a lot of time."

"This may be a stupid question," Vickers said, "but wouldn't this place be totally covered up by now? After twenty-five years it would seem like there'd be quite a bit of snow on top."

"Good question." Devlin rubbed his chin. "I do think Eternity Base is most likely totally covered over by now, but not from snowfall. There isn't much accumulation down there, but the wind would pile ice and snow up against any exposed structure. However, we do have a plan for that.

"As I explained, we can get pretty close if we find these mountains. Once we do that, we land and use sonar to try and find the base. It's similar to the way fishermen look for schools of fish. We have two backpack sonar sets at the base, which are used for research on the ice cap. We can use those to shoot down into the ice as we ski along the azimuth. The metal and different density of the base ought to show up clearly. According to our information, Eternity Base covers a large area underground."

Conner wondered what contingency the builders had designed to find the place if it was covered up. She doubted very much that they had overlooked that major problem when they'd built it. "What's the weather like?" she asked.

Devlin walked over to a table and switched on a radio set. "Let's find out. We have high-frequency contact with our base, and just last month we finally got the people over at McMurdo to give Aurora Glacier the weather reports. Before that we were on our own." He glanced at Conner as he fiddled with the radio. "We're not quite rich enough yet to have satellite communications."

Conner returned the look, trying to determine what he meant by that. This trip was going to be even more intriguing than she had thought.

Conner thought it was interesting that McMurdo hadn't been giving weather reports to the Our Earth people. Typical government mentality. Our Earth represented a potential threat, so the party line was probably to ignore them, or to make their life as miserable as possible. On the other hand, she imagined that the Our Earth people wouldn't exactly ingratiate themselves to the various government personnel down there.

Devlin fiddled with the dials and then picked up the microphone. "Aurora Glacier, this is Auckland. Over."

There was no answer, and he repeated the message. Finally the radio crackled with a woman's voice. "Auckland, this is Aurora Glacier. Over."

"What's the weather look like? Over."

"The latest from McMurdo at 1900 Greenwich mean: present readings. Temperature minus 29 degrees Fahrenheit. Winds north, northwest at 23 knots. Barometric pressure 29.4 rising. Ceiling 1,200 feet, overcast. Visibility 4 miles with some blowing snow.

"Forecast is for the temperature to rise to minus 21 degrees Fahrenheit and the winds to continue at the same. Ceiling is expected to go up to around 1,500 feet with continued broken clouds. Visibility to extend to almost 5 miles. Over."

"Great. We'll give you a call once we're in the air and tell you when to expect us. Over."

"Roger. See you then. Out."

Lallo was looking worried. "That sounds like pretty bad weather to me."

Devlin smiled. "Actually that's good weather. The forecast is for eight hours, plus two on the far side for a safety margin for the military's C-130 flights, which are a little faster than we go. That report is a combination of inputs from d'Urville, the Russians at Minsk Station, the Aussies at Wilkes, and several others. McMurdo collates them and then broadcasts every thirty minutes. Five hours out from McMurdo is our point of no return. That's when we get the latest weather relayed from Aurora Glacier and the pilot makes the decision whether to continue on or turn around and head back."

The door leading to the hangar slammed open and Swenson stood there, wiping off his hands with a grimy towel. He spoke with a strong Australian accent. "We're topped off and I've got all your gear loaded. We'll be ready to roll at first light as long as the weather holds."

He stomped up to the front of the room. "I've got extra fuel tanks on the wings and two bladders in the back all hooked up. We should have enough petrol to make it there."

"Should have?" Vickers echoed.

Swenson smiled. "Just a phrase. It's a good airplane—a Cessna 411, if that means anything to you—but Antarctica is a bit out of its normal range, so we have to pack on all that extra fuel.

"I assume Devlin has told you about the point of no return. It's not only because of weather but also because of the fuel situation. Once we go past that point, we've got to make it to Aurora Glacier Station because we won't have enough fuel to turn around and come back." The burly man shrugged.

"All right. Here's your safety briefing. We run into trouble, you do what I say without asking any questions. We go down in the ocean, the raft is under the copilot's seat. That's the one up front that I'm not sitting in. You'd better hope we stay afloat long enough to get the raft inflated and out the window because if you get dunked, the cold water will kill you in less than a minute.

"We go down on land and I don't make it to give you advice, then my advice now is stay with the plane. It's got an emergency transponder on board, and even if that gets busted, the plane is going to be the biggest thing rescuers could find. You go wandering around on the ice, you'll last a little longer than if you'd gone in the water, but not by much. The end result will be the same.

"There are first aid and emergency kits on board the plane. They're marked in red and you can't miss 'em." Swenson smiled. "Any questions?" The other five people just stared at him. "All right then. See you in the morning."

Devlin pointed at some boxes lined up against the wall. "I've got some cold weather gear here. Let's get your equipment squared away before I show you where you'll spend the night."

ATLANTA, GEORGIA. Falcon read the brief reply from ISA headquarters that he'd picked up at the dead drop. His initial feeling was one of relief. Since the ISA had no record of Eternity Base, there was nothing to this mission. He'd been worried about it for the past several days. If the place did exist, the potential embarrassment was great. That was not something Falcon wanted to get involved in. He had no idea why the army would have built something in Antarctica, but he'd worked with the government for more than twenty years now and learned long ago not to apply logic and common sense to anything he came across.

Falcon got up and looked out his high office window, down onto the streets, slowly rolling his head to stretch his neck. "No," he said to himself, the bad feeling returning. Complacency was bad. Just because the computer held no record didn't mean there was nothing to the story. Conner had too much information. Too many pieces. The most chilling piece was the MIA aircrew.

Falcon felt the uneasy knot tie together in his stomach. If the U.S. Army built Eternity Base, then the ISA *had* to have some record of it. Since there was no record, logic said that it didn't exist. Falcon threw out logic and went with the opposite supposition. Suppose it did exist? What did that mean? If Eternity Base was real, then someone had built this place using government resources yet had also managed to keep it a secret from the government.

Falcon sat down at his desk and wrote out another message to ISA headquarters for immediate transmission.

— eleven —

AUCKLAND, NEW ZEALAND, 28 NOVEMBER 1996. Conner stole her hand down Devlin's stomach and started to slowly caress him awake. His eyes opened about the same time he was hard and she pushed aside the covers to straddle his body.

"You have to leave before everyone else is awake," she whispered as she lowered herself onto him.

"Good wake-up call," Devlin replied, his hips rising in rhythm with her strokes. After a few minutes he swung a leg out and they rolled over, Devlin assuming the upper position. Conner wrapped her legs around his back and was just beginning to build toward orgasm when an insistent rapping at the door distracted her.

"Stop," she hissed at Devlin, who was himself just reaching a point of no return. Conner put both hands on his chest and pushed. Devlin's eyes were unfocused with pleasure. "Stop!" Conner insisted. "Someone's at the door."

Devlin came to a unsatisfying halt and she rolled out from underneath him. Throwing on a robe, she went over to the door. She waited until Devlin had grabbed his clothes and snuck into the bathroom before cracking open the door.

Her sister, Sammy, stood there with a man behind her. She pushed in without saying a word and the man followed, shutting the door behind him.

"What the hell are you doing here?" Conner exclaimed as she tightened the belt on her robe.

The man with Sammy held up a hand and pointed at Devlin's shoes next to the bed and then at the bathroom. "Is someone in there?"

Conner blinked and tried to sort out her thoughts.

"Is there someone in there?" Sammy repeated the man's question.

"What business is it of yours?" Conner replied, astonished at what was happening.

Sammy shook her head. "This is no time for games. We need to talk. Now."

"Devlin, come out," Conner called.

Devlin came out, his hastily thrown-on shirt still unbuttoned.

"Who are you?" Sammy asked.

"Who's he?" Conner retorted, pointing at the man with her.

"This is Dave Riley. He's a friend of Colonel Pike's."

Conner frowned. Pike had been an associate of their dad's. If Riley was involved with Pike, that meant he was involved in some sort of spook work. "Devlin, meet my sister, Sammy. Sammy—Devlin. He's with Our Earth." The two shook hands. "Now tell me what you're doing here."

Riley shook his head. "We need to keep this as tight as possible."

Conner rolled her eyes. "I trust Devlin."

"It doesn't matter if you trust him," Riley replied quietly. "It's Sammy's life that's on the line."

"What do you mean 'life on the line'?" Conner asked.

Sammy looked at Devlin. "Are you here to help my sister find Eternity Base?"

"Yes."

"All right. Then he can stay."

"I recommend against it," Riley urged. "You have to consider the legal aspect of what's happened."

Sammy laughed. "I think it's a little too late for that."

"Would someone tell me what the hell is going on!" Conner demanded.

Sammy grabbed a chair and sat down. "I suggest you all get comfortable. It will take a while."

Conner checked the clock next to the bed. "We only have an hour before we have to head out to the airfield for our flight to Antarctica."

Sammy nodded. "I'll be done in twenty minutes. You need to hear this before going any farther."

She launched into a description of what had happened to her from the moment she'd faxed the photos and ended her tale with their arrival in New Zealand only an hour previously.

When her sister finally fell silent, Conner ran a hand through her thick hair. "You have no idea who this man you killed worked for?"

Sammy shook her head. "Most likely the government, which is why Riley and I are here. The only way we can get out of this is to find the base and subsequently figure out who built it and why it is so important that someone is willing to kill to hide its existence."

"This is hot. Real hot." Conner's mind was already running, trying to figure new angles to the story. "Since you escaped, we're a step ahead of them. That means we've got to keep moving."

"Maybe not," Riley said.

Conner swung her head around and looked over at Riley, who was sitting cross-legged on the floor. He'd kept quiet until now. "Why do you say that?"

Riley looked up at her. "Because the man your sister killed said that you were not his problem. That says to me that whoever he worked for knows about you and this news team. So you might not be a step ahead."

Conner shook her head. "No. We have to be. You say you were kidnapped in the morning. We were in the air by six that evening."

"We caught up with you," Riley noted.

Conner met his eyes. "You got my sister here safe and sound. That was what you were paid to do and you did it. This is no longer your concern. I'll take care of things from here on out."

Riley's face was expressionless. "She's not out of danger until we figure out who was behind the attack on her. In fact, I would say that she's in more danger now than if she had gone with me to the safe house in North Carolina like the colonel wanted." He shrugged. "But my staying or going is not up to you. It's up to Sammy."

"I'd like you to come with me," Sammy said, looking at Riley.

It was Devlin who objected now. "We're going to be tight as it is flying down there. We appreciate your warning, but you two really have nothing to offer our expedition."

Sammy finally showed some of the temper that Conner had been so familiar with as a child. "These people tried to kill me because I gave you this story! You two are acting like this is some academic problem. This is real shit. I don't—"

"Hold on!" Conner stepped up to her sister, placing her hands on her shoulders. "Take it easy, Sam. I'm sorry. It's just that you've taken us off guard." She looked at Devlin. "Can we fit them on the plane?"

Devlin looked decidedly unhappy but reluctantly nodded.

"All right. Let's get our stuff together and we'll head out to the airport in fifteen minutes."

AIRSPACE, SOUTH PACIFIC OCEAN. "Roger, Aurora Glacier. Passing point of no return and coming in. Out." Swenson turned in his seat to face the seven passengers and yelled over the whine of the engines. "Weather is satisfactory all the way, so we're continuing on."

Conner didn't know whether to be relieved or not as she squirmed in the copilot's seat. It was amazing how such a simple thing could push all other thoughts out of her mind. The urge to urinate had crept over her an hour ago and was now overriding all attempts at higher level cognitive thinking.

She twisted her legs for the fortieth time, taking care not to hit the copilot's peddles on the floor. At least she had more space up here than the six people in the back. They sat among a jumble of equipment with scarcely enough room to move an elbow. Surreptitiously, she unbuckled her seat belt, hoping that would ease the pressure.

"Here," a quiet voice whispered in her ear. Riley slipped her a camouflage-patterned poncho liner and a large lidded plastic jar. She turned her head, but he'd already slumped back with his eyes closed. The other four men and her sister also all seemed to be sleeping. She glanced over at Swenson, who was quietly whistling to himself, eyes fixed forward.

Conner's face was beet red as she briefly debated what to do. The laws of physiology made that determination for her. If she didn't do it, she knew she'd probably wet her pants well before the remaining four hours of flight were up. She draped the poncho liner over her lap.

It was a difficult process with all the layers of clothing, but she felt much better when done. She screwed the lid on the jar and placed it between her feet on the floor of the plane.

Two hours later, Swenson's voice intruded on the numbing roar of the plane. "There's Antarctica."

Conner, along with the others, peered out the right side. "That's Cape Adare," Devlin announced.

Dark peaks, streaked with snow and ice, poked through the low-lying clouds. To the left, through a few gaps in the clouds, the sea ice stretched as far as the eye could see.

As they continued south, they flew parallel to the coast, and the ocean turned into the Ross Sea. More peaks appeared, and Devlin called out the ranges as they went by: the Admiralty Mountains, the Prince Albert Mountains, and, finally, the Royal Society Range.

Swenson began to drop altitude as a single massive mountain appeared straight ahead above the clouds, set apart from the others to the right. "That's Mount Erebus," Devlin pointed out "Aurora Glacier Station and McMurdo are both set on the base of Erebus on the far side. It and Mount Terror make up most of Ross Island. Captain Ross—for whom the island, the sea, and the ice shelf are all named—christened both mountains after the two ships he used to explore the Antarctic."

"There isn't a long runway," Swenson told them as they descended. "We land on the Ross Ice Shelf itself because it's the flattest thing around. The reception party should have marked out a reasonably good stretch for us. We don't need much," he added in way of encouragement.

Conner watched the slopes of Erebus come closer; then they punched into a thick cloud layer and the view was blanketed. She remembered reading in her notes that an Air New Zealand DC-10 had crashed into Mount Erebus in 1979, killing all on board. She started tapping her fingers against the side of the plane as it was buffeted by the wind. Waiting for the clouds to break, she started imagining a wall of snow-covered stone appearing out of the gray ahead.

Suddenly the clouds parted and they were in the clear again. The plane was low now and Swenson banked hard left, over land.

"That's McMurdo Station," Devlin yelled. Conner pushed her nose against the glass and looked below. The sprawl of buildings and numerous large storage tanks surprised her; McMurdo was much larger than she had imagined. Somehow she had pictured the primitive settlement in the old science fiction movie *The Thing*: a few Quonset huts huddled in the snow. She guessed there were at least forty buildings down there.

"All right. Everyone buckle up." Swenson swung out over the ice, flying very low. They roared over a snow tractor with a large red flag tied to the top. Swenson pulled up and did another flyby. A man on top of the tractor was holding a green flag pointing in a northeasterly direction.

On the third pass, Swenson finally dipped his wings down. With a hiss and then a steady rumble, the skis touched the ice, and a thin mist of snow plumed up on either side. Gradually, they slithered to a halt. Swenson turned the plane around and taxied it back to the tractor. Conner could now see that the tractor had a flatbed trailer hitched to it with several drums piled on top.

The silence as Swenson turned off the engines was as shocking as any loud sound. They'd lived with engine noise for eight and a half hours. As their senses adjusted, the steady whine of wind bouncing off the skin of the plane became noticeable. With the airplane's heater off, the temperature immediately started dropping inside.

"Everyone bundle up." Devlin was cinching down his hood. Conner made sure that everything was on before finally pulling the bulky mittens over her hands. She had arranged for the gear with Devlin over the phone and was very grateful he had followed through. What she called winter clothes back in Atlanta would not have done the job here.

Devlin had also come up with an extra set of gear for Sammy. The only one who did not need to be outfitted in New Zealand was Riley. He had pulled his own cold-weather equipment out of his duffel bag. He was wearing a Gore-tex camouflage parka and overpants that Conner was determined wouldn't appear in any of their shots—much too militaristic. The three men and her sister were dressed the way she was—a bright orange parka and pants over a pile jacket and bib pants that zipped on the sides and the crotch. The polypropylene underwear next to their bodies would wick away any moisture from their skin. Large boots—Devlin had referred to them as Mickey Mouse boots—covered their feet, which were encased in thick wool socks.

Conner had not introduced Sammy as her sister but had identified Sammy and Riley as a security team sent by SNN. Her crew had taken that in stride, since all of them had worked with security personnel on various overseas assignments.

Swenson swung open his door and Conner took a quick gulp as a blast of cold air slammed into her lungs. Swenson scrambled out and Conner followed suit, her feet crunching in the snow. She'd never felt such cold. The air stung her face, the only exposed part of her body. Her skin rebelled, trying to shrink from the pain of the cold and she felt her muscles tighten as if somehow she might be warmer if she could make herself smaller.

The other members of the party piled out and stood looking around. To the north, Mount Erebus was a solid wall reaching up into the cloud cover. To the south, an endless line of ice disappeared into clouds that seemed to touch the horizon. To the west, the Royal Society Range blotted out the space between cloud and ice. The mountains looked amazingly close, as if you could walk there in an hour or two, yet Conner knew they were almost a hundred miles away. If they got nothing else from their trip here, they'd have some spectacular film footage.

The tractor kicked to life, drawing her attention away from the scenery. It roared up, treads clattering, placing the trailer alongside the plane. The driver, looking like a bear in his garments, waved down at them, pumping his fist. He seemed to be in a rush.

"Let's off-load," Devlin called out.

As they busied themselves transferring the gear from plane to trailer, Swenson used a sledge-hammer to drive pitons into the ice—one for each wing, one for the tail, and one for the nose. Rope attached to each piton secured the plane to the ice.

Once all the equipment was off the aircraft, Devlin gave Conner a boost up onto the wooden platform that made up the floor of the trailer. She tried to get as comfortable as possible among the bags and cases. The other members of the party climbed on board, and all grabbed on for dear life as the driver threw the tractor into gear and roared off toward the looming form of Mount Erebus.

Devlin leaned over and yelled in Conner's ear. "Welcome to Antarctica."

— twelve —

AURORA GLACIER STATION, ANTARCTICA. Sammy's first glimpse of Aurora Glacier Station confirmed what she had expected. The large, squat, boxy building looked more like several trailer homes sealed together than a research station. The bright red building sat on the ice, several hundred yards from the base of Mount Erebus; just to the right a cluster of antennas was tied off to a tower. A colorful banner reading "Our Earth" was strung along the front. Aurora was located six miles from McMurdo Station.

It had taken the tractor almost forty-five minutes to get them off the ice shelf and here to the station. They pulled up in front with a clatter, and a couple of people stepped out of the building to greet them. As Devlin did the introductions, Sammy could see Riley hanging back. His camouflage cold-weather suit contrasted with the bright outfits of the station personnel, and their lackluster handshakes on meeting Riley were a predictable reaction.

"Let's get our equipment indoors," Devlin ordered.

Sammy helped Riley haul his duffel bag inside. They were directed down a short corridor and into a small room containing three sets of bunk beds and not much else. Riley dumped his gear onto one bed and went back out to help Conner's crew with the camera and radio gear.

Sammy stood with Devlin, Conner, and Swenson in the mess hall/meeting room as Devlin briefed a skinny, bearded man on their mission to find Eternity Base. Devlin had introduced him as Peter Mc-

Cabe, Our Earth's foremost Antarctic expert. When Conner showed him the faxed photocopy of the picture, McCabe sat down at the table and looked at it for a long time.

"This looks familiar. It's rare that you have three nunataks that close to one another." He pulled out a large chart. "Show me again where you think this place might be based on the air time."

"Two hours by C-130 comes to roughly five hundred miles." Devlin traced a half arc around McMurdo Station.

"It's not to the west," McCabe announced firmly. "That would put it very close to the French station there, and I've been in that area quite a bit lately so I'd certainly recognize these peaks if they were there."

He stared at the map, his eyes boring in as if he could see the actual terrain by just looking at the two dimensional paper. Sammy took the opportunity to glance over at Riley, who had just joined the group. He seemed unconcerned about the whole situation. Ever since their conversation at the airport, he had been very quiet, talking only when directly questioned. Sammy had spent most of their many hours in the air sleeping and recovering from her ordeal.

McCabe turned the map around and placed the photo on it. He tapped a spot on the far side of the Ross Sea. "It's here. I'd be willing to bet that middle peak is Mount Grace. The one on the right is McKinley Peak. The lower one on the left must be this one that has no name."

Devlin shook his head. "Are you sure? I'd have thought they'd put the base farther south." He pointed at the map. "Down here along the Shackleton coast, perhaps."

McCabe looked up. "No. That's Mount Grace. I knew I'd seen that silhouette before. To the south of it is the glacier where they launched the Byrd Land South Pole traverse in '60. When you fly out in that direction you put the glacier on the right and McKinley on your left. Then it's open ice until you hit the Executive Committee Mountain Range."

Conner spoke for the first time. "How soon can we take off again?" she asked Swenson.

The pilot was chewing on the end of his bushy mustache. "Ah, well, missy, the plane, it can take off right now. The problem is the pilot. I just put in ten nonstop hours and I could use a couple of hours to rest. How about in four hours?"

Sammy could tell that Conner wasn't very happy about the delay. She half expected her sister to order the pilot to take off immediately. But Conner sighed and looked around the table. "All right. It's presently three-fifteen local time here. We take off at seven-fifteen. The—"

"What about darkness?" Lallo interrupted. "We won't be able to find the place in the dark."

Devlin laughed. "There is no night in the summer down here. The sun gets a little lower on the horizon, but it never sets."

"As I said," Conner continued, "I want everyone gathered in this room ready to go at six. That will give us plenty of time to make it down to the plane and be in the air at seven-fifteen. Are there any questions?" she asked.

Riley leaned forward in his chair. "I'd like about thirty minutes to give a little class on how to operate in the cold—particularly how to properly wear your clothing and about cold-weather injuries."

Conner frowned and looked at her watch. "I have to do a transmission back to Atlanta in twenty minutes. I need to get ready to do that, and Vickers has to set up his equipment. Then we all need to get a nap, because it might be our last opportunity to sleep for several days. I really don't see the need for it anyway. We're going to be inside the plane."

"As long as things work out, you'll be inside the plane," Riley replied. "But if things go to crap, you're going to be on the ice."

"Devlin will be with the party, so we'll be able to draw on his experience," Conner countered.

Devlin seemed amused by Riley's comments. "Have you been to Antarctica before, Mr. Riley?" he asked.

"No."

Devlin's lips parted. "Ah. Well, then, what background are you drawing upon for all this information you wish to impart?"

Riley looked him in the eye. "I spent some time in the Special Forces, and we did a lot of work in winter environments. I've been above the Arctic Circle in Norway and Alaska on operations, and I've done quite a bit of work in mountainous regions including the Rockies and the Alps."

Devlin shook his head. "None of that really compares to what you face down here."

Riley shrugged, but his voice was sharp. "It's cold, right? There's a lot of ice and snow, right?" Sammy felt sorry for Riley; she'd dragged him into this when he probably had no desire to even be here.

Devlin spoke as if to a child. "Yes, but it's much colder here, and there's more snow and ice. The terrain is also very unique. I'm not sure that Norway can compare—"

"All the more reason to know what you're doing." Riley held up a hand. "But you're the expert." He looked over at Sammy. "I'm going to get some sleep. I'll see you all at six."

Riley left the conference room and reappeared almost immediately, his duffel bag over his shoulder. He headed toward the door leading outside.

"Where are you going?" Conner asked.

"I'm going to sleep outside. I'll be on the lee side of the building when you want me." With that he stepped outside and the door slammed shut behind him.

"You brought a weird man with you, Sammy," was Conner's only comment before turning to her crew and giving some more instructions.

Sammy tugged on her parka and went outside after Riley. She found him on the far side of the building, digging in the snow. He briefly glanced up at her, but she said nothing, watching his actions.

After completing a slit in the snow, he removed the bungee cord from around an insulated sleeping pad and laid the pad in the bottom of the trench. He unscrewed the valve on the top corner and the pad quickly expanded to full size—a foot and a half wide by six feet long and about an inch and a half thick.

Then he pulled his sleeping bag out of a stuffed sack, released the cinches, and unrolled the bag. He stretched a poncho across the top of the trench and secured the ends with snow, leaving an opening just large enough to crawl into. All done, Riley put the shovel down in the hole and put his bag in a place he had dug out near the head.

"Why are you sleeping out here?" Sammy finally asked, unable to restrain her curiosity.

Riley looked up at her. "I hate sleeping that close to a bunch of people. I'm a very light sleeper, and the slightest noise wakes me up." He gave the tiniest hint of a smile. "Hell, tell the nature lovers in there that I'm just loving nature."

"What's that?" Sammy asked as he started to slip into a thin bag.

"It's a vapor barrier, or VB, liner that goes inside the sleeping bag," Riley explained. "The liner keeps my perspiration inside it. Makes for a damp sleep, but it's better for me to be damp than the bag to be. I can dry out. I might not be in circumstances where I can dry out the bag. And a wet sleeping bag will kill you here."

He proceeded to slide all the way into the trench until the only thing showing was his face. Sammy leaned over. "I appreciate your help."

Riley nodded. "No problem."

"I'm sorry my sister isn't being very nice."

Riley closed his eyes. "You're not responsible for her, Sammy. She's got a job to do."

She turned back toward the warmth of the station. "Have a good sleep."

"You too." Riley's muffled voice floated out of the trench in the snow.

"You all set, Ms. Young? I've got a clear bounceback from the satellite." Vickers did a last check on his equipment.

"Yes." Conner pulled a 3.5-inch diskette with red markings on it from her computer and handed it to him. He slipped it into what looked like an external disk drive for a computer, except it was connected to his satellite communications (SATCOM) transmitter/receiver. The transmitter in turn was hooked—by way of a twenty-five-foot cable snaking out the cracked open window—to the small dish antenna he had placed outside in the snow, oriented at the proper azimuth and elevation to hit the designated satellite.

Vickers checked his watch. At exactly 0600 Greenwich mean, he hit the send key. The disk whirred as its information was relayed to the transmitter and then sent out. After five seconds it stopped.

"All done. We have about nine minutes before the receive." Vickers was already at work on the small keyboard built into the radio, preparing it for the incoming message.

Conner wondered how Riley was doing out in the snow. He was a strange man. Devlin had come to her and told her it was crazy for Riley to be outside, but Conner figured that Riley had made his bed, literally, and now he had to sleep in it. Besides, she wasn't responsible for him, Sammy was.

At ten minutes after the hour the disk whirred again—this time for less than two seconds. Vickers removed the disk and handed it to Conner, then went outside to retrieve the dish.

Conner took the disk and slid it into her laptop. She entered the appropriate program, and the screen glowed:

SNN TRANSMIT/RECEIVE
ENTER CODE:

Conner punched in her personal code and hit the enter key. The disk whirred, the screen cleared, then the message from Atlanta was displayed.

TO CONNER YOUNG 392993
FROM STU FERNANDEZ 483772
DTG 280400 NOVEMBER 96
NO NEW INFORMATION HERE
RECEIVED YOUR MESSAGE CLEAR
GOOD LUCK
END MESSAGE

Conner hadn't really expected anything. She dumped the message into the hard drive memory and shut down the computer. Time to get some rest before the long "night" ahead. She hoped her sister was already asleep. She didn't particularly want to talk to her now.

She entered the women's bunk room and wasn't surprised to see Sammy sitting on her bunk, wide awake. It was the first time they'd been alone since she'd shown up in New Zealand. Conner ignored her and stretched out on another bed, fully clothed.

"Are you having fun?" Sammy asked.

Conner turned her head. "What do you mean by that?"

"I show up in New Zealand and I find you in bed with someone. I tell you that my life was threatened and that I killed somebody. And your reaction is basically wondering how big a story it will be."

Conner looked back up at the ceiling. "Come on, Sammy. I'm sorry about what happened to you in St. Louis. There's nothing I can do about it now. Getting this story is as important to you as it is to me."

"Is that why you're screwing Devlin . . . 'cause he can help you get the story?"

Conner lifted herself up on an elbow. "Listen. Who I sleep with is—"

The door burst open and Riley stood there. "The mess hall, now!" He was gone as quickly as he'd come.

Conner and Sammy scrambled out of bed and rushed to the mess hall to find Riley leaning over an unconscious Swenson. The pilot was slumped in a chair, his clothes covered with melting ice and snow.

"What happened?" Conner asked.

"I found him outside, lying in the snow." Riley was checking the pilot's bare hands for frostbite. "Another five minutes and he'd have frozen to death."

"How'd you find him?" Sammy inquired.

"I heard a noise. Sounded like the main door slamming shut. I don't know." Riley shrugged. "Something just didn't seem right, so I got up and checked."

As Riley spoke, the other members of the team filed in until all were assembled.

"So what happened to him?" Conner wanted to know. "Did he fall and knock himself out?"

Riley shook his head. "I don't think so." He broke open a medical kit, pulled out some smelling salts, and waved them under Swenson's nose. The pilot gagged briefly and then his eyes flickered open. He reached for his head and moaned. Conner stepped behind him for a closer look. Through the thinning hair on the back of Swenson's head, a large purplish bruise was visible.

Conner moved in front of Swenson. "What happened?"

Swenson tried shaking his head, but the pain got the better of him and he held still. "Shit. I don't know. I was going down the corridor to take a piss and someone whacked me on the back of the head. That's all I remember."

Eight sets of eyes met, then shifted uneasily from one to another. The silence lasted for almost a minute.

Riley looked at the other men. "Was anybody awake when Swenson left?"

All three men shook their heads. Riley turned to Conner. "When I came in, all three were in their beds and appeared to be sleeping. You two were in your room. The three people from Our Earth were all accounted for also."

"That leaves you then, doesn't it?" Devlin observed.

Riley shrugged. "Then it would have been pretty stupid of me to rescue him, wouldn't it?"

Conner decided to take charge before things got out of control. "Are you able to fly?" she asked Swenson.

Swenson nodded carefully. "Aye. I don't think I have any permanent damage." He got up, a bit unsteady on his feet.

"Then we leave now." Conner turned to Vickers and Lallo. "Get your gear ready to go. We leave for the plane in fifteen minutes."

After Conner's crew left the room, Devlin turned to her. "What about whoever knocked him out? I don't think it was chance that our pilot was attacked. Somebody is trying to stop us from getting to Eternity Base."

"That's why I want to leave right away," Conner replied. "If we wait around here any longer, whoever it is will have a chance to do something else, like maybe sabotage the plane."

"So we're going to fly with a pilot who just got conked on the head?" Sammy asked.

"I don't have time for this," Conner said. "He said he can fly."

"The odds are," Riley said, "that we'll be transporting our problem with us to Eternity Base—if we find it."

"Once we find the base," Conner declared, "it will be too late. We'll have the story." She pointed at Sammy. "It's the same reason you came down here. The key to stopping these people is to find out who built the base."

Sammy shook her head. "But whoever it is has to be pretty power-ful to have been able to infiltrate your team so quickly."

Conner looked her sister in the eye. "I don't think whoever tried to kill Swenson is from my team."

Sammy looked at Riley and then back at her sister. "Are you accus-ing Riley?"

"I'm not accusing anybody. I'm just being realistic," Conner retorted.

Sammy bristled and Riley stepped between the two women with his hands raised. "Let's chill out," he suggested. "Conner's right. We need to get to Eternity Base first. Standing around yacking isn't going to do us any good." He looked from one woman to the other. "All right?"

Sammy nodded. "All right."

"All right," Conner echoed.

— thirteen —

ROSS ICE SHELF, ANTARCTICA. Conner could hear Vickers humming the theme song from *The Wizard of Oz* as the plane picked up speed. Swenson pulled in the yoke and the heavily laden Cessna bounced a few times, then clawed into the air. Reaching sufficient altitude, the plane banked and headed for the search area.

Their course followed the edge of the Ross Ice Shelf to the east. Ross Island faded behind them, and after an hour Roosevelt Island appeared below and then slid to the rear. They slowly closed the distance to the Ford Mountain Range, looming up in front of them. As they approached the first mountains, Swenson increased power; the wings groped in the thin air for even more altitude until the Cessna had sufficient height to clear them.

The plane was as crowded with people and equipment as it had been on the flight from New Zealand. Conner, Kerns, and Riley were on the left side of the plane, one in front of the other; Vickers was in the copilot's seat; and Devlin, Sammy, and Lallo behind Vickers on the right. They'd loaded all the camera equipment along with one backpack of survival gear for each person. If they found the base, Conner wanted to be prepared to stay and get her story.

Although the magnificence of the peaks that jutted out of the white impressed Conner, what struck her more was the sea of ice that swept the flanks of those mountains. It was hard to imagine an ice sheet almost two miles thick. Devlin had told her that the ice was so heavy it had forced most of the bedrock surface of Antarctica below sea level; if the ice were removed, the land, relieved of the pressure, would rise above sea level.

Swenson had piloted them over a glacier and through a pass, putting them on the opposite side of the mountain range. Now they flew along the southern edges, looking to their left, searching for the three mountains. Conner had taped the photocopy of the picture against the bulkhead above the left side window, and she and Devlin were scanning in that direction. As Devlin leaned over her right shoulder, she tried to ignore his close proximity, but his body was generating a warmth that was welcome in the frigidness of the plane. She wondered if Sammy was right: was she attracted to Devlin as a person, or because he could be of use to her at the moment—a way to Eternity Base, a warm body on a cold airplane.

Swenson flew straight up the middle of the mountain chain. The weather was remarkably clear, and the peaks seemed startlingly close. Conner felt as if she could reach a hand out the window and caress the rock. She glanced right at the map board on Devlin's lap. He had their route marked on the plastic cover with a grease pencil.

"Everyone look carefully. McKinley should be coming up soon," Devlin yelled. His words disappeared into the whine of the engines without any reply from the others.

"That's McKinley," Swenson shouted a short while later. He immediately banked to the left, and the nose of the aircraft settled on a northerly route.

Riley reached forward and tapped Devlin on the shoulder, gesturing for the map board. Devlin passed it back and Riley oriented himself, checking the map against the terrain features he could see below.

"Can we move to the right a little bit?" he called out to Swenson. Riley ignored Conner's annoyed look. Taking her silence as assent, Swenson changed course slightly to the right.

Visibility was unrestricted, and far out to the front through a gap in the range, they could even see the ice pack on the coast. To the left and right, isolated mountaintops poked out of the white carpet of ice.

"There. That's it," Riley calmly announced, pointing. Three peaks, against a backdrop of other nunataks.

Conner looked up at the paper taped on the fuselage and then out again. She leaned forward and tapped Swenson on the shoulder. "There. We're pretty close on the right azimuth."

Conner leaned across to Devlin. "What do you think, Devlin?"

Riley broke in. "You have to consider the fact that the photo was taken from the ground. We're up much higher. Ask Swenson to drop down and let's see how they look."

The pilot circled down until they were barely a hundred feet above the ice. He pointed the nose straight at the peaks, and all eight of the plane's occupants stared ahead.

Conner was the first to break the silence. "That's it. Lallo, get us a shot as we go in."

NEW YORK, NEW YORK. The North Korean ambassador's aide studied Loki's latest report, which had been forwarded in response to his highlighting. This Antarctic thing was very strange. Loki had done a good job summarizing all the information available, but it raised more questions than it answered.

The aide rewrote the information for forwarding. Although there was nothing of apparent importance to his native country, one never knew when something that seemed irrelevant could prove useful. At the very least there was the possibility that the United States could be embarrassed if this secret base actually had been built. That was always good, particularly now.

FORD MOUNTAIN RANGE, ANTARCTICA. "Patience, missy," Swenson called over his shoulder. "We don't want to be buckling our landing gear out here. It's a long walk back."

Conner ignored the missy comment and concentrated on the three peaks. Swenson was on his fourth pass over the floor of the basin, looking for a spot to land. Conner had no doubt that they were in the right place. It had to be. The peaks matched, and the basin was surrounded on three sides by mountains. The bowl was perhaps ten miles wide by twenty long, open to the south. If they could get down and match the azimuth on the picture with the mountains in the background, she knew they could get close. Very close.

The passes had revealed no sign of any structure, but that didn't surprise Conner. The ice and snow would have covered the above-surface portions of Eternity Base many years ago.

"All right. I've got something that looks like it might work. Everyone make sure you're buckled up."

Conner's hands clenched the back of Swenson's seat as he slowly let out the yoke and reduced throttle. The ice crept up, closer and closer.

"Let's be hoping there are no crevasses," Swenson muttered. The skis touched and they were down—at least for the moment.

"Oh, shit!" Vickers yelled from the right front seat as they became airborne again, bouncing over a small ridge and then slamming into the ice once more.

The plane was shuddering, and the right wing tipped down as the ski hit a divet. They turned slightly right, then straightened. When the plane finally stopped, Conner's fingers had made indentations in the imitation leather on the back of Swenson's seat.

"Well, that was fun." Swenson turned around. "What do you want to do for an encore, missy?"

Conner rubbed her hands to restart the circulation and looked about. "Can you taxi along the ice until we get on the right azimuth to line up the three peaks like in the photo?"

Swenson looked around outside the aircraft. "Well, I certainly can do that, but the ice might not allow it." He looked at Devlin. "What do you think?"

Devlin licked his lips. "Actually the ice should be all right here. We're on a pretty solid base. You have to worry about crevasses when you're on a glacier, but we're on the polar ice cap now. Should be all right."

"Let's do it," Conner ordered.

"To the right," Riley said. Conner looked at him questioningly. "If you want to line them up, go to the right," he repeated.

"To the right," Conner confirmed.

Swenson increased throttle and worked his pedals. The Cessna slithered along.

"Hold it," Conner called out after three minutes of very slow moving. "What do you all think?"

They looked to the north.

"Yes." Riley was the first to answer.

"Yes." Devlin echoed him. The others said nothing.

"Let's get skiing." Riley unbuckled himself. He slapped Devlin on the shoulder. "Which do you want? North or south?"

Devlin slid to a halt and looked back over his shoulder. The plane didn't look very far away, but he estimated he'd come at least four miles. He reached for the sonar emitter slung over his shoulder and pointed it down. As he pressed the trigger, he watched the small screen on the back. After five seconds he slid it back over his shoulder and continued onward.

Every thirty push-offs of his right ski, he halted and repeated the process. The skiing felt good, but Devlin was getting tired and he knew he'd be sore tomorrow. The skis were not true cross-country skis but rather a specially made hybrid that Our Earth used down here. A combination binding connected at the toe and rear. The rear binding could be unlocked for cross-country movement such as this, or locked for downhill.

Devlin had chosen to go north, so he had the mountains to his front. His course was centered on the middle peak ahead. It was very hard to judge distances, but he estimated that the mountains were only about four to five miles away. He sensed he was going slightly uphill as he continued on. The surface wasn't as flat as it had appeared from the air, and he wondered how Swenson had managed to find such a smooth spot to land. Occasionally, Devlin crossed a low ridge of compressed ice and had to traverse his way up and over in order to stay on line.

Twenty-seven. Twenty-eight. Twenty-nine. Thirty. The echo just below the surface shocked Devlin, it was so unexpected. He blinked and stared at the sonar emitter screen for ten seconds. It was still there. Devlin looked around the immediate area. The surface ice was relatively even except for a six-foot ridge running at an angle across his front. There was no sign of anything man-made.

He pulled off his backpack, slid out one of the thin plastic poles with a flag attached, and stuck it in the ice. Then he began to ski, only ten paces now, trying to search out the dimensions of whatever was under the ice. He continued to receive a positive response as he approached the ridge. Devlin traversed up the small incline and stood on top of the buckled ice. His flag was more than eighty yards away. This had to be the base. He noted an outcropping from the ice ridge about ten yards away and skied along the top to it. Snow had piled up, forming a block perhaps fifteen feet to a side and eight feet high. Devlin aimed the sonar into the snow pile. Positive response. There was something in there too.

Devlin looked to the south. His view of the plane was blocked by a large ridge he had crossed about a mile back. He secured the sonar over his shoulder and skied down off the ridge and back to his ruck. Throwing it over his shoulder, he set out to the south with long glides on the skis. He forgot about being tired.

Conner shivered. She considered asking Swenson to crank the engine and turn on the heat, but she held off. They had only so much fuel and they'd been on the ice now for more than an hour. The windows had fogged over from the breathing of the occupants, and she used her mitten to wipe a small hole in her porthole so she could peer out.

A figure appeared on the horizon, skiing toward the plane with smooth, powerful strides. She kept the glass clear and watched the bundled man come closer.

"One of them's back," she announced.

Vickers swung open the side door and the wind swirled inside, removing what little body heat had built up in the plane. The skier stepped out of his bindings and passed the skis to Vickers, who slid them along the floor. The man stepped in and the door was shut behind.

"Anything?" Conner asked as the man slid down his parka hood. She recognized Riley.

"Nothing." He slumped down in his seat and leaned back. "I went about eight miles out and took a slightly different route back and picked up nothing."

There was a roar as Swenson started the engines. In a minute welcome heat poured out of the vents, and the windows slowly started clearing.

"Let's taxi north and pick up Devlin on his way back," Conner suggested.

Swenson shook his head. "Uh-uh. I know where the runway is safe for take off." He pointed out the front window. "Right back the way we came. Plus there's too many small ridges that way. We wouldn't get far."

"Besides," Riley added, "we don't know if Devlin is taking a straight route back. Even though it isn't likely, we might just miss him."

Conner sighed and resumed her vigil out the window. She didn't like waiting. Swenson shut off the engines after five minutes, and the heat quickly dissipated out the skin of the plane.

Swenson turned in his seat, tapping the headset he wore. "I just got the weather report from McMurdo. It doesn't sound encouraging. They only give another three to four hours max of good weather and then we're going to get hit with high winds, which means very low visibility."

Conner wondered what was taking Devlin so long. He should have been back a half hour ago according to the plan.

Twenty minutes later, Vickers called out. "I see him."

Conner leaned over and looked out the opposite side porthole. Devlin was moving rapidly to the plane. They opened the door as he arrived, and he threw in his backpack, followed by the skis and himself.

"Anything?" Conner asked.

"Yes."

She waited for an explanation, but Devlin was busy cleaning the snow off his boots and then shutting the door. "Well?"

Devlin removed his snow goggles and smiled at Conner "There's something under the ice about three miles from here." he said, "I checked it as much as I could and left a flag there. It's pretty big, whatever it is—at least eighty yards long, maybe more. It's either your base or a big flying saucer that got buried under the ice."

Everyone in the plane looked at Conner expectantly, waiting for her instructions. Devlin accepted a cup of coffee from Vickers's thermos and cradled it in his hands, absorbing the warmth.

"Can we land up there?" Conner asked him.

Devlin nodded. "I think there's a good level area to the north of the spot. I couldn't tell for sure because I didn't ski over it, but I think it's worth a look." He looked forward toward Swenson. "It runs northwest-southeast."

Swenson shook his head. "We've got bad weather coming. If we don't head for home now, we may get stuck out here."

Sammy spoke for the first time. "What happens if we're stuck out here?"

Devlin shrugged. "We have our emergency gear, but it depends how long the weather stays bad. It could stay bad for a week, in which case it would be an awfully long time to be cooped up in this plane."

"I don't think staying here's a good idea," Riley threw in.

"What if we get into the base?" Conner said.

"What?" Devlin was confused.

"What if we get into Eternity Base? It would be out of the wind. They probably left supplies in there."

Riley was shaking his head. "Even if what Devlin found is Eternity Base, he said it was all covered up. How are we going to get in?"

Devlin was considering the idea. "They had to have an access shaft, and actually I think I found it when I was checking out the dimensions. Something is covered with blown snow next to an ice ridge."

"We've got shovels and pickaxes in the plane's gear. Let's give it a shot," Conner argued.

"I don't like it." Riley shook his head. "If you want my opinion, we go back to Aurora Glacier and wait until we get good weather. We know where the place is now and can come back."

Swenson agreed. "I don't like the idea of staying here, missy. I think we ought to go back."

Conner leaned forward in her seat. "We're going to have to weather out this storm somewhere—either at Aurora Glacier or here.

If we stay here, at least we won't get caught in the bad weather flying back. Plus, remember we'd still have that forty-five-minute tractor ride back to the station. I think landing up near the base site and trying to dig in is the better option."

Time was the most precious commodity Conner had now. She made a command decision. "Let's try to land near the site."

— fourteen —

FORD MOUNTAIN RANGE, ANTARCTICA. The second landing had been smoother than the first, and the plane was now staked down three hundred yards to the north of the ice ridge. Next to the ridge itself, Sammy, Riley, and Vickers were hacking at the ice and snow on the protuberance while Kerns and Devlin swept away the loose debris with shovels. Conner and Lallo were capturing their actions and the surrounding terrain on film.

It was obvious that the object underneath this snow was man-made. The shape was too linear to have occurred naturally. Riley swung the pick, and a section of ice splintered off. His next swing almost broke his hand as the point bounced off something solid. With his gloves he began wiping away ice and snow, exposing metal.

"I've got something," Riley yelled. The others gathered around and stared at his discovery. The metal was painted white, and the pick had gouged the smooth surface.

"Let's clear it out," Devlin said, dropping his pick and grabbing a shovel. Shoulder to shoulder, Riley and Devlin used the edges of their shovels to enlarge the clear space on the metal. Soon they had exposed a flat sheet of metal almost three yards wide by two high.

Devlin stepped back and looked. "This has to be some sort of surface shaft."

"Where's the door then?" Sammy asked.

"There are four sides," Riley replied as he began excavating around

117

the corner to the right. Vickers joined him. Without a word, Devlin and Lallo started around the corner to the left.

As they dug, they actually were leveling the area around the shaft, making it flush with the surface of the ice on the nonridge side. The wind had picked up and snow was beginning to lift and blow across the basin.

Riley worked smoothly, trying not to break into a sweat. As his body heat rose, he removed his parka and stuffed it into his rucksack. He advised the others do the same.

A yard from the edge, Riley discovered a seam in the metal. He scraped away the ice up and down the seam and then to the right. Gradually a door appeared. On the far right side he discovered a spoked metal wheel. Once the door was completely uncovered he stepped back. The rest of the party had gathered around.

"Do you think it will work?" Conner addressed the question to Devlin.

Devlin ran his hands along the seam. "I don't know. It ought to. It shouldn't have frozen up—the temperature here never gets above freezing so there isn't any moisture. Let's give it a try."

Riley moved back as Devlin gripped the wheel and leaned into it. The metal didn't budge.

"Here, let me try." Vickers placed the handle of the pick through one of the spokes of the wheel and squatted down. Slowly he started to exert pressure upward.

"Watch out!" Riley yelled, just as the wooden handle broke. The free piece ricocheted off the door and hit Vickers in the head. Dazed, he fell back onto the ice.

"Damn." Vickers sat there rubbing his head through the parka hood. "That hurts."

Sammy found it darkly amusing to get this far and maybe not be able to get in. But what truly worried her was the weather. The sky was dark with clouds and the wind was really howling now, knifing through her clothes. They needed to get out of the wind, and there were only two choices: into the base or back to the plane.

She looked at Vickers again; something dark was seeping through the hood. "Shit," Sammy muttered. "Stay down," she ordered as Vickers tried standing up. She carefully pushed aside the big man's hood. The inside was caked with blood that had already frozen. The gash from the wound wasn't hard to find on his bald head. It was about three inches long but didn't appear to be deep.

"What's wrong?" Conner asked.

Without answering, Sammy opened the first aid kit attached to her rucksack and pulled out a sterile gauze pack. She quickly tore it open and then put her mittens back on before pressing the cloth against the cut. It immediately turned bright red.

"He got cut. It's not deep, but scalp wounds bleed a lot because the blood vessels are right on the surface." Sammy looked up. "We need to go back to the plane now and settle in. Hopefully this thing will blow over quickly."

Swenson shook his head. "I don't think so, mate. McMurdo says this is a big front. We may be stuck for days."

Sammy took a deep, icy breath as she considered the situation. "All right." She looked at Conner. "Here, you hold this and replace it every couple of minutes. Make sure you keep the pressure on. We need to stop the bleeding. There's some more gauze in this pack here."

She gestured to the men. "Let's all get on this thing." They grabbed hold of the wheel. "On my count of three, counterclockwise. Ready? One. Two. Three." All leaned into the wheel and strained. "Again. One. Two. Three." The second attempt was also a failure.

"All right. Take a break for a second."

Riley looked at the wheel. "Let's do it again, but let's try it the other way—clockwise."

The men reassumed their positions. Sammy coordinated their effort. "Ready? One. Two. Three." With a loud screech the wheel moved ever so slightly. "Again. One. Two. Three." More than nine hundred pounds of man and woman power leaned into the wheel again. It turned almost a full inch.

"Again." Inch by inch, the wheel turned. After five minutes of struggle, Sammy estimated they had done one complete revolution, yet there was no indication that they'd unlocked the door.

They continued on, the wheel moving a little easier now. After another five minutes the wheel stopped and wouldn't budge.

"I think we've gone as far as it goes," Devlin said. "I'd say it opens inward. It makes sense. You want doors to open in down here because the outside could be blocked with snow."

Riley examined the joints of the door. There was an overlap on the outside—another indication that the door opened inward. "All right. Stand back."

Riley lay down with his back wedged against the ice, then he put his feet on the bottom of the door and pushed. Seeing what he was doing, Lallo and Swenson joined in, pushing on the sides with their arms. With a low creak, a small gap appeared on the right side near the wheel. As they kept up the pressure, the door slowly swung wider and wider, Riley scrambling along the ice to keep his leverage until finally the opening was wide enough for a person to slip through.

"Hold it!" Conner called out. She peered around the edge of the door. In the darkness she could just make out a metal landing and staircase. Eternity Base beckoned.

"Light her up," she said to Lallo.

The cameraman pulled the cover off his camera rig. A bright light just over the lens came on. Conner slipped through the door, Lallo following, recording the entry. The stairs did a ninety-degree turn and then seemed to descend directly down. An open area next to the stairs had a pully system on top, suggesting that was how supplies were lowered. Shining the light down, they could make out wood planking about fifteen feet below. Something else was at the bottom of the stairs, but from their position they could spot only a vague outline.

Lallo leaned over the railing and froze as his light illuminated the scene. What a moment ago had been only a meaningless shape now assumed the form of a man. He was lying at the base of the stairs, face down, hands stretched out in front of him, almost an act of supplication.

Conner stumbled backward into Riley. "What's wrong?" he asked as he kept her from falling.

"There's someone down there!" she hissed.

Riley let go of her and walked forward, peering down. After a few seconds he gestured to her. "Come on. Everyone else stay put."

Conner cautiously followed Riley down the metal steps. The form still hadn't moved. When they reached the bottom, Riley shone his light on the body, revealing a figure clothed in army issue clothes. Three black holes punched a line across the back of the man's jacket, surrounded by a red frame of blood. Riley knelt down and turned over the body. Sightless eyes peered out from a young face, forever frozen in the surprised grimace that must have come as the bullets slammed into his back.

Riley looked closely at the face of the corpse, marveling at the frozen preservation. He wondered how long the man had been dead. He didn't realize he was thinking aloud until he heard Conner's quiet reply. "He's been dead for about twenty-five years."

— fifteen —

ETERNITY BASE, ANTARCTICA. Conner, after her initial shock seemed to be on track. She was supervising Lallo as he filmed the body from different angles.

"How long do you think he's been down here?" Sammy asked, as the rest of the party piled up their baggage in the dimly lit space at the base of the stairs. Riley glanced over at Sammy. "Your sister seems to think he's been here since the base was closed down in '71." He moved back to the body and began checking the man's clothing, cracking the frozen fabric. The man wore unmarked army fatigues under olive-drab cold-weather gear—old-style-issue gear, Riley knew. There was no name tag on the man's shirt.

Riley pulled a poncho out of his rucksack and gently draped it over the body. "Whoever he worked for shot him in the back to keep him from talking about what he saw here. Judging by the size of the wounds, I'd say it was a small-caliber gun—probably a .22. You have to be damn good to kill someone with a gun that small."

Conner turned to the rest of the group. "We've got to find out everything we can about this place. I want to know who built it and why, and then I'm going to nail their asses."

Conner began organizing the group. She stared down the corridor, trying to pick up details. Devlin's flashlight reflected off the metal sides of the corridor and faded out after thirty feet. The ceiling, ten feet above, consisted of steel struts holding metal sheeting that blocked out the ice and snow. Conduits, pipes, and wires crisscrossed the ceiling, going in all directions. The corridor itself was about ten feet wide; the floor was made up of wood planks, each separated by a few inches to allow snow and ice to fall through the cracks to the sloping steel floor below.

It was as cold down here as it was outside, but at least they were out of the wind. Riley pulled a sleeping bag from his backpack and helped Vickers into it.

In the excitement of actually entering the base and the horror of finding the body, Conner had forgotten about Vickers's wound. "Is he going to be all right?" she asked Riley, who was examining the bandage with his flashlight.

"Yeah. We could use some heat, though."

"There ought to be some sort of generator or space heaters down here," Devlin said, playing his light around the immediate area.

"You think they would still work after all this time?" Conner wondered.

Devlin coughed nervously, the sound echoing off the walls and ceiling. "Oh, yes. Antarctica is the perfect place to preserve things. The body is proof of that—the man looks the same as the day he died. Think about it. The temperature never gets above freezing. There's no moisture. No bacteria.

"There are supplies in Shackleton's hut on Ross Island that were placed there in 1907 and are still edible today. I have no doubt that if we can find the power source down here, or even a portable heater, we can get it going." He pointed his flashlight at a lightbulb set in a cage on the ceiling. "We might even get the lights on."

Conner peered down the dark corridor again. "Where do you think we'd find that?"

Devlin shrugged. "I don't know. Let's take a look."

Conner turned back to the rest of the party. "Sammy, you and Riley stay here with everyone. I'm going with Devlin to see if we can get the power on or at least find a portable stove or something."

Riley nodded, busy wrapping a binding around the dressing on Vickers's head. The bleeding appeared to have finally stopped. "Those of you staying here, break out your sleeping bags and get inside. No sense losing any more heat than you need to."

Devlin and Conner walked side by side down the wood planking. After thirty feet the walls disappeared on either side and they entered a cross corridor. To the left the corridor opened on two doors, one on either side, and then ended about ten feet in. To the right the corridor also opened on two doors. The right-hand corridor ended just beyond the doors, but not cleanly. A pile of snow and ice blocked the way.

Devlin shone his light where pipes on the ceiling disappeared into the pile. "Looks like that's where some ice buckled the ceiling."

"Let's try the doors," Conner suggested. They turned left and tried the door on the left side first. It wasn't locked and opened easily. The light of the flashlight revealed a room about thirty feet long and ten feet wide, full of electronic equipment. Conner remembered Freely telling her about the prefab units that had been flown in to make up the station. This was obviously one of them.

After a few moments' inspection, Devlin turned back for the door. "Looks like some sort of communications setup. We need to find either a storeroom or the power plant." He pointed his light at several large boxes hanging from the ceiling. "It looks like each of these units is heated separately with electric heaters and the corridors are kept at normal temperature. This setup reminds me very much of what I read about Eights Station."

Conner remembered Eights Station from her research. It had been established at the base of the Antarctic Peninsula in 1962 and had consisted of eight prefab units flown in by C-130 and buried under the ice, just like this.

"How would electric power be generated here?" Conner asked.

"Most likely oil-burning generators. That's what runs the majority of the bases here, although they would have had to airlift all that oil. At McMurdo they bring it in by ship, so it's not a major logistical problem. Here, I don't know."

"The man I talked to who helped build this place said they brought in quite a few bladders of fuel."

Devlin nodded. "Then we need to find whatever burns that fuel."

Next they went to the door straight across the corridor. This unit was a nicely designed living quarters with three sleeping areas, each separated by a thin wall. Traversing the entire length, they came to a door on the far side. They exited that and were faced with another side corridor extending off to the right and a door directly in front.

"Let's go straight through until we get to the end. There's supposed to be four of these in line, according to my source," Conner said. "If there's nothing in this row, we'll work up the middle one."

Devlin swung open the door and they stepped in. Large stainless steel tanks lined both sides of a narrow walkway. The tanks were open on the top, and banks of dead lights hung low over them. There were pumps and various tubes arrayed throughout the room.

"What is this?" Conner asked.

Devlin shined his flashlight inside one of the tanks. "I don't know. It reminds me of something I've seen before, but I can't place it right now."

They walked the length of that unit and through another door. Devlin pushed open the door to the last unit.

"Ah, this is more like it," he said as he swept his flashlight over the machinery inside. "This must be the power room. Look, there's a control panel." He walked over to a console full of dials and switches. "There's the 'on' for the master power, but I'm sure we have no battery power." He pressed the button with his thumb. Nothing.

"There must be a small auxiliary generator to start the main." He flashed the light on the other side. "Here we go."

Conner watched as he knelt down next to a medium-sized portable generator and unscrewed a cap. He shone his flashlight inside. "It's even got fuel. Hold the light while I prime it."

Conner hovered over Devlin's shoulder as he worked. She didn't know what he was doing, but he obviously did. After about five minutes he stood. "All right. Let's give it a shot." He took hold of a knob attached to a cord and pulled.

"Shit," he muttered when the cord didn't move. He pulled more carefully, and the cord slowly unwound. Then he squatted and exploded upward. The engine turned over once with a burp. "Damn. This thing is stubborn."

Conner didn't say a word. She found it remarkable that they were trying to start a generator that had been in frozen limbo for twenty-five years. The concept of a place where nothing deteriorated or rusted was hard to grasp.

After five more tries, the engine coughed, sputtered, and turned over for almost ten seconds before dying.

"I've got it now." Devlin adjusted the choke and pulled once more.

The generator sputtered again and then roared to life. Devlin let it run on high for a few minutes before he turned down the choke.

"All right. Let's see how we get the main started while that warms up." He took the flashlight from her hands and played it over the control panel. He laughed. "They've got all the instructions right here, almost as if they were expecting someone who didn't know how to run this thing. Hell, it's even numbered.

"We've already accomplished step one by getting the auxiliary started. OK. Two is to open up the main fuel line." He moved to the left of the console and looked up. "Here's the valve."

Conner heard a few seconds of metal screeching.

"OK. We've got fuel. Now we prime this baby." Devlin worked for a few minutes, following the instructions step by step. "Last—but not least—we open the power line from the aux to the main generator and give it some juice."

Conner watched as lights flickered and glowed on the console. Gradually they steadied. Devlin looked over the gauges. "Ready?" he asked.

Without waiting for an answer, Devlin pressed the starter button. The lights on the board dimmed, and they heard a sputtering noise behind the console. The sputtering shifted to a whine and then a rhythmic rumble after thirty seconds.

Devlin was examining another row of controls to the right. "Here's a bunch of switches labeled north, middle, south, east, and west tunnels." Conner looked over his shoulder at the schematic of the corridors of the base. At least she could get oriented now. The surface shaft where they had come down opened onto the north end of the east corridor.

Devlin threw all the switches, and light suddenly streamed in through the open doorway. "All right!" he yelled.

Conner flicked on the light switch just inside the doorway. She squinted as the room was flooded with bright light from the overheads. "What's that for?" she said, pointing at the other end of the room.

Devlin turned. The far end of the unit was filled with a massive control panel with uncountable gauges. It made the main generator board look puny. A three-by-three panel with a triangular warning sign was recessed into the left side. Devlin walked the twenty feet to look over the setup.

"Oh, my god. I don't believe it. I don't fucking believe it."

Conner hurried up to him. "What's the matter?"

Devlin turned to her, his face ashen. "This is the control panel for a nuclear reactor."

— sixteen —

ETERNITY BASE, ANTARCTICA. "How could they put a nuclear reactor down here? I thought reactors were huge and had lots of safety devices and all that," Sammy asked. It was the first time she had said anything since Devlin and Conner had returned from their recon mission. The members of the team were huddled in their sleeping bags, listening to an excited Conner finish her report on the base.

"I say we go to the first set of living quarters you found and set up," suggested Riley. In answer to his own proposal, he threw his gear over his shoulder, helped Sammy to her feet, and headed off. They left the corpse in the corridor, covered with a blanket, letting the cold continue its task of preservation.

Entering the room, Riley switched on the ceiling heaters as the rest of the team settled in. Devlin was still agitated by their most recent discovery—more than he had been over the discovery of the body. He answered the question Sammy had asked out in the corridor. "Mc-Murdo had a nuclear reactor: the U.S. Navy set it up in '61 and got it on line in '62. They thought it would alleviate the problem of bringing in all the fuel oil every summer and would be a cheap and effective way to keep McMurdo supplied with power."

"What happened?" Vickers was seated on a chair, leaned against the wall, obviously feeling better.

"The plant was closed in '72—the year after this place was built. They had a leakage of coolant water into the steam generator tank. The navy shut the thing down, and it took them three years to remove

128

it. When we get back to Aurora Glacier Station, I can show you where the reactor was. They put it on Observatory Hill right near Erebus, which in and of itself wasn't too smart, since Erebus is still an active volcano.

"They shipped the reactor and a hundred and one drums of radioactive earth back to the United States and buried them somewhere. But even that didn't make the site clean enough. The navy had to dig out more earth and ship it back. The site wasn't opened up for what the military termed *unrestricted use* until 1979."

"There's no way they could have left a reactor down here unattended for twenty-five years," Conner said. "I don't know much about them, but I do know they require constant attention."

Devlin nodded. "You're right. But this one is off line. The plan must have been that when they reoccupied this place, they'd bring the rods with them and use the oil generators until they could get the reactor on line. But, even so, the fact that the U.S. government put a nuclear reactor—even one without the nuclear fuel—down here and abandoned is unbelievable."

Lallo was more concerned with immediate matters. "What now? We have to wait out the storm, but what do you want to do in the meantime?"

Conner stood in front of the group. "We need to explore. Now that the lights are on, we should be able to figure out what this place was built for and maybe who built it." She looked at Vickers. "Can you work?"

Vickers nodded. "The bleeding has stopped. As long as I don't hit my head again I should be all right."

"OK." Conner was all business. "Let's get out the cameras and take some initial footage. I want to start at the top of the staircase and work our way in, as if we were entering for the first time."

Kerns and Vickers started opening the cases of camera and sound equipment. Devlin grabbed his flashlight and headed for the door. "I'm going down to the power plant to see what I can find out about the actual reactor. They must have offset it from this base, and maybe I can find the location."

The room rapidly emptied until Sammy was left with Riley and Swenson. The pilot walked over to one of the beds and flopped down on it. "I'm going to catch me some shut-eye so I'll be ready to fly when this storm does break." With that he pulled the pillow over his head.

"Let's take a walk," Riley suggested to Sammy.

They could hear Conner and her camera crew clattering on the stairs in the access shaft. Riley walked to the doorway straight across the hall and entered the first unit that Devlin and Conner had explored.

Riley switched on the lights. It was obvious this was some sort of communications setup. Against the walls were several radio consoles with chairs in front of them. Riley flicked the on switch for one, and the set hummed. "They've got a lot of redundant commo equipment here," he remarked to Sammy. He pointed. "That's an HF—high frequency—radio. That looks like a SATCOM—satellite communications—rig. I used both types when I was in the service."

He fiddled with the knobs, trying to see if he could get something. A dull hiss was all that came out of the speakers. Riley suddenly slapped his hand on the panel in disgust. "Shit. Sometimes I'm so dumb. The antennas probably blew away a long time ago, if they ever put them out."

Sammy pointed to the far left corner of the room where a large number of wires ran into a shaft that disappeared into the ceiling. "That must be where the antenna wires run up next to the entrance shaft."

A transmitter on the other side caught her attention. Several large boxes containing long-lasting batteries surrounded it. A placard on the front read "Eternity Base Transponder. Frequency: 45.83."

"What's this?" she asked.

Riley came over and examined the set. "That's how the builders of this base planned to find it once it was covered over. The transponder is set to be initiated by a plane's radio. The pilot dials up the proper frequency—45.83—on the radio and presses his transmit button. That turns on this transponder. The pilot then homes in on the radio beacon.

"It's the same system set up at small airfields. It allows pilots to turn on the airfield light when they approach at night and the tower isn't manned. The antenna is probably built into the roof of the access shaft."

Riley looked at the various gauges. There was no juice left in the batteries, but they were now slowly recharging with the main power on. Even the cold of Antarctica couldn't have kept the batteries alive for twenty-five years.

The two left the radio room and moved on to the next unit. It was another set of living quarters, except this one was more lavish. There were two bedrooms and a small living room. Sammy moved into the smaller bedroom and immediately spotted a large blue binder conspicuously placed on top of the bed. An envelope was taped to the outside of the binder. PETER was written in block letters on the outside of the envelope.

Sammy carefully peeled off the envelope. It was sealed. She stuffed it in her pocket, then picked up the binder and rejoined Riley, showing him only the binder.

With the reenactment of the entry into the base completed, Conner guided her crew to the first unit to the right. She narrated as she led the way. "I have labeled the various units according to their row and column for identification purposes. The row nearest the entry shaft is row A. The next will be row B and so on. The column farthest from the shaft is column one, the middle column is column two, and the one closest to the shaft is column three. Thus we have just left unit A3, which appeared to be a communications setup.

"We are now entering unit A2." Conner went into the living quarters that Riley had exited just minutes earlier. She led Lallo, Kerns, and Vickers through the three rooms, making comments as the camera's eye took in everything. Then she went back out into the tunnel.

"This tunnel, designated the north tunnel on the power supply board, is blocked heading to unit A1. We might be able to get to that unit by going up the west tunnel. We intend to work our way over there.

"Unit B3 is living quarters where we have temporarily left our equipment and where our pilot is catching some sleep." She opened the door directly across the corridor. "We are now entering unit B2."

The first thing that caught her eye as she went through the door was Riley and Sammy at the electric stove. "As you can see, some of our party are already at work using the equipment here to prepare a meal."

Riley ignored the camera and continued stirring a large pot on top of the electric stove. "Dinner will be ready in about thirty minutes."

Conner led the way through the kitchen and dining area. "This appears to be the central area for meals and probably was designed to double as the meeting area for the community that was to live here."

They went through the door and into C2, which turned out to be another set of living quarters. Then they crossed over to C3, which contained the strange metal tanks and light fixtures that she and Devlin had discovered earlier.

She spent more time in D3, making sure they got complete coverage of the control panel for the nuclear reactor. As she narrated, she noticed that the grating to the left of the panel had been removed, revealing a dark tunnel. A small sign above the tunnel read "Power Access Tunnel." She assumed that was where Devlin had gone.

"Here we have the controls for a nuclear reactor. We can only assume that the radioactive rods were never put in place, so the reactor is inert and not dangerous at the moment. This base, according to our sources, was established in 1971, just one year before a similar experimental nuclear reactor at McMurdo Station was shut down at great expense to the American taxpayer.

"That, however, does not explain the secretive manner in which this base was built and the way its presence was completely obliterated from government records. Nor does it explain the listing of the aircrew who helped build this airbase—the only aircrew that knew where this base was—as missing in action in Vietnam, when in reality they were here on that day, flying the last mission out of Eternity Base.

"Even more ominous, it does not explain the attempt on the life of the worker from the Records Center who discovered the existence of this base. Nor do we know why the man at the entrance of the base was killed."

Conner slashed her finger across her throat. "Cut."

"Good," Vickers said. "That'll be a real catchy intro. It'll sure make them sit up in Atlanta when we send it."

"Let's get the rest of this place on tape," Conner ordered. "They can edit it in Atlanta."

She led the way to the next unit, D2, which turned out to be an extremely well-stocked library. Not only were there numerous books on the shelves but several file cabinets full of microfiche and three microfiche readers set up on tables.

Unit D1 was a dispensary with enough equipment to outfit a minor surgery and shelves well stocked with drugs.

C1 was an indoor greenhouse. Large banks of lights lined the ceiling, and trays filled with frozen soil were held in floor-to-ceiling racks. There were also lights on the bottom of each rack. Someone had spent a lot of time making every inch of space functional in the small room.

The west tunnel was blocked halfway up between B1 and B2 by the buckling of the ice ridge. Unit B1 itself was crushed halfway through. Conner stood next to a wall of ice while Lallo filmed her against the white backdrop. "Here we see that Eternity Base did not totally live up to its name. Despite the remarkable preservation of most of the base and its equipment, as evidenced by the quick startup of the generators and the lights, we see that Mother Nature did not totally spare the base. This destruction is the result of pressure formed by two sections of ice meeting each other and buckling up to form a ridge on the surface."

Conner went back into the main center tunnel. They'd been in all the units except A1, which was blocked. She now turned her attention to the set of large double doors that were on both ends of the main tunnel. She and Vickers pulled open the set to the west. A large dark tunnel appeared. Groping inside the doors, Conner found a lever, which she pulled down. Sparks sputtered out of the ceiling and then nothing. Using the camera's klieg light, they probed the darkness, only to be met by the same wall of buckled ice that blocked off unit A1. It had cut across the base diagonally and continued on through here.

"Let's try the other side." Conner led the way down the main cross tunnel and opened the doors there. She threw the lever and gasped as large arc lights went on, revealing a massive tunnel burrowed out of the ice, extending almost two hundred yards straight ahead. There was a clear central passageway, but the rest of the twenty-yard-wide tunnel was crammed with mountains of supplies.

Conner moved down the aisle, letting Lallo photograph the labels on the boxes. Most of it was food. The last fifty yards of the storage tunnel housed a dozen snowmobiles, a bulldozer, a backhoe, several snow tractors of various sizes, and two large cabins on skis that looked as though they could be hooked up to the back of the larger tractors.

The tunnel ended at a metal grating that ramped up, extending to the white ceiling. "What do you make of that?" Conner asked.

"I think that's how they planned on getting these vehicles out of here—and how they got them in," Vickers replied. He pointed at sections of metal grating stacked to the side. "They could run the bulldozer up the ramp and put down the grating as they went until they reached the surface."

Conner looked at her watch. "Let's send this off and then go to the mess hall and get some food."

They retraced their steps back to the east tunnel and turned right until they got to the shaft. At the base, Vickers pulled out the small cassette in Lallo's camera. He gave it to Conner, who attached a special drive to her portable, that digitized the pictures and stored them on the disk. Taking the disk from her, Vickers headed for the surface to burst everything to Atlanta.

Conner, Kerns, and Lallo went into the mess hall, where Riley was ladling something into Devlin's bowl.

"What did you find?" Conner asked as she sidled up to Devlin.

"I went down the access shaft to the reactor, but it was blocked by ice about fifty yards in. I assume the reactor is out that way another hundred yards or so."

"The reactor is five hundred yards straight line distance from the power room. Southwest," Riley added. "As you guessed, the rods aren't in. They were supposed to be brought in and put in place when the base was activated."

Conner and Devlin both turned and looked at him. "How do you know that?" Conner demanded.

"Your sister found the instruction book for this Tinkertoy set," Riley said, holding up a large blue binder.

Sammy reached into her pocket and pulled out the letter. "I also found this."

— seventeen —

INTELLIGENCE SUPPORT AGENCY (ISA), HEADQUARTERS SOUTHWEST OF WASHINGTON, D.C. Another exciting Monday morning. Bob Weaver rubbed his eyes as he looked at the message lying on top of his in box. He had no idea what the connection was between all the requests for information (RFIs) listed in it, but he also knew it wasn't his place to know. He was just here to find and forward. He started typing in the data, looking for answers to the questions:

Any further information on Eternity Base?

Confirm information that U.S. Air Force C-130, tail number 6204 from 487th TAS, Clark Base, Hawaii, was reported as MIA 21 December 1971, Vietnam.

Determine actual location U.S. Army Engineer unit, B Company, 67th Engineer Battalion, from August 1971 through December 1971.

Run file on David Riley, former U.S. Army. SSN 906-23-5482.

Run file on Randall Devlin, member environmental group Our Earth. SSN unknown.

Run file on Peter Swenson, Australian national, pilot.

Run file on Samantha Pintella. SSN unknown. Works U.S. National Personnel Records Center, St. Louis, MO.

Priority request.

Falcon 2100Zulu/11/27/96

ETERNITY BASE, ANTARCTICA. "Hydroponics!" Devlin exclaimed, looking at the diagram of the base and the label for unit C3. "I knew I'd seen that somewhere before. They have a setup like that at UCLA."

"What's hydroponics?" Lallo asked.

"It's the cultivation of plants in water rather than soil. They set aside unit C3 to grow food just like the greenhouse in C1, except this one uses water instead of dirt." Devlin shook his head. "But I don't understand why they'd need to dedicate two units of their base to growing food when they have the ice storage tunnels." He pointed down at the diagram. "The one blocked ice tunnel to the west looks like it's as large as the one to the east. That's a lot of food and supplies."

"It doesn't seem as though they were counting on a resupply," Conner remarked.

The binder listed the locations of equipment and supplies along with instructions for the use of various equipment, but it didn't say anything about the purpose of the base or who was supposed to use it.

"Look how far away they offset the reactor," Devlin commented. "More than a quarter mile. All that ice in between serves as a very effective shield for the main base."

Conner focused on the one unit they hadn't been able to look at. "Check out the label on unit A1: special supply and armory." She glanced up. "We have to get into that. If we can record weapons on tape, we have a direct violation of the treaty."

"What about the letter?" Devlin prompted. "Will you open it?"

Riley handed Conner a pocketknife with the blade open. She slit the top of the letter and pulled out a one-page hand-written note.

"Read it aloud," Devlin said.

Conner cleared her throat and began reading.

21 December 1971

Peter,

If you are reading this, then your fears were justified and I suppose this was all worthwhile. It seems odd to write this knowing that if it ever enters your hand I shall be dead. Of course, I will have much good company—if one may call the world's population company.

I do not envy you or the special friends you deem worthy of survival here. Until today I saw Eternity Base as a cradle, but

your final delivery this morning leaves me with little optimism.
The courier who delivered the final shipment will guard your
base until you arrive or until the ice claims the base, as per
your instructions.
May you enjoy your kingdom.
Glaston

Glaston—sounds a lot like Claxton, the name Freely had mentioned, Conner thought. They now had the name of the murderer.

"The bastards set up a survival base down here!" Devlin exclaimed.

Riley looked at Devlin and shook his head. "You mean you just figured that out? Hell, why else do you think someone would put something like this down here and stock it so full of supplies? Why do you think they have the greenhouse and the hydroponics?"

Devlin was rubbing his chin. "Well, they certainly picked the best continent to put it on. In the event of an all out nuclear exchange, there are no worthwhile targets in Antarctica. The winds off the coast would keep the fallout to a minimum. And we've already seen how the cold and lack of humidity preserve things."

"Let's remember also that this base was set up in 1971 when the Cold War was still going strong," Lallo added.

Devlin was still focusing on the base. "They were smart—not only putting it in Antarctica but in this specific location. It's as remote as you can get. Straight north of here you hit the South Pacific Ocean. A spot there is the world's farthest point from dry land. Without having an intermediary base like McMurdo, it would be almost impossible to fly straight to this location."

"There's in-flight refueling," Riley disagreed.

"Yes," Devlin admitted irritably. "But you have to admit that this is the most isolated location you could possibly find."

Riley ignored Devlin and turned to Conner. "You've got your story. What do you want to do now?"

"Aren't you guys interested in the identity of Peter?" Sammy asked. "That seems to be the key question, wouldn't you say? He had to be the one giving the orders and in charge of this place. He's the one we want. After Glaston," she added.

"I don't think we're going to find the answer here," Riley said.

"Well, you don't need to be in any rush, whatever you want to do."

Swenson spoke for the first time. "I just poked my head out the door and the weather's totally gone to crap." He pointed over his shoulder as Vickers stormed in wearing his cold-weather gear. "And your man here has some more good news for you."

Vickers slid his radio gear onto the table and forced open the lid. The metal looked as if it had been smashed with an ax. "Someone got to my gear. The transmitter is destroyed. We won't be sending any messages."

"And we won't be flying anywhere either," Swenson added. "We're cut off from the rest of the world."

"Who had access to your gear?" Riley asked.

Vickers laughed bitterly. "Shit, everyone. It was lying there in the corridor with the other equipment while we were running around doing all that other stuff. It could have been anyone."

Conner stood up. "All right. Everyone calm down." She pointed. "I want my crew to go to the other unit where the baggage is and wait there. I'd like to talk to Sammy, Riley, and Devlin."

When the four were alone she looked at Sammy. "Have you been with Riley the entire time since we entered the base?"

"Listen, Conner. You've got no proof of anything, so don't go making accusations. I—"

"Just answer my question, damnit!" Conner banged her fist on the tabletop.

It was Riley who answered. "No. We weren't together the whole time. I went to the east tunnel and got some food supplies while she started getting things ready for the meal." He leaned forward. "But I didn't smash the radio."

"How do we know that?" Devlin countered.

Riley didn't even spare him a glance as his eyes bored into Conner's. "Because it was stupid, and I don't do stupid things. If I wanted to keep you from finding this place or getting the story out, you can be damn sure you all wouldn't be here right now."

"Why do you say it was stupid?" Sammy asked, forestalling Conner's angry reply.

Riley finally broke eye contact with Conner. He slumped back in his chair. "It was stupid because I know how we can still send a message to Atlanta."

— eighteen —

SNN HEADQUARTERS, ATLANTA, GEORGIA. Stu Fernandez pressed the play button on the remote and showed edited scenes of Conner's tape of Eternity Base. Conner's recorded voice echoed through the room, five thousand miles away from where she was. Stu had cut the tape down to six minutes of what he felt were the best parts. The picture was grainy—the result of the video being digitized and converted into a format that could be read by a computer and easily transmitted.

SNN had worked to perfect the computer video-burst transmission technique because it saved sending a large video transmitter and receiver on assignments. The picture had been transmitted the same way Conner's messages had been—encoded by a special digital recorder onto disk and then burst out over the SATCOM radio. This capability allowed SNN news teams to travel light and move farther and faster than normal teams. This method had proven its worth the previous year when dramatic pictures of the massacre of a Kurdish village in Iraq had stunned Americans who were complacent with a "victory in the desert."

Stu knew it was a good sign that the entire six minutes ran without an interruption. The tape faded out with a picture of Conner standing in front of the nuclear power plant control console. Stu flicked on the lights and waited.

Parker was the first to speak. "Very good. I like it. Superb."

"When do you want to run it, sir?" Stu asked.

Before Parker could answer, John Cordon, his assistant, quietly spoke. "I recommend we hold off until we have the complete story. Presently, there's no chance another network can cut in. We have an exclusive as long as we keep it quiet. I suggest we get the entire story and then play the whole thing before anyone can react. Let's give Ms. Young a chance to uncover all she can.

"We need to do a lot of background. Try to find out who this Glaston fellow is. We have more questions than answers, and we need to get as much information as possible before going live with this."

Legere nodded. "I concur, sir. If we play this now, there are going to be planes from all the other networks heading down to Antarctica."

"Conner and her people are weathered in right now, so they can't go anywhere," Stu added. "We can get their digital video, but as you can see, the quality is not the greatest. I'd like to have the original tapes before I put it together. Plus, if we can get Conner back here, she can do voice-overs and in-studio presentations. She also said they've had some problems in the party. Someone damaged their radio gear, and she wants another SATCOM team sent down."

"We also don't know who the dead man is," Cordon said. "We don't want to be broadcasting until we can get an identity on him."

Parker stood. "I agree that there's no rush. We need to make sure this stays confidential here in Atlanta. I want no leaks. Tell Ms. Young she can take as much time as she likes, but to be damn sure she has everything she can get before she leaves."

"Yes, sir." Stu smiled as the SNN executives filed out of the room. He and Conner were in the big time now.

ETERNITY BASE, ANTARCTICA. Sammy worked the small tractor's plow, carefully scraping away slivers of ice from the blockage. The controls were similar to those on the forklift she occasionally used in the Records Center, so she had taken charge of the tractor when they'd started it in the supply tunnel. She was enjoying the work, but she wished the corridors were large enough to bring out the bulldozer. She was sure it could punch through in no time. As it was, the small tractor was difficult to maneuver in the narrow confines of the west tunnel.

The other members of the party—minus Swenson, who was seated in the mess hall reading a book—were standing in back of her, Lallo filming and the rest watching. Riley's jury-rigged radio, using parts from the commo room, had worked just fine, and Conner had made contact with Atlanta. Whoever smashed the radio had to be getting desperate.

Nothing more had been said about the radio or what had happened to Swenson back at Aurora Glacier Station. Sammy sensed that her sister was at a loss for what to do, and everyone else seemed equally helpless. With no obvious suspect, each member was eyeing the others with equal suspicion.

Easing down on the accelerator, Sammy pushed the corner of the plow blade into the ice. She'd been at it now for fifteen minutes and had worked through almost five feet of ice and snow. Of course, she reminded herself, they might not find anything on the other side. The ice may have crushed everything behind the cave-in.

After scraping off another six inches, she dropped the blade, drew back the debris, and piled it against the wall of unit B1. She rolled forward again and dug in the blade. The tractor suddenly lurched, and Sammy had to slam on the brakes as the blade broke through. She backed off and shut down the engine.

Riley came forward with a flashlight and shone the light through the hole. They could see wood planking on the floor—the extension of the west corridor.

"Let's use the shovels," Sammy advised. "I don't want to take too much of a chunk. For all we know, that ice is the only thing keeping the ridge from coming down farther."

Side by side, Riley and Sammy enlarged the hole until it was big enough for a person to slip through. "After you," Riley gestured.

Sammy slid through, followed by Conner and Devlin. Riley came last, playing his light at their feet so they wouldn't trip. They moved up to where the north and west corridors intersected. Devlin went to the door of unit A1 and swung it open. The four stepped in. The glow of the flashlights lit up a well-equipped arms room.

"Unbelievable," Conner muttered as they examined the weapons racks.

Riley tried the light switch on the off chance that the power might still be connected, but the power lines must have been cut when the ceiling came down. He walked along the racks, noting the weapons. Two dozen M16s. Four M60 machine guns. Several M79 grenade launchers. Various pistols. The sides of the unit were stacked with boxes of ammunition and other military supplies. Looking at the stencils on them, Riley noted both plastic explosive and TNT. There were also several types of mines. "Why did they need all this stuff?" Sammy asked as she picked up a pistol.

"For the same reason they built this place," Riley answered. "The kind of mind that would plan and build Eternity Base, and kill the people who knew about it, would have to border on paranoid. This place was designed to be used after a nuclear war or something equivalent. For all these people knew, the war might still be going on when they got down here. Maybe they were worried about who was going to be in charge once the smoke and radiation cleared. The Russians had several bases already set up in Antarctica in 1971."

Riley moved past the weapons racks. Two large crates, each about twelve feet long by three feet wide and high filled the end of the unit, one on either side of the far door. He played the light over the stenciling on the outside: MACHINED GOODS.

"What's that?" Sammy asked.

"Don't know," Riley replied. He tried the lid, which didn't yield.

"Do you think we could string power to this unit so Lallo can tape all this?" Conner was asking Devlin.

"I suppose so. Maybe we can find some extension cords and run them from B1, through the hole and up here."

Conner was leaning over, looking closely at an M60. "I have got to get this on film."

Riley grabbed a bayonet off one of the shelves. Army standard issue model M9, he noted as he slid the knife free of the scabbard. He placed the point under the top of the right crate and pushed it in. Putting his body weight on it, he levered up. With a loud screech the top moved half an inch.

"What did you find?" Conner asked. She and Devlin came over and watched.

"I don't know," Riley grunted as he pushed again. He slid the blade around and carefully applied pressure every foot or so. Slowly the top lifted. Riley put his fingers under the lid and pulled up. The top popped off and he pushed it to the side. A slim, cylindrical gray object, pointed at one end with fins at the other, was inside, resting on a wood cradle.

"They put a fucking bomb in here?" Devlin exclaimed.

Riley bent over to examine it with a growing feeling of coldness in his stomach. He noted the suspension lugs where the bomb could be attached to an aircraft. A serial number was stamped on a small metal plate, halfway down the casing. Riley read the ID and then slowly straightened.

"That's not just a bomb." His words were totally flat. He was too numb to have any emotion.

"What do you mean?" Sammy asked as she looked up at him.

"That's a nuclear bomb."

"Bullshit." Devlin was staring into the crate with wide eyes. "How can you know that?"

Riley felt a surge of irritation break through his shock. He pointed his flashlight at the bomb. "I was on a nuke team when I first arrived in a Special Forces Group. A nuke team's mission is to emplace a tactical ADM—that's atomic demolitions munition. We were supposed to infiltrate behind enemy lines, put the bomb in the right spot, arm it, and then get the hell out before it blew. That mission was phased out several years ago when they decided cruise missiles could do the job just as well with no chance of compromise."

Riley glanced at Devlin. "I know you believe that all government workers are idiots, but we were very well trained on nuclear weapons. They take a little more brain power to properly employ than it does to shoot a gun.

"Each nuclear weapon has a special serial number—and this one has the proper designator for a nuclear weapon. If I remember correctly, this looks like an MK/B61, which is a pretty standard nuclear payload for planes." He looked back at Devlin in the dim light cast by their flashlights. "You may know something about nuclear reactors, but I know about nuclear weapons, and that's a goddamn nuclear weapon."

"What about the other box?" Sammy asked.

Riley used the bayonet on that one, levering up the lid. It opened to reveal a similar bomb. Riley checked the serial number. "Another one."

Sammy seemed mesmerized by the cold gray steel. "You said you know about nuclear weapons. Can that thing be detonated?"

Riley closed his eyes briefly, trying to remember. "There are a lot of safety devices on a nuclear weapon. We had to pass a test every three months that required us to flawlessly complete forty-three separate steps to emplace and arm our nuke.

"A standard nuclear weapon has an enable plug, a ready/safe switch, a separation-timer, pulse thermal batteries, a pulse battery actuator, a time delay switch, and a whole bunch of other things that all have to be operated correctly and in the right sequence. But if someone knows what he's doing, and has enough time to tinker with it, I have no doubt that he could initiate it—except for one thing. You can't even begin without—" Riley stopped and blinked.

"What one thing?" Sammy asked, finally looking up from the bomb.

Riley turned and headed out of the unit.

"Where are you going?" Conner yelled after him. When he didn't answer, they followed.

Riley made his way directly to the mess hall. Swenson looked up as Riley stormed in and grabbed the blue binder off the counter. He thumbed through, turning to the index. He had started reading the material from the beginning but had gotten only halfway through. Now he ran his finger down the index as the others crowded around. He stopped at Emergency Procedures.

Riley rapidly flipped through the binder until he got to the appropriate section. The first page referred them to the operating manual for the reactor in the power room if there were any problems with that. The second page was about getting the tractors out of the east ice storage room using the ramps. The third page consisted of a hand written note. Riley recognized the handwriting from the note that had been taped to the outside of the binder.

The PALs and arming instructions are in the safe.
Glaston

Riley closed his eyes. "Oh, fuck!"

"What does that mean?" Sammy asked as she peered over his shoulder.

Riley opened his eyes and looked at her. "Let's go out in the hallway." He led Sammy, Conner, and Devlin out, taking the binder with him. He spoke quietly. "As I was telling you, if someone knows what he's doing, he can get by all the safeties on those bombs but one. The first and most critical safety is the permissive access link, or PAL. That's the code that allows you to even begin to arm the bomb. The code and bomb are never kept together for security reasons. The MK/B has a multiple-code six-digit switch with limited try followed by lockout. That means you get two shots at the right code; if you get it wrong both times, you don't get a third shot—the bomb shuts down."

Riley stabbed his finger down at the paper. "Except it appears that the PALs for those two bombs are here in the base." He turned back to the index and scanned. "Here." He turned to the page displaying a diagram of a unit. "The safe with the PAL codes and arming instructions is located in unit A2."

— nineteen —

COLORADO SPRINGS, COLORADO. Peter hit the speaker button on the phone as he continued to peruse the computer printout in front of him. "Peter here."

"It's me," a woman's voice said.

Peter smiled as he recognized the person. "Yes. What can I do for you?"

"My man failed. They found the base and the packages."

The computer printout was forgotten as Peter sat back in his seat. "Are they going to release the story?"

"Not right away. It's still being kept in tight. The plan is to wait until a support team gets down there and they can go live."

"Then we have some time?"

"Yes."

Peter nodded. "All right. Release the information about the bombs to the other party as you did the initial information. Let's see how they handle it. They are already interested, and this should whet their appetite. In fact, I'll send you some additional information over secure modem. I'll make the other arrangements."

For the first time the voice sounded uncertain. "Are you sure I should—"

"Do as I say," Peter ordered. "I will take care of everything else."

SNN HEADQUARTERS, ATLANTA, GEORGIA. Stu Fernandez stared at the computer screen in confusion. There was a SATCOM message from Conner logged in only ten minutes ago, yet he couldn't access it. Not only wasn't the message addressed to him, he couldn't even get the computer to show him a copy of the message—it was keyed only for the password of the person to whom it was addressed. He looked at the ID code number and frowned. Who was 634822?

Stu went to the directory and punched up the code. "What the heck?" he exclaimed as the screen cleared and the identification came up:

ID Code 634822: J. Russell Parker

Stu had never had a reporter send a message past him. Why was Conner addressing a message directly to the CEO? What was so important that he didn't have a need to know? Who was the producer of her special anyway? Did it have anything to do with the destruction of the satellite radio? All those questions raced through Stu's mind and then he sighed. He sure wasn't going to ask J. Russell. He'd find out when the time came.

UNITED NATIONS EMBASSY, NEW YORK, NEW YORK. The ambassador's aide frowned as the secretary entered the meeting room and hurried over to his chair. "Mister Kang, there is an urgent message for you," she whispered in his ear.

Kang made his excuses to the delegation of trade bureaucrats from Poland, then walked swiftly to his office. The encoded message sat on the center of his desk, only the word URGENT readable, the rest in unintelligible seven-letter groups. He unlocked the safe behind his desk and pulled out the one-time pad.

Writing out the letters in long hand, he deciphered the message on a single sheet of paper with a hard plastic board beneath it in order not to leave an impression copy. As the words coalesced into meaning, Kang felt both excited and confused.

News team has discovered Eternity Base.

Inert nuclear reactor found at base. No evidence of rods ever being emplaced, but reactor core could not be reached.

Appears to be a base designed for select personnel to survive a nuclear war or similar disaster.

Weapons found in armory.

Two U.S.-manufactured nuclear weapons, serial numbers
NTB-486929-350-98 and NTB-486929-350-56; both suspected
model type MK/B 61 included in armory.

Arming codes and instructions for nuclear weapons also
contained in safe at base.

Information being held here at highest level—eyes only
J. Russell Parker. U.S. authorities currently not being notified.

News team is weathered in. Extent or duration of storm
unknown.

Uncertain what reaction will be here. Expect they will hold
information in attempt to have exclusive story.

Will continue to monitor and relay information as soon as
possible. Have more detailed information on situation that I am
in process of encoding.

Loki. 291435Z NOV 96.

Kang didn't even try to sort out the various pieces of the puzzle. He
immediately pulled out another one-time pad and transcribed the letters of the message verbatim as quickly as his hand could write.

Done, he rapidly walked up the stairs to the fourth floor of the
brownstone that served as his country's U.N. embassy. A stone-faced
guard in an ill-cut three-piece suit stood before a heavy steel door.
Despite Kang's rank of full colonel in the army and having worked in
this building for three years, the guard still demanded to see his identification card. Kang didn't mind. If the guard had not asked, Kang
would have minded very much, because his secondary role at the
embassy was security chief.

Satisfied, the guard opened the door and Kang stepped into a small
foyer, the door shutting behind him. There was a peephole in the next
steel door; an oversized eye appeared and then the door opened.

"Yes, sir?" The technician on duty showed more proper respect for
Kang's position.

Kang thrust the encoded message into the man's hand. "Send this
immediately. Urgent priority."

ETERNITY BASE, ANTARCTICA. "Latest weather from McMurdo calls
for at least another twenty-four to forty-eight hours of this storm,"
Conner informed the group gathered around the mess table.

Swenson nodded. "Aye. I took a look about twenty minutes ago and couldn't see more than ten feet from the door. The wind is howling. I hope my plane is all right."

The warm air from the electric heater overhead blew gently across Conner as she looked around the room. So far, the only ones who knew about the nuclear weapons were her sister, Devlin, and Riley. She'd sent the information in a coded message to Atlanta forty-five minutes ago on the radio Riley had put together, and the reply had been encoded along with the weather report that Riley had just picked up.

Parker's orders were to sit tight. He was rushing a larger support team from Atlanta down to their location. They ought to be in Antarctica as soon as the weather cleared. Upon their arrival, Parker wanted Conner to go live on regular SATCOM feed with the story.

Until then there was little her team could do. She herself had a lot of work to do, preparing what she would say. "I suggest we all get some sleep. When we get up I'd like to dig out the west tunnel and completely open up the way to unit A1. Until then there's really nothing that needs to be done."

She could tell that her team took that information with relief. They were all exhausted and immediately headed off to B3 to go to bed. Sammy and Riley waited for everyone else to leave. Conner eyed her sister and the security man warily.

When they were alone, Sammy got up and moved to the seat next to Conner. "What's the plan from Atlanta?"

Conner acted surprised. "What do you mean?"

"Come on, Constance. You've been tied to the SATCOM shoestring ever since we got down here. I have to assume that you've already sent word to your superiors about the nukes. You've been up and down those stairs almost nonstop for the last couple of hours. I want to know what the plan is."

"I do too," Riley added. "You need to tell us what's in those coded messages."

"You really don't have a need to know." As soon as she said it, Conner realized she'd made a mistake. She hadn't meant to be abrupt, but she was tired and excited at the same time and not thinking straight.

"Listen, lady." Riley's face was taut. "This isn't a fucking game anymore. Those are nuclear weapons in there, not toys. Those things are supposed to be under strict control, yet here we have two abandoned in the middle of Antarctica. That worries me. It worries me a lot. Because we're the ones who are sitting on them now."

Conner gave a little ground. "They're sending another news team down from the States. It'll have the capability to do high-quality transmissions straight from here. When they arrive, we go live with the story."

"Then what?" Sammy asked.

"What do you mean?"

"I mean what do you think is going to happen then?"

Conner hadn't really thought that through. "Then I suppose the government takes its bombs back and we return to Atlanta, and this is a hot story for about a week, or until some other crisis knocks it out of the headlines."

Riley leaned forward. "Has it occurred to you that you're going to be doing quite a bit of damage to the United States by airing this story?"

Conner choked back a laugh. "Hey, they put those things down here. Not me. I just report the news."

"Has it occurred to you," Riley persisted, "that the people who built this place and put those weapons down here are probably all retired or dead by now? Why do you think no one has been down here in so long? Why do you think the batteries on the transponder were dead?"

Conner shook her head. "It doesn't matter. We just report it."

"We just report it," Sammy said. "Is that it? What about these bombs?"

"Let's take it easy," Riley interceded. "We still don't know who was behind the building of this base. We need to stay focused on that as far as the story goes. As far as reality goes, Sammy is right—we need to be concerned about those two bombs."

"Who knows about the bombs in Atlanta?" Sammy asked.

"Only one person," Conner said firmly. "Mister Parker, who runs SNN."

"Are you sure?"

"Yes. I coded the message for his eyes only, and the only one who can uncode it is Mister Parker." Conner turned to Riley and asked a question of her own. "What kind of damage could those bombs do if one of them went off?"

Riley shook his head. "That depends."

"On what?"

"On what they're set at. I think the MK/B has four settings for yields ranging from ten to five hundred kilotons. So it depends on the setting."

"You mean you can change the power of the bomb by flipping a switch?"

Riley gave her a weak smile. "Pretty neat, huh? The theory is the bomb is set for required yield prior to a mission, depending on the target profile. I'm sure there's an access panel on the casing that opens to that control. I for one don't plan on messing with it."

"Well, for instance, what will a ten-kiloton blast do?" Conner felt somewhat embarrassed to be asking this. Somehow, she felt she ought to know more about the subject.

"A kiloton is equal to a thousand tons of TNT. So ten kilotons is ten thousand tons of TNT. If it blew here, it would take out this base but not much more than that.

"There are five effects of a nuclear explosion. Most people think of only two—the blast and the radiation. The blast, which is the kinetic energy, uses about half the energy of the bomb. That's what blows things up: it's the shock wave of compressed air that radiates from the bomb at supersonic speed. If the bomb goes off underground, that wave is muffled, but it takes out whatever it blows near, creating a crater. If it's an airburst or above surface, then the blast does more damage. You have to worry about not only the original wave but also the high winds that are generated by the overpressure. We're talking winds of more than two hundred miles an hour, so it can be pretty destructive.

"There are two types of radiation: prompt and delayed. Prompt is what is immediately generated by the explosion and uses about five percent of the energy of the bomb. It's in the form of gamma rays, neutrons, and beta particles. We measure those in rads. Six hundred rads and you have a ninety percent chance of dying in three to four weeks."

"How many rads would these bombs put out?" Conner asked.

Riley shrugged. "I can't answer that. It depends on the strength of the blast, whether it goes off in the air or underground, your relative location to ground zero, and how well shielded you are. Usually you'll die of blast or thermal before you have to worry about prompt radiation.

"If you survive the initial effects, then you have to worry about delayed radiation—also known as fallout. However, with the strong winds down here, the fallout would get dispersed over a large area. And there aren't many folks here to be affected by it. In a more populated and less windy area, fallout can be devastating.

"The other two effects are thermal and electromagnetic pulse. Thermal causes damage in built-up areas because it starts fires. If you're exposed to it, the flash will blind and burn you even before the blast wave reaches you. Thermal uses up about one-third of the energy of the bomb.

"Electromagnetic pulse, known as EMP, is the one effect that few people know about. When the bomb goes off, it sends out electromagnetic waves, just like radio except thousands of times stronger. Those waves will destroy most electronics in their path for a long distance."

Riley was depressed. He'd buried all those facts deep inside his head and had refused to dig them out for a long time. "The bottom line is that no one really knows exactly what impact nuclear weapons will have on people. There are too many variables. The only times they've ever been used against people—at Hiroshima and Nagasaki— were so long ago, and those bombs were so different from what we have now, that the data is not very valid.

"I think Nikita Khrushchev, surprisingly enough, summed up nuclear war quite well. He said the survivors would envy the dead."

Conner and Sammy were silent for a few minutes as the implications of what Riley had said sank in.

Riley was lost in his dark thoughts. He remembered the debates in the team room about their nuclear mission. Most had been worried about simple and more personal things such as whether there was actually a firing delay in their ADMs, as they had been told. Many believed that once the bombs were emplaced and initiated, they'd go off immediately. Why would the powers-that-be risk an hour's delay to get the team to safety? Riley had spent his time worrying about more global effects. He'd read all that was available about nuclear weapons, mesmerized and repelled by the destructive power he could carry on his back.

"What if there's a fire down here? Would those bombs go off?" Conner interrupted his thoughts.

"It has thermal safety devices that would prevent accidental detonation due to fire," Riley replied.

"How do you think the bombs got here?" Conner asked. "I thought you said those things were tightly controlled."

"How did this base get here?" Riley replied. "Your guess is as good as mine."

Sammy pointed at the blue binder. "Do you think we should open the safe?"

Riley shook his head. "I looked at it. It's set in the ground and requires a combination. We don't have that. I recommend we don't mess with it. You've got the bombs. You don't need the codes." Riley suddenly stood.

"Where are you going?"

"I need to start earning my money." He looked at Sammy. "You want to give me a hand?"

"Sure," she replied.

With that they were gone. Conner speculated for a few seconds about what Riley might be up to, but then dismissed her sister and Riley from her mind as she opened up her portable computer and got to work, preparing her story.

SNN HEADQUARTERS, ATLANTA, GEORGIA. Falcon carefully read the reply from ISA headquarters.

No further information on Eternity Base.

Confirm information that U.S. Air Force C-130, tail number 6204 from 487th TAS, Clark Base, Hawaii, was reported as MIA 21 December 1971, Vietnam..

Actual location U.S. Army Engineer unit, B Company, 67th Engineer Battalion, from August 1971 through December 1971 was Chi Lang, Vietnam, OPCON MACV-SOG.

Falcon scanned the page-long printouts for pertinent information on the people he'd had checked out. The fact that Riley was an ex–Special Forces man who'd run counterterrorist operations caught his attention. He wondered if there was a connection between that and the MACV-SOG cover-up. There were so many classified organizations conducting various operations that Riley could still be working for the government.

This whole damn thing didn't make much sense. The end of the message indicated that his superiors thought the same.

Request all information you have on Eternity Base.
Priority One.

Slowly he put the papers down on his desk. The report had yielded no significant information. Eternity Base's cover had been backstopped all the way through the classified files in the ISA's database. Although Falcon knew such a thing was in the realm of possibility—especially for something that had happened so long ago—it meant that the secret of Eternity Base could be a bad story publicity wise. Since they didn't know what the base was or what the original cover story had been, there was no way to plan for damage control.

Falcon typed into his computer and studied the data that Young had already sent. His forehead wrinkled in concern as he saw that the last transmission had been coded only for Parker's ID and password. Why had she done that? What had she found that was so important—more important than the existence of the base and the finding of the body? Falcon was worried about what Parker now knew that he didn't.

Falcon tapped a finger against his teeth as he pondered the situation. Wheels were turning, but he wasn't sure where they would lead him. His fingers flew over the keyboard as he searched other databases. He stopped when he found the order from Parker sending the new support team to Antarctica ASAP. Why hadn't he been informed of that? Falcon slammed a fist down on his desktop in frustration. Damn Parker and his penchant for secrets.

Falcon reopened the data file on information that Young had sent prior to the coded message. There had to be something that would help him figure out what was going on.

— twenty —

KAESONG, NORTH KOREA. The headquarters for the North Korean Special Forces is located twenty-five miles north of the famous border city of Panmunjom. This puts it in close proximity to the demilitarized zone, where many of its units' covert activities are conducted. Tonight, however, Gen. O Gulc Yol, the army chief of staff and former commander of the Special Forces Branch, had his eyes focused on a map that had never before been unfurled in his operations room. The fact that his staff had even been able to find the map on such short notice was quite an accomplishment. General Yol had been awakened by the duty officer and given Kang's message from New York just forty-five minutes ago.

Yol pointed a gnarled finger, broken many times in hand-to-hand combat training, at the map. "It is there, sir."

There were only two people in the world to whom General Yol would have shown such deference. One was Kim Il Sung, the leader of North Korea for forty years, who had died two years ago. The other was the man who presently stood opposite him looking at the map—Kim's son, Kim Jong Il. "It is very far away," Yol said.

"Yes, sir, but it is a golden opportunity. It gives us a lever that is the perfect solution to the problem that has kept us from implementing the Orange III plan."

Kim, designated heir to Kim Il Sung, rubbed the side of his face. He had watched his father slowly die without having seen completed

155

his dream of uniting the two Koreas. It was unthinkable that his father's life-long vision had not been realized. He would not allow the same thing to happen to himself.

The recent reduction of American forces in South Korea had left that threat a paper tiger. Kim had no doubt that his massive army—sixth largest in the world—could now overcome their enemies to the south. The problem was that the Americans still held a real threat—tactical nuclear weapons.

Korea is a land of mountains and narrow plains. It is along these narrow plains that any offensive movement has to advance. And tactical nuclear weapons were the ideal countermeasure to such movement. If that one factor could be removed, the entire balance of power in the peninsula would shift to the North's favor.

In late 1991, the United States had removed all tactical nuclear weapons from the peninsula in a gesture meant to force the North Koreans to abandon their nuclear weapons program. The North ignored the gesture for the simple reason that it was seen as an empty one. The Americans maintained enough tactical nuclear weapons on the planes, submarines, and cruise missiles of the Seventh Fleet to more than make up for the lack of land-based ones.

Orange III was the classified operations plans (OPLAN) for a northern invasion of the south. Unfortunately, to Kim Jong Il's mind, his father had not approved the implementation of the plan because of the high risk and cost potential if it failed—and fail it most likely would if the Americans used their nuclear weapons.

The fact that the North Koreans had their own small arsenal of nukes did not change that balance for two simple reasons: First, they had only limited abilities to project those weapons a few hundred miles into the South—and, of course, they could never touch the United States itself. Second, tactical nuclear weapons favored the defender, not the attacker.

North Korea had even opened its nuclear facilities to international inspection in 1992, having already made two dozen weapons and secreting them. They'd done that in exchange for political concessions from both the South and the Americans. For the past several years they had played the nuclear card close to their chest; there was not much more they could hope to gain in the political arena.

But now, *now,* there was a window of opportunity. This new information, if it was used properly, could make Orange III a reality.

Kim looked up at his old friend. "I cannot believe that the American government has abandoned two nuclear weapons and that this so-called news organization has not notified the military of their presence."

Yol smiled, showing stained teeth, the result of constantly smoking cigarettes. "Imperialists are like that, sir. This news organization is more concerned with profit than duty and country. They will keep it a secret so they can have the story all to themselves."

Kim thought it was all too strange. He just couldn't understand Americans. "But the bombs? How could they have just been left there?"

"I don't know, sir. But the fact is they are there. Unguarded for the moment. And we must seize the moment." Yol emphasized each word in the last sentence.

Kim was more cautious than his military chief. "Could it be a trap set by the Americans? Could they have discovered our source at SNN?"

Yol considered that very briefly. "I do not believe Loki has been compromised. I also see no reason for the Americans to go through such trouble to set up a trap. It is a trap only if they know of both the Orange III plan and Loki's existence. Even then, they cannot expect us to launch a mission based on such information. I believe they would not have put the weapons so far away if they had considered such a trap."

"But can we use these weapons?"

Yol held up the message he'd received from Kang. "The codes and instructions to arm the weapons are at the same base."

"How much time do we have?" Kim asked.

Yol sat back down in his chair. "It will take the second American news team about twenty-four hours to arrive in New Zealand. Then they must wait until the weather is good enough to fly down to Antarctica, which will take another eight or so hours. And from what my intelligence officer tells me, the bad weather can last for weeks. When they finally arrive at the base, they will announce their story."

"It will take us at least twenty-four hours also," Kim remarked, looking at the wall map of the world. "In fact, I don't believe we can reach Antarctica from here with any aircraft we have. And we certainly cannot refuel anywhere en route."

Yol had already thought of that. "I have had my staff working on this since the message first came in. They concur with your analysis, sir. The distance is too great to be reached from here. Additionally, the Americans and their South Korean lackeys keep too close a watch for us to even try launching a team by air from any of our bases here."

Yol's finger slid across Antarctica and up into the Atlantic Ocean until it came to rest on a spot in Africa. "Here is our answer, if you will give me permission, sir."

"You have a plan then?"

Yol smiled. "Yes, sir."

Kim settled back in his seat. "Let me hear it."

Yol tapped an intercom button, and three officers carrying charts and paper bustled into the room. A Special Forces lieutenant colonel started talking, his pointer beginning at the same spot in southwest Africa. As he progressed, the pointer made its way south to Antarctica and then north again—but not to the Korean peninsula.

At the end of fifteen minutes, Kim had caught Yol's enthusiasm. The briefing officers wrapped up and left the room, leaving the two of them alone. Kim Jong Il had worked with General Yol for his entire adult life. He had only one question for his old friend. "It is a very daring plan. You think you can do it?"

"Yes."

"Send the messages."

ISA HEADQUARTERS, SOUTHWEST OF WASHINGTON, D.C. "How the hell can there be a base put in by our military that we don't know about?" General Hodges demanded, his forehead glinting in the overhead lights.

No one at the table ventured an answer. Hodges hadn't truly expected one. Thirty-one years in the military intelligence community had taught him that not only didn't one hand know what the other was doing in the U.S. government, but that fingers on the same hand were often in the dark as to the action of the other fingers.

"Do we have anything to work from?"

Weaver, the analyst who worked with Falcon, their source at SNN, spoke up from the far end of the table. "We have a name from a letter that was left at the base."

Hodges swung his flint-hard gaze down the table. "What's the name?"

"Glaston. Apparently he was the man in charge of construction in 1971. He worked for ISA from '62 through '79. Direct action section. Code three alpha."

"I want this man Glaston." Hodges turned to a man in a three-piece suit. "I want him ASAP. You have priority one authorization."

"Yes, sir." The man headed for the door.

— twenty-one —

LUBANGO, ANGOLA, SOUTHWEST AFRICA. Major Pak Roh Kim read once more the message his radio operator had decoded twenty minutes ago. It was the longest message he had ever seen transmitted over high frequency radio in his twenty-one years with Special Forces. He was holding a complete operations plan for a new mission that was to commence immediately.

Pak's face twisted in a sneer as he read the concept of operations. Those desk-bound fools in Kaesong! He looked up at the thatched roof of the hut that comprised his team's headquarters. Pak was a small man, less than five and a half feet tall and weighing no more than a hundred and twenty pounds. He was the spitting image of Bruce Lee, the major difference being that Pak had actually killed many more men than the actor had ever simulated killing in his movies.

"Get me Lim," he snapped at Kim Chong Man. As his executive officer scurried out to the airstrip, Pak leafed through the pages of the OPLAN, his mind trying to rationalize the words in front of him. This was going to be difficult, very difficult.

Pak had been in Angola for a year and a half now, advising the Movement for the Popular Liberation of Angola (MPLA) government forces in their thirty year war against the UNITA rebels. In Pak's personal opinion, the real reason he and his men were here was to gain combat experience. The MPLA would never defeat the rebels, especially since the Cubans had pulled out and run back to their island with their tails between their legs. Now one hundred and twenty North Korean Special Forces soldiers were supposed to do what thousands of Cubans hadn't been able to accomplish.

Pak had run more than his share of classified missions, so he was no stranger to being awakened in the middle of the night and handed an OPLAN. This one, however, was different in several important aspects. The first was the fact that it was an operation outside of his immediate area of operations. The second was the strategic significance of the mission. It all looked very nice on paper, but implementation was going to require great sacrifices and effort.

Typical bureaucratic thinking, Pak snorted. This was the same type of thinking that had almost gotten him killed in a DMZ infiltration tunnel north of Seoul two years ago. He and his team should have been pulled out at the first sign of compromise, but indecision in the chain of command had left them in there long enough for the South Koreans to flood the tunnel. Pak shuddered as he remembered the torrent of water pouring in and the muffled screams of the men who didn't make it out.

Lim stepped in and snapped a salute, breaking Pak out of his black reverie. "Captain Lim reporting as ordered, sir."

Pak looked at the short man in the flight suit with unveiled disgust. "What is your aircraft's range?"

Lim blinked. "It's sixty-five hundred kilometers with a one-hour reserve, sir."

"We need to go ninety-seven hundred kilometers."

Lim stared nervously at the major. "Then we will have to refuel somewhere, sir."

"If we had someplace to land and refuel, I would have told you that." Pak's voice was ice cold. "We need to travel ninety-seven hundred kilometers without refueling."

"That is impossible, sir."

"Make it possible. You have one hour to be ready to leave." Pak turned his gaze to his XO, who had come in behind the pilot. "Bring in the team and I will brief them."

ETERNITY BASE, ANTARCTICA. Sammy sat down with her back against the crate containing one of the bombs and watched Riley, who was examining a rifle. They had run a power line into the armory, and now the overhead lights worked, along with the heat. They'd spent the past two hours doing what Riley referred to as "what-if" work. Sammy was happy to stay busy.

Riley pointed up at the heater, which was blowing out warm air. "The weapons are sweating now, and when they get exposed again to subfreezing temperatures they're going to freeze up."

Sammy shrugged. "I don't think my sister is too worried about that."

Riley put down the rifle and sat across from her. "I have to agree with that." He looked around. "I wish I had a beer. I suppose they didn't put any alcohol down here because it would have frozen. I'm not too sure I would have liked living in a survival shelter without beer."

"How could the government have lost track of these weapons?" Sammy asked, tapping the crate.

Riley sighed. "These bombs are either a closely guarded secret or a complete oversight. Crazy as it sounds, the latter is most likely the truth. If someone from the government knew about these things, there would have been some monitoring of this place."

Sammy disagreed. "That man who showed up in St. Louis certainly was keeping very good tabs on this place. He must have gotten on to me either through SNN or from the data runs I made on the computer at the Center."

Riley shrugged. "I don't know. We have that name—Glaston. If we can find out who he worked for, then we'll have some answers. I'm more worried right now about who tried to kill Swenson and trashed Vickers's radio. If whoever it is works for the same people who sent that man to St. Louis, then they really have their act together. That's why I wanted to prepare for the shit to hit the fan."

"If we can get into the reactor itself, I think we ought to move the stuff we gathered into that," Sammy suggested. "It would be an ideal place to hide."

Riley nodded. "That's a good idea. Let's get back and join everyone else."

They negotiated the corridors to the unit where the rest of the party was sleeping. As Sammy reached for the doorknob and started to push, Riley screamed "NO!" He grabbed her by the shoulders, rolling to the left, his body on top of hers as they hit the wooden planks on the corridor floor.

The sharp, devastatingly loud crack of an explosion split the air. Sammy felt a strong current of air rush by her and Riley, and she heard the sounds of splintering wood and tearing metal. Then came a brief moment of absolute silence until excited voices started from inside the unit.

Riley rolled off Sammy and sat up, his back against the wall, as the door opened and the rest of the party surged out into the hallway, Conner in the lead. "What happened?"

Sammy just shook her head, trying to clear her ears of the ringing. She turned to Riley for the answer. Riley pointed up, and everyone's eyes followed. A scorched black mark on the ceiling and the remnants of a piece of wire were all that was visible. "Our saboteur has turned to more direct means to try and solve his problem. Someone put a Claymore mine up there and rigged it to blow when the door opened."

LUBANGO, ANGOLA, SOUTHWEST AFRICA. "I have prepared the plane to fly ninety-seven hundred kilometers, sir." Captain Lim stood underneath the massive nose of his plane.

"How?" No congratulations. Pak didn't believe in them.

"Normal range is sixty-five hundred kilometers. If we also use the one-hour reserve fuel supply, our possible range is extended to seven thousand one hundred twenty-five kilometers. We will make the additional two thousand five hundred seventy-five kilometers by using three of the fuel bladders here at the airfield. I have loaded them on board, and we will hand pump the fuel from the bladders to the main tanks as we progress."

Pak nodded. His narrow eyes watched the team members loading their gear on board the aircraft. They'd been instructed only to gather their equipment. Pak wanted to wait until they were in the air before fully briefing the team.

"May I inquire where we are going, sir?" Lim held up his flight charts. "I need to plan a route."

"South." Pak answered.

Lim frowned. "South, sir? To South Africa?"

"No. Straight south. Over the ocean."

"But, with all due respect, sir, there's nothing to the south."

Pak turned his coal black eyes on the pilot, cutting him off. "You fly the plane, captain. Let me worry about everything else. We take off in ten minutes."

Lim saluted stiffly and retreated into the belly of his plane. Pak stepped back and ran his eyes along the silhouette of the Soviet-made IL-18. It was an old plane, built in the late fifties. Four large propeller engines mounted on its wings reminded one of an old-style airliner. The Russians had dumped the obsolete plane on their so-called North Korean allies in exchange for desperately needed hard currency. The plane was the way Pak and his fellow commandos had traveled to Angola, and it was their only way out and back to North Korea. Taking the plane meant that the other Special Forces men would be stranded. Pak was sure the people in Kaesong hadn't thought of that either, or if they had, they felt this mission was worth more than these men.

Kim snapped to attention before him. "All loaded, sir!"

Pak nodded. "Let us board."

ETERNITY BASE, ANTARCTICA. "But why try to kill you two? What would that accomplish?" Devlin's eyes were riveted on the shattered wall of the next unit. The thousands of steel ball bearings projected by the mine had torn large gashes in the surface.

Riley held the remains of the igniting wire in his hands. "Desperation. Whoever it is tried to stop us from getting here by trying to kill our pilot. That failed. Then they tried to keep us from communicating our discovery by damaging the satellite radio. That failed when we used the equipment already down here.

"Now he—or she—has no choice but to somehow get rid of everyone here. They tried to start with Sammy and me. It was just luck that I saw the trip wire running from the top of the door." He looked at Swenson. "You would be last, since that person needs you to fly out of here. Unless, of course, you're the person. Or if whoever it is can pilot the plane."

"But," Devlin protested, "the base would still be here. And Atlanta has tapes."

Riley looked at Conner. "Has SNN played those tapes on the air yet?"

She shook her head. "No. They're waiting until we have the complete story."

"If there's a leak at SNN, it's also possible that the tapes have been compromised." Riley gave a twisted smile. "Not only can't we trust anyone or any organization back in the real world, but we can't trust each other here."

"What do we do now?" Sammy asked.

"We stick together in groups of two or more," Riley suggested. "If one half of a pair ends up dead, then we have to assume the live half is the culprit."

Conner stood. "All right. I agree. From here on out no one goes anywhere alone. We will also have at least two people awake at any one time."

"I also suggest we go to the arms room and see if any weapons are missing," Riley said. "Whoever took that mine might have taken some other goodies that we don't want to be walking into."

Conner headed for the door. "Everyone goes."

CAPE COD, MASSACHUSETTS. The old man was jogging slowly along the deserted beach, leaving a trail of footprints just above the surf line. His head was slightly bowed, the sparse white hair reflecting the setting sun. His head cocked slightly as the sound of helicopter blades crept over the sand, but his feet kept their steady rhythm.

A shadow flashed over him and a UH-60 Blackhawk helicopter flitted by, less than thirty feet above the ground. The man's feet finally came to a halt as the helicopter flared, kicking up sand. The old man covered his eyes as the wheels touched and two men in unmarked khaki hopped off.

They ran over to him. There was no badge flashed or words spoken. They were all players and knew the rules. The old man allowed them to escort him onto the aircraft. It lifted and immediately sped off at maximum speed to the west, toward nearby Otis Air Force Base.

The incoming tide washed over the footsteps, and within twenty minutes all traces of the lone jogger were gone.

— twenty-two —

ETERNITY BASE, ANTARCTICA. The tension was palpable. Riley looked up from the crates where he'd been counting ammunition. "We've been through everything, and we have one M16, four magazines, and eighty rounds of ammunition missing. That's besides one Claymore, but we know where that went."

Conner was biting the inside of her mouth as she tried to figure out the next move. "Should we search for the rifle?"

Devlin waved his hands about. "It could be anywhere. And if we found it, we still wouldn't know who stole it. Any one of us could have come in here and taken it."

Riley agreed. "A search would be a waste of time. There is one thing I think we have to do, though."

"What?" Conner asked.

"We need to make sure these bombs can't be used. We need to destroy the PAL codes."

"How do you propose we do that?" Devlin asked.

"I blow up the safe that holds them."

"No." They all turned to look at Sammy. "Destroying the codes doesn't do anything. If our saboteur was sent by whoever built this base, then that person could already have the PAL codes."

Conner rubbed her forehead. "You've got a point there."

"Then we neutralize the bombs by another means," Riley said. He pointed at the two crates. "I told you that these bombs have a six-digit

166

PAL code that allows limited try followed by lockout. I'll enter two wrong codes and cause both bombs to go into lockout. That will mean they can't be exploded."

"Bullshit!" Everyone looked at Devlin in surprise. "How do we know you don't already have the codes like Sammy said. You could arm the bombs with the correct six digits instead of entering the wrong ones."

"Why would I do that?" Riley asked.

"I don't know!" Devlin turned to Conner. "Listen to me. What's to stop Riley from arming the bomb with a time delay? Then he kills us or just holds us at gunpoint and leaves, taking Swenson with him. If one of those bombs goes off, all evidence of this base will be gone."

Riley was shaking his head. "That's stupid. You can hold a gun on me while I do it."

"That still won't do us any good if you arm the bomb," Devlin argued. "We wouldn't know how to stop it. We'd all have to leave and the base would still blow. You'd have achieved your mission of destroying the real evidence of this base.

"You're also the only one among us with the military training necessary to do the acts of sabotage we've already had. You're the one who would know how to rig that mine—and that would make it more than just luck that you avoided it."

Vickers spoke for the first time. "You know, it's quite a coincidence that Riley is the only one of us who was involved in all three incidents."

"What do you mean?" Conner asked.

"He's the one who found Swenson. He says he just happened to wake up and find him out in the snow. He's the one who figures out how to replace the destroyed transmitter so quickly, almost as if he'd known what had happened. He's the one who just happens to see the trip wire for the mine and saves himself and Sammy. It would have been real easy for him to have avoided all those disasters if he was the one who planned them."

"But why would I do that?" Riley didn't seem overly concerned by the accusations.

Vickers pointed at the bomb. "To make us trust you enough to arm the bombs."

Riley shook his head. "If I had the PAL codes, I could have armed them at any time. I wouldn't need your trust."

"Hold it!" Sammy yelled. "We're all going a little nuts here. None of you are making much sense. Let's calm down a little."

"What if someone other than Riley enters a six-digit code on the bombs?" Lallo asked. "Pick six numbers at random and enter them."

Riley laughed, the sound incongruous in the air of fear and mistrust that permeated the room. "Well, I'd have to say we run into the same problem. Since I know I'm not the person doing all this stuff, I trust myself, but I certainly don't trust any of you. If you're not going to allow me to lock out the bombs because you don't trust me, I'm certainly not going to allow any of you to do it either."

Conner slapped her hand on a crate of ammunition. "Forget about the goddamn bombs for a minute. Our real problem is that someone here is trying to stop us from getting out this story about the base. Even if the tapes in Atlanta have been compromised, we can still get the truth out. Once the support team gets here, we can go live on satellite feed and that will mean whoever it is has failed. Until then we have to stick together and work together. There's nothing else we can do."

"I don't like the idea of being cooped up in here with a killer on the loose," Devlin muttered.

"Well, there isn't anything you can do about it," was Conner's reply. She looked around the room, from one person to another. "Let's continue on with the work we planned. We stay in parties of at least two from here on out, though."

"I still think we ought to open up the power access tunnel to the reactor," Devlin suggested.

"Good idea." Conner turned to the rest of the team. "Riley, Sammy, and Devlin work on opening up the reactor tunnel. Kerns, Vickers, and Lallo work on the west tunnel. I'll be with the group down at the west tunnel. We'll meet back at the mess hall in four hours."

SAFE HOUSE, VICINITY FREDERICKSBURG, VIRGINIA. The old man looked up as the door opened and two men walked in. The short one was carrying a briefcase, the taller one nothing. The short man placed the briefcase on the desk, and they both stared at the old man.

Finally, he could take it no longer. "What do you want?" Not a word had been said to him since he'd been picked up on the beach, flown into Otis Air Force Base, cross loaded onto a military jet, and flown down here. He knew that the men were from his government because their procedures and resources were too complex for a foreign government operating in the United States.

The taller one, whom the old man had correctly guessed was in charge, spoke. "We need information, Mr. Glaston. Or should I say Colonel Glaston, U.S. Army, Retired?"

"What information?" Glaston asked warily. In twenty-three years of duty, most of it with the ultrasecret Intelligence Support Agency, he'd participated in more than his share of covert operations, any one of which might interest these people.

The tall man reached into his pocket and laid an ID card on the desktop. "I'm with your old organization, Mr. Glaston. We need information on an operation you were involved in that we have no record of." The short man flicked one of the locks on the briefcase.

Glaston frowned as he searched his memory. "What are you talking about? Everything I did at ISA was fully debriefed and recorded."

"Eternity Base?" the tall man simply asked.

Glaston felt a sledgehammer hit him in the chest. "I've never heard of it."

The short man pressed the second lock and swung up the lid. He turned it so Glaston could see inside. Various hypodermic needles were arrayed along the top, and serum vials were secured in the bottom. The tall man gestured at the contents with a wave of his hand. "The art of interrogation has developed to much higher levels than when you retired. We're less crude and much more effective.

"You know, of course, that everyone talks eventually." The tall man reached in and pulled out a needle, holding it up to the light. "With these sophisticated drugs, that eventually comes much sooner. Unfortunately, the side effects cannot always be controlled. I would like to avoid resorting to such methods." He laid down the needle. "Why is it that we have no records of Eternity Base?"

Glaston considered his options. "What do I get out of this?"

The tall man shrugged. "It depends on what you tell us."

Glaston sighed. He knew what the tall man had said was true—he would talk sooner or later. He'd been on the other side of this desk too many times not to know that. Jesus, to have it come to this all because of that stupid base! He slumped back in the chair.

"I was the ops supervisor for the construction of Eternity Base in late 1971 in Antarctica. It was a group of buildings—twelve to be exact—that were buried under the ice. The sections—"

"We know what's down there," the tall man interrupted. "What we want to know is who was behind the op and why."

That meant they'd found it, Glaston realized. That, in a strange sort of way, relieved him. He'd often thought about the base over the past twenty-five years, wondering if it had ever been shut down and the bombs removed. "I worked directly for Lieutenant General Woodson."

The two men exchanged glances. They both knew that Woodson had been head of the ISA in the early seventies. "How did Woodson give you this assignment?"

"Personal briefing." Glaston sighed again. If they'd been down there they'd found everything, and it wouldn't do him any good to hold back. Except for the plane. That he could never mention. He hoped they hadn't turned up any information on that.

"It was an unofficially sanctioned mission—no paper trail and denial if uncovered. Woodson brought me back to Washington from Vietnam, where I was doing liaison work between CCS—Combat and Control South, MACV-SOG—and the Agency. Trying to keep the Green Beanies and the spooks from each other's throats.

"When I got to D.C., Woodson told me he had a mission that could be very profitable to both of us and had the president's blessing." Glaston ignored the disgusted looks the two men exchanged. If they hadn't done work for cash yet, they would someday. It was much easier to put your life on the line with a substantial bank account to back you up. A government pension wasn't enough for this line of work.

"Who was Woodson working for?"

"Someone with the code name Peter. I had a number in Colorado where I contacted him. I don't know who Peter was, and I certainly don't remember that phone number. It was probably a cutout anyway."

"Woodson never told you who the place was for, or even what it was designed for?"

"It was easy to see what it was designed for. It was a survival shelter. As far as the who goes, it had to be somebody with a lot of money and resources, along with leverage at the White House. Woodson and I supplied the manpower and the aircraft; Peter supplied all the equipment."

"What happened to the C-130 that was doing the flights from McMurdo to the base?"

Glaston's heartbeat escalated. "It went down a couple of hours out of McMurdo on the way home. I had to cover it up somehow, so I used the MACV-SOG cover."

The tall man looked at him dispassionately. He turned to his partner. "I'll be back in an hour. Prep him."

"Wait a second!" Glaston yelled as the short man pulled out a vial of clear liquid and picked up the nearby needle. "I'm telling you everything. You said if I cooperated, that wouldn't be necessary." He thought briefly of the courier and realized that finding his body must be the reason they were doing this to him.

"I said it depended. You just told us you did freelance work while at the ISA. You broke the rules, and now we're going to find out what other rules you might have broken in your career."

The short man approached with the needle.

AIRSPACE, SOUTH ATLANTIC OCEAN. As Captain Lim approached, Major Pak looked up from the plans he and his XO were studying. Pak was impressed that Lim had waited almost eight hours before coming out of the cockpit to talk to him. The interior of the IL-18 was stripped bare except for Pak's team, their equipment, and the fuel bladders. The team was spread out on the vibrating steel floor, either sleeping or preparing their equipment for the infiltration.

"Sir, may I speak to you?" Lim inquired.

Pak nodded.

"Sir, as captain of this airplane it is my duty to inform you that we do not have enough fuel, even with all this, to make landfall in this direction." Lim waved a hand at the bladders. "In two hours we will be too low on fuel to turn around and make it back to Angola."

"There's land ahead," Pak quietly remarked.

Lim blinked. "We are heading for the South Pole, sir. There are no all-weather airstrips suitable for this aircraft down there."

"I know that," Pak responded. "My team will parachute out, and then you will attempt to land on the ice and snow farther away to ensure operational security. I will leave one of the members of my team on board to help you travel to our exfiltration point."

Lim blanched. "But, sir—" He halted, at a loss for words.

Pak stood. "But what, captain?"

Lim shook his head. "Nothing, sir." He turned and retreated to his cockpit.

Senior Lieutenant Kim looked at his team leader. "Our captain is a weak man."

Pak turned his attention back to the papers. "Are you satisfied that your men know the parts of the plan that they need to?"

Kim nodded. "Yes, sir."

"Have you picked who will stay with the plane?"

"Yes, sir. Sergeant Chong has volunteered."

"Good."

Kim scratched his chin. "The only thing I don't understand, sir, is why we are doing this."

No one else would have dared say that to Pak, but the two of them had spent four years working together. They'd infiltrated the South Korean coastline three times and conducted extremely successful reconnaissance missions there. They owed their lives to each other.

"There are two U.S. nuclear weapons at our objective."

Kim didn't show any surprise. "But you briefed us that there is only a news team there. No military."

"Correct."

Now Kim was surprised. "You mean these two bombs are unguarded?"

Pak nodded. "Yes. Our objective is to seize those weapons along with their arming codes and instructions. And to leave no trace of our presence there."

"How will we do that, and what will we do with the weapons? I thought our government already had nuclear weapons."

"We are not going back home with the weapons." Pak shook his head. "The rest is not for you to know yet, my friend. You will be told when it is time. Suffice it to say that if we are successful, Orange III will be implemented and it will succeed."

Pak leaned back in his seat as his executive officer moved away. Although this whole plan had been jury-rigged on short notice, there was much precedent for the entire operation. The primary wartime mission of the North Korean Special Forces was to seize or destroy U.S. nuclear weapons. Pak had participated in the drawing up of plans for direct action missions against overseas targets, including the U.S. Seventh Fleet bases in Japan and the Philippines, and even Pearl Harbor in Hawaii.

North Korea had never been shy about striking at enemies outside its own borders, and the Special Forces (SF) had been involved in every action. In 1968 thirty-one Special Forces soldiers had infiltrated across the demilitarized zone (DMZ) and made their way down to Seoul to raid the Blue House, home of the South Korean president. The mission failed, with twenty-eight men killed, two missing, and one captured.

Shortly after that attack, on 23 January 1968, People's Korean Army (PKA) Special Forces men in high-speed attack craft seized the USS *Pueblo*. Later that year, a large SF force of almost a hundred men conducted landings on the coast of South Korea in an attempt to raise the populace against the government. It failed, but such failures didn't daunt the North Korean government. In 1969, a U.S. electronic warfare aircraft was shot down by the North Koreans, killing all thirty-one American service members on board.

As security stiffened in South Korea during the 1970s, North Korea moved its attention overseas, not caring about the international effect. In 1983, three PKA Special Forces officers planted a bomb in Rangoon in an attempt to kill the visiting South Korean president. That mission also failed. Later in 1983, four North Korean merchant ships infiltrated the Gulf of California to conduct monitoring operations against the United States mainland. One of the ships was seized by the Mexican authorities, but that didn't prevent the North Koreans from continuing such operations.

Pak knew that history, and he also knew more than the average North Korean about the changes that had been sweeping the world in the nineties. Living in Angola, he had been exposed to more information than the tightly controlled society back in his homeland ever received. The breakup of the Soviet Union had never been acknowledged by Pyongyang, except in cryptically worded exhortations to the people, telling them they were the last true bastion of communism in the world. Pak truly believed he was part of the last line in the war against western imperialism—especially with the Cubans running home. If this mission succeeded, he would strike a blow greater than any of his Special Forces predecessors. That was enough for him.

— twenty-three —

ETERNITY BASE, ANTARCTICA. They'd managed to clear not only the west tunnel of ice, but also the entryway into the west ice storage area. That room was as large as the east one, but there was no ramp at the end. It was also stocked full of supplies and food. Conner's team had taken footage of the entire event.

Right now, Sammy was lying behind Devlin and Riley in the power access tunnel, which was made of corrugated steel tubing approximately three feet in diameter. They'd been digging here by hand for two hours. Removing the ice was slow work, because it had to be put on a blanket and dragged the length of the tunnel, then Sammy would dispose of it along the south ice wall.

It probably would have been easier to go up to the surface and use the sonar to find the reactor, then try to dig out its access shaft. The only problem with that plan was the weather. Sammy had gone up the main surface shaft several hours ago with Riley and Devlin to take a look outside. Visibility was close to zero as the wind lashed the countryside with a wall of white. Ten feet from the doorway, a person would be lost and would find his way back only with a lot of luck. It was hard to believe Vickers's latest radio message that the storm was actually lessening in intensity.

Remembering the blowing snow and the icy talons of cold ripping at her clothes through the open door, and thinking about the frozen body lying at the foot of the stairs, brought to mind something Sammy had read in Conner's binder during her two-hour guard shift: the fate of Capt. Lawrence Oates, a member of Scott's ill-fated 1911–12 South Pole expedition. Scott's party had arrived at the South Pole after man-hauling their sleds most of the way, only to discover a tent and note that Norwegian Roald Amundsen had left behind, proving that he had beaten Scott there by a month. On their return trip, the party was running out of food and was in the middle of a blizzard. Oates, who was suffering from severe frostbite, walked out of the campsite into the blowing snow, sacrificing himself so the party could continue on more quickly. His noble gesture was all for naught, though, because the rest of Scott's party died only eleven miles from a supply depot. Eight months later their bodies were discovered along with Scott's journal relating the sad tale.

"I've got an opening." Riley broke Sammy out of her snowy reverie. He was poking his shovel through the ice. Together, Riley and Devlin scratched away to widen the opening. The tunnel continued on ahead for another ten feet before angling off to the right.

"Let's see what we have," Riley said, as he led the way.

Sammy crawled along on her hands and knees behind Riley and Devlin, her Gore-tex pants sliding on the steel. Fifty more feet and they reached a thick hatch. Riley turned the wheel and the door slowly opened. Another two hundred feet. Then another hatch. They squeezed out the second one and could finally stand. A small shielded room opened out onto the reactor's core. Radiation warning signs were plastered all over the walls. Sammy looked through the thick glass at the slots where the rods were to be inserted in the reactor core itself. In front of the glass was a small control panel with a few seats.

"Unbelievable." Devlin shook his head. "They really thought something this poorly constructed could work. No wonder the one at McMurdo had to be taken apart."

"You have to remember this was twenty-five years ago," Riley reminded him.

"Hell, even twenty-five years ago someone should have had more common sense." Devlin ran his hands over the thick glass separating them from the core. "Why are people so stupid?"

"Let's get Conner. She'll want to get this on tape." Devlin reentered the access tunnel and headed back. Riley and Sammy stayed a few seconds, checking out the room, and then followed.

AIRSPACE, ANTARCTICA. Pak watched as Sergeant Chong finished securing the steel cable that would hold their static lines to the roof of the airplane, just in front of the aft passenger door. Pak had never jumped out of an IL-18, but he had heard that it had been done. The IL-18 was not specifically designed for paratroop operations, but the team was making the best of the situation, which seemed to be the overriding concept for this whole mission. Everything about the operation was being improvised due to the time constraint, and Pak didn't like that.

He looked out a small porthole at the polar ice cap glistening below. They were flying at the plane's maximum altitude. Pushing up against the glass and looking forward, Pak could make out a dark line indicating the storm blanketing Lesser Antarctica. The OPLAN had told him about it. Jumping into the high winds was going to be extremely dangerous, a factor the bureaucrats at Special Forces Command seemed to have overlooked.

Pak checked his watch. They were less than an hour and a half from the target. "Time to rig!" he yelled.

Splitting into buddy teams, the nine men who would be jumping began to put on their parachutes, Sergeant Chong helping the odd man. Pak threw his main parachute on his back and buckled the leg and chest straps, securing the chute to his body and making sure it was cinched down tight. The reserve was hooked onto the front. Rucksacks were clipped on below the reserve, and automatic weapons were tied down on top of the reserve.

After Sergeant Chong inspected all the men, they took their seats, each man lost in his own thoughts, contemplating the jump and the mission ahead.

Pak pulled the OPLAN out of his carry-on bag and checked the numbers in the communications section. With those in mind, he waddled his way up the aisle toward the cockpit.

ETERNITY BASE, ANTARCTICA. The wind had actually diminished, although it was still kicking along with gusts up to thirty-five miles an hour. Visibility was increasing to almost fifty feet at times. The slight break in the storm could last for minutes or hours.

Below the surface, in the base itself, the party was taking turns sleeping. Vickers, Kerns, and Lallo were seated at the doors to unit B2, standing guard on the sleepers and each other.

In the communications unit, A3, all was quiet. The lights had been turned off since Conner finished videotaping hours earlier. There was no one in the room to notice the small red light that suddenly flickered and came alive on the transponder. Someone had initiated the beacon using a radio on the proper frequency, and it was now pulsing out the location of Eternity Base to any receiver within a three-hundred-miles radius in all directions.

— twenty-four —

WALTER REED HOSPITAL, WASHINGTON, D.C. The young nurse looked up from her romance novel as the doors at the end of the corridor opened. Four men appeared, one pushing an empty wheelchair. The nurse glanced up at the clock behind her work station, wondering what they wanted this early in the morning. They trooped to a halt at her desk, and the older man in front slid a piece of paper out of his briefcase. The other three men flanked him, their faces expressionless.

"I'm Doctor Wallace. This is the transfer order for one of your patients. We'd like to pick him up immediately."

The nurse frowned. At four in the morning? "I'll have to get the intern on duty to sign off on that."

The man gave a grimace that seemed intended as a smile. "We'll wait."

Two minutes later the intern stood before the men scratching his head as he read the order. "This is a legitimate transfer, but normally the patient's doctor is the one who signs off on the transfer. The intern shot a pointed glance at the clock on the wall. "That's usually why they occur during regular duty hours."

Wallace seemed not to have heard. "The paper is in order. Note the signature by the hospital director. Please sign."

The intern had noted the signature. That effectively relieved him of responsibility. Still, he knew that the patient's doctor would probably give him a dose of grief. "All right," he finally said, taking this easiest course of action. His pen scratched in the proper spot.

"He's in three-nineteen," the nurse offered.

Wallace inclined his head and the three men strode down the hallway.

"He's hooked up to monitors and IVs," the nurse said as she stood. "They're going to need help unhooking him."

Wallace held up a hand, the command implicit in the gesture stopping her. "One of them knows how to do it."

In three minutes the men reappeared, one wheeling the chair, the IV carried by another. The third held a bag containing the patient's possessions. The patient appeared to be semiconscious and didn't say a word as they passed by. The party was gone in record time.

"That's strange," the nurse muttered, the intern barely picking it up.

"What is?"

"The patient, General Woodson, always was very alert."

The intern shrugged. "Nobody, especially not a man who's had half his guts removed for cancer, likes being jerked out of bed at four in the morning."

The nurse shook her head as the intern headed back to his cot. She'd have sworn that Woodson looked drugged. But that wasn't possible; they had him on only a mild pain suppressant. She picked up her novel. Within a few minutes, General Woodson's transfer was forgotten as she plunged back into the heroine's perils in Victorian England.

Thirty minutes later a figure slipped in the fire door at the other end of the corridor and moved to room 319. The man quietly opened the door and stepped into the room, drawing a syringe out of his pocket at the same time. He halted, surprised by the empty bed. He checked the chart at the foot of the bed to be sure that it had held his target. Replacing the syringe, the man retraced his steps and departed the hospital.

He went to the first pay phone he could find and dialed the number he'd memorized when assigned this mission.

"Peter here."

"This is Lucifer. The target is gone. I was too late."

There was a long moment of silence. "All right. Your contract is over." The phone went dead.

AIRSPACE, FORD MOUNTAIN RANGE, ANTARCTICA. Sergeant Chong was wearing a headset that allowed him to communicate with Captain Lim in the cockpit. Chong stood next to the rear passenger door, his hands on the opening handle. A rope was wrapped around his waist, securing him to the inside of the plane. The plane itself was being buffeted by winds, and the men tried to keep their balance as the floor rose and fell. Up front the pilots were flying blind, eyes glued to the transponder needle, praying a mountainside didn't suddenly appear out of the swirling clouds.

"One minute out, sir!" Chong called to Major Pak.

Pak turned and looked over his shoulder at the men. "Remove the coverings on your canopy releases!" The jumpers popped the metal covering on each shoulder. These metal pieces protected the small steel cable loops that controlled the connection of harness to parachute risers; pulling that loop would release the risers on that side, separating parachute from jumper. Doing this in the air would result in death, but Pak had a reason for taking this dangerous step prior to exiting the aircraft.

Pak shuffled a little closer to the door, his parachutes and rucksack doubling his weight. "Open the door!" he ordered. He reached down and activated the small transmitter/receiver attached to his right forearm, as did the rest of his team.

Chong twisted the handle and the door swung in with a whoosh. They'd depressurized a half hour ago and were flying in the middle of the storm, Lim keeping the plane on track with the transponder. They were at an estimated altitude of 1,500 feet above the ice.

Snow swirled in the open door, along with bone-chilling cold. Pak didn't even bother taking a look—he wouldn't have been able to see more than a few feet anyway. The plan was to jump as soon as Lim relayed that the needle focusing on the transponder had swung around from front to rear, indicating they'd flown over the beacon. The one-minute warning was Lim's best guess, meaning the needle had started to shiver in its case in the cockpit.

Pak grabbed either side of the door with his mittened hands, his eyes on Chong, waiting for the go. The seconds went by slowly. Pak realized he was losing the feeling in his hands, but there was nothing he could do about it.

Chong suddenly stiffened. "GO!" he screamed.

Pak pulled forward and threw himself into the turbulent white fog. Behind him, the other eight men of the team followed.

Pak fell to the end of the eighteen feet of static line, which popped the closing tie on his main parachute pack. The pack split open and the parachute slid out, struggling to deploy against the wind. Pak felt the jolt and looked up to make sure he had a good canopy.

He couldn't tell what the wind was doing to him, nor could he see the ground. With numbed hands, Pak reached down to find the release for his rucksack so it would drop below him on its deployment line and he wouldn't land with it attached.

He was still trying to find it when he hit the ice. His feet had barely touched when his sideways speed, built up by the wind, slammed his head into the ice, the helmet absorbing some of the blow.

Pak blinked as stars exploded in his head. Now the lack of feeling in his hands truly started working against him. He scrabbled at his right shoulder with both hands, trying to find the canopy release; he'd never have been able to find and pop the cover under these circumstances, thus the release in the plane before the jump. The wind took hold of his parachute, skiing him across the surface, his parka and cold-weather pants sliding along the ice, his head rattling on the bumps.

Finally his numb fingers found the cable loop. Pak pushed his mittened right thumb underneath, grabbed his right wrist with his left hand, and pulled with all the strength in both arms. The riser released and the canopy flopped over, letting the wind out. Pak lay on his back, trying to gather his wits. He knew he should be up and moving but his head was still spinning.

Pak had no idea how long he'd been lying there when a figure appeared out of the snow, right wrist held before his face, the receiver guiding in on Pak's transmitter. The small face of the receiver blipped a red light along the edge, indicting the direction of the team leader's device. By following that red dot, the team could assemble on Pak.

The bundled-up soldier immediately ran to the apex of Pak's canopy and started S-rolling the parachute, gathering it in. Pak finally turned over and got up on one knee. He popped the chest release for his harness and slipped it off his back. He pulled out his weapon from the top of the reserve and made sure it was still functioning.

As Pak was stuffing his parachute into his rucksack, other figures appeared out of the blowing snow. He could see that two men were hurt: Sergeant Yong had a broken arm that the medic was working on and Coporal Lee was limping. Pak counted heads. Seven. One was missing.

"Where is Song?" Pak yelled above the roar of the wind.

When there was no immediate answer, Pak quickly ordered the team on line. "Turn off all receivers!" He pushed a button on his transmitter and it became a receiver, picking up the different frequency of Song's wrist guidance device.

Pak headed in the direction the red dot indicated, his team flanking him on either side. His first priority was to account for all personnel. He broke into a trot, his men keeping pace, Yong and Lee gritting their teeth in pain. Pak was actually very satisfied that eight of the nine-man team had survived the jump. He'd expected at least 25 percent casualties.

They found Song; fortunately his body had jammed between two blocks of ice, otherwise it might have been blown all the way to the mountains. As two men ran to collapse the parachute and gather it in, Pak knelt down next to his soldier. Song's eyes were unfocused and glassy. Pak unsnapped the man's helmet. As he pulled it off he immediately spotted the caked blood and frozen, exposed brain tissue that had oozed through the cracked skull.

Pak looked up at Senior Lieutenant Kim. "Have two men pull him with us to the target."

Pak took off his mitten and quickly reset his wrist transmitter/receiver to the transponder frequency. He turned his face into the wind. The target was in that direction.

ETERNITY BASE, ANTARCTICA. "Don't stay too long," Riley called from the stove as Vickers zipped up his parka. "The food will be ready in about five minutes."

Vickers picked up his radio. "Who wants to go with me?" he asked as he headed for the door.

Devlin hopped up from his chair. "I'll join you. I'd like to take a look outside. Feeling a little cooped up in here."

"I'll go too." Kerns grabbed his parka and hurried out after the other two.

Riley glanced around the mess hall at the remaining members of the party. Lallo had recovered the instruction manual for the nuclear reactor from the control room and was poring through it. Conner was staring intently at whatever was displayed on the screen of her portable computer. Swenson was kicked back in a chair, slowly sipping a cup of hot chocolate. Sammy was sitting at the table reading Conner's background binder, trying to keep her mind from black thoughts.

Riley lifted the ladle and blew on it. He'd learned the art of expedient cooking from his team; they had put together all sorts of concoctions inside number ten cans and cooked them over a fire in the field. He tasted his stew. It needed more Tabasco sauce.

Pak stopped abruptly and peered through the driving snow. Something large loomed directly ahead. He moved forward ten feet on his hands and knees until he could identify the surface shaft, about forty feet in front of them. Using hand and arm signals, he sent two men scurrying around each flank to encircle the entrance.

There was a black wedge open on Pak's side, and he could make out some movement there. Staying low, he continued forward, slowly closing the distance. He halted as soon as he saw a small antenna dish set in the snow, just outside the doorway. His team was poised behind him, waiting for his instructions.

Pak stayed in position. He didn't want to interrupt if a communication was being transmitted. The lack of movement allowed the cold to penetrate his body and coil around his skin, sending sharp pain messages to his brain. Pak ignored them. He silently worked the bolt on his weapon, making sure it wasn't frozen.

After five minutes, three figures appeared in the doorway. One bent over and hooked something into the satellite dish, then went back in. The other two just stood there peering out, almost directly at Pak.

* * *

Devlin shivered under the lash of the cold, but a few minutes' release from the claustrophobic underground base more than made up for the pain. Vickers had just gone back in, having hooked up the cable to the satellite dish. Kerns was standing next to Devlin, gazing out at the storm.

The shots sounds like muffled pops, and Devlin turned, astounded to see Kerns pirouette into the snow, bullets tearing through his body. Devlin stared at the blood seeping from Kerns for a split second and then looked up, first into the muzzle of an M16 and then at Vickers' face.

"Please! Don't," Devlin begged, raising his hands in futile defense as the man's finger tightened on the trigger. Devlin stood rooted to the spot, mesmerized by the gaping muzzle, when Vickers suddenly jerked to the side, like a marionette pulled offstage. The sound of gunfire thundered through the howling wind.

Pak moved forward at the run, his team dashing behind him. In two seconds he'd closed half the distance to the door. Pak fired another sustained burst from his AK-47, and the man with the M16 was slammed against the white steel, slowly sliding down to the ground, a long smear of blood on the wall tracking his descent. As Pak shifted his weapon, the second man dove for the door. The man who had been shot was crawling for the opening, yelling after his comrade.

Pak slipped on the ice but immediately rolled back to his feet, keeping his eyes on the door. He was twenty feet away when it started to swing shut. The wounded man reached forward, trying to crawl in; his hand was almost crushed as the door closed with a clang.

One of Pak's men rolled the wounded man over, kicking his rifle away. A black face stared up with wide eyes. Pak looked at the blood-encrusted parka; the man would soon be dead, from either the cold or loss of blood. Pak lowered the muzzle of his AK-47 and fired twice, then turned as his team gathered around.

He pointed at the door. "Lieutenant Kim! Open this!"

— twenty-five —

ETERNITY BASE, ANTARCTICA. Riley met Devlin halfway down the stairs of the shaft. "What the hell happened?"

Devlin slumped down on the metal steps, his breath coming in ragged gasps. "It was Vickers!"

"What?" Riley asked, grabbing him by the arm.

"It was Vickers." Devlin was dazed. "He killed Kerns and he was trying to kill me! And then they shot him."

"Who shot him?"

"I don't know! Some men with guns!"

Riley looked up the stairs. "Where is Vickers now?"

"Outside. He's dead. Kerns is dead!"

A dull echo sounded from above as two shots rang out. Riley let go of Devlin and sprinted up the remaining stairs. The door was shut. Riley slid the blade of the broken pick through the wheel and jammed it against the side wall.

The rest of the party assembled on the stairs around Devlin, yelling confused questions at him. They'd heard the initial rifle fire and had followed Riley here from the mess hall to see what was happening.

"Everyone shut up!" Riley yelled sharply. He knelt down next to Devlin. "All right. Tell us what happened. Who shot Vickers? Who's up there right now?"

Devlin took a deep breath. "Vickers had gone inside after hooking up the satellite dish, and I went out with Kerns. Then Vickers came back out with the M16 and shot Kerns. He was getting ready to kill me when someone else shot him. I could see the blood. They kept shooting—I could feel the bullets going by me—so I dove for the door and just got in. I managed to get it shut." Devlin looked up. "That's all I know."

"Did you see who they were?" Sammy asked.

Devlin shook his head. "No. I caught a glimpse of several people moving out there. I think Vickers must have seen them and maybe that's why he started shooting. Or maybe he just didn't want the message to go out. I don't know."

Riley craned his head up. There were no more sounds from the door. That worried him.

"Who could have done that?" Conner asked.

"Someone who wants us dead or who wants the goddamn bombs, or both." Even as he answered, Riley knew what the immediate course of action had to be. "All right. Listen up and do what I say. I don't know who these people are. For all we know they could be Americans, but one thing's for sure: they aren't friendly. They've already killed Vickers, and I don't think they'd hesitate to shoot any of us.

"Sammy, you take Conner, Swenson, and Devlin to the reactor. I want you to wait by the first door. If you hear Lallo or me, open it. If it's anybody else, retreat and shut the second door, securing that one too. You all should be safe in there."

He turned to the cameraman. "You come with me."

"What are you going to do?" Conner shook herself out of her shock.

"What I should have done when we first found the bombs."

"Maybe we can talk to these people," Devlin suggested tentatively.

Riley grabbed him by the shoulders. "Kerns and Vickers are dead. You would be too if you hadn't acted so quickly. If they get in and catch us, we'll *all* be dead. We don't have time to stand here and discuss things." He pushed Devlin toward the corridor. "Move!"

The four headed off down the east tunnel. Riley sprinted for the armory, with Lallo puffing along behind. He threw open the door and headed directly for the cases lining the wall, calling over his shoulder, "Grab two M16s and two pistols!"

Riley looked at the bombs. He wasn't even sure which access panel opened onto the PAL keypad. On the top side of each bomb were at least six metal plates secured with numerous Phillips-head screws. He didn't have time for that. He needed a more expedient way to neutralize the bombs.

He used a bayonet to open a crate of 5.56mm ammunition. He threw a couple of bandoliers over his shoulder and tossed two more to Lallo. "The magazines are in that locker. Start loading."

Riley then grabbed a crate marked C-4 and tore off the lid. He took out several blocks of the plastique explosive, then looked for caps and a fuse. He found them on the other side of the room. For good measure, he grabbed a few other items.

Lallo was still fumbling with his second magazine, loading it round by round, when Riley finished collecting what he needed.

"There's a speed loader in each bandolier," Riley explained. "Here . . ." He pulled a small metal piece out of the green bag. Taking ten-round clips, he used the speed loader to slam them down into the magazines, leaving out the last two rounds on the second clip. Eighteen rounds per twenty-round magazine: it echoed through Riley's brain almost like a chant as he quickly loaded six magazines. The last two rounds were left out to prevent the magazine spring from overcompressing and malfunctioning.

Riley slammed a magazine home in each weapon and handed one to Lallo. "You know how to use this?" Lallo shook his head. Riley was already regretting his decision not to take Sammy or Swenson instead.

"Come on." As Riley led the way out of the armory, he gave his quickest class yet on the M16: "This is the safety. It's on right now. If you want to fire, you push it to semi. Then you aim and pull the trigger. Got it?"

"Yes."

"All right." Riley kicked open the door to unit A2.

"What are we doing here?" Lallo asked nervously.

"We're going to destroy the PAL codes and instructions for the bombs. Keep an eye on the corridor."

Riley knelt down and laid out the explosives before him. As he was unwinding the fuse the sharp crack of an explosion roared through the base. Riley dropped the explosives and grabbed his M16. He'd run out of time.

* * *

Pak was the first to leap over the door. Kim's charges had blown the door off its hinges and into the top of the stairwell. Weapon first, Pak sidled down the stairs, his men right behind, the muzzles of their weapons searching every corner.

Stopping short of the first intersection, Pak deployed his men in two-man teams. He'd gotten a sketch of the layout of the base with the OPLAN, so he had an idea of where he was and what lay ahead. He signaled for two teams to head down the east tunnel, clearing in that direction; he would take the rest directly to A2 to secure the codes and then to A1 for the bombs.

As the first two men stepped forward into the intersection, a burst of automatic fire ripped into them, slamming both to the floor. Pak slid the muzzle of his AK-47 around the corner and blindly fired a magazine in that direction as Kim pulled one of the men back under cover. The other lay motionless in the center of the intersection.

"Smoke," Pak ordered.

Lee took a grenade off his combat vest, pulled the pin, and threw it into the north tunnel. Bright red smoke immediately billowed out and filled the corridor.

"Go," Pak ordered, gesturing his instructions.

Two men stepped out into the corridor and moved slowly forward, while two more sprinted down the corridor to loop around and catch whoever had done the firing from the flank.

Riley was sure he'd hit two of them. All he'd seen were two men bundled up in dark-colored clothes. He and Lallo were just to the south of the intersection of the north and west tunnels, using the corner of B2 to protect themselves.

He gave the smoke enough time to completely fill the corridor and then pulled the trigger, emptying eighteen rounds into the fog. As he smoothly switched magazines, his answer was dozens of rounds of return fire ricocheting off the walls.

"They're going to try and flank us," Riley whispered to Lallo. "Let's go."

Weapon ready at his waist, Riley moved into the smoke-filled corridor, heading for the door on the north end of B2. He opened it, and just as he slid in, he spotted two figures out of the corner of his eye.

He quietly shut the door behind Lallo as the two men passed by, moving toward their old location.

Riley made his way through the mess hall to the far door. Were the flankers already around, or were they right in front of the door? Screw it, Riley thought. He swung the door open and stepped out. No one.

He opened the door to C2 and hustled Lallo through, then across into the south tunnel. As they moved out into that hallway, Riley could hear voices behind them, yelling in a foreign tongue. He recognized the language with a quiet chill—Han Gul, Korean.

"All right." He leaned against the outside wall of the library. Lallo was looking at him with large eyes; the knuckles on the hands gripping the M16 were turning white. Riley whispered his plan. "We have to cross and get into the generator room. If these guys have their shit together, they've left someone overwatching the east tunnel.

"We go together—you on the right, me on the left. If there's someone there, I'm going to fire. You keep going no matter what. If I don't make it, go to the access tunnel to the left of the control panel. Crawl down it until you come to the first hatch. Devlin should be on the other side. Call out and have him open it, then go in and make sure you seal that hatch and the next one. Do you understand?"

Lallo nodded.

"Ready? GO!"

Riley stepped out, weapon tight in against his shoulder, aiming up the tunnel. He and the two Koreans at the other end fired simultaneously. Riley could sense—whether it was by sound or feel, he couldn't quite say—bullets passing by him.

In the second and a half it took to cross the corridor, he had emptied his magazine, as had the two men. Miraculously, Riley was untouched. He slid into the safety of unit C3.

The scream that tore through the air informed him that Lallo hadn't been as fortunate. Riley spun around. The cameraman was lying in the middle of the tunnel, hands grasping his left leg, blood pouring over his fingers. His M16 lay on the floor, forgotten.

Even as Riley started to move out to pull him to safety, a burst of automatic fire walked up the floor, sending chips of wood flying. The rounds stitched a pattern across Lallo's midsection, the velocity of the rounds punching him three feet down the south tunnel where he came to rest, dead.

Riley turned and ran through the door to the power plant, hoping the Koreans would move cautiously down the corridor. He slid into the power access tunnel. There was no way he could replace the grate from the inside, so there would be little doubt about which direction he had gone. He'd have to trust the strength of the double hatches.

He crawled the distance to the first hatch and pounded on it. "It's me, Riley." The wheel slowly turned and the door opened. Riley slid through, pushing past Sammy. "Shut it."

"Where's Lallo?"

"Dead." Riley slumped against the corrugated steel tubing that made up the wall. "Secure it."

Sammy flipped over the latch, locking the handle.

Riley looked around the tunnel and pulled off one of the green bags he had draped over his shoulders.

"What are you doing?"

"They blew in the door to the shaft, so they can probably blow this one too. I want to leave them a little surprise."

AIRSPACE, COASTLINE, ANTARCTICA. Captain Lim craned his neck, looking out the window. They had just cleared the last mountains and broken into an intermittent cloud cover, leaving the storm behind. The sea of ice that surrounded Antarctica was spread out below as far as he could see to the north. There was no way he could land on that.

"We must turn back and try landing on the ice cap!" he pleaded with the impassive Sergeant Chong. "We are almost out of fuel."

Chong fingered his slung AK-47 and took a deep breath, held it, and pulled the trigger. The first round blew the copilot's brains against the right windshield, smearing it with red globules.

"What are you doing?!" Lim screamed, twisting in his seat, his eyes growing wide as the gaping muzzle of the AK-47 turned toward him. "If you kill me there will be no one to fly the plane!"

Chong's finger increased pressure on the trigger.

"Please!" Lim begged.

Chong shot him through the chest three times, the third round blowing the pilot out of the seat. Without hands on the controls, the plane continued to glide forward smoothly. Chong reached over Lim's body and pushed down on the yoke. The nose of the plane turned downward.

When the angle got too steep, the plane plummeted out of control toward the ice-covered water. The nose hit first. The rest of the plane crumpled and compressed as it punched through the ice into the freezing saltwater below.

In five minutes a black smear on the ice was all that was left to mark the grave of the IL-18.

ETERNITY BASE, ANTARCTICA. Pak looked at the unprimed C-4 lying in front of the untouched safe and frowned. Someone in the news party had been very smart but not quick enough.

"Open that safe, but make sure you don't destroy the contents," Pak instructed Lieutenant Kim.

Kim slid off his backpack and pulled out his explosives, molding the plastique with his fingers, shaping the charge.

Sergeant Jae stuck his head in the door. "They are down a tunnel that is blocked by a steel door, sir!"

Pak nodded. "Blow the door and kill them." Jae turned and sprinted away.

Pak checked his watch. Chong was most likely dead by now, along with Lim and his copilot. Song's body was in the shaft. Nam had been killed in the first burst when they'd crossed the intersection, and Ho had been wounded, although not severely. Yong had a broken arm and Lee had sprained his knee. That left three wounded and four healthy men. Not good.

"Clear!" Kim yelled as he finished priming his charge.

He unraveled his det cord as they exited the unit. "Firing!" Kim pulled the igniter, and a soft burp of explosion echoed out the door. Pak walked in and checked the results. The door of the safe was off its hinges, the contents untouched. Pak pulled out the papers and leafed through until he found what he needed. Kim gathered his supplies. "I will assist Sergeant Jae."

Pak nodded his concurrence, engrossed in translating the documents.

"What are you doing?" Devlin asked. They had secured the second door and now Riley was lining the tunnel ten feet in from the door with small white packages linked together with green cord.

"If they get through the first door and then get through this one, I'm going to blow the tunnel. That ought to stop them."

"We'll be trapped then!" Devlin exclaimed.

"If we don't do it, we'll be dead."

A deep explosion sounded, reverberating down the tunnel. "That's the first door," Riley said grimly. He halted and waited, listening. A second, sharper explosion sounded, followed immediately by screams, faintly heard through the thick steel of the door. "That's the Claymore. That'll make them think twice about taking out this door."

Pak looked at the mangled remains of Sergeant Jae. The corrugated steel tunnel had intensified the effects of the antipersonnel mine, channeling the thousands of ball bearings in a devastating tornado of death. Jae's body had absorbed the majority of the impact, but some of the quarter-inch steel balls had gotten by him, and Yong's right arm and leg were perforated. Sun had given Yong a shot of morphine and the screaming had stopped.

Kim came crawling back through the blood. "I can still blow the second door, sir."

"I know." Pak rubbed his chin. Someone in the news party certainly knew what he was doing. Pak had not expected such a fight. In fact, he had not expected any fight. He had been so concerned with simply getting here that he had not sufficiently war-gamed possible events upon arrival. Now was the time to cut his losses.

"Leave the door," Pak announced.

Kim looked up at his team leader in surprise. "But they are still alive in there. Our orders are to leave no trace."

Pak nodded grimly. "I know."

— twenty-six —

ISA HEADQUARTERS, SOUTHWEST OF WASHINGTON, D.C. "General Woodson has been uncooperative, sir."

Hodges scowled. "I want to know what they did down there! I gave you priority one for Glaston, and you have it for Woodson too."

"Yes, sir." The man turned and left.

Hodges aimed his black gaze at Weaver. "Anything from Falcon?"

"No, sir. There was another message forty-five minutes ago from Antarctica, but that was also eyes only for Parker."

"Falcon has no idea why this Young woman is doing that?"

"No, sir."

"Tell him to find out."

ETERNITY BASE, ANTARCTICA. "What the hell is going on?" Conner asked of no one in particular. She was slumped in a chair in the reactor room next to Devlin.

Riley was seated on the floor with his rifle near the tunnel entrance to the reactor. He held a fuse initiator in his hand. Sammy sat beside him, a pistol in her lap.

Swenson leaned against the thick glass separating them from the reactor core. "Well, we're in a mess now," he said.

"I'm surprised they haven't blown the second door yet," Riley remarked.

"Maybe they just wanted the bombs, and they've taken them and left," Devlin offered hopefully.

194

"But how did they know the bombs were down here?" Conner wondered aloud. She was trying very hard not to think about the fact that Vickers, Kerns, and Lallo were dead. Since she hadn't seen their bodies, it didn't seem quite real.

"You must have a leak at SNN." Riley's words were spoken flatly.

Conner shook her head. "My messages about the bombs were encoded, and Parker is the only one who could have decoded them. You said these people spoke Korean. How could the Koreans have found out about this?"

"That really doesn't matter now," Devlin cut in. "We need to decide what we're going to do."

"Do?" Riley laughed bitterly. "There's nothing we can do."

"If they're stealing the bombs, we need to stop them," Devlin said, getting out of his chair.

Riley stood up and walked over. He thrust out the M16. "Here. You take this and go stop them. Of course, they've probably rigged that door on the other side just like I rigged it on this side. But, hey, I'm not going to stop you, if that's what you want to do."

Devlin didn't take the weapon. "What do you suggest?"

"I suggest we sit tight for now." Riley pointed at the three bags piled in the corner. "There's food in those. Enough to last us a week or so. We also have three sleeping bags. Even if they turn off the power and we lose the heat, we'll be able to survive until someone notices that you aren't making contact on the radio and they come to see why. Or your support news team arrives."

"Why did you put food and sleeping bags in here?" Conner asked. She'd noticed them when they'd first entered and had wondered about that.

"Just earning my money," Riley replied. "Once you found those bombs and sent word back to Atlanta, I figured there was a chance we might get some visitors. I get paid to 'what-if' and 'worst-case' things. Except I didn't expect our visitors would come in shooting. I was thinking more in terms of spooks from our own government. Your sister figured this room would be a good place to hole up until your support team got here and we could scare off the bad guys with publicity.

"If I'd known something like this was going to happen, I would have destroyed those PAL codes and instructions when we first found

them. But I didn't, and now we're in here and they're out there, and
there isn't a damn thing we can do about it."

Riley pointed up. "There's a hatch in the ceiling that probably
opens onto an access tunnel to the surface, but there's nothing up
there for us either."

"You said they spoke Korean," Sammy said. "You mean they're
from North Korea?"

Riley's answer surprised her. "I don't know. Both North and South
speak Han Gul. I've been to South Korea several times so I recognize
the language. But those might be South Korean troops out there for
all I know. There are a lot of people in the world who'd like to get
their hands on a U.S.-made nuclear bomb and wouldn't be too concerned about who they'd have to kill to do it."

"But they'll never get away with it!" Conner said. "I mean, how
can they cover this up?"

Riley shrugged. "I don't know. I don't even know how they got
here. They couldn't have landed a plane in that weather. Maybe they
jumped, but if they did in those winds they're better men than I. How
they plan on getting away is something else I don't know. But I can
tell you one thing: whoever is in charge has thought of answers to
those questions or those men wouldn't be out there."

"Do you think they'll steal our plane?" Devlin asked.

Swenson laughed. "Hell, they can steal it, but they sure aren't
going to take it anywhere. You can't get off the ice in this weather."

Riley agreed. "I doubt they'll steal it. They could try to walk out.
For all I know they came here on some sort of oversnow vehicle and
are going to use that to leave. They're hard soldiers, and they're
used to operating in cold weather. They've already taken several
casualties, but I don't think they expected any opposition. From here
on out they'll be ready for us if we make a move. So I say we sit
tight."

Conner was at a loss for words. She felt as though they ought to be
doing something, but Riley's cold logic made sense.

"So you say we just let them walk away with two nuclear weapons?" Devlin demanded.

Riley looked over at Conner and their eyes met. "Like our boss
here said—we didn't put those bombs down here, so they're really not
our problem, are they? In fact, since these men are most likely here

because of a leak at SNN, and since Vickers was the one who killed
Kerns and tried sabotaging this whole mission, I would say you two
have the greatest sense of responsibility for this mess."

Riley's words were met with silence.

The MK/B 61 nuclear bomb weighs 772 pounds. Using the same
small tractor that Sammy had used to clear the way to the armory,
Pak's men pulled the first bomb along the hallway to the east ice
storage tunnel. There they placed it on a large sled and secured it
with ropes.

Corporal Sun had started the large bulldozer and was up on the
steel grating ramp, cutting away at the ice with the blade, aiming
for the surface. As soon as Sun cut through, they would take the
large SUSV tractor and head out. The SUSV consisted of a large
engine section on treads, which could seat three men up front, and
a second section on tracks, which was pulled along and could fit ten
men and all their supplies. Pak watched his soldiers' efforts for a few
minutes and then went back to the armory.

SNN HEADQUARTERS, ATLANTA, GEORGIA. As soon as Falcon turned
on his computer and accessed the message log, he noted that a second
message had been sent directly from Antarctica to Parker more than
an hour ago. The reply from ISA headquarters urgently requesting
more information spurred him to action.

He went down to the computer center in the basement. The graveyard shift workers were eyeing the clock, ready for relief. The supervisor's office was dark, and Falcon used his master access card to
electronically unlock the door. He sat down behind the desk and
booted up the main computer. He knew this was the one terminal in
the entire building that had open access to all information in the data
banks, regardless of coding. It was necessary to allow the computer
supervisor to do her job.

Falcon's fingers flew over the keyboard as he ran through directo-
ries, looking for the correct file. In less than a minute he had it. He
opened up the first "eyes only" message for J. Russell Parker from
Conner Young. He glanced down the screen as he ingested the
decoded message. Halfway through he froze, his stomach executing a
backward somersault.

"What are you doing, Mr. Cordon?" Miss Suwon stood in the doorway, hands on her hips, her diminutive form blocking the exit.

The words barely registered on SNN's executive vice president of
operations. He hit the command and exit keys, sending the screen
back to the opening prompt. "I had to check on something for Mr.
Parker," he muttered absentmindedly as he stood.

"No one is to have access to my computer without proper authorization," Miss Suwon warned as she strode across the room and
claimed her seat. "What file were you in?"

"I had authorization." Cordon simply turned and walked out. Miss
Suwon, even an irate Miss Suwon, was very low on his priority list.
He took the elevator up to the main lobby and strode out into the
street. The rising sun was battling with the night's chill, but Cordon
didn't notice. He walked to the closest pay phone. When he picked up
the receiver there was no dial tone. Broken.

Cordon dashed across the busy street to the 7-Eleven and checked
the pay phone on the building's wall. This one functioned, and he
quickly punched in an 800 number.

The other end was picked up on the second ring. A mechanical
voice answered. "Yes?"

"Falcon. One three six eight."

"Verifying." There was a short pause as both his code name and
number were checked and his voice pattern was run through the ana-
lyzer. The echoing machine voice came back. "Go."

"Priority one message. Reference file Falcon Seven Three. News
team has found two U.S.-manufactured nuclear weapons at Eternity
Base. I repeat, two U.S.-manufactured nuclear weapons at Eternity
Base. PAL codes and instructions are also present at base. That is all I
have for now. Will try to find out more. Verify."

"Message received." The machine affirmed that his message had
been copied.

"Out." Cordon hung up the phone and leaned against the store's
wall.

ETERNITY BASE, ANTARCTICA, 30 NOVEMBER 1996. The way was
clear, and Sergeant Sun had managed to drive the SUSV up the
uneven ramp to the surface, where it sat rumbling on the ice cap, the

sled hitched behind it. Major Pak walked back down the ramp and across the base to the armory where Sergeant Yong was propped up, back against the wall, his weapon on his knees. His wounded arm and leg were swathed in bandages. The bodies of Jae, Song, and Nam were laid out in the hallway under ponchos.

Pak couldn't find the right words to say good-bye to his soldier, so he simply stood in front of him and saluted. Yong looked up and returned the gesture with his non-wounded arm. Before he had second thoughts, Pak turned and swiftly walked back to the east ice storage room. He climbed up the ramp and crunched across the ice to the SUSV. He got into the cab and nodded at Sun. The medic threw the vehicle in gear, and the treads slowly started turning. At a crawl of ten miles an hour they headed away from the base. Pak directed the driver to their one last stop before heading for the mountains lining the coast. The sled bobbed along in its wake, with cargo securely tied down.

PENTAGON, ALEXANDRIA, VIRGINIA. General Hodges didn't like the role reversal. The hastily assembled officers and senior administration officials were bombarding him with questions, and Hodges, unfortunately, didn't have many answers. Being the bearer of bad news had a historically poor rating.

The ranking officer in the room, the army chief of staff, General Morris, listened to the confused questioning for five minutes before he cut to the heart of the matter. "Gentlemen, we have to accept the fact that SNN knows about these two bombs, and there is nothing we can presently do to make that knowledge disappear. Given that, there are two courses of action we have to pursue.

"Our primary concern must be to secure the bombs. I say that is primary because of the potential physical threat they represent. Our secondary concern is to find out where these bombs came from and how they ended up at this base. Attached to that second concern is to find out why and how this Eternity Base was built."

Morris looked around the room to make sure everyone, particularly the president's national security adviser, was following him. With the chairman of the Joint Chiefs in the Middle East, this problem was his problem. "In line with the first, I am going to have certain military forces alerted and deployed to the Antarctic to secure the weapons and remove them."

"Won't that violate the Antarctic accord?" an air force general asked.

Morris bit off a sarcastic reply. "The accord has *already* been violated. It is now time for damage control, and we have to get those bombs out of there.

"To help solve the second problem, the various intelligence organizations have all been notified and are investigating this situation." He swung his gaze to General Hodges. "I want your source at SNN to find out everything they have on this situation. I also want everything you've received from the two personnel you've already detained in connection with this incident."

Morris fixed his gaze on a full colonel at the end of the table. "What do we have that can get there ASAP to secure those weapons?"

The colonel looked at the large map at the end of the room. "To be honest, not much, sir. I think the closest ground forces would come from either Panama or Hawaii. Elements of the Third Fleet are operating off Australia. The big problem is that we have no way to deploy forces by air without an inflight refuel. That's the most isolated place in the world—a minimum flight of two thousand miles from the nearest land."

"I don't want problems. I want results."

"Yes, sir."

VICINITY ETERNITY BASE, ANTARCTICA. Kim laid the satchel charge in the middle aisle of the Our Earth plane. They'd just located it, parked four hundred meters away from the base, and Major Pak had directed Kim to destroy it. He estimated that thirty pounds of explosive would more than do the job. Kim pulled the fuse igniter and hopped out the door. He ran back to the SUSV and clambered into the cab, next to Pak. The driver immediately threw the vehicle into gear and they headed away.

Three minutes later, the dull crack of the explosion sounded through the blowing snow; the flash was lost in the white fog. Thirty miles directly ahead lay the coast.

— twenty-seven —

ETERNITY BASE, ANTARCTICA. "I wonder why they haven't cut off the power?" Swenson asked.

"Maybe they don't care if we're hiding in here," Conner suggested.

"Maybe they've already left," Devlin added. "Surely they wouldn't want to hang around any longer than they had to."

The five of them were sitting in a semicircle, facing the hatch. There had been no noise for quite a while. Sammy had to admit that she was surprised the power was still on and that the Koreans hadn't tried to finish them off. The more she thought about this, the more it didn't make sense. She was still missing too many pieces in the puzzle, and the puzzle kept getting more complicated.

Sammy nudged Riley. "What do you think about all this?"

Riley considered his reply for a few seconds. They were all deferring to him now out of default. He was the one who came up with a plan, and that was why they were alive now. "This whole thing doesn't make sense. Skipping the issue of why the Koreans—be they from the South or North—would want two nuclear bombs, we're left with the question of how they think they can get away with this.

"Even if they had wiped us all out and tried to make it look like an accident—say a fire destroying the base and all the bodies—they've got to know that Parker's been told about the bombs. The United States would then send a team down here to search, and when they didn't find the bombs, the heat would be on."

"Maybe they were hoping there would be enough time for them to get away before anyone discovered that the bombs were missing," Conner offered.

"True," Riley agreed. "But then they should have killed all of us." He shook his head, which was beginning to throb with a splitting headache. "They've got a long trip back to Korea with those things, and what are they going to do with them once they get there?"

"Whatever happens," Devlin said, "the U.S. government is going to look pretty stupid. How could they have put two bombs down here and then just forgotten about them?"

Riley had been thinking about that. "There're a lot of ways that could have happened. You all probably don't realize the sheer numbers of atomic weapons the United States has. If I remember correctly, there were more than three thousand of these MK/B 61s built. And that's just one of several types of weapons in the inventory. There're easily over ten thousand U.S.-made nuclear weapons in various places all over the world. Add in the former Soviet Union's, and it's a wonder one hasn't turned up in the wrong hands before this."

"Well, let's pray these two never get used," Conner said. "That's one story I never want to cover."

"Amen to that," Swenson added.

Devlin suddenly stood up. "I can't sit here any longer and just allow this to happen."

"What are you going to do?" Conner asked.

"Riley's probably right—the access tunnel is most likely booby-trapped," Devlin said. He pointed to the ceiling. "I say we go up to the surface and come back down the main shaft. They won't expect us to be coming that way—that's if they're still here. Or we go for the plane."

Swenson, Sammy, and Conner all turned to Riley, looking for his opinion. "Well," he said, "we're going to have to get out of here sooner or later, but I think it's safer to wait for later and let someone come to us. If we get out and the weather still isn't good enough to take off, then we're stuck out on the surface if the Koreans are still in the main base. Plus, the Koreans have probably destroyed the plane. It's the logical thing for them to do."

"Someone won't come here for several days at least," Devlin countered.

"I still think we ought to wait," Riley quietly replied. "You don't have a plan beyond getting to the surface."

"Let's at least see if the shaft is blocked," Conner said.

Riley couldn't find any way to refuse that request. "All right." He grabbed one of the chairs and slid it underneath the trapdoor in the ceiling. The door was held in place by two latches. The first one came free easily enough, but the second was more stubborn, resisting Riley's efforts. After a few minutes Swenson took his place and gave it a try. On the third attempt the latch slid free and the door swung down, sending Swenson sprawling on the floor.

"You all right?" Riley asked.

"Aye, mate."

Riley stepped up on the chair and shined his flashlight into the shaft. It was clear for five feet, then another hatch blocked the way. "They sure put a lot of doors in this place," he remarked.

Devlin tried to make himself useful, if only with knowledge. "That's to keep in the radiation once they powered up the plant. It's the same reason this place is offset a quarter mile from the main base and the tunnel has those turns in it. They shielded the reactor not only with these walls but also with all the ice between here and the main base. They probably planned on using this room only for occasional maintenance checks."

Riley grabbed the inside lip of the first door with his gloved fingers and lifted himself up. There were rungs in the wall, and he could stand on the six inches of frame that rimmed the first door. The second door was similar to the first, and Riley went to work on the latches.

Both moved relatively easily. He knelt down to let the door swing open over his head. Shining the light up, Riley wasn't surprised to see the shaft blocked by ice, about ten feet above his head. He carefully dropped back down into the reactor room.

"It's filled with ice. I'm not sure how much of the shaft is blocked." He looked at Devlin. "How far below the surface do you think we are?"

Devlin shrugged. "Hard to say. If we're on line with the main compound, then I'd say about thirty feet under. But the access tunnel slopes down a bit, which makes sense since they would want to have more ice on top to help shield it. I'd say we might be as deep as fifty to sixty feet below the surface."

Riley didn't fancy the idea of digging through thirty feet of ice, or more if the entire shaft was blocked. On the other hand, the plug might be only a few feet thick. "I'll take the first shift digging." He looked around. "I'll knock the ice down, and you all pile it up in that corner."

Riley took the entrenching tool from his ruck and tucked it inside his parka. He also unsnapped a twelve-foot length of nylon rope that was attached to the outside of his ruck, then wrapped the rope about his waist and around each leg, making an expedient climbing harness. He tied two loops in the ends of the rope and connected them with the snap link that had held the rope to his ruck. Then he climbed back into the shaft and up the rungs.

Reaching the ice, Riley clicked the snap link on a rung and sat back in the harness. He reached inside his parka, pulled out the e-tool, and unfolded it. Carefully pulling up his hood to protect his head, he used the point of the shovel to break off chunks of ice, letting them fall down the shaft to the floor. He worked mostly by feel—the reflected light from the room below barely lit the shaft.

It was the sort of mindless work that Riley enjoyed. It took his thoughts off the sight of Lallo lying in the corridor, bullets slamming into his body. And it didn't allow him to think about the fact that he had killed again today. There would be plenty of time to think about that after they got out of here.

HOWARD AIR FORCE BASE, PANAMA. Major Frank Bellamy watched the confusion in his men's faces as they were handed the cold-weather clothing that the battalion sergeant major had scrounged out of the central issue facility. The fact that the facility even had cold-weather gear in the first place was a little surprising, but they were Special Forces after all—ready to go anywhere at a moment's notice. Just because they were stationed in Panama didn't mean they wouldn't be sent to someplace not as temperate.

Bellamy grabbed the red webbing that served as seats on the side of the MC-130 Combat Talon as the plane suddenly stopped on the runway and then slowly turned. The roar of the engines easily penetrated the plane's metal skin.

The loadmaster was yelling at Bellamy to get his men seated for takeoff. Bellamy ignored him. Air Force people always acted as though they were the most important thing in the world and the other services were just training aids to support them. What difference would it make if his men were seated on the web seats or standing in the middle of the plane if they crashed on takeoff, Bellamy had always wondered. They'd be dead either way.

Bellamy was the company commander for C Company, 3d Battalion, 7th Special Forces Group (Airborne). He'd received the alert direct from Special Operations Command forty minutes ago, and in that time he had gathered together two of his teams—the ones who weren't out training—and gotten them and their gear loaded onto this MC-130. The twenty-six men were now crowded in the rear of the aircraft, trying to sort through the rapidly loaded equipment. Halfway up the cargo bay, a large black curtain blocked the view forward. Bellamy knew that behind the curtain were banks of electronic equipment manned by air force personnel.

With a slight bump, the brakes released and the plane rumbled down the runway. The loadmaster must have told the pilot that the soldiers had ignored his order to sit down, because the nose of the plane suddenly lifted and they immediately began climbing at an extreme angle.

"Assholes," Bellamy muttered as he lurched backward and reluctantly took his seat.

His XO, Captain Manchester, sat down next to him and yelled into his ear. "Where are we going?"

"Antarctica," Bellamy screamed back.

Manchester took that news in stride. "What for?"

"Fuck if I know," Bellamy replied. "All the alert said was to get our butts in gear. I'm supposed to get filled in once we're airborne and SOCOM gets its shit together and calls."

Manchester nodded and leaned back in his seat, closing his eyes. No sense worrying about what they didn't know. Bellamy had the same attitude. He bunched up a poncho liner behind his head and was asleep in less than ten minutes after takeoff.

EIGHTH ARMY HEADQUARTERS, YONGSAN, SOUTH KOREA. The U.S. Eighth Army commander, General Patterson, steepled his fingers and contemplated his staff G-2. The G-2 was the officer responsible for intelligence, and it was at his request that the other primary staff members of Patterson's headquarters were gathered in the situation room at almost eleven o'clock at night. The G-2 had just spent twenty minutes going over his recent intelligence data. He'd finished only a minute ago, and the rest of the room was waiting for Patterson's reaction.

"OK. Let me see if I have this straight. All these indicators that you've just briefed add up to level four activity across the border. Am I correct?"

"Yes, sir," he answered. Contrary to what many nonmilitary people think, it is impossible to launch a large-scale military campaign without certain preparations. These preparations are watched carefully by the intelligence agencies of all the armed forces in the world and are the basis for predicting the actions of their potential enemies. Noting some of those activities across the border in North Korea was what had caused the G-2 to become concerned and call this meeting.

"How many times have you seen this?" Patterson asked.

"We saw it during Team Spirit back in March. The North went up to level two then, but that was expected because they do it every year during that exercise. We haven't seen an unexpected four like this in the eight months I've been here."

"What do you think the reason for this is?"

The G-2 wasn't about to conjecture. "I couldn't say, sir. However, I must point out that the activity seems to be southern directed." He gestured at the map on the wall behind him. "The satellite imagery definitely shows the V and II PKA Corps moving to forward assault positions along the border."

"They may be doing this just to get us to deploy our forward elements into their battle positions so they can ID them," pointed out the operations officer, the G-3. "They can pull those units back just as quickly as they move them forward."

"Our sensing equipment is also picking up some tunneling activity in the DMZ," the G-2 added. "We haven't pinpointed it yet, but it's the most extensive we've heard since '94 when Kim Il Sung died."

Over the years three tunnels under the DMZ had been discovered and neutralized. It was estimated that at least eighteen more tunnels had yet to be found, each one large enough for an estimated 8,000 troops an hour to pass through.

Patterson frowned. Level four was the first stage of intelligence alert to possible invasion from the north. By itself, it required no action on his part other than to inform subordinate commanders. Level three—if it came to that—required the restriction of all personnel to base and a one-hour alert status for every unit. Level two required forward movement to defensive positions and the initiation of movement of reinforcements from U.S. bases outside of the Korean peninsula—the real version of the Team Spirit exercise that was conducted every year. Level one meant that war was possible with less than a ten-minute warning.

"How far are they from reaching level one?" Patterson asked.

The G-2 bit his lower lip. "I'd say minimum of seventy-two hours, sir, if they're committed to it. More likely a week. If we get any of several intelligence nodes passed in the next eight to twelve hours, we will be at level three."

Patterson nodded. "All right. Inform me immediately if I have to go to level three alert. I want all major subordinate commanders notified about the level four. That includes all reinforcing units. I'm going to personally call the CG of the 25th in Hawaii and update him. I'll also call the war room in the Pentagon." He turned to his air force and naval commanders. "Please notify your respective personnel to go to level four alert."

ETERNITY BASE, ANTARCTICA. Conner had watched the steady stream of ice splatter down the chute for the past fifteen minutes. Now Riley's feet appeared as he lowered himself into the room. "Who's next?" he asked, shaking ice flakes off his parka.

Devlin zipped up his jacket. "I'll go."

Swenson stood. "No. I'll go. I need the exercise to warm up. You take the next shift."

Riley took the rope off his own waist and wrapped it around the pilot, then he filled in the rest of the group on his progress. "I got about four to five feet in. Most of the metal tubing is still good. It almost looks like the ice came in from the top, or else we haven't reached the break in the wall yet. Let's hope the ice didn't crush the metal together."

Swenson cinched the rope around his waist. "All set."

Riley pointed. "I hung the shovel on the top rung."

"OK." With a weary smile, Swenson pulled himself into the tube.

The temperature in the reactor room had dropped considerably due to the open hatch and the slowly melting pile of ice in the far corner. Conner had gone through the bag of supplies and retrieved crackers and canned fruit cocktail. She handed a can to Riley as he sat down on his ruck.

"Thanks." Riley smiled. He held up a can of fruit. "C rations. I haven't seen these since '84."

Conner returned the smile, then glanced over at Devlin. He looked worn and scared. The main emotion she felt for him right now was pity. She sat next to him with her food and he spoke to her for the first time since they'd started digging.

"I liked the story you did on me."

Conner was surprised he brought that up now. "It was the best interview I ever did." She touched Devlin's shoulder. "I mean that."

"I'm sorry I didn't call you." Devlin's words were almost choked.

"It's OK," Conner whispered in his ear.

On the other side of the room, Sammy rolled her eyes. She didn't want to hear this—not because of the implied intimacy between the two, but because she could see that Devlin's nerves were frayed. As far as Sammy was concerned, things were going to get worse before they got better, and they couldn't afford for anyone to come apart at the seams.

Sammy poked around in her can of fruit cocktail and tried to ignore Devlin and her sister. Conner put an arm around Devlin and started talking very quietly into his ear. They sat that way for a few minutes, interrupted only by the sprinkle of ice from the hatch as Swenson continued to dig away.

Sammy was surprised when Riley slid over until their legs were touching and started talking to her. "You have any thoughts about what you're going to do when you get back to the real world?"

Sammy forgot the murmuring across the room and turned her attention to Riley. "Not really. I just want to get this over with."

"I doubt that you'll be able to go back to your old job, regardless of how this turns out." Riley regarded her for a few seconds. "I know I haven't said much since we met at the airport, but that's because I've been concentrating on the job." He considered that statement for a second. "All right, that's not entirely true. It's also because I'm not very good at talking to people. It's also because I've been very caught up with my own loss."

Sammy met his eyes. "I appreciate that. I'm not really sure how I feel myself. Why don't you tell me what happened? You said earlier—"

She never finished analyzing those feelings as her world went upside down. It was as if a large hand grasped the reactor room and lifted it, tumbling everyone to the floor. The lights went out and a tremendous roar, like thousands of locomotives charging by, deafened Sammy's ears. Her last thought as she was thrown across the room was regret that she and Riley hadn't finished their conversation.

— twenty-eight —

ETERNITY BASE, ANTARCTICA. The fact that the epicenter of the blast was underground muffled the kinetic effect of the explosion but utterly disintegrated Eternity Base, producing a puckered crater more than a quarter mile wide. The fireball lashed across the ice, searing the surface for more than two miles in every direction. The refreezing of the briefly melted ice produced a landscape that resembled sheets of glistening glass.

The immediate radiation was absorbed by the ice in a relatively short distance. The delayed radiation in the form of strontium 90, cesium 137, iodine 131, and carbon 14 was grabbed by the howling winds; as the elements rose in the atmosphere, the radiation began spreading over a large area.

VICINITY ETERNITY BASE, ANTARCTICA. The flash and thermal energy bathed the snowy plain in dulled white light—the swirling snow having lessened the effect—the heat at a bearable level here, more than fifteen miles from the epicenter of the blast. Five minutes before the hour, Pak had turned the vehicle so the rear pointed directly toward the base, but still the shock wave split through the storm and slammed into the back of the SUSV with gale force. The vehicle actually lifted a foot off its rear tracks before rocking back down and continuing on its way.

Pak said a silent prayer for Sergeant Yong, who had volunteered to remain behind and detonate the bomb and not slow them down with his wounds.

MCMURDO STATION, ROSS ICE SHELF, ANTARCTICA. More than five hundred miles to the west of Eternity Base, needles on seismographs at McMurdo Station flickered briefly and then were still. Scientists scratched their heads, perplexed at the cause of the burp in their machines. Dutifully they recorded the data and forwarded it back to the United States. Over the next twenty minutes, other Antarctic stations forwarded the same data as their machines registered it.

The two favorite theories bandied about at the various U.S. stations were either an earthquake or a massive split of ice falling off the ice shelf into the ocean. They were both wrong.

RUSSKAYA STATION, ANTARCTICA. The senior scientist at the Russkaya Station looked at the various reports on the seismic disturbance and noted that a strong electromagnetic pulse had just washed over his station. The former might be explained by an earthquake or ice breaking, the latter by a severe sunspot. Together, they added up to only one answer—a nuclear explosion. But how? Why? Most importantly, who?

Ah, well, the scientist shrugged, that was for people much more important than he to worry about. He wrote up a report and had his radioman send it over the one transmitter that had survived the EMP—an old tube radio that had been here since the base opened. All the modern solid-state circuitry radios had been fused by the electromagnetic pulse.

ETERNITY BASE, ANTARCTICA. Sammy checked her body from head to foot, making sure all the parts were still functioning. Everything seemed all right. She sat up and turned her head from side to side, listening. Someone was moving nearby.

The total dark was the worst. Eyes wide open, she could see nothing. Suddenly a small light flared next to her and, in the glow, she saw Riley holding his flashlight.

"You OK?"

Sammy nodded. "I think so."

Riley swiftly ran the light around the room. Devlin appeared to be unconscious, with several boxes of supplies piled on top of him. Conner was moving groggily, hands on her head.

Riley ignored both of them and jumped to his feet. He shone his light up into the shaft. A pair of feet disappearing into ice were all he could see twenty feet above. Riley turned to Sammy. "Hold the light for me. Swenson's buried." He rapidly climbed up.

Reaching the feet, Riley hooked one arm through a rung and squeezed one of the feet with his free hand, just to let Swenson know help was here. He hooked his fingers and tore at the ice, pulling away chunks. The cold helped to numb the pain as he tore his fingernails. Riley worked by feel, the glow from the light in Sammy's hand doing little good this far up.

"Is he all right?" she called.

Riley kept working. He had yet to get any sort of reaction from Swenson. "I need help! Get up here."

Sammy climbed up to just below Riley. "When I get him free I'll need your help to lower him down. He's unconscious." He shoved his arm up along Swenson's chest and pulled hard. A large chunk of ice broke free, bounced off Riley, and tumbled below. He felt Swenson's body shift and quickly grabbed the rope that was still hooked to a rung, easing the body down.

"Get him!" he yelled as he tried to unhook the snap link with numbed and bleeding fingers. Sammy had one arm wrapped around Swenson's body, but Riley couldn't unsnap the anchor. "Fuck it," he muttered and pulled out his knife. The razor-sharp blade parted the rope with one swipe.

Riley reached down to help Sammy with Swenson. Together they lowered the body to the reactor floor. Riley jumped down out of the shaft as Sammy pointed the flashlight at the man's face. The eyes were closed. Riley used his good hand to feel Swenson's neck. He leaned over and placed his cheek next to the pilot's mouth to see if he could pick up any breath. No breath, no pulse.

Riley tilted Swenson's head back and blew in three quick breaths. He linked his fingers together and pressed down through the bulky clothes on the chest. Within ten seconds he was into the cardiopul-monary resuscitation (CPR) rhythm.

He didn't know how long he'd been at it when Sammy slid in on the other side and relieved him. Riley sank back on his haunches, his arms and shoulders burning with exhaustion. The pain from his hands was now a deep throbbing. Sometime during this process, Devlin must have regained consciousness, because he was sitting up, holding his head between his hands. Sammy had checked Conner and him and they both seemed to be all right.

Riley gave Sammy an estimated five minutes, then he took over again. Still no movement or sign of life. Riley shut down his mind and concentrated on the routine.

"He's dead." Sammy's voice barely penetrated Riley's mind. He kept on. Finally he felt Sammy's arms wrapping around him from behind. "He's dead, Riley. You can't bring him back." Riley allowed the arms to pull him away from the body.

"How're Devlin and Conner?" Riley asked as he finally accepted the reality of Swenson's death.

Sammy aimed the light across the room. "How are you?" she asked quietly.

Devlin lifted up a haggard face. "What happened? Earthquake?"

"I don't know." Sammy looked at her sister, who appeared to be disoriented. "Are you OK?"

"I think so."

Devlin repeated his question. "What happened?"

Riley wanted to laugh at the naivete of the question, but the feeling died just as quickly as it came. They were past the petty stuff now—way past. "One of the bombs went off."

Sammy looked about the room. "How could we have survived?"

Riley answered succinctly. "A quarter mile of ice between us and the blast center. The low yield—ten kilotons. An underground burst, which helped contain much of the energy. Being in this reactor, which was built to contain radiation and is heavily shielded. And a lot of luck."

"I don't think we've been very lucky," Sammy disagreed. "We started with eight people. We've got four left."

"Why did the bomb go off?" Devlin asked dumbly.

"To leave no trace," Riley replied. "There's nothing left of Eternity Base now except this reactor. They have the other bomb free and clear, and no one will ever know it's gone."

"There's us," Sammy countered.

Riley conceded that point. "They probably underestimated the protection the reactor gave us. As far as the Koreans are concerned, we're history." Riley thought about what he had just said. "We may well be history, too, if we don't get up to the surface." He looked around in the dim glow cast by the mag light. "We can talk about what to do when we get out. If we stay here, we'll die."

PENTAGON, ARLINGTON, VIRGINIA. General Morris looked up as General Hodges rapidly entered the situation room. He didn't like the look on his subordinate's face.

Hodges wasted no time getting to the point. "Sir, several research facilities in Antarctica have picked up a seismic disturbance. We've analyzed the reports." Hodges swallowed. "Sir, based on the triangulation and the size of the shock wave, we believe there has been an approximately ten-kiloton nuclear explosion at the location we have been given for Eternity Base."

"What about imagery?" Morris asked.

"We've taken some satellite shots, but nothing can be made out through the cloud cover. That large storm front still covers most of Lesser Antarctica."

"What's the status on our unit heading down there?"

"We've alerted a Special Forces unit in Panama. They're on board a Combat Talon. Estimated time of arrival is 0500 Zulu tomorrow."

Morris turned to the situation room's operations officer. "What fleet assets do we have in that area?"

The officer looked up at the large world map that encompassed the entire far wall. "Nothing in the immediate area. The Third Fleet has a carrier group near Australia."

"Order them to head south as quickly as possible."

"Yes, sir."

He turned back to Hodges. "What about the fallout?"

"Should be minimal, sir. The winds will sweep it out into the South Pacific. As I said, it was a very low yield."

That didn't make Morris feel much better. "What about the Russians? Have they picked it up?"

Hodges sighed. "They must have, sir. They have a research station less than three hundred miles away from the Eternity Base location. General Kolstov has been notified."

Morris took a moment to collect his thoughts. "All right. I have to contact the president."

— twenty-nine —

SNN HEADQUARTERS, ATLANTA, GEORGIA. The computer log showed there had been no contact with Eternity Base for almost five hours. A message had been sent more than two hours ago, but no acknowledgment was received. The support team that Parker had dispatched was sitting in New Zealand, unable to go any farther until the weather cleared. Cordon shut down his computer and put on his suit jacket. It was time to get all the information, and there was only one man who could give him that. He made his way down the hall to the corner office of the CEO.

After checking with the secretary, Cordon entered. Parker was busy on the phone and waved for him to take a seat. Cordon settled into the large leather chair that faced the desk and waited impatiently.

Parker finally hung up. "What can I do for you, John?"

"We seem to have lost communications with the Antarctic team. They didn't acknowledge a message sent a little over two hours ago."

Parker frowned. "Are you sure the problem isn't on this end?"

"Yes, sir. I had everything checked. I did notice, though, that there were two messages sent to your access code only, and I was wondering if they might have anything to do with this lack of communication. Perhaps you told them not to make contact?"

"No." Parker shook his head. "I gave no such instructions."

Cordon proceeded to play his hand. "There's something else I've

216

found out from one of my sources." Cordon's present position was a direct result of those "sources." He often supplied SNN with information that no one else could. It had not yet occurred to anyone at the news show that Cordon might be a two-way conduit for hard-to-find information, thus increasing the flow from each side. He was known as Falcon to one side and as vice president of operations to the other.

"Seismic detectors have picked up a disturbance in the vicinity of Eternity Base. The cause hasn't been determined, although my source suspects an earthquake."

He could see that he had Parker's full attention now. "An earthquake? Do you mean our team could be in danger?"

"Well, it's kind of funny," Cordon replied. "My source told me that an earthquake was the only logical explanation he could think of, but one of his colleagues said it looked more like the signature for a nuclear blast."

Cordon felt no sympathy as Parker blanched. "Nuclear blast?"

"Yes, sir. Of course no such thing is possible down there, so . . ." Cordon paused. "Are you all right?"

"Oh, my God!" Parker turned to his computer and hit some keys. "Come here. I need to show you something."

ETERNITY BASE, ANTARCTICA. Riley felt at home in the dark. Gravity told him which way was up, and that was all he needed. He'd found the shovel still lodged in the ice where Swenson had been digging, and he continued the work. The explosion seemed to have loosened the ice, as it broke free more easily. Riley estimated he had made almost fifteen feet so far. The surface couldn't be far ahead.

Thirty feet below, the mag light made the tiniest glow as Devlin, Conner, and Sammy cleared away the ice. Riley shoved the steel tip of the shovel upward, and a large block broke free. Riley swung up again and sparks flew as steel hit steel.

"I need the light," he yelled. A small pinprick of brightness appeared below and grew stronger as Sammy climbed up to join him. Riley reached down for the light and examined the ceiling. It was apparent now why the shaft had filled with ice. The hatch was breached, half open. Riley played the light around. Both hinges on the far side of the hatch had succumbed to time and pressure; they had popped. The problem was that Riley had no idea how much ice was on top of the hatch. He handed the light back to Sammy.

He unhooked himself from the rung and, after warning Sammy, stepped down one rung and then pushed his feet against the near wall and allowed himself to fall across the three-foot-wide tube. He was braced now, in the classic chimney climb position. Inch by inch, Riley edged himself up until the edge of the hatch was at eye level. Cautiously, he kept his balance with one hand while he used the other to probe through the foot-and-a-half opening into the ice. Small pieces fell out, bounced off his stomach, and tumbled below.

"I'm going back down," Sammy called out as she beat a hasty retreat.

After five minutes, Riley was in a position where he could brace his feet on the hatch itself. It took him a few more minutes to realize that he could dimly see. There was light from above, penetrating the ice.

TASMAN SEA. The *Kitty Hawk* was one of the oldest aircraft carriers still on active duty with the U.S. Navy. Built in the early sixties, it had been extensively refitted in 1991 and then assigned to the Third Fleet operating out of Pearl Harbor. It was at present steaming east in the center of Battle Group 72, a collection consisting of the *Kitty Hawk,* two Aegis cruisers, two destroyers, four frigates, two resupply ships, and two submarines hidden underneath the waves.

They'd just completed a joint training exercise with the Australian navy. Admiral Klieg, the battle group commander, was taking this opportunity to correct several of the deficiencies he'd detected in some of his ships during the exercise. Early this morning he was on the bridge of the *Kitty Hawk,* watching as his ships reacted to a practice alert, when his staff operations officer brought him a classified message for his eyes only.

Klieg examined the flimsy message under the red glow of the battle station lights. He took a minute to think, then he addressed the waiting operations officer. "Call off the present training exercise. All ships, battle cruising formation. Flank speed."

"Heading, sir?"
"Due south."

FORD MOUNTAIN RANGE, ANTARCTICA. The SUSV was two and a
half hours out from Eternity Base and had traversed twelve miles in
that time. Since the explosion the cab had been silent, each man lost
in his own thoughts and worries. It was Kim who broke the silence.
"Sir, you said I would know the plan when I needed to. Could you
tell me when that will be? We have already lost half our party. If we
lose you, I will not know what course of action to take. Nor will I
know what to do with that." Kim nodded over his shoulder at the sled
bobbing along in their icy wake.

Pak's real reason for not including Kim in the entire plan was that
he hadn't believed it would work, and he knew his XO would have
thought the same thing. In fact, Pak still didn't believe they would be
able to accomplish the entire mission despite the fact that they had
been successful so far, albeit with the loss of five men, seven if he
counted Captain Lim and his copilot.

But now, Pak realized, he had to brief Kim. They were committed,
and there was definitely no turning back. And, for the first time, he
felt they had a chance to succeed.

"We are on our way to a rendezvous with a ship—the *Am Nok
Gang*—that will pick us up off the coast. We will determine the exact
location of pickup when we reach the shore and can establish radio
contact with the vessel. The frequency to make contact is 62.32. Our
call sign is Tiger; theirs is Wolf.

"We will load aboard the ship and immediately head for our target.
It will take us an estimated four more days of sailing to reach the
target."

"Which is?" Kim pressed. He knew of the *Am Nok Gang*. It was
one of two dozen merchant ships the North Koreans used for infiltration purposes while maintaining a facade of legitimate maritime operations.

"Pearl Harbor, Hawaii."

Kim blinked. "The Seventh Fleet!"

Pak gave a weary smile. "We are not to destroy the target, at least not at first. The plan is that the mere threat will allow our government to blackmail the U. S. government to do, or perhaps I should say not do, two things. One is not to deploy their reinforcing units to South Korea in the face of higher levels of readiness. The second is not to use nuclear weapons once the border has been breached."

Kim thought about it. "Do you believe that the United States would accede to such blackmail?"

Pak shrugged. "The United States stood still when a handful of their citizens were taken hostage. The threat of tens of thousands of people killed in a nuclear explosion might make them change their mind and question the worth of their allegiance to the South. They blinked when they suspected we had nuclear weapons. Even if it doesn't cause them to do as we wish, destroying their facilities at Pearl Harbor—now that Subic Bay is closed—will greatly reduce their ability to project forces into the Pacific."

"But how are we supposed to smuggle this bomb into Hawaii? How are we supposed to hide, especially once the threat is made?"

"According to the operations plan, that is up to our initiative. As you know, the *Am Nok Gang* has high-speed infiltration craft in its hold. If we can get close enough to the Hawaiian Islands, we can make it.

"We do have an advantage: the Americans do not know we have the bomb. They will think the explosion at the base was an accident and that both the bombs were destroyed and the news people killed. They will not be looking for us until we are already in position."

"Then how will they believe we have the one bomb?"

"Once we are in position, our government will give them the PAL code that arms the bomb, along with its serial number. They will believe that."

Kim leaned back on the rocking bench and regarded his commander. "We are going to invade the South?"

Pak nodded. "I would assume they are already mobilizing to do so."

"Do they really think we can succeed?"

"We have so far," Pak answered evenly.

Kim shook his head. "But it is a long way from here to Hawaii. And then—"

"I know," Pak cut off his XO. "I know all that. But it is too late to question anything. We must do as ordered."

ETERNITY BASE, ANTARCTICA. "What about radiation?" Conner asked. The crater that had been Eternity Base lay two hundred feet away. The edges of the crater were jagged, and Conner had no desire to get any closer.

Riley was tightening the straps on his rucksack. "We escaped the initial radiation because of the shielding of the reactor room. Residual is already up in the atmosphere and will follow the winds. We're all right." Finished with his pack, Riley checked the others, making sure they were ready to go.

Go where was the key question, Conner realized. She'd been so happy to make it out of that dark hole that she'd thought of little else. Now, with the wind lashing her face and the cold seeping into her bones, she wondered what the plan was.

Riley handed her a small backpack. "Let's see if the plane might have escaped the blast." He pointed at the white fog on the other side of the crater. "We'll walk around."

"But none of us can fly," Devlin protested.

"I'm not thinking of flying," Riley replied. "I want to see if the radio is still intact. It's most likely the EMP has destroyed its circuits, but it's worth taking a look." He glanced at the three of them. "Are you ready?"

With two nods of agreement and a blank look from Devlin, they set out. It took fifteen minutes to circumnavigate the crater with a good two hundred yards of safety margin. Conner was surprised at how easy it was to walk on the ice. A thin layer of snow covered the ice cap, and she felt as though she was just sliding along, the brittle snow barely covering the toes of her boots. The problem was the wind and the snow that blew with it. She had to keep her head bowed and the hood of the parka pulled in close. She was walking like that when she bumped into Riley's back.

"Shit," he was saying. "They blew the goddamn plane. Either that or the bomb blast did this. Either way it doesn't matter."

Conner lifted the edge of her hood. There was little to indicate that a plane had been here. Scattered pieces of metal littered the ice.

"Where now?" she asked.

Riley didn't say a word; it was Devlin who answered. "The nearest base is Russkaya, about seventy miles to the northeast."

"Let's get going, then," Conner said.

"No." At first Conner didn't believe her ears. But Riley repeated himself, turning to face the three of them. "No. We go after them."

"After who?" Devlin asked, but Conner already knew the answer. "The Koreans."

"But how?" Conner asked. "We don't know which way they've gone."

Riley considered that for a few seconds. Conner wondered what thoughts were running through his head. His advice and actions so far were the reason they were still alive. Whatever he was going to say, they owed it to him to listen.

"They're heading for the coast," Riley finally answered.

"How do you know that?" Conner asked.

"Because it's their only option. They couldn't have landed a plane in that storm." He pointed at the ground. "And that's the direction their tracks go."

Conner turned and saw the tread marks leading off to the north.

"But they're probably very far ahead of us," Devlin protested. "And they've got a vehicle."

Riley agreed. "They must have taken one or two of the oversnow vehicles from the storage shed. They're certainly not pulling that bomb with manpower. They have a big head start and are moving much faster than we can on foot. Nevertheless, we need to go after them."

"What do you mean 'need'?" Devlin asked.

Conner found it interesting that Riley and Devlin now seemed to have switched camps. She was uncertain about her own feelings. She was so happy simply to have survived that she found it hard to focus on the future.

"They've already shown they are willing to use the bomb. We have to assume they have the other one. It's up to us to stop them." Riley was resolute.

"You didn't want to stop them before!" Devlin shouted. "Maybe none of this would have happened if you'd listened to me."

"We couldn't do anything before," Riley said. "I miscalculated—I didn't think they'd use one of the bombs here, and I didn't think they could get away. Now that I know they actually have a chance of getting away, I have to do everything I can to try and stop them."

Devlin turned away. He seemed defeated. Riley looked steadily at Conner. "How do you feel? The three of you could stay here. The weather seems a little better. I'm sure there'll be someone flying out here in the next twenty-four hours."

Conner felt like curling up in a little ball and blocking this whole crazy week out of her life, but she knew that wasn't possible. Reality was here in the form of a chilling wind and a gaping crater in the ice. This was not the time or place to stand around debating things. Besides, it was not in her nature to stay behind and wait.

Sammy had been listening quietly to the conversation and now she stepped to Riley's side. "I'm with you."

Devlin waved his arms, gesturing at the terrain around them. "It's crazy. We could pass a quarter mile away from them and miss them. And what will we do if we find them?"

"We stop them," Riley answered, slinging the rifle over his shoulder.

Devlin looked into Conner's eyes. "I say we stay here. If we go wandering around on the ice cap, we might never make it out alive, whether we run into the Koreans or not. The blast had to be picked up. People will come to investigate once the weather clears."

Riley put on his pack. "Make your decision now."

"Conner, please stay here," Devlin pleaded.

Conner picked up her pack. What Riley had said down in the reactor was right. She had helped cause all this. She looked at her sister, then at Devlin. "We need to try, Devlin."

Devlin reluctantly shouldered his pack.

Riley's voice was flat. "All right. We go after them. But you three have to listen to me and do what I say without asking questions. This is my area of expertise."

They all nodded.

Riley pointed. "This way." With long strides he was off into the blowing snow, Sammy at his side, Conner and Devlin falling in behind.

— thirty —

PENTAGON, ARLINGTON, VIRGINIA. General Morris rubbed his forehead as Hodges came into the situation room. His conversation with the president had not gone well. The secretary of defense was on his way back from the West Coast to take over the operation, but in the meantime the monkey was on Morris's back.

"What is it?" he demanded as Hodges took a seat across from him. He was trying not to slay the bearer again, but it was difficult.

"We have the serial numbers on the two bombs, sir. They were on the aircraft carrier *Enterprise* in 1970. Both bombs were loaded on the wings of an A-7 Corsair, which was lost overboard during a typhoon and never recovered."

Morris felt the pounding in his head grow stronger. "Where?"

"In the Pacific, to the east of the Philippines."

"Were they really lost or was that a cover?"

"Our data says they were really lost."

"So how the hell did they end up at this place?" Morris demanded. "Who recovered them?"

"I assume the same person who built the base, sir," Hodges replied. "Anyone who could support that could also support the undersea recovery of the bombs."

"Anything from your two guests?"

"Not yet, sir, but we'll get something. We're close. From what we've received so far, I would say that it appears Eternity Base was a privately funded enterprise using government support."

Morris closed his eyes. He didn't doubt that for a moment. Billions of dollars a year were spent by the government on various secret projects. Who was to say that some influential civilian couldn't do the same thing, especially if that civilian had the proper connections in the military industrial complex. "I want a name."

"Yes, sir."

Morris opened his eyes as an imposing figure in a medal-bedecked uniform stomped into the room.

Morris stood. "General Kolstov. Welcome."

The Russian general wasted no time on a greeting. "I understand there is a problem. A nuclear one."

Since the president had informed the Kremlin of the source of the nuclear explosion, a liaison officer from the embassy representing all of the countries of the former Soviet Union had been assigned to the Pentagon to follow the situation. It was part of the nuclear disarmament and control treaty that both countries had signed the previous year. Any incident involving nuclear weapons was to be monitored by both countries to ensure there would be no confusion or misunderstanding that might lead to unfortunate consequences.

Morris wasn't sure which he hated worse—having a civilian superior riding herd on him or the presence of General Kolstov in the Pentagon war room. Still, he had to admit that the provision was a good idea. He knew that if his people had picked up an unknown nuclear explosion in Antarctica and the Russians had reported it as an accident—an accident that had no logical explanation—he'd sure as shit want to have someone sitting in on their investigation. Morris wasn't sure he'd buy a story of two bombs lost overboard and suddenly reappearing at a mysterious base. He wasn't sure General Kolstov was going to buy it either.

SOUTH PACIFIC. The merchant ship *Am Nok Gang* cruised south at a steady twenty knots. The captain stalked the bridge, unable to sleep. He watched as an iceberg, long ago spotted by his lookouts and radar, slipped by a mile from the port bow, the constant sunlight reflecting off its slopes.

This was insanity, the captain knew, but he dared not say it. The political officer's cabin was next to his, and that man, not the captain, held the ultimate control over the ship. They'd received the order from

Pyongyang less than twenty-four hours ago, and there had never been any question but to obey.

The captain shook his head. The fools! How could he pick up someone off the coast of Antarctica? Obviously no one had bothered to look up the facts. The ice pack surrounded Antarctica the year round, giving up slightly to the sea in the summer but never allowing open water to reach the coast. The captain knew the history of these waters. He'd spent thirty-two years of his life in Antarctic waters on the annual whale hunts. North Korea was one of the few rogue nations that still ignored the international outcry against the ravages of the hunt.

The captain knew that Capt. James Cook, the first to sail around Antarctica, from 1773 to 1775, had never once spotted land, the ice pack keeping him well out of landfall. The first party ever to land on Antarctica and spend the winter had not succeeded until well over a century later, in 1895. And in the century since, men in ships had been able to accomplish little more in these vicious seas.

But now, *now,* the idiots in Pyongyang wanted him to pick up people off the *coast* of Antarctica! The captain silently laughed to himself—as if a simple command could make it happen. He would see what the political officer had to say when they hit the ice pack in the morning. Maybe he would order the ship to fly over the ice! Whoever was to be picked up would have to come to them, not the other way around.

The captain twisted his head and peered into the distance as the lookout phoned in another iceberg off the port bow. The false dawn of the time piece was a long way off.

FORD MOUNTAIN RANGE, ANTARCTICA. The SUSV stuttered, pivoting to the right and not moving forward. Pak grabbed the dashboard and turned a quizzical look to his driver. "What is wrong?"

"I don't know, sir. It is not responding."

"Stop." Pak zipped up his coat and then opened his door. He climbed down to the snow. The answer stared him in the face. The track on the right side was gone. Pak peered back. It was thirty feet to the rear, laid out in the snow like a long, thick metal snake. One of the linchpins holding it together had snapped in the bitter cold.

Kim joined him. "What now, sir?"

Pak's reply was terse. "We walk."

Kim didn't question. He rapped on the door to the rear cargo compartment and yelled in his instructions. Ho and Lee began unloading the gear. Sun left the driver's seat and joined them around the sled. They unhooked the tow rope and rigged it to be pulled by men.

Kim used his last satchel charge on the SUSV. The party moved out to the north, all the men straining in the harness. Twenty minutes out a sharp crack from behind told of the destruction of the vehicle.

Riley was channeling his anger into his legs, pumping steadily as the miles flowed beneath them. The anger had started smoldering low in his gut from the minute he'd seen the bullet holes in the soldier's back at the base of the stairs. Then when Devlin had raced down the shaft and told them that Kerns and Vickers were dead, it had piled more fuel on the fire. The last two shots had really ignited it. He'd been on the other side of this kind of ruthlessness before, but it had been for a better cause. Or at least he'd thought it had been a better cause.

Riley was more than willing to go on without rest, but he knew that wasn't smart. His plan was to halt the party every fifty minutes for ten minutes of rest. Every other hour, he would break out his small stove and cook up something hot—soup or coffee. They would go slower that way, but in the long run they would cover more miles. Years of experience in Special Forces, marching with the merciless weight of a rucksack on his back, had taught him that it was the long haul that counted.

They continued to follow the tracks in the snow: two treads and a deep impression in the middle. Occasionally the trail would disappear, covered by blown snow, but it was easy to pick up again. The Koreans were heading due north as directly as the terrain would allow. Riley didn't permit himself to dwell on the fact that they were probably moving two to three times faster than he was.

"Does the sun shine all the time?" Kim asked as the five men huddled together next to the large sled, trying to share some warmth during the short break Pak gave them every so often.

Pak looked up. The storm had lessened two hours previously, and visibility had increased to almost a mile. "We will have no night." Pak's best estimate was that they were less than five miles from the coast. The only map he had was one he had torn out of a world atlas stolen from a schoolroom prior to their departure from Angola. It was totally useless for navigating. He was offsetting his compass based on the map's notation of magnetic south, but he wasn't confident that he was taking the quickest possible route.

Pak's main goal was to head north—as best he could tell—and also stay on the lowest possible ground, skirting around mountains. Despite the bomb's weight, the sled pulled easily behind the five men—as long as they were on level ground. They'd just spent the past forty-five minutes traversing back and forth—getting the sled up and over a large foothill—making only two hundred horizontal meters in the process.

Pak directed them to the left, along the edge of a massive wall of ice that shot up into the sky, where the polar ice cap had ruptured itself against rock. He hoped they could continue bypassing such formations and make it to the coast on schedule. They'd already lost quite a bit of time hauling the sled.

"Let's move," he ordered. The five men staggered to their feet and placed themselves in the harness.

AIRSPACE, PACIFIC OCEAN. "I'm awfully thirsty down here, big brother."

"Roger. I've got what you need."

The Stratotanker KC-10 dwarfed the MC-130 Combat Talon as it jockeyed into position, closing in less than forty feet above and to the front of the smaller aircraft. In the rear of the tanker, seated in a glass bubble, the boom operator toyed with his controls, directing the drogue boom toward the refuel probe on the nose of the Combat Talon. As the cup fit, he flicked a button on his yoke, locking the seal.

"We're in," he spoke into his mike, verbally confirming what the pilot 120 feet in front in the cockpit could already see on his control panel. "Pumping."

The two planes were at 25,000 feet, cruising at 350 miles per hour yet maintaining their relative positions with less than a two-foot variance at any moment. Jet fuel surged through the hose, filling up the almost dry tanks of the Combat Talon. The umbilical cord stayed in place for two minutes.

"I'm full down here, big brother."

"Roger. That'll be fourteen ninety-five." The drogue separated and the KC-10 started gaining altitude, pulling away.

"Roger. Do you take checks?"

The Stratotanker banked hard right, turning back toward home.

"Your credit is good. Good luck and good hunting."

FORD MOUNTAIN RANGE, ANTARCTICA. Riley worked the bolt of the M16, making sure it moved freely. He pushed the magazine release and caught the aluminum box as it fell out. He pushed down on the top bullet, making sure the spring was still functioning correctly, then he replaced the magazine and loaded a round into the chamber. Looking up, he noticed Sammy watching him, her eyes framed by the frosted edge of her hood.

"Do you think we'll catch them?" she asked. He could see that she was shivering. That was bad—he thought he'd planned enough rests for them to make up for the loss of heat. It was hard for him to factor in the others' needs with his desire to catch the Koreans.

Riley glanced over to where Devlin and Conner were wrapped together in a sleeping bag, trying to conserve their warmth, then he returned Sammy's gaze. "Not unless we get lucky."

"Then why do you want to go after them?" The words came out in puffs.

Riley laid the rifle across his knees. His face hurt from the cold and the skin on his cheeks felt like crinkled parchment as he spoke. "Several reasons. I didn't see much sense in doing anything before. I figured we'd get out alive if we did nothing, and I also figured these guys would get caught. I was wrong on both counts: we're lucky to be alive, and these people are getting away. That's two mistakes, and I don't want to go for number three."

"But what can we do if we catch them?"

"I'll figure that out when we get there," Riley replied. He didn't like to admit this, but it was the truth. He had no plan. "We have to catch them first," he said, getting to his feet. "All right. Let's move out."

"We're never going to catch them," Devlin said, peering out from his bag. "I say we stay still—we're losing too much energy walking."

Riley held back his anger. "Listen. If you want to, you can head back to Eternity Base and camp out in the reactor room. Or you can head for the Russian base. Or you can stay here. I don't care. You do whatever you want to." He picked up his pack. "Time to move out." Sammy stood and started putting her gear in her backpack.

Conner slid out of the sleeping bag, then spoke to Devlin. "We can't split up now. It would be too dangerous. Come on, Devlin, let's go. Please."

"We should have gone after them at the base like I wanted to," Devlin complained. "We'll never catch them here. We need a break. We've been moving for over eight hours now."

Riley started walking along the track, and Sammy moved with him. After twenty yards he looked over his shoulder. Conner was talking to Devlin, her head bent close to him. Riley went another twenty yards and looked again. They were following.

SAFE HOUSE, VICINITY FREDERICKSBURG, VIRGINIA. The two men walked down the underground corridor, the squeak of their shoes echoing off the cinder block walls. "I got everything out of Glaston," the short man remarked. "He put the bomb on the C-130."

"Why?"

"To keep the location secret, and for five hundred thousand dollars. His rationalization was that they were losing over fifty thousand men in Vietnam for no reason, so five more wouldn't make much difference. He also killed the courier who accompanied the bombs down there—some SF guy who worked OPCON to Combat Control South, MACV-SOG. He says the SF guy didn't know what was in the crates, but he couldn't take a chance."

"Shit," was the tall man's only comment. "Nothing more on Peter?"

"No."

"Let's do the old man again." They stopped at a thick steel door.

"He's a tough old bird. But if we give him another shot, he'll be gone," the short man warned. "His heart can't handle it."

The tall man's face didn't show the slightest sign of emotion. "We've had a nuclear detonation. We need the name. Give him another shot." He opened the door and they walked in. General Woodson was seated in the same wheelchair they'd used to take him out of the hospital. His eyes peered up, unfocused, trying to see who had come in.

The short man shrugged—it wasn't his responsibility. He walked over to the table and charged the needle.

McMurdo Station, Ross Ice Shelf, Antarctica. The twin-engine plane skidded to a halt and the tractor rumbled up to it. The side door opened and a skinny man with long hair poking from beneath his parka hood hopped out and ran over to the driver of the tractor. The SNN support team had finally arrived.

"Hear anything from Atlanta?"

"Yeah. They say sit still."

The man was incredulous. "We bust ass to get here and they want us to sit on our butts! What the fuck is going on?"

The driver of the tractor was just the messenger. "Damned if I know. Get your stuff on the wagon and I'll get you all settled in."

— thirty-one —

FORD MOUNTAIN RANGE, ANTARCTICA. Walking along with her head bowed, eyes following the trail, Sammy almost tripped over the tread. She looked up and saw the circle of debris from the tractor twenty yards ahead.

"What happened?" Conner asked. "Did they have an accident?"

"Looks like they threw a track," Riley answered. "They must have destroyed the tractor. So they're on foot now, pulling the bomb."

"We might catch them then," Sammy said, feeling a surge of adrenaline.

"Yes." Riley didn't even bother to look at the others. He walked past the wreckage and on the other side found footprints and the furrow formed by the sled that carried the bomb. He set out at an even quicker pace.

EIGHTH ARMY HEADQUARTERS, YONGSAN, SOUTH KOREA. The staff was assembled for the daily 1000 briefing. The mood in the war room was deadly serious as the speaker approached the podium. General Patterson sat in the first row, facing the front. The G-2 was the lead briefer as always, and today he had a rapt audience.

"Sir, unless there is a drastic change in data trends, we are currently less than two hours from going to a level three threat. Our intelligence indicates the entire People's Korean Army is mobilizing. There are also unconfirmed reports that first- and second-stage reserves are being given their mobilization orders. The South Korean 4th Infantry Division destroyed one infiltration tunnel when the exit was opened. Their sector of the DMZ is north of Kumsong." The G-2's pointer slapped the map. "No report on ROK or PKA losses."

Patterson ran a hand through his thinning gray hair. Since taking command of the Eighth Army a year ago, he'd known he was in the most volatile military theater in the world. The two countries were still technically at war, more than forty years after most people thought the Korean War had ended. In those forty years, thousands of people—Korean and American—had died in what the politicians liked to term *incidents*. But what was brewing now was no incident.

The accord that the two countries had signed in 1991 promised better relations, but it had barely been worth the paper it was printed on. As long as Kim Il Sung's son ruled, then only united Korea would be under his direction.

"No indication of any drawback?" the G-3 asked.

"No, sir."

Patterson wasn't willing to wait two hours. Most of his combat troops were based less than an hour's flight time from the border, vulnerable to a quick air strike. Although the carefully mapped intelligence plan for North Korean mobilization and preparation for war was accurate, Patterson also remembered that there had been a very good intelligence plan in 1941 in Hawaii. It hadn't worked too well.

Patterson had authority to go to level three. Level two required presidential approval. He had been here long enough to know one thing: the North Koreans were determined to go through with this.

"All U.S. forces will go to level three. I will inform my South Korean counterpart and the Pentagon."

FORD MOUNTAIN RANGE, ANTARCTICA. "Hold on!" Pak yelled as he felt the rope give way through his gloves. Lieutenant Kim and Sergeant Lee—at the tail end—wedged their bodies behind the sled to keep it from sliding back down the hundred-foot incline they had just laboriously negotiated.

"Pull," Pak exhorted Sun and Ho. They tried to get a better grip on the icy rope in the front. Ho slipped, the rope burned out of Pak's grip as the entire weight of the sled bore down on the two men in the rear.

Lee screamed as the eight-hundred-pound sled snapped the leg he'd wedged up against the lip. Kim threw himself out of the way as the sled ran over Lee's twisted leg and rocketed to the bottom of the incline before finally turning over.

Pak slid his way down the hill to Lee. He didn't need to probe for the injury in Lee's thigh: white bone had pierced the many layers of clothes and was exposed to the brutal cold.

Kim joined him, and their eyes met as they looked over the injury. Lee's face was twisted as he forced himself not to scream again.

"We can pull him on the sled," Kim suggested weakly.

Pak was angry at his executive officer for even saying that. With five men they had barely been able to pull the sled. Now they were down to four.

Pak slowly stood and took a deep breath.

"I will take care of it, sir," Kim said, obviously realizing the foolishness of his earlier comment.

"No." Pak put his mittened hand on Kim's shoulder. "I am the leader. It is my responsibility." He looked down. "Do you wish for some time?"

Lee shook his head and closed his eyes. Pak pulled his AK-47 from where it hung across his back and slipped his index finger into the trigger finger in his mitten. He fired twice, both in the head, then turned and walked away. Behind him, Kim took two thermite grenades off his harness. He grabbed Lee's weapon, then placed one grenade on top of Lee's face and one on his chest. He pulled both pins and followed his commander.

They went to the bottom of the hill. The puff and glow from the thermite grenades flickered on the incline above them as they struggled to right the sled. The fire had burned out by the time they accomplished that and started the sled back up the hill, using longer traverses this time to prevent a repeat of the accident.

AIRSPACE, SOUTH PACIFIC OCEAN. Major Bellamy listened through the headset as the pilot updated him on the situation. "The weather over the target is still too rough for you all to jump in. We're going to head to McMurdo Station and let you jump there—the winds are much lower. We've received word that you will load onto a platform there, and that will take you out to the target."

"What kind of platform?" Bellamy asked.

"Unknown. That's all I've got."

"Roger."

Bellamy put down the headset. They'd received the news about the nuclear explosion several hours ago. Bellamy hadn't been thrilled with the idea of jumping right on top of that. As far as he knew, their job was to secure the site, but the information he was getting over the radio was confusing. The biggest unanswered question was why the bomb had gone off.

FORD MOUNTAIN RANGE, ANTARCTICA. Sammy sensed something different and halted. As she peered ahead, trying to figure out what had alerted her, she realized that it was the lack of something that had caught her attention. She turned around and looked back—Conner and Devlin were almost a hundred yards back and moving very slowly. She had no idea how long Riley and she had been pulling away from them. What had been missing was the noise of their shuffling feet on the ice as she concentrated on keeping up with Riley.

"Hold it," she called out to Riley.

He turned. "What?"

Sammy pointed, and together they retraced their tracks.

"What's the matter?" Sammy asked her sister when they came up to them.

She pointed at Devlin. "He says he can't feel his feet."

"Sit down," Riley ordered Devlin.

Riley shrugged off his backpack and knelt down next to him. Devlin's skin was white, and he was not fully aware of his environment. His lips were pale blue and he was shivering uncontrollably: the early symptoms of hypothermia. If allowed to progress much further, Devlin would go into true hypothermia, and Riley knew he couldn't do anything about that—not in this environment.

"Get in your sleeping bag," Riley ordered Conner. "Zip your bag with his and try to get him warmed up."

Devlin looked right through him. He started walking off, back in the other direction. Riley caught up with him. "What are you doing?"

"I'm going to get help," was the barely coherent reply.

Riley grabbed his arm and dragged him back. He took off Devlin's backpack and pulled out the sleeping bag. "Get in this. You're not in any shape to go looking for help."

Riley quickly dug through Conner's backpack and pulled out her bag and sleeping pad. He laid them out, unzipped the bag, and helped her into it. After making sure that Devlin was bundled up next to her, Riley pulled out his portable stove. Sammy crawled into her own bag to keep warm. Riley pumped up the stove, squeezed starter gel around the nozzle, and lit it. When it was running smoothly, he pulled his canteen from the vest pocket of his parka and poured water into his canteen cup.

Riley made a cup of instant soup and split it between Devlin and Conner. He forced it down Devlin's throat, getting the warm liquid to his stomach. In the early stages of hypothermia, circulation to the hands and feet is reduced as the body tries to maintain temperature in the vital organs. Riley knew that no matter how well insulated Devlin's extremities now were, they would not warm unless the central core of his body was warmed. He also knew that this situation was precipitated not only by the cold but by lack of fluid intake. They had to give up an hour or two of traveling to ensure that they would be able to keep going.

It was now a grim equation: using her own body warmth, Conner had to raise Devlin's heat production higher than his heat loss. Riley could feel the cold gnawing through his joints, so he attached his bag to Sammy's and crawled in.

"What are you doing?" Sammy mumbled as Riley pressed up against her.

Riley didn't say anything. Wrapping his body around hers, he managed with great difficulty to get the two bags zipped together. He could feel her drawing off his warmth like a heat vampire.

"You need to stay awake for a little while," he exhorted her. "At least until we get your blood circulating properly. Then you can rest. You're not too far away from going hypothermic yourself."

"Too tired," she muttered.

Riley considered the situation. He'd been taught the best way to deal with someone who was going into shock or hypothermia was to talk with them and try to keep their mind involved. If the mind led, the body hopefully would follow. He'd have to make it very interesting to rouse Sammy. Riley thought for a minute and then decided.

"Hey, Sammy. Did I ever tell you about my friend Donna Giannini?"

"What?" A little spark of interest from Sammy. "You haven't told me much about yourself or anyone in your life."

"Donna and I were engaged. Sort of," Riley amended with a pang of regret. They'd just accepted that they would always be together. "She got killed last month in a robbery. She was a detective in the Chicago Police Department."

"I'm sorry," Sammy said.

"We met under very strange circumstances," Riley told her. He remembered flying up to Chicago, chasing after the dangerous creatures that had escaped from a lab in western Tennessee, and being greeted by Giannini, the detective assigned to the case. "Kind of like how you and I met," he said.

"Tell me about it," Sammy said, her eyes now fully open.

Riley launched into the story, telling her about genetically engineered killing machines called Synbats, which he had pursued through the woods of Tennessee and into tunnels under Chicago. When he was done, Sammy was fully alert, and he felt they should get moving again. They could leave Conner and Devlin behind and move ahead on their own. Riley could feel the time clock going. How far ahead were the Koreans?

But he was exhausted, and his own body was close to being hypothermic. His hands were already flirting with frostbite. Aw, fuck it, Riley decided—even as another part of his mind screamed *no*—an hour or two of rest would be worth it if they could move faster. He hugged Sammy tighter and closed his eyes, feeling her head nestle against his shoulder.

SOUTH PACIFIC OCEAN. The flight deck of the *Kitty Hawk* was packed with rows of aircraft. F-14 Tomcats, E-2 Hawkeyes, S-3A Vikings, F-18 Hornets, and A-7 Corsairs competed for valuable parking space. On the port side of that crowded deck, the elevator from the first-level hangar lifted into place smoothly, bringing up another aircraft. It was the only one of its kind on the carrier.

The most unusual thing immediately noticeable about the aircraft was that the two engines at the end of each wing were pointing straight up, with massive propellers horizontal to the gray steel deck. The aircraft remained on the elevator as it came to a halt. Slowly, the two blades began turning in opposite directions.

After a minute of run-up, the aircraft shuddered and the wheels separated from the deck. Sliding slightly left, the aircraft gained altitude as the swiftly moving ship passed beneath it. At sufficient height, the propellers slowly changed orientation, moving from horizontal to vertical as the entire engine rotated and the airframe switched from helicopter mode to airplane. When the engine nacelles on the wing tips locked into place facing forward, the CV-22 Osprey caught up with the *Kitty Hawk* and passed it, racing toward Antarctica, 1,900 miles away.

The tilt rotor operation of the Osprey made it the most valuable and unique transport aircraft ever built. Congressional budget cuts and interservice squabbling had killed the program back in 1990, but this particular aircraft was one of eight produced by Bell-Boeing during the original prototype construction. The eight, flown by Marine Corps pilots, had been deployed to the various carrier groups to allow maximum flexibility of use. That innovative deployment idea was now paying dividends.

PENTAGON, ARLINGTON, VIRGINIA. Secretary of Defense Torreta did not seem pleased to be sitting in the situation room at ten o'clock at night after a flight back from the West Coast. General Morris ran a hand along the stubble of his beard as the secretary gestured for him to continue with his situation update.

"The Combat Talon is three hours out from McMurdo Base. The Osprey has just taken off from the *Kitty Hawk;* it will arrive at McMurdo in five hours. The Special Forces soldiers will cross load to the Osprey and fly out to the target site."

"We still have no imagery of what happened there?" Torreta inquired.

"No, sir. The weather is clearing, but the site itself is still cloud covered. We have a viewing opportunity by satellite only every three hours as it passes over."

Torreta glanced at the notes his aide had prepared for him. "What's the problem in Korea?"

Morris frowned at the change in subject. "Intelligence has picked up enough North Korean activity to justify a level three alert."

"Yes, yes, I know that," Torreta replied testily. "But what's this message regarding the *Kitty Hawk* Carrier Group from the Eighth Army commander?"

Morris hated airing service conflicts in front of civilians. "General Patterson wants the group to move north to be in better position to support him if something occurs on the peninsula."

"Does the man understand we have a nuclear problem?" Torreta demanded.

"No, sir. That information is under a need-to-know basis."

"Well, I don't want to see any more messages like this. One problem at a time. The president is not happy. He's already had to talk to the Russian president about this incident, and that proved to be somewhat embarrassing since he doesn't have all the answers himself. I want this mess secured and cleaned up. Do I make myself clear?"

"Yes, sir." Morris had long ago learned not to argue with his civilian superiors, but he strongly disagreed with the present prioritizing of events. This Korean thing was much more significant than Torreta thought. Since the breakup of the Warsaw Pact and the quick victory in the Gulf, many people were getting complacent about the potential for war. Korea had been hot for more than forty years, and sooner or later the smoldering below the surface would break out into flames.

Morris looked over his shoulder at the electronic wall map displaying significant military—U.S. and foreign—deployments throughout the world. He had a feeling he was missing something very important.

— thirty-two —

ICE PACK, TWENTY MILES OFF THE RUPPERT COAST, ANTARCTICA.
The *Am Nok Gang* picked its way through the ice, barely crawling at three knots. Every so often the ship had to back out of a dead end and try to slip left or right. The captain was in constant communication with his shivering lookout eighty feet above the bridge in the crow's nest, trying to find a route through the piles of ice. Occasionally, the captain would use the reinforced bow of the ship to smash through thin ice, but large chunks, some hundreds of yards in width, were more than a match for his steel ship. Those had to be bypassed.

The horizon far ahead was a mass of clouds, but the captain knew that if the clouds lifted, he would be able to see the shore. So far his radio operator had not heard a single transmission on the designated frequency. The captain hoped that the people he was to pick up were ready for him because he did not want to wait, sitting in the ice pack. Ships had been crushed as the ice froze around them. The captain wanted to move in and out quickly and get this mission over with as soon as possible.

FORD MOUNTAIN RANGE, ANTARCTICA. Riley opened his eyes and tried to orient himself. He felt strangely warm, which was a very nice feeling. He twitched his fingers and was surprised to find them wrapped around a body. Then it all came back to him—the stopping, the climbing in the sleeping bag with Sammy to warm her up, the talking. He must have dozed off. The thought of giving up the warmth of the bag was extremely discouraging.

Riley waited a few more seconds, then unzipped the bag and crawled out. His movements woke Sammy, who blearily opened her eyes.

"What's up?"

"Get your boots on before they freeze up," Riley told her. "They're in the waterproof bag near your stomach. We need to get moving."

He peered up—the sky was clearing. The sun hadn't broken through yet, but the clouds were much higher, and he could see farther along the ice than at any period since the storm started. The wind had also died down. Riley checked his watch—he'd been asleep for almost two hours. He wasn't happy about losing that time, but he'd had no choice.

He glanced over at the other sleeping bag lying on the ice. There was no movement from Devlin or Conner.

"Wake up!" he called out as he started packing his gear.

Conner heard the voice as if from a far distance. She cracked her eyelids. She could feel Devlin's weight along her side, and she turned to look at him. His eyes were wide open and staring at her. It took a few seconds before she realized that they were unfocused and glassy. The pupils in the center were black orbs looking into the depths of wherever Devlin had allowed himself to be dragged.

"Oh, my God!" Conner cried as she scrambled out of the bag.

Riley hurried over and quickly examined Devlin. He looked up with a grim face. "He's dead."

Conner was shaking but not from the cold. "You mean he died there, right next to me?"

Riley zipped up the sleeping bag, closing it over Devlin's face. "Yes."

Sammy looked at the inert bulge in the sleeping bag. Things had gone to crap from the moment she faxed those pictures, and it certainly wasn't getting any better. There's only one way to atone for what has happened, she thought. "Let's go."

Conner looked at her sister with wide eyes. "We're just going to leave him here?"

Riley finished stuffing his sleeping bag into his backpack. "There's nothing else we can do. We can't haul the body."

"But you just can't leave a man like this," Conner protested.

"There's nothing we can do," Riley repeated. "We know the location, and when this is over we can send people here to recover the body."

Sammy watched the internal debate played out on Conner's face. Her eyes turned in the direction of Devlin's body, then back to the north where the sled holding the nuclear bomb had left its trail. Then back to Riley. Then to her. "All right."

The increasing visibility had an inverse effect on Pak's optimism about making it to the coast; it revealed a massive ridge lying directly across their path. There was no way around it. The ice rose more than a thousand feet in moderately steep waves for the next three miles.

Pak had given his men a one-hour break earlier, but it had done little to restore the energy they were burning pulling the sled and fighting the cold. He could sense his men looking at him and at the ridge, their eyes shifting from one to the other. Not a word was said.

Pak leaned forward, the rope around his waist pulling tight. The other men joined in, and they began to traverse to the right, angling their way uphill.

AIRSPACE, VICINITY MCMURDO STATION, ROSS ICE SHELF, ANTARCTICA. The MC-130 Combat Talon leveled out, boring straight in for Mount Erebus, twenty miles away. In the rear, Major Bellamy checked the rigging of the static lines for the two bundles, one hooked to each cable. The bundles were tied down on the back ramp. Bellamy's men were standing now, parachutes on their backs, close to the edge of the ramp.

They all felt the plane slow down, and the loadmaster looked at Bellamy. "Three minutes out."

A gap appeared in the top rear of the aircraft, and freezing air swirled in. The back ramp leveled off while the top part ascended into the tail, leaving a large open space. Bellamy stared: the view was spectacular, with the entire Ross Ice Shelf laid out below to the east.

"One minute," the loadmaster yelled through the scarf wrapped about his face, trying to be heard above the roar of the engines and the air.

"One minute," Bellamy relayed to his men, all hooked up to the left cable. He edged out, right behind the bundle. The red light glowed in the darkness of the upper tail structure.

"Stand by," the loadmaster yelled. He leaned over one of the bundles with a knife in his hand, while another air force man did the same on the other side.

The light flashed green, and the loadmaster severed the nylon band holding down the bundle. It immediately was sucked out the rear of the plane. The other bundle went out at almost the same time.

Bellamy waddled out after it, hands over his reserve, chin tucked into his chest. He felt as though he was passing straight through the static line and deployment bag of the bundle as he stepped off the edge of the ramp. Three seconds of free fall were followed by the snap of the deploying chute.

Bellamy guided on the two bright red parachutes of the bundles as he descended. The ice rushed up; he stared straight at the horizon and bent his knees. With a grunt he hit the ice.

Gathering in his chute, Bellamy watched as the rest of his men hit in a long line of white parachutes along the track of the aircraft. He could also see a large snow tractor rumbling toward him, pulling a sled. The tractor stopped and two men hopped off, one wearing an air force parka and the other in civilian garb and sporting a large beard.

The military man introduced himself first. "I'm Lieutenant Colonel Larkin. This is Doctor O'Shaugnesy, McMurdo Station leader. We—"

"What is your purpose here?" O'Shaugnesy interrupted.

Bellamy blinked and looked at the civilian, then at Colonel Larkin. "Didn't you brief him?"

Larkin wearily nodded. "I briefed him."

"If you expect me to believe that you and your men are conducting rescue practice, then you must take me for a fool," O'Shaugnesy snorted. "Do you have any weapons with you?"

Bellamy spread his empty hands wide. "Of course not." Asshole, he thought to himself. O'Shaugnesy and the entire scientific community at McMurdo were almost totally dependent on the U.S. military for support, yet they acted as if they owned the place. Bellamy had not been thrilled about putting all his weapons in the bundles, but he had followed orders. One of these days public relations was going to destroy a mission.

Larkin interposed himself between the two. "Your other aircraft is en route, major. It should arrive in about four hours. In the meantime, we'll put you up in the airstrip control tower." He turned to O'Shaugnesy. "Doctor, I did you a courtesy by obliging your request and bringing you out here. I ask that you not harass Major Bellamy and his men. They will be out of your station as soon as possible."

Under the distrusting eye of O'Shaugnesy, Bellamy's team gathered together and loaded the two bundles on the sled. The men jumped on board, and they all moved out for the main base, three miles away.

ICE PACK, EIGHT MILES OFF THE RUPPERT COAST, ANTARCTICA. "This is as far as we can go," the captain informed the political officer. The bow of the *Am Nok Gang* was securely wedged in ice, and less than a hundred yards to the front, a large iceberg blocked the way.

The captain knew he could probably do some more maneuvering— trying to find the thin ice—but he also had to get back out, and he felt this was as far in as he could go and still be able to turn around.

The political officer stood next to him, peering out the glass of the bridge at the mountains looming in the near distance. They looked less than a mile away, but the captain knew they were farther—he just didn't tell the political officer that. A large glacier, probably the same one that had spawned the iceberg in front of them, split the mountains to the right front.

"All right. We wait." The political officer turned and went back to his cabin.

FAR SOUTH PACIFIC OCEAN. With the assist of the hydraulic catapult, the E-2 Hawkeye roared off the deck of the *Kitty Hawk,* dipped down below deck level, and then rapidly gained altitude as it headed southeast. Upon reaching 10,000 feet altitude, the twenty-four-foot-diameter radome on top of the fuselage began turning at a rate of six revolutions per minute. Inside the fuselage, the three controllers watched their screens as an area three hundred miles in all directions from the aircraft was displayed before them. In three hours, Eternity Base would be in range.

VICINITY RUPPERT COAST, ANTARCTICA. They were three-quarters of the way up the ridge when Pak finally called a halt. It was less than a mile straight line distance to the top, but the wide traverses would more than triple that distance.

"Rest," Pak ordered. "I will be back shortly." Pak had to know whether or not the coast was just beyond this ridge. He was aware that dedication to duty went only so far; his men were at the limits of their capabilities. They needed some positive news.

Leaving his three men huddled together next to the sled, Pak untied the rope from his waist and headed straight up the ridge, ignoring the screaming pain of exhaustion in his thighs. His breath crackled in the brittle air as he made his way to the top.

As he climbed, Pak's thoughts turned to home, a place he had a feeling he would never see again. Even if they made it to the *Am Nok Gang*—if the ship was there—and the ship made it to Hawaii—and they managed to infiltrate with the bomb—and . . . Pak stopped that train of thought. He reminisced about his mother and regretted never having married so his mother would have a daughter-in-law to take care of her in her old age. He was an only son, and his dedication to country had taken him away from his family, leaving his parents alone.

The top was not much farther. Pak slipped and fell, almost tumbling back down, but he dug the metal folding stock of his AK-47 into the ice and stopped himself. Getting to his feet, he made the remaining distance.

Cresting the ridge, Pak stopped and stared, his heart lifting. The ocean—at least he assumed it was the ocean under all that ice—was less than three miles away. Sweeping in from his left and descending to the ocean was a large glacier.

Pak scanned the area for a long time. Then his eyes focused on a black speck just to the side of a large iceberg—the ship! It was far out on the ice sheet but within sight. Pak turned and headed back down the slope.

"Look!" Riley exclaimed.

Sammy squinted through red-rimmed eyes. She had no idea what he was pointing at. In fact, she had a feeling she was in a dream—a very bad one at that. She wished she could dream of warmth and comfort and lying in front of a fireplace with—

"There," Riley grabbed her and pointed again. "Near the top of the ridge of ice."

Sammy seemed to remember lying safe and warm in a pair of strong arms. Was that a dream too? Or had that been reality and this a dream? Which was which? Then she saw it—tiny black figures against the white background, just below the top. An oblong shape on the ice to their left rear. Reality came flooding back.

"Is it them?"

"Yes." Riley's voice held an edge she had never heard before.

"How far away do you think they are?"

"It's hard to tell. Maybe four, five miles."

It looked closer than that to Sammy. Four or five miles sounded like forever. "Can we catch them?"

"It depends on how far away the coast is," Riley replied. "They've got the high ground on us."

Instead of immediately running off toward the Koreans as she expected him to, Riley turned and looked at her. "Are you all right?"

"I'm tired, I'm sad, and I'm cold. But I can make it." Sammy was surprised as soon as she said it, but it was true.

Conner stepped up next to her and wrapped an arm around her shoulders. "We can do it, sis."

Riley's face was windburned, and the stubble of a two-day beard competed with the raw flesh for surface area. When he smiled at the two of them, the lines around his eyes and cheeks cut deep divets. "All right. Let's go."

As they approached a small ice ridge, the Koreans disappeared from view. Riley was leading the way up when he caught sight of something black off to the right. He headed in that direction.

"What's that in the snow?" Conner asked as she also spotted the unnatural object.

"Wait here," Riley told her. He walked forward and stared for a few seconds until he recognized what he was looking at. When he quickly turned away, he bumped into Conner. Sammy was standing next to her.

"I told you to wait back there."

"I'm not a child who you can tell what to do and what not to do." Sammy looked over his shoulder. "What is that?"

"One of the Koreans. Or what's left of him," Riley replied.

Now Sammy could recognize the pieces of white bone and the charred flesh. Thankfully there was no smell. "What could have done that to him?"

"I don't know how he died, but someone put a couple of thermal grenades on the body so it couldn't be identified." Riley tapped her on the shoulder. "Let's keep going. This means they'll be moving even slower."

Pak collapsed. Getting to the top of this ridge, pulling the sled, was the hardest thing he had ever done in his life. His entire body reverberated with pain overlaid with exhaustion. He lay there panting, feeling the sweat freeze on his skin. He knew he needed to do something, but he couldn't move. Not now. He wanted to be home again, lying on the tiled floor of his parents' house, feeling the heat rising through the floor from the burning coal he had to load every evening, hearing his mother in the kitchen pounding cabbage for the kimchee.

Pak roused himself. "The radio," he called out. Ho pulled a package off the sled and handed it to him. With fumbling fingers inside his mittens, Pak unwrapped the radio. He hoped it would work. They had encased it in metal foil to protect it from the EMP blast of the bomb, but he had little faith in the recommendations of scientists.

Pak threw the antenna out on the ice. Taking off his mittens, he swiftly dialed in the correct frequency and turned on the radio. By the time he put his gloves back on, he had lost the feeling in all his fingers. A distant part of his mind told him that was bad, very bad.

He pushed the send on the handset with a palm. "Tiger, this is Wolf. Over."

As each second of silence ticked by, Pak's heart fell.

"Tiger, this is Wolf. Over."

"Wolf, this is Tiger. Over."

Pak felt a wave of relief. "This is Wolf. We are within sight. Over."

"Roger." There was a brief break of squelch, as if the other station had gone off the air. Then the voice came back. "Do you have the package? Over."

"Yes. Over."

"Roger. We will wait for you. Out."

AIRSPACE, ROSS SEA. "What language does this sound like?" the SIGINT (Signal Intelligence) operator aboard the E-2 Hawkeye asked the other four men on board. He played back the message he had just intercepted.

No one could identify it, although the pilot suggested it was Oriental. "Where'd you pick it up?"

"Low-power, high-frequency radio coming from the southeast."

"Airborne platform?" the pilot asked.

"Negative. I don't think so—the signal was fixed," the SIGINT operator replied.

"I've got zip on the scope," the radar operator told him. "We're the only thing in the air other than the blip down near McMurdo."

"Relay it back to the ship. Maybe they can figure it out," the pilot ordered.

"Roger."

MCMURDO STATION, ROSS ICE SHELF, ANTARCTICA. The Osprey slowed as its engines switched from horizontal to vertical. Major Bellamy watched in amazement as the aircraft slowly settled down in a whirlwind of snow. He'd heard of the Osprey but had never seen it in operation. In fact, he could have sworn that the program had been canceled. Simply watching the aircraft land made him question the wisdom of such a decision.

"Let's go," he yelled. His men followed him, hauling their two as-yet-unopened bundles. They crowded into the cargo bay, while the crew chief ran out to coordinate the refueling. Hoses were run from the fuel blisters, and JP-4 fuel was pumped as Bellamy's men settled in. Bellamy went forward into the cockpit.

The pilot looked over his shoulder as Bellamy poked his head in. "Captain Jones." He nodded at the copilot. "Lieutenant Langron. As soon as we're topped off, we'll be lifting."

"Major Bellamy. Have you heard anything about the target site?" Jones shook his head. "Nothing. We've got a Hawkeye in the air, and it should be in radar range of the site soon. I'm not sure if that will give us anything, but at least we'll know if we're the only ones in the sky."

Bellamy frowned. He'd expected something more.

"We're full," the pilot announced.

Bellamy made his way to the rear. His men had opened the bundles and were passing out weapons, each man receiving a type suited to his specialty and talents: silenced MP-5SD submachine guns, PM sniper rifles, SPAS 12 shotguns, M249 Squad Automatic Weapons (SAW), LAW 80 rocket launchers, and sidearms. If there was anybody left alive at the target site and they were antagonistic, Bellamy's men were ready.

AIRSPACE, ROSS SEA. The radar operator stared at his screen. "Shit, there's still nothing out here," he muttered to the man on his left. He'd never seen such a blank screen: not a single aircraft in a six-hundred-mile radius, the Osprey having disappeared as it landed at McMurdo.

He flipped a switch, and the radar went from air to surface. This was a different story. He tried making sense out of the jumbled mess on his screen. The surface bounceback was very cluttered, even where the sea should be. He was used to a flat reflection where ships stood out in stark relief to the ocean. Here ice formations broke up that image, creating a confusing disarray.

The naval officer began sorting out the screen, trying to see if there was anything identifiable. He fiddled with his controls, adjusting and tuning, like a kid playing a computer game.

"Hey, I've got something here," he told the SIGINT operator. Keying his mike, he relayed his report back to the *Kitty Hawk*. "Big Boot, this is Eye One. We have a surface target, bearing zero nine three degrees true. Distance, two hundred seventy-three miles. Speed zero. Over."

"This is Big Boot. We copy. Out."

— thirty-three —

RUPPERT COAST, ANTARCTICA. Pak had been tempted to pile his survivors on board the sled and ride down the glacier, but wisdom had prevailed and they lashed themselves to the rear of the sled as a human brake, keeping the bomb from getting away from them only with great difficulty.

They'd gotten off of the glacier less than ten minutes ago, and now they were on top of the ocean, making their way across the ice pack. In most places the ice was so thick they couldn't tell the difference between it and the polar cap, but in other places the ice thinned out and, with the snow blown off by the wind, the ocean could be seen below. These areas were dangerous, and Pak had his men skirt around them. He estimated another four to six hours until they arrived at the *Am Nok Gang,* which was now hidden by the surface ice.

PENTAGON, ALEXANDRIA, VIRGINIA. General Morris listened to the intercepted message as he tried to shake the cobwebs of sleep out of his brain. "That language sounds familiar," he remarked.

"It's Han Gul—Korean," Hodges informed him.

Morris felt a chill hand caress his spine. "Where did the Hawkeye say this originated?"

Hodges tapped the map. "Here, along the coast due north of Eternity Base. It was someone on the shore communicating with a ship the Hawkeye has located in the icepack right here, eight miles off the coast."

"Do you have a translation of the message?" Morris asked.

"Yes, sir." Hodges pressed a button on a tape player and an unemotional voice spoke in English:

> Station One: Tiger, this is Wolf. Over.
> Station One: Tiger, this is Wolf. Over.
> Station Two: Wolf, this is Tiger. Over.
> Station One: This is Wolf. We are within sight. Over.
> Station Two: Roger. Do you have the package? Over.
> Station One: Yes. Over.
> Station Two: Roger. We will wait for you. Out.

"Oh, sweet Jesus," Morris muttered to himself. He spoke up. "Do you have an ID on the ship?"

"No, sir. The E-2 is more than two hundred miles away and at its fuel limit range. They just have a radar image. They're launching another E-2 right now to replace it, and that plane will be able to get in a bit closer."

Morris turned to the duty officer. "Get the SECDEF here ASAP, and also General Kolstov."

He looked at the situation map. The *Kitty Hawk* was still 1,100 miles from Eternity Base, more than a thousand from the Korean ship. "What's the range on your attack aircraft from the carrier?" he asked the naval duty officer. "More specifically, do you have anything you can put on station over that Korean ship?"

The naval officer didn't even have to consult his notes. "Not yet, sir."

"When?"

"We'll be able to launch some Tomcats in about three hours. They won't have much time on station—less than twenty minutes—and they'll have to carry a minimum armament load."

Morris stared at the situation map. The pieces were falling into place, even though he wasn't sure what they all meant. The North Koreans had one bomb and were making for the ship. Once they made it on board, it was going to be a very ticklish situation. But it definitely fit in with the alerts they were hearing from the peninsula. Morris wondered what the North Koreans were going to do with one nuclear weapon. There was a variety of answers, none of them good.

If Hodges's source at SNN hadn't alerted them, the whole thing might have been overlooked—even the explosion, since no one would have initially thought of a nuclear weapon. The reaction here definitely would have been much slower. Damn, the sons of bitches almost got away with it, he thought. They still might, he reminded himself.

"How about the Osprey with the Special Forces men?" he asked.

"Just lifted from McMurdo. A little less than three hours out."

"Divert them directly to the coast."

"Yes, sir."

Morris looked up as General Kolstov strode in. He idly wondered how the Russian managed to appear so unruffled after being dragged out of bed so early in the morning. The uniform was immaculate. Kolstov's bald head gleamed under the overhead lights.

"I understand you have something new?" The English was perfect also.

"Yes." Morris quickly filled him in on the data picked up by the Hawkeye, then played the translation tape. He concluded with his best estimate of the situation: "I think this has something to do with the mobilization intelligence we are picking up in North Korea."

Kolstov raised an eyebrow. "You did not inform me of the situation in Korea."

"I didn't think it was applicable."

Kolstov nodded. "Yes. Hmm. Well, I was aware of the situation there from my own sources." Morris knew he meant the coded radio messages that poured in and out of the Russian embassy. He had no doubt that the Russians kept a close eye on their sometime ally the North Koreans.

"What are you going to do?" Kolstov asked.

"From the message it appears that the ship is waiting for a party on foot that has one of the bombs. We're going to have to stop it."

"What if the party boards the ship before you can stop it?" Kolstov was looking over Morris's shoulder at the situation board and could easily see that there were no U.S. forces in the immediate vicinity of the ship.

"Then we stop the ship," Morris coldly replied.

"Ah, my American friend. You have no right to stop that ship in international seas."

Morris bristled. "My job is to get that bomb back." He knew they never should have let the goddamn Russians in on this. The guy was going to give him bullshit arguments about freedom of navigation when a nuclear weapon was involved.

Kolstov appeared not to have heard. "In fact, my friend, you are not even certain that 'the package' referred to in the message is your lost bomb. What if you attempt to board that ship and you are wrong?"

Morris bit off his words. "They've already detonated one bomb. That proves they are capable of doing it. I have no doubt that they would detonate the second. I will not allow that ship anywhere near a potential target. And I am sure this is tied in to what is presently happening in North Korea.

"We have the potential here for all-out war on the Korean peninsula, and I believe that your government is in agreement with mine that we don't want war. I am willing to take the chance I am wrong, but I will stop that ship."

"Ah," Kolstov said. "But what if your boarding that ship constitutes an act of war in the eyes of the North Koreans? What if they are drawing you into a trap?"

That hadn't occurred to Morris. This whole thing was so vague he wasn't sure about anything. "Could be," he conceded. "But we're going to make sure."

Kolstov held up a hand, palm out. "My friend, perhaps in the interest of world peace, I might be able to help you with your little problem."

Morris thought he would rather crawl naked over broken glass for a mile. But he forced a smile. "What do you have in mind, my friend?"

RUPPERT COAST, ANTARCTICA. "How are you feeling?" Riley asked as they collapsed to their knees on the crest of the ridge.

"Tired," Sammy replied.

"Ditto," remarked Conner.

"Are either of you sweating?"

"No," they answered in turn.

"Good. Drink half your canteen. I'll melt some more ice in a minute." Riley pulled his own canteen out of the flap pocket of his parka—the only place it could be carried and not freeze—and took a deep drink of the chilly water.

He peered down to the ocean, scanning in sections. "Look—out there!" The ship lay like a black bug miles out in the ice pack.

"Where are the ones on foot? Have they reached it yet?" Conner asked.

"The ship doesn't appear to be moving, and I don't think they could have gotten there that quickly." Riley brought his gaze in closer. After a minute he spotted them. "There. See that large square iceberg? To the left and in."

"They're halfway out there." Conner's voice sounded resigned. "We'll never catch them."

The walk up the ridge had just about wiped out Riley. A quarter of the way up, Conner had started stumbling from exhaustion, so he'd taken Conner's pack and strapped it on top of his own. For a little while she'd done better, but he could tell she was at the limit of her resources. Sammy seemed to be doing better than her sister, which for some reason didn't surprise Riley. When he'd first met Sammy in St. Louis, he'd sensed her strength.

"You two stay here. I'll go after them alone." Riley knew if he didn't catch the Koreans before they got on the ship, the chase was in vain.

Sammy shook her head. "I'll go with you. If it's a choice between being tired and being cold, I choose tired. As long as I keep moving I'll be all right."

"I'm not staying here alone," was Conner's only comment.

Riley was too numb to argue. He took out the stove and got it started. He emptied his canteen into the metal cup and placed it on top of the stove. Once the water was boiling he scooped up ice and melted it, gradually filling their canteens.

"Are you ready?" he asked as he put away the stove.

Sammy stood. "Do you think we can catch them?"

In reply, Riley took two snap links and slipped them through small loops at the end of his twelve-foot length of rope. He reached under Conner's parka and hooked one end to her belt. He hooked the other to Sammy's and then himself to the center.

"What's this for?" Sammy asked.

Riley pointed to the left, where the deceptively smooth surface of the glacier glistened a quarter mile away. "We're going to make up some time going down."

SAFE HOUSE, FREDERICKSBURG, VIRGINIA. The tall man sat in the shadows, watching his partner work Woodson under the glare of the track lighting.

"Who was Peter?"

Woodson blinked, trying to see in the face of the bright lights. The drugs had altered the chemical balance of the old man's brain; reality was no longer a valid construct for him, nor would it ever be. But the two men wanted answers, and they'd keep on until Woodson could no longer think.

"Peter? Peter?" Woodson muttered.

"Peter," the short man intoned. They'd been at this one question for two hours now.

The tall man could barely hear the next words. "The keeper of the gate."

The short man glanced over at his partner and turned down the lights to half power. "The keeper of the gate?"

"The keeper. Yes. The keeper."

"What gate?"

"To the base." Something must have clicked in Woodson's brain, for the information began spilling out. "Peter made up the list of who would come in. There were fourteen. He picked them all."

Woodson hesitated a few seconds, then continued. "It was his ace in the hole. The base. The last refuge."

"Why did he put the bombs—" The short man halted as the tall man made a chopping motion with his hand. He mouthed, "Stay with Peter."

"Who is Peter?"

"The gatekeeper . . . the builder. The man with the money."

"A name."

"Peter."

"His real name."

Woodson blinked and his face settled into normalcy for a brief moment. "Bradford P. Kensington." Woodson gave a dreamy smile. "He uses his middle name for people like me."

The two interrogators exchanged glances. The tall man stood and headed for the door; this had just gone to the highest echelons, and he wanted nothing further to do with it.

RUPPERT COAST ANTARCTICA. "Ready?"

Sammy looked up at Riley and weakly nodded. Conner had a death grip on Sammy and didn't say a word. The two women were wrapped in a nylon poncho, lying on their backs inside a sleeping bag, heads cushioned with their backpacks. Riley's M16 was on Sammy's chest, her hands wrapped around it.

Riley began walking, the rope tightening around Sammy's and Conner's waists, pulling them along on the ice. He accelerated to a jog, the slope helping increase their speed. Satisfied, he flopped down on his stomach, his Gore-tex parka and pants sliding on the ice.

Linked together, the three tobogganed down the glacier, Riley trying to control speed and direction with the point of his entrenching tool. As they rattled over bumps in the ice, Sammy thought to herself that they'd all be very black and blue, if they survived.

They were three-quarters of the way down to the coast, Sammy too numb to feel anything anymore, when Riley broke through the ice into a crevasse. His yell gave Sammy less than a second to react. As her feet slammed against the far side of the break, she did the only thing she could do, raising the M16 up across her body and desperately jamming the muzzle of the weapon into the ice. She and Conner started sliding down. The poncho and sleeping bag fell off and disappeared into the depths. Sammy came to an abrupt halt, bracing herself against the rifle, and then felt a tremendous jar as Conner reached the end of the rope and dangled below.

Suddenly there was no more weight on the rope. Sammy held still, not believing she was alive. Her feet and back were pressed up against the walls, and the rifle, dug into the ice, kept her in a precarious balance across the mouth of the crevasse. Carefully, she looked down.

The crevasse widened and descended into a blue darkness as far as she could see. No sign of Riley. Conner was standing there, her feet on a narrow ledge of ice, looking up, eyes wide with fear. Sammy followed the rope with her gaze until it disappeared under an overhang of ice.

"Riley!" she cried out.

"Yeah. Are you all right?" The voice echoed off the walls.

"I can't move!" she replied.

"Hold still! I'm on a small ledge down here. Let me try to climb up."

Sammy wasn't about to go anywhere. She could hear Riley working with his entrenching tool below her. The minutes passed and she felt her feet shift slightly on the ice, her heart going to her throat. How far would she fall if she slipped? she wondered. Would the fall kill her, or would she lie there broken but alive, waiting in an icy grave for the cold to take its final toll, preserved like the body at the base?

"Hang tough," Riley called up. She could hear his labored breathing. Finally, out of the corner of her eye, she could see him. He had reached up and was digging out a hold in the ice with the shovel so he could haul himself up. It was a slow process. Sammy wasn't sure how long she could hold on, her numbed hands wrapped around the rifle, all feeling in her feet already gone. She assumed her feet were still at the end of her legs.

Riley had passed Conner and was almost at Sammy's level. She carefully turned her head to look at him. He gave her a very forced smile. "Some ride, eh?"

He was now wedged as she was—his back and feet against the ice. She watched as he squirmed his way up to the lip. He disappeared over the side, then his head reappeared. "Okay, I'm anchored up here. Sammy, you come on up first."

Sammy shook her head. "I can't feel my feet."

Riley puffed out a deep breath. "All right. I'll pull you up. When I yell, you pull your feet out. OK?"

"Can you do it?"

"I'll do it." He was gone. Sammy anxiously waited. "Ready?"

Sammy briefly closed her eyes. "Yes."

"Let go."

Sammy tucked her knees in and fell for an interminable split second. Then the rope tightened down on her waist, causing her to exhale sharply. But the rope stopped her fall. She scrabbled at the ice with her dead hands and feet, trying to help Riley as much as she could. Inch by inch, she went up until she could slap an arm down on the surface. The pressure on the rope was maintained, and she continued up until she could get her waist over and roll onto the surface.

She lay there, savoring the sight of the open sky. Riley crawled up next to her and collapsed, throwing an arm over her and pulling her in tight. "You all right?" he asked.

"Yes," she whispered.

"Let's get your sister up here." Together the two leaned into the rope and hauled Conner to the surface. When she flopped down on the ice and stared up at the sky, Riley leaned over her.

"Do you want to go on?"

Conner shook herself, and with great effort she managed to stand. "Yes."

ISA HEADQUARTERS, SOUTHWEST OF WASHINGTON, D.C. "What does the president want done?" the bald man at the end of the table asked General Hodges.

"The president wants the matter kept quiet." Hodges nervously fingered his eelskin briefcase.

A snort of laughter. "That's damn near impossible. What's his second choice?"

"He needs to satisfy the Russians that this wasn't a government-sponsored action in Antarctica that malfunctioned and that we're trying to cover ourselves by this story. We need to pick up Kensington."

"Kensington is the second richest man in America," the bald man replied. "He's supported every Republican president for the past thirty years." He picked up a file. "Since we uncovered the name, we've done some checking. The facts fit. Kensington helped us recover the codes from that Soviet sub off Japan back in '68 using his oil exploratory deep-sea minisub. Apparently he used the same minisub to recover the two nuclear bombs on that A-7.

"Kensington has had extensive contact with many government agencies—"

"To include this one!" Hodges threw in.

The bald man acknowledged that with a tilt of his head. "Yes, including this one. And the CIA. And the FBI. I understand he also paid people to do covert work for the Republican Party. That would make interesting news.

"Kensington had the government contacts, the subsidiary companies, and the money to get Eternity Base built as his own personal bomb shelter. We've discovered that his nuclear power plant in Utah had a contingency plan to load rods onto a plane with a three-hour notice. The specifications fit the power plant at Eternity Base.

"Kensington also is the man behind a very large number of defense manufacturing companies in this country. Even with all the cutbacks, he still has his finger in a lot of pies.

"I wonder what names would be on the list of people that Kensington planned to bring down to Eternity Base in case of nuclear war. I'm sure we would not want that to become public record.

"There are other things we've discovered, but we won't go into them right now." The bald man closed the file with a snap. "Again. What does the president want done?"

"Kensington has gone from an asset to a liability." Hodges stood. "I'll inform the president that it will be taken care of."

The bald man did not seem happy with the decision, but he nodded. "All right."

— thirty-four —

RUPPERT COAST, ANTARCTICA, 1 DECEMBER 1996. "Come on!" Pak exhorted his three exhausted partners. "There's the ship."

The four leaned into the rope, and the sled creaked along the ice, making way toward the ship now slightly less than two miles away.

"How close . . . do you . . . have to . . . get?" Sammy asked, trying to catch her breath as they crossed a high point where two sheets of ice had buckled together.

"A quarter mile at maximum. I'd like to get closer than that," Riley replied. They were at least three-quarters of a mile behind the Koreans. Riley's best estimate was that it was going to be close, very close.

He hadn't mentioned the additional problem of weapons on board the ship. If it carried weapons, Riley had to assume that once he fired on the party pulling the sled, the ship would return fire. He didn't fancy the idea of being caught out on this ice in a running gun battle—the forseeable conclusion wasn't favorable for him and the two sisters.

As they went along, Riley noticed black spots on the ice about three hundred yards to the left. He dropped down, out of sight, pulling Sammy and Conner with him. An ambush? He raised his head and peered at the figures, finally realizing what he was looking at. Seals were lying near a water hole they'd broken in the ice. It was the first sign of animal life they'd seen.

260

* * *

"There they are!" the political officer exclaimed, pointing off the starboard bow.

The captain trained his telescope in that direction. "There are four men, and they are pulling a sled with something on it."

"I want you to gather a party of men to go out there and help them."

The captain wasn't thrilled with that idea. His men were civilians, and he didn't want to risk them on the ice. But he turned to his executive officer and reluctantly relayed the order.

Seven hundred yards off the port side, the ice suddenly erupted, three long black shafts pushing through. The shafts abruptly widened and a massive black conning tower appeared, tossing aside the ice like child's blocks. The ice behind the tower split to reveal a long black deck sloping 150 feet behind the tower. The exposed portion of the vessel was almost as long as the *Am Nok Gang.*

"What is that?" the political officer gasped.

"A submarine," the captain replied, stunned at the sight.

"I know that, you fool," the officer snapped. "Whose submarine? American?"

"I don't know."

"What should we do?"

The captain turned to look at the officer. "There is nothing we can do." He nodded at the black hull. "We wait to see what *they* do."

Pak and his men halted, staring past the ship at the submarine. He knew in his heart that it was all over. Even if they made it to the ship, the Americans would never let them sail away. He wondered how the plan had failed.

"Sir?" Kim turned to him for instructions.

Pak looked at his executive officer. "We go to the ship. Quickly."

The four men strained against the rope.

Riley started sprinting as soon as the submarine broke surface, leaving Sammy and Conner behind, yelling at them to stay put. He passed four seals around a small circle of open water. The distance was now down to five hundred yards. Another two hundred and he could fire.

* * *

The present Hawkeye on station was the third one rotated in; the earlier ones had exhausted their fuel supplies and returned to the *Kitty Hawk*. The radar operator had picked up the sub as soon as the mast breached the ice. Now he was busy guiding in the Osprey and the two F-14 Tomcats from the *Kitty Hawk,* matching the glowing green dots representing the planes with those of the ship and submarine.

"Eagle One, this Eye One. Assume heading eight seven degrees, range one hundred fifty kilometers and closing. You've got a sub on the surface, about seven hundred meters to the east of the ship. Over."

"Roger. Out." The acknowledgment from the pilot of the lead Tomcat was heard in the operator's left ear. In his right ear was the tactical center of the *Kitty Hawk* demanding information.

"Eye One, this is Big Boot. Do you have an ID on the submarine yet? Over."

"Negative. Over."

"Eye One, what is Eagle's ETA? Over."

"ETA five minutes. Over."

Pulling at the front end of the rope, Pak felt the ice crackle beneath him. He halted and looked down in surprise. In his haste he'd run onto a thinner portion. There was no way it would support the weight of the bomb, twenty feet behind him.

"To the left," he ordered Kim, Sun, and Ho.

As they turned, the thin ice exploded upward, and Pak caught a glimpse of a massive black and white snout rising into the air. The snout split in two, revealing rows of glistening white teeth. The forward half of the creature slammed down onto the ice, half out of the water, and the teeth closed on Kim.

The XO's scream was cut short as the killer whale slid back with its meal into the hole it had just made in the ice. Pak pulled out his knife and desperately slashed at the rope around his waist as he was dragged toward the hole. He succeeded just inches short of the freezing water. Ho and Sun were not so fortunate. Scrabbling at the ice as they moved inexorably toward the hole, the men were pulled in. Pak had a last glimpse of Ho's pleading eyes as the rope, still attached to Kim and Sun, drew him under the ice.

Pak quickly cut the rope attached to the sled and scrambled away from the thin ice.

"What happened?" screamed the political officer.

"Killer whale," the captain curtly replied, saying a mental prayer for the three men. "That's how they hunt seals." He removed his eye from the telescope and turned to look at the political officer. "Men. Seals. Not much difference is there? What do we do now?"

They both twisted their heads as two gray jets came roaring in low over the ice from the west.

"Big Boot, this is Eagle One. Over."

"This is Big Boot. Over."

"Roger. We've got a visual on the sub. You've got one Russian Delta class boomer on ice. Over."

There was a pause. "Roger. Maintain station and await further instructions. Break. Viking Two, break from patrol and head for target site, maximum speed. Over."

"This is Viking Two. Roger. Out."

Aboard the E-2 the radar operator exchanged a worried look with the SIGINT operator. The Delta was the largest submarine in the world and carried twelve missile-launch systems for multiple-warhead ballistic missiles. What was it doing here?

The Viking diverted by the *Kitty Hawk*'s tactical operations center was its primary antisubmarine defense system—a plane totally dedicated to killing submarines, carrying both torpedoes and depth charges for that purpose.

The radar operator checked his screen. He estimated another fifty minutes before the Viking arrived. He had a feeling that whatever was being played out below would be over long before the Viking arrived.

His eyebrows raised at the next message from *Kitty Hawk*. "Eagle One, this is Big Boot. Delta submarine is to be considered friendly. I say again. Delta submarine is to be considered friendly. Out."

Riley came to a screeching halt after witnessing the whale attack. He looked down and realized he could see a dark shape through the ice. He quickly sidled left to thicker ice, figuring that if he couldn't see the whale through the ice, it couldn't see him.

He twisted his head and watched as the two planes with U.S. Navy markings flew by once more. About fucking time, he thought. Of course, they couldn't spot one man on the ice.

Riley moved forward more slowly, aware that the lone man ahead had a weapon that could kill him as easily as the whales could.

Pak glanced up as American planes flew by. He looked to the whaling ship and beyond it to the submarine. He could not pull the bomb by himself. There was only one thing left to do. He reached inside his parka and took out a sheet of paper.

Pak bent over the gray carcass of the bomb. He had done this once before, so he knew the preliminary steps. He stripped off his gloves—ignoring the knife of cold that stabbed into every joint—and flipped open the latch on the control access panel.

"The submarine is signaling us!" the ship's executive officer exclaimed.

The captain swung his telescope around to port. A light on the conning tower was flashing international Morse code. "Copy!" the captain ordered. Something was going up one of the tall black masts on the conning tower. The captain focused on that. Halfway up, the wind caught it. A Russian flag unfurled.

The captain pulled back from the telescope and turned to his executive officer. "What does the message say?"

The XO ran a tongue over his lips and glanced at the political officer.

"Go ahead!" the captain insisted.

"Sir, it says: L-E-A-V-E-N-O-W."

The captain ran his eyes over the familiar lines of his ship. Slowly he reached for the speaking tube. "Engine room. Port engine. One-quarter, reverse."

"What are you doing?" the political officer demanded, grabbing the captain by his coat.

"I am going home," the captain replied.

"You cannot. I forbid it!"

The captain pointed out the window to the left. "The Russians are there, and they say leave." He pointed up. "The Americans are there, and I believe they want us to leave. We have no weapons." He pointed out to the ice. "He is alone out there. We cannot help him." The ship shuddered as the engines engaged for the first time in hours and the newly formed ice cracked around the hull. "We leave."

Riley picked his way through the ice, avoiding the thinner sections and at the same time making sure he was out of sight of the Korean. He wondered what the man would do now—there was no way he could pull the bomb by himself.

Riley's head snapped up as he heard the throb of engines and the crack of ice. The civilian ship was moving very slowly, turning away. He looked farther and saw the flag above the submarine. It didn't make sense, but he didn't care. It was over. He continued forward, going slower, making sure he didn't expose himself to a chance shot from the man trapped on the ice.

"Big Boot, this is Eagle One. The ship is leaving. Over."

"Roger. Break. Eye One, this is Big Boot. Status of the Osprey? Over."

"Fifteen minutes out. Over."

"Roger. Break. Eagle One. Is there anything on the ice? Over."

"Wait one. Over."

Pak winced as a jet screamed overhead again, barely thirty feet above the ice, but he didn't look up. His numbed fingers continued working.

"Big Boot, this is Eagle One." The naval flight officer in the backseat of the Tomcat glanced down at his video display and flicked the controls. The TV automatic target identification system blanked and then showed in slow motion what the camera had picked up on the previous pass.

"Uh, this is Eagle One. We've got four figures on the ice. One with . . ." The officer peered closer. "One with our object. It is not on board the ship. I say again. It is not on board the ship. Over."

"Roger, Eagle One. Go to altitude and maintain position. Stinger will take care of this when they arrive. Over."

"Roger. Out."

Riley did a quick peek over a block of ice, then stopped and took a slower look. The Korean was leaning over the bomb, a hundred yards away, and his arms were moving.

"Oh, shit!" Riley exclaimed. He stood up and began running.

— thirty-five —

RUPPERT COAST, ANTARCTICA. With shaking fingers, Pak punched in the six-digit code, one number at a time. He cursed as his numbed fingertip slipped on the fifth digit and struck the wrong number on the numeric pad inside the access panel. The LED screen cleared, and Pak took a deep breath. Once more he began.

Riley was less than fifty yards away. He threw the M16 to his shoulder and stared down the iron sights. The head of the Korean wavered in them. Riley drew in a frigid breath and held it. The sights steadied and he pulled the trigger. The comforting recoil of the weapon was erased as the round impacted with the ice that had jammed into the barrel when Sammy used it to break her fall. Riley felt the pain in his hands as the breach exploded.

Riley realized his error in a heartbeat as the Korean lifted his head at the sound of the small explosion and stared at him, their eyes locking over the bomb.

Where had he come from? Pak wondered as he swung up his AK-47, pressing the metal folding stock into his shoulder. His eye never left the other man's as he lined up the front sight post with the rear and pulled the trigger.

The rounds roared across the fifty yards, slamming into the man and throwing him onto the ice. Pak let the weapon fall back on its sling and checked the piece of paper again. What number had he been on? His fatigued mind struggled to remember.

Riley's breath came in deep, painful gasps. His right side was on fire, and he could feel the blood seeping into his layers of clothing. He knew he had to move. He put every ounce of energy into his legs. Nothing. Riley tried to scream, but a moan was all he managed. He focused his mind: he had to stop the Korean, or the Russian sub would be destroyed and he would die.

Pak tried to concentrate on the LED screen. Yes, he was up to the fourth number. He held his finger over the keys. He had no feeling in his hand anymore, so he guided it down by sight. When the dead finger rested on the proper number, he pushed.

The fifth now. Pak looked at the number on the code sheet. He matched it with the keyboard. His right hand would no longer hold steady. Pak took his left hand and placed it over his right forearm, steadying it. He pushed down and glanced up at the LED screen. The ENTER sign was still flashing on the top. Yes, the five were correct.

Pak checked the sixth number. He forced his finger over and down. He hesitated as he thought of his family, so far away in Korea. Pak sighed. With his finger an inch away from the keyboard, stars exploded on the right side of Pak's head. He rolled away from the bomb onto the ice and looked up, trying to see his attacker.

A figure loomed above. Pak put his arms up to block the blow that swung down on him. He felt his left forearm shatter as steel hit bone. The pain brought his foggy mind into sharp focus. Pak was desperately reaching for his AK-47 on its sling when he stared into the greenest eyes he'd ever seen. A woman!

She swung the shovel again. He rolled away from the next blow but slid much farther than he'd intended, trying too late to slow his momentum.

Sammy collapsed to her knees, dropping the bloody entrenching tool as the Korean fell into the water hole. She started to stand when the man suddenly surged out of the water and grabbed her left forearm with his right hand.

The Korean pulled her down to the edge of the hole. He looked up at her, his dark eyes boring in. Sammy felt herself drawn in by them, bending over, her face lowering down to the water so close to being frozen. The entrenching tool blurred by the side of her face and smashed into the Korean's head. His grip loosened on her arm and he slipped beneath the surface. Sammy collapsed to the ice and Conner slid down beside her, dropping the e-tool and wrapping her sister in her arms.

For a long minute, they held onto each other. Then they stood. There was no sign of the Korean. The bomb sat alone on the ice near them. Sammy and Conner carefully walked over to it. The cover on the control panel was off.

"Oh, shit," Sammy muttered. She turned away and looked back. "Dave!"

— thirty-six —

RUPPERT COAST, ANTARCTICA. Riley had managed to crawl almost ten feet, leaving a trail of red on the ice, before he could go no farther. A logical part of his mind recognized that he was going into shock from the combination of loss of blood and cold, but the fact didn't bother him very much. It would be only moments before the Korean finished entering the code and the bomb went off, so oblivion wasn't far off either way.

As he retreated into unconsciousness, a persistent voice calling his name intruded. With great difficulty, Riley cracked his eyes and peered up. A sharp blow across his cheek barely elicited a response from his frozen skin.

"Wake up, goddamnit!"

Riley found a scrap of energy and tried to focus. "What?" he muttered.

"The Korean was messing with the bomb. We stopped him, but I need to know if he finished arming it." Sammy leaned close. "Are you hurt bad?"

"I'm all right," Riley said. "Take me to the bomb."

As Sammy grabbed his arms, the pain brought him fully alert. He tried to help with little pushing motions of his feet as Sammy and Conner dragged him across the ice.

"I can't land on the ice," the pilot said for the third time. "This aircraft needs fifty-six inches of solid ice to support it, and you can't tell that by looking out the window." The Osprey's engines were in the helicopter position and they were cruising at forty knots above the ice.

Bellamy accepted the inevitable. "All right. Then give me a hover and we'll fast-rope out."

"OK."

Bellamy turned to Captain Manchester and signaled. Manchester and an NCO began rigging the fast rope to bolts in the ceiling of the Osprey, while Bellamy looked out over the pilot's shoulder. He could see both the submarine and the ship, which was slowly making its way out of the ice pack.

"Where's the bomb?" he asked.

The pilot did a gentle bank right. "There," he pointed.

The sled was a long black spot on the ice. Bellamy noted the three figures, two dragging one, less than twenty feet away. He ran back to the rear of the plane as his team lined up on the rope.

"There're three people on the ice near the bomb. They make a move for it, take them out."

The first man nodded and slipped the selector switch on his MP5 sub off safe. The plane came to a halt, and Manchester threw open the door.

Sammy and Conner propped up Riley so he could look at the LED screen. He scanned it for ten long seconds and then shook his head. "He entered five of the six numbers on the PAL code. You stopped him before he could enter the last one. It's all right. We're safe."

They looked up as the Osprey came to a hover overhead and a thick rope uncoiled out the door. Riley watched the first man slide down with the MP5 over his shoulder, quickly followed by a line of men, slithering down to the ice less than thirty feet away.

"Get me away from the bomb," he told the women. "NOW!"

Sammy grabbed his jacket and pulled him back, the bomb between them and the men, just as bullets cracked by overhead.

"Cease fire!" someone was yelling. "We don't want to hit the bomb. Alpha team, fan right. Bravo, cover."

"I think we'd better surrender," Riley suggested. "Just keep your hands far away from your sides and start yelling in English."

"Don't shoot! Don't shoot!" Sammy and Conner called out as four men rushed up, weapons at the ready.

"Freeze! You on the ground—hands away from your sides."

"He's wounded," Sammy informed them.

"Step away!" One of the man carefully rolled Riley over while another kept a weapon on him. "Shit," the man muttered as Riley's blood-encrusted jacket came into view.

"Berkman, get over here. We've got some work for you."

As the medic went to work on Riley, Major Bellamy checked the bomb. His heart gave a jump when he noted that five of the six numbers for the PAL code were entered. They'd been just in time. He didn't understand what had happened or who these three people were, but he didn't need to. His job was to simply secure everything. The powers-that-be would determine what to do about the prisoners.

He had one of his men do a quick bore sample to check for ice depth, and once he found a good spot, he ordered Manchester to land the Osprey. As soon as the aircraft settled down, he loaded the bomb, the prisoners, and his men on board and they lifted, heading back for the *Kitty Hawk*. As they took off, the Russian submarine slowly sank under the surface. There was nothing left except Riley's blood and the rapidly retreating Korean ship.

— thirty-seven —

SNN HEADQUARTERS, ATLANTA. Cordon looked up from the computer screen as his door banged open and Stu Fernandez stormed in. He quickly blanked the screen. "What's wrong?"

Fernandez leaned forward, both hands on Cordon's desk. "The tapes are gone."

"Which tapes?"

"Conner's Antarctica tapes. Both the original and the edited version. They're gone and no one knows where they are."

Cordon frowned. "They weren't signed out?"

"No."

"Well, don't you have a backup?"

"No. If you remember, you told me not to make copies, for security reasons."

Cordon rubbed his chin. "Hmm. OK. It's not a big deal. We'll have the originals from Conner as soon as she links up with the support team. Just have her retransmit."

Fernandez shook his head. "That's another problem. We've had no contact with her for twenty-four hours. And someone ordered the support team to stay at McMurdo Station and not go forward to Eternity Base."

Cordon held up a hand. "Listen. Just calm down. Mr. Parker is handling this whole situation personally. I suggest you get back to work and don't worry about Eternity Base. Everything is being taken care of there. It is no longer your concern."

"That's my story!" Fernandez fumed. "Conner's mine. You can't—"

"Go back to your office." Cordon's voice was ice cold. "If you want to continue working here, I suggest you drop this whole subject."

Fernandez pulled his hands off the desk and regarded his boss for a few seconds, then he turned and left.

When the door slammed shut, Cordon turned off the computer. He took his briefcase and left the building, walked three blocks, and turned the corner. He had to wait only five seconds before a car with tinted windows pulled up to the curb and the back door opened. Cordon got in and the car pulled away.

"Do you have them?"

Cordon pulled out the two tapes and handed them over.

DENVER, COLORADO. The Apache helicopter raced up on the Bell Jet Ranger and matched speed to the left of the smaller aircraft. The 30mm cannon that hung under the nose of the attack gunship turned until it was pointing directly at the Jet Ranger. The Apache pilot keyed his radio.

"Helicopter tail number four seven six, you are directed to assume a heading of one six five degrees. You are to make no radio transmissions. You have ten seconds to comply."

The gunner in the front seat of the Apache nervously caressed his trigger and waited. The Jet Ranger made no change in course.

"You have five seconds."

The gunner had destroyed numerous Iraqi tanks during the Gulf War and had no doubts about what his 30mm cannon could do. He couldn't believe the other aircraft was ignoring them.

The pilot counted down. "Four. Three. Two. One." The pilot switched to intercom. "What's wrong with the guy?"

The gunner looked in his sight and zeroed in on the cockpit. The pilot was staring straight ahead, not even acknowledging their presence. There was someone in the backseat. "Try another frequency," he suggested.

The Apache pilot did that, still getting no response. "Put some rounds across his front."

The gunner let loose a five-round burst, the tracers flitting across the front of the Jet Ranger. Still nothing.

The Apache pilot keyed his radio to a different frequency. "Tango One Niner, this is Hawk. We are getting no response from the target. They are not acknowledging our warnings. Over."

"This is Tango One Niner. Are you over open land? Over."

The pilot glanced down. Nothing but openrange land for miles, which was why they had picked this intercept point. "Roger. Clear as far as I can see. Over."

"Put the target down. Over."

"What!" the Apache pilot exclaimed, forgetting radio protocol.

"I say again. You are ordered to shoot down the target and give us the grid of the wreckage. We will take care of it from there. Over."

The gunner looked over his shoulder at the pilot sitting behind him. "Are they serious?" he asked over the intercom.

"Fucking A, they're serious. Put him down."

The gunner shook his head. Orders were orders. They'd been told that this helicopter was being used by some drug smuggler. The gunner's finger curled around the trigger, and he placed the crosshairs on the engine compartment. His finger twitched and 30mm bullets tore into the other aircraft, shredding metal.

The Jet Ranger plummeted straight down. The Apache pilot descended until they were at a hover over the smoldering wreckage. There was no way anyone could have survived the crash. He radioed in the site; within ten minutes an unmarked Blackhawk helicopter was on the scene, and they were ordered to depart.

USS *KITTY HAWK* OFF THE COAST OF ANTARCTICA. "I told them about Devlin, but they insisted they had to take us directly back here," Conner fumed. "They said they would send out some planes to recover his body."

Sammy shrugged. She wasn't as worried about the dead as the living. Riley was propped up on the bed, his chest swathed in bandages and an IV hooked into each arm. He'd been unconscious ever since they'd brought him in from surgery. The doctor had said his prognosis for recovery was good.

There was a marine guard outside the wardroom door, and Conner had been pacing back and forth ever since Riley had been wheeled in fifteen minutes ago. Sammy was too weary to discuss anything right now. No one would tell them anything; she had a feeling they were waiting for someone to arrive, someone who would give them the "word," whatever it was.

"They wouldn't even give me any paper to write on," Conner complained as she finally sat down.

Sammy lay on the bed next to Riley, closed her eyes, and let sleep overtake her.

EIGHTH ARMY HEADQUARTERS, YONGSAN, SOUTH KOREA. "Sir, we have a reversal of several key indicators. Elements of the PKA I Corps are reported to be standing down. Three merchant ships that we have been tracking, ships that were suspected to have PKA Special Forces troops on board, have turned back."

Patterson nodded. He knew that the message he had just received from the Pentagon had a lot to do with that. Apparently the Russians had talked to their former friends in the North and informed them that it would not be in their best interest to conduct offensive operations against the South. There had also been a veiled reference from General Morris that the *Kitty Hawk* battle group had been involved in a joint U.S.-Russian operation that had affected events here. The message between the lines to Patterson had been clear: don't complain about the deployment of Seventh Fleet elements anymore.

For the time being, things on the peninsula would stay the same—a wary watching across barbed wire and antitank trenches. "Inform all units to reduce to a level four alert status."

ISA HEADQUARTERS, SOUTHWEST OF WASHINGTON, D.C. General Hodges impatiently tapped his fingers on the arm of the chair. "What about Kensington?"

The bald man raised his eyebrows. "What about him?"

"Why did he build Eternity Base?"

"You know why from the interrogation of Glaston and Woodson. Bomb shelter. Home away from home until the world cooled off enough for him to return. Because he wanted to and he could."

"Why the bombs, though?"

The bald man steepled his fingers. "Because he had them. Because Kensington was a man of immense power and he wanted to maintain that power after money no longer mattered. There was a certain paranoiac logic to it all that I find quite fascinating."

"Was?" Hodges inquired.

The bald man smiled. "Mr. Kensington had an unfortunate helicopter accident earlier today. The exact cause of the crash is still being investigated with the aid of some of the men from my office."

Hodges ran a nervous tongue over his lips. "The president wants this whole thing buried deep. There can't be a scandal."

The bald man leaned back in his seat. "We're holding Glaston for a while to see if we can find any other operations he may have been involved in. Then he will be terminated. General Woodson, most unfortunately, died of heart failure due to his recent cancer surgery. A terrible shame for a man who gave so much to this organization."

"What about the reporter from SNN?"

"We're handling it."

"How did the North Koreans find out about the base?"

"That's been taken care of also."

Hodges stood. "It's closed then?"

"It's closed."

USS KITTY HAWK, SOUTH PACIFIC OCEAN. The door swung open and a man in civilian clothes stepped through, immediately closing the door behind him. Conner reached over and tapped Sammy on the shoulder. "We've got company."

Riley's eyes flickered. Sammy gently shook Riley and he came awake with a grimace. The man stood there looking at the three of them for a little while, then spoke. "We've recovered Mr. Devlin's body. Tentative cause of death is extreme hypothermia."

The man pulled over one of the plastic chairs and sat down. "We have a problem here that also happens to be your problem. To put it bluntly, the words 'Eternity Base' must never be mentioned publicly."

"What!" Conner exploded. "You're crazy."

The man didn't even blink. "Let me explain the facts to you. First, Eternity Base no longer exists. We've landed men there to sterilize what little is left, including the reactor.

"Second, you have no record of the base. The pictures from the Records Center have been taken care of. By the way, I am sure you would not like to see any legal action taken against your sister for breaking her contract with the government by sending you copies of those pictures." The man looked at Sammy with a cold grin.

"Your equipment disappeared in the explosion and you have nothing. The—"

"Atlanta has copies of my video," Conner countered.

"As I was just about to say—your headquarters in Atlanta has somehow managed to misplace the two copies of your tape."

Conner stared at the man and then turned to Sammy and Riley, who had yet to say a word.

The man wasn't done yet. "As a matter of fact, you might say the circumstances surrounding the deaths of your crew and Mr. Devlin and Mr. Swenson are very murky. We have only your word on that issue. Some might suggest that the three of you had a hand in their deaths, especially Mr. Devlin's. At the very least you might be found negligent in his death."

Conner just continued to stare, holding back the angry words that wanted to spew forth. Now was not the time or place to fight.

Riley broke the silence, his voice barely more than a whisper. "What's the deal?"

The man seemed to relax for the first time. "As I said—no word of Eternity Base." He looked Conner in the eyes. "I believe you will find that your boss, Mr. Parker, has already agreed to that."

Conner slumped in her chair. As if sensing that he had her on the ropes, the man offered a handout. "In exchange for your cooperation, we are willing to offer you an exclusive on the 'real' story: the dramatic rescue by a joint U.S.-Russian military task force of the survivors of your news team covering an ecological story. We have quite a bit of footage—including shots of the Russian submarine that helped rescue you—enough to make an interesting piece."

The man stood. "Mr. Parker has also been informed of improved future cooperation between SNN and various agencies of the government. I am quite sure he is very satisfied with the possibility of several exclusive leaks of information. I am certain you will also see the advantages of your cooperation."

He looked at Sammy. "And I even believe they still have your old job waiting for you back at the Records Center, perhaps even a promotion."

He walked to the door and stopped. "I will assume I have your agreement." He stepped out.

— thirty-eight —

ISA HEADQUARTERS, SOUTHWEST OF WASHINGTON, D.C., 2 DECEMBER 1996. The bald man looked up from his desk as the investigator walked in. "Everything filed satisfactorily?"

The crash investigator nodded. "The FAA is satisfied it was structural failure."

"Good." The bald man looked closely at the young man standing across from him. "What's wrong?"

The investigator pulled out a briefcase and laid it on the desk. He flipped open the top and extracted a burned piece of metal laced with wires.

"What's that?" the bald man asked.

"It's part of a helicopter autopilot relay system. We've traced it to a prototype designed by Bell-Boeing."

The bald man regarded the other with unblinking eyes. "You found two bodies, right?"

"Yes, sir."

"Their dental charts matched Kensington's and his pilot's, didn't they?"

"Yes, sir."

"But . . . ?" the bald man asked, watching the hesitation in his subordinate.

The man took his lead. "But, sir, I believe it was a setup. I think the two men inside were dead when the Apache approached. Someone

280

was flying that chopper by remote control. I think the bodies were rigged with false dental work—the whole thing. It's hard to do, but if you have the money it's possible."

"And Kensington had the money," the bald man concluded. He appeared to think about this scenario for a while. "All right. This is closed. You are to tell no one about it. Do you understand? The president would not be happy to hear this." He pointed at the report and the wreckage. "Leave that with me."

The investigator nodded vigorously, glad to be done with the mess.

The bald man waited until the door closed, then picked up his secure phone.

KAUAI, HAWAII. "Peter here."

"This is Andrew. The case has been closed."

Kensington nodded. "Good."

"Can you tell me why you got the North Koreans involved? You almost caused a damn war."

"We could use a war," Kensington said. "Good for business."

"Well, your business is over. Is that clear?"

Kensington frowned. He didn't like being talked to in such a manner by a hireling. "Are you threatening me?"

"Jesus Christ—don't you get it? We've had a nuke go off. People killed. Armies on the verge of combat on the Korean peninsula. All you can say is that you played it that way because it would have been good for business? You're fucking nuts, and I've got the goods on you. So you lay low. I don't want to hear from you again. I've covered your ass for the last time. From now on, no amount of money will work." The phone went dead.

Kensington hung up the phone and went back to surveying his island paradise. The house was built into the side of an extinct volcano, the lush jungle of Hawaii stretching out below it down to the cliffs facing the pounding surf. The view was spectacular and the location was isolated. The old man's eyes were as sharp as they'd ever been, and he used them to soak up every detail. "It is over," he announced.

"How did you know it would work?" The other occupant of the room was seated on a leather divan.

Kensington waited a few moments before answering, as if the question surprised him. "Actually," he said, "it didn't work. Optimally, I would have gotten through all this without my name being revealed."

Kensington picked up a glass and took a drink. "But it really doesn't matter, does it? With enough power you *make* things work, and I came out of this alive when they were ready to kill me. I must admit, it worried me when your man was unable to stop the team from discovering the base. Then I knew it had to be destroyed, and I tried to find a way to do that. The North Koreans were very handy."

The woman shrugged. "Mr. Vickers was the best I could come up with under the short notice. Also, you must remember I didn't know that Riley would be a factor. Without his influence, it would have been much easier. And weren't you worried about it getting beyond Antarctica?"

"I was prepared to make a profit out of a bad situation if it got out of Antarctica," Kensington said.

"How did you know *my* people wouldn't succeed in their mission?" she asked. "You helped them by giving me the transponder code for the base, so I could forward it to Kang."

Now Kensington laughed. "How can anyone succeed unless I let them? When you control the information going to both sides, you can certainly assure that neither side succeeds. You should know that after working for me *and* North Korea for all these years. SNN was certainly the place to be to both acquire and manipulate information." He sighed. "There would have been some good profits to be made if your people had succeeded and Orange III had been implemented. We haven't had a good war for quite a while, but there will be other opportunities."

He swung his chair so he was directly facing her. "Now, my dear, no more questions." He picked up a briefcase and put it down on the desktop. "Here is your payment. Your tenure at SNN was most advantageous. I don't understand why you are going back to your home country. I can find you work that will put your assets to better use."

Miss Suwon got up and walked over to the desk. She looked at the briefcase, then at Kensington. "I am returning home because money is not everyone's god."

Kensington laughed again. "It works for everyone I've ever encountered." He pointed at the briefcase. "You came here for that, didn't you?"

"No, I didn't."

Kensington frowned. "I won't pay you more."

"Yes, you will."

Kensington pressed a button. "I don't appreciate this. You're messing with the wrong person."

Miss Suwon smiled, and Kensington's confidence slowly dissolved when no guard came rushing in.

"You goddamn . . ." he sputtered, then collected himself. "All right. I'll get you more money."

"I told you," Suwon said, "that money is not the issue."

"But you said you wanted me to pay you more . . ." Kensington's voice trailed off.

"And you will." Suwon leaned forward and placed her hand on his.

"Hey!" Kensington yelped, retracting his hand and looking at the back of it. "What was that?"

She turned her hand over. A small needle was cupped between her fingers. "Ricin. A most powerful toxin. You will be dead in a minute." Suwon picked up the briefcase. "You know, we wanted those nuclear weapons. Many good men died trying to get them."

"Wait!" Kensington shouted. "You can't do this!" He grabbed his chest and struggled for air.

"It is already done."

— epilogue —

AUCKLAND, NEW ZEALAND, 5 DECEMBER 1996. Riley looked over at Sammy and Conner and gave them a weak smile. "Are we having fun yet?" The three were alone for the first time since being flown from the *Kitty Hawk* by military plane and escorted to this hotel. The government was obviously satisfied that the three had acceded to the demands of its agent. Riley was lying on the bed, his right side swathed in bandages.

The phone rang and they all turned and looked at it. There was only one person who knew they were here—besides the government. Riley picked up the receiver, spoke briefly, then put it back down.

"Colonel Pike is here," he announced. Conner and Sammy relaxed. A few minutes later there was a knock on the door and Sammy let Pike in, giving him a big hug as soon as the door was closed.

After Sammy let him go, Pike walked over to Riley. "Thanks for helping me when I asked you, Dave."

"No problem, sir."

"How's the wound?"

"Healing," Riley said. He knew Pike had information for them, and he waited as the colonel introduced himself to Conner and talked for a few minutes.

Finally, Pike looked at all three of them. "Well, what now?"

Conner rubbed a hand through the tangle of her dark hair. "Do you think we have any options?"

284

Pike shrugged. "Not really. The government's covered it's tracks. Not only that, they hold a few hammers over your heads. If you say anything, Sammy will lose her job. I checked in Atlanta—SNN doesn't have any tapes. So you don't have any evidence. You'll probably be fired too," he nodded at Conner, "if you make waves."

"Sammy and Riley were there," Conner said. "They'll back me up."

Riley coughed, which made him wince. He shifted position very slowly. "My word isn't worth much. They also have a thing or two they can hold over my head."

Sammy sat in the chair next to the bed and studied Riley with her green eyes. "What about Kerns and Vickers and Lallo and Swenson and Devlin? Are we going to write them off?"

"The government has already issued a cover story to explain their disappearance," Pike said.

Sammy didn't seem to hear the colonel. She continued talking, her voice cracking with emotion. "I didn't ask what the powers-that-be are doing. I asked what *we* are going to do." She looked at Riley. "Are we—you and I and Conner—going to forget about them?"

"You need to drop this and get on with your life," Riley said. "You need to forget about the dead."

Sammy poked her finger at him. "That's pretty good advice from a man who can't erase his own ghosts."

Riley regarded her for a long time without saying a word.

Pike cleared his thoat, regaining their attention. "I have some more information that will interest you." He reached into the small briefcase he'd carried with him and pulled out a folder. "Do you recognize any of these men?" He laid out a half-dozen photos on the bed next to Riley. They were all black and white pictures of young men in uniform.

"That one," Riley immediately said, tapping a photo. "He's the body we found in Eternity Base."

Sammy and Conner nodded their agreement.

Pike picked up the photo and looked at the back. "Sergeant Michael Palmer. A member of Command and Control, Military Assistance Command, Studies and Observation Group."

"MACV-SOG," Sammy said. "Same as dad."

"Same as your dad," Pike confirmed. He paused, and his lined face seemed to grow even older. "I did some arm twisting in DC before I left, using what you'd told me over the phone. There's lots of butts on the line because of this Eternity Base incident, so I got some of my contacts to talk more than they normally would have—people are trying to cover their ass.

"This whole operation in Antarctica was started by a civilian—my sources wouldn't give me a name—but it was supported by the forerunner of the present Intelligence Support Agency, a secret group with a large budget that runs most of the covert operations for the Pentagon.

"Because this organization could cut orders and use the resources of the military, they often used personnel and units without those people being aware they were participating in a covert operation or knowing what the mission was. A good example is the engineer company that was diverted from Vietnam to construct Eternity Base."

Pike held up the picture. "Another example is Sergeant Palmer, here. He was used to escort the nuclear weapons down to Eternity Base. For maintaining the security of the base and the fact that the bombs were there, he was killed."

"So we have another of the piece of the puzzle," Sammy said. "We can find more."

"That's not why I'm telling you this," Pike cut in. "I'm telling you this because through the same source I also received another photo." He reached into his shirt pocket, pulled out a small picture, and handed it to Sammy.

"Dad" was her only comment as she cradled the photo in her hands.

"What happened to him?" Conner asked, tenderly taking the picture from her sister and looking at it.

"Killed in a plane crash in South Korea on 5 January 1972," Pike replied.

"South Korea?" Sammy said. "But he was MIA in Vietnam."

"He was in Vietnam," Pike confirmed, "but he got sent on a mission to Korea, and that's where he died. Since they couldn't report that, they made up the MIA story."

"What mission?" Sammy demanded.

Pike looked at her and shook his head. "I don't know, and we aren't going to find out. Trust me on that. I cared about your father too—and many other men who disappeared—but . . ." Pike paused. "It was a dark world we were all in back then, and your father knew the risks of what he did for a living. I was given this information so that you would know that he's dead. That's it."

"But what about Michael Palmer?" Sammy asked. "Does his family know how he died? Helping build Eternity Base for somebody who could pull the strings to get it built? And getting shot in the back for doing his duty?"

Pike had no answer to that.

Riley suddenly spoke. "All right, Sammy. I'm with you. What are you going to do?"

Sammy blinked to hold back the tears as she looked at the photo of her dad one more time. "I'm going to fight them."

Riley winced again as he adjusted his position slightly. "They have all the cards. They'll crush you. But I'm with you regardless."

Sammy turned from him and looked at her sister. "Are you with me, or are you going to play by the rules?"

It surprised her when Conner smiled. "They won't crush us, sis. I can play the game better than they can and make my own damn rules." She reached under her shirt and pulled a 3.5- inch diskette out of her waistband. "I have the original video of the base—including the body, which we can now indentify, as well as pictures of the bombs and their serial numbers—digitized on this." She glanced at Riley. "You weren't the only one who prepared just in case someone showed up."

A faint smile of respect crossed Riley's face, but his words were wary. "You know what's going to happen. Even if you get someone other than SNN to run that, they're going to come down on you hard."

Conner replaced the diskette. "I know." She stood up and went over to the bed and sat down next to her sister. Taking Riley's free hand and one of her sister's, she squeezed them between her two hands. "But I think we can do it. We have to if we're going to live with ourselves."